The Meddling Matriarch

by

Cheryl A. Cornell

Christmas in the Castle

The Meddling Matriarch

COPYRIGHT © 2025 by Cheryl A. Cornell

Cover Art by *Tina Lynn Stout*

The Wild Rose Press, Inc.
PO Box 708
Adams Basin, NY 14410-0708
Visit us at www.thewildrosepress.com

Publishing History
First Edition, 2025
Trade Paperback Print ISBN 978-1-5092-6398-1
Digital ISBN 978-1-5092-6398-1

Christmas in the Castle
Published in the United States of America

Acknowledgments

My thanks to everyone at The Wild Rose Press for their continued support. A special thanks to my very patient editors Roseann Armstrong and Josette Arthur and to Tina Lynn Stout for the beautiful cover art.

Chapter One

Eleanor was exhausted and exhilarated at the same time. The last weeks spent getting ready to leave her home outside of Birmingham and then traveling to Southampton to meet Mrs. Cornwell had sped by. Their time on the ship to America had felt like a whirlwind.

As the horse-drawn wagon progressed from the train station toward Tuxedo Park, New York, she'd tried to take in her new surroundings. But the drive had gone too quickly to appreciate all the sights. She hoped in time she would be able to see the whole town.

Now they stopped before a gigantic stone structure with several stories. A large porch shaded the entry, and a huge turret window ran the height of the three-story home. In the distance she saw the gates of the actual town. Apparently, she was to live near but not inside its walls.

She'd done some traveling around England with her mother before she passed away, and the home reminded her of trips to London where she'd seen beautiful castles and residences. They'd seen other castle-like homes, but she never considered she might actually live in one and make it her home. The family estate she'd grown up on wasn't nearly as beautiful as this structure.

"It looks like a castle from a storybook," she whispered, but the driver—Daniel, as he'd introduced himself—didn't seem to hear her. With a deep breath, she wondered if she'd really live there. Would she become the Christmas bride promised in Mrs. Crane's correspondence? She had a moment of anxiety, her hands sweating inside her gloves. She was old enough to know not every promise turned out as described.

"There seem to be so many acres," she mused. The grounds were larger than her family's estate in England. Running it would be a big responsibility.

Daniel helped her down the wooden step. "I'll take your trunks around back." He drove off before she could ask any questions.

She took a few moments to gaze at her new home and tried not to gape. The front door swung inward, and a small child ran toward her. His brown curls encircled his head like a halo. He hugged her around the legs.

Without thinking, she let her gloved fingers tousle his hair. "Hello."

"Hello." The child stepped back to look at her. He had beautiful brown eyes.

"I'm Eleanor. Who might you be?"

Before the child could answer, a female voice echoed from the entry. "Alfred, where are you?"

The child turned and looked over his shoulder. In a whirl of black fabric, a woman rushed out and grabbed his hand. She tugged him toward the house. "You know better than to go outside without me." She gave him a pat on the bottom, and he scooted inside. "Go on now, up to the nursery," she instructed him. The woman didn't pause to give Eleanor a look.

Nobody came to greet her, so she moved inside the grand three-story entrance and pulled the door shut behind her. She found so much to look at that she turned in circles to take in the space. She could picture it decorated for the holidays and her wedding to George Crane. Would they find a large tree where they could have their wedding photo taken? She exhaled an exasperated breath, knowing her life was still in flux. Yet she pictured what the space might look like if she were in charge of decorations. Still, nobody came.

"Hello," she called but got no answer. "Hello, is anyone here?" Again, no answer.

A wall clock struck three. Wandering the rooms without an invitation would be rude, especially since all the interior doors were closed. She took off her gloves, hat, and cape. She folded the cape and put it and the other items on the bench under the staircase. The small mirror in her travel case told her that her hair could use some repair, so she finger combed it in place. She stowed the case under the bench. She desperately wanted a cup of tea but wouldn't go uninvited looking for the kitchen.

She sat and leaned against the wall. Exhaustion overrode polite society rules, and she relaxed and closed her eyes for a moment. The hall clock chimed four, and she woke with a start. She stretched and debated what to do.

Technically, this wasn't her home...yet. She settled against the wall and waited.

****

Phillip Crane bustled through the rear door into the empty kitchen. Margaret and their two maids would still be at the church setting up for the wedding tomorrow. He lifted the kettle and shook it. It held enough water for tea, so he put it on the burner and headed upstairs to check on Alfred, his son.

He came into the main hall, then halted at the sight of the sleeping woman. "Damn," he whispered. He'd gotten busy on the land and forgotten she was due to arrive today. He gave her a once-over and found himself staring. The woman was just one more problem his younger brother, George, had created. He shook his head. How was he supposed to tell this bride her expected husband had run away?

He knew from Grandmother's gossip that the girl— Eleanor, he remembered—was considered plain with no prospects for marriage. She had two younger brothers who would fight over the family estate. He'd seen the photograph his grandmother sent. It was three years old, but time had been kind to the woman. Gone was the girlish air, replaced by an adult woman in her late twenties. On the other hand, no sane woman on the East Coast would agree to marry George with his reputation. He'd had thirty-two years to sully the family name.

Phillip had been married by age thirty-two and now had a three-year-old son. He'd moved to this plot of land near Tuxedo Park, whereas George had stayed in Newport, Rhode Island, and continued his womanizing ways. When George realized Grandmother Agnes was serious about him changing those ways, possibly arranging a bride for him, he'd left Newport and settled farther south on the East Coast.

But George's funds were running out. His grandmother had told him to marry the girl she was importing from England or get a job. The word *job* had sent him running for parts unknown. It was too late to cancel the bride-to-be, and for the last few months, no one had heard from George. So now it was up to Phillip to break the news to the woman. She had no groom waiting.

He gathered his thoughts and turned back to the

kitchen, leaving the kitchen door open behind him. He stood at the stove and waited for the kettle to boil. Eleanor wasn't stunningly beautiful, but she was pretty if viewed from a certain angle. Her light-blonde hair was fashioned in the latest puffy style. Her suit seemed functional. It was a sturdy, dark-brown fabric without much embellishment. She had beautiful hands with no rings on her fingers. He'd glanced at the cape, gloves, and hat on the bench beside her. They were of good quality but not new or fashionable.

That didn't matter to him. Seeing her today, he knew his first impression of the woman in the photo had been accurate. He was attracted to a stranger who was supposed to marry his brother. The fact that he was attracted to her—and had been since seeing her image— bothered him more. She was the opposite of the woman he'd married. This woman could be a problem for him if she stayed in the house. His mind reeled from the idea he might touch her one day, kiss her one day, and even have her as his own. His thoughts were not conducive to a healthy brother- and sister-in-law relationship.

All he could hope was that she wasn't enamored with George. Rather, the arrangement had been made with her future in mind. Maybe she would leave quickly and quietly when she found out she had no groom waiting. Then his life would go back to normal. He didn't need thoughts of romance and a wife to complicate his world.

The kettle whistled. Phillip turned and saw the woman jolt awake. She stood and straightened her skirt. She glanced around, then walked into the kitchen with her hand outstretched and gave him a polite smile.

"Eleanor Sterling. You must be George." With her

hand still reaching out, she added, "I'm so glad to finally meet you. During the voyage with Mrs. Cornwell, she told me all about your lovely town and castle." She paused for a breath. "This entry will look stunning at the holiday for our wedding."

"No, I'm not George. I'm Phillip Crane, his older brother." He took one step toward her and shook her hand. He immediately dropped it. "Come, the kettle is boiling."

He walked back to the stove and moved the kettle to the side. His heartbeat felt out of pattern—he'd never had this kind of intense reaction to any other woman. He was attracted to the woman who was his brother's bride-to-be. He silently cursed the cornflower-blue eyes that studied him.

"It's a lovely kitchen, large and well appointed," she said. "In fact, the home reminds me of a castle."

"Not a castle, just a stone home."

"Will I be seeing George soon? I'd like to freshen up before meeting my fiancé."

"Not today." He hated the cryptic tone to his voice.

"Oh. When, then?"

Phillip glanced over his shoulder to look at her and turned away. He moved around the kitchen, taking down two cups and three saucers and placing them across the table from each other. "We're an informal household compared to what you're probably used to." He motioned for her to take the seat across from where he stood. "Well, Eleanor, do you prefer Elle, Ellie, or Eleanor?"

"I only answer to Eleanor," she said. "Younger brothers can be cruel and rhyme anything to be disrespectful." She gave him a half smile, and he looked away.

He moved to a counter and grabbed the tea canister. He poured hot water from the kettle into a teapot, swirled it, and placed the kettle back on the stovetop. He poured out the water in the teapot and replaced it with fresh water. After he measured out four spoons of tea into the pot, he set it on a pad in the center of the table and grabbed a strainer. He was glad he had the task of making tea. It gave him time to gather his thoughts.

Grateful his hands were still steady when lifting the pot, he reached for her cup and positioned the strainer over it while he filled it with the brew. He repeated the process in his cup and set the pot down. He laid the strainer on the third saucer. Finally, he pulled out the chair across from her and sat heavily.

"The tea smells wonderful and is appreciated." She took several sips of the brew.

"Do you want milk or sugar?"

"No, thank you. This is fine. It's been a long day of traveling."

"When did you get here?" He stared at the far end of the room, refusing to look directly at her but viewing her in his peripheral vision. Her slim fingers cradled the cup, and he felt a stirring that was long forgotten.

"Just after two o'clock. Your driver met me at the train."

"I'm sorry you were left alone. There is a wedding tomorrow morning, and the whole town is helping to decorate the church."

"That's nice, as it should be with the community pitching in. With the fall colors…"

"Yes, as it should be." He sipped his tea but still didn't turn to look at her.

"When I got here, a young boy met me. He is adorable, almost angelic."

Phillip laughed. "Trust me when I say he is not angelic at all, completely the reverse."

"Oh," she said. "Is there a reason you won't look at me?"

He put his cup down, stood, and paced to the far side of the kitchen. "I figure you'll appreciate the truth. George has gone away…"

She hesitated, then rose. She studied him for a moment. "Away for work or to get away from marriage?"

He turned and looked at her. "Marriage. Or any adult responsibility."

"I'm confused. The correspondence… I have the letters from Agnes Crane."

"Sit and enjoy your tea. I know all about the letters and the arrangement my grandmother brokered."

" 'Brokered'?"

"Yes, the financial arrangement with your father, a dowry of sorts." He sank into the chair, relieved the truth was out.

"That explains why he was so happy to see me go. In the beginning, he made it seem it was for travel and education abroad. It wasn't until the approaching travel date that I was made aware of the marriage. When I was on the ship as Mrs. Cornwell's companion, she gave me the letters. I'd hoped I was misreading them, but eventually, with the proof in hand, I knew better. Your use of 'brokered' just solidified the situation for me."

Her head dropped for only a moment, and she took her seat. She looked up at him with those blasted cornflower-blue eyes. He had to look away.

"George didn't want to marry…or marry me? He never met me or even saw me. We never corresponded. How could he dislike me out of hand? Did he see a photo of me and decide he couldn't be attracted?" She lifted her cup and put it back without drinking.

"He disliked the commitment." He stood and reached for the strainer. He refilled her cup and then his, but he remained standing and watched as she carefully lifted the hot cup. "The photo didn't arrive until after George left. He never saw it."

She placed her cup on the saucer. "I suppose it's better that he didn't take one look at me and run." She picked up the cup again. "What happens now? Am I to be returned to England?" Her voice quaked.

"I think there should be no decisions made abruptly. Why not enjoy the home and town as a respite until I get an answer from Grandmother? I believe she has notified your family and is waiting for their input."

Eleanor placed the cup down yet again, stood, and paced to the end of the room and back. "Their input was to send me away at the first chance they got. They won't want to reverse the deal." She dropped into her chair and sipped the tea.

"George may return. He's just running scared of the commitment." He reseated himself across from her.

"Does everyone in town know he jilted me?"

"No. Most know they haven't seen him lately, but we didn't announce your arrival in case you met and chose to return home."

"I don't have a home to return to," she whispered.

"Why not enjoy our hospitality until we hear from Grandmother?" He'd practiced that statement just for this moment.

"Just what you wanted—a guest with no prospects. I'll try to make myself useful while I'm here."

Her soft voice hit him on a gut level. "You don't have a strong British accent."

"I've been trying to curb it. I wanted to assimilate, not force my heritage on everyone I met."

"That makes sense." He drank from his cup. "Grandmother will figure out something for the long term, but for now, you're a guest. I'd prefer to introduce you as a family friend instead of George's fiancée. It will make life easier for you. Most people know George hasn't been seen around here for a long time. They assume he's in Newport or traveling."

The rear door opened and shut.

"Margaret, I'm glad you're here. This is our…guest, Eleanor Sterling. Margaret, Miss Sterling."

"Just Eleanor." She stood and reached to shake the woman's hand.

"Welcome, Eleanor. Give me a moment, and I'll take you up to your room." Margaret removed her hat and shawl and placed them on a peg in the back hallway. "Come, I'll take you up."

Eleanor nodded to Phillip. "Thank you for the tea, Mr. Crane."

He stood but didn't verbalize any of the twenty thoughts that ran through his mind. "See you at supper." He turned and left by the rear door.

Outside, he stormed to the workshop he used as an office. "Damn you, George," he muttered several times. He slammed the workshop door and paced the length of the room. A black cat startled from its sleep and ran to the other side of the building.

Until he heard back from Grandmother, he and

Eleanor were stuck in limbo. For now, he had to keep his distance. Being near her sent his body into overload.

His wife, Ida, had passed away three years ago after giving birth to their son, Alfred. Raising the child and finishing the house had kept him occupied. He shook his head, thinking how sad that she'd never gotten to see the finished structure or live there. Ida had been staying in Rhode Island with his grandmother until the birth of Alfred. She'd traveled back and forth twice at the beginning of the building process. Now he realized she hadn't been interested in making design decisions about their soon-to-be home.

When her pregnancy was revealed, Ida had stayed with Agnes, saying the traveling caused too much stress. He received a telegram about her difficulty with the birth. He took the next train north and managed to get there two months before she passed.

Everyone—even Ida—knew she wouldn't survive the complications of childbirth. She reinforced her desire that he take Alfred and give him the life they dreamed about in the new home. They had time to say their goodbyes, but the time wasn't long enough. She made him promise to find a new wife, a kind woman who would accept their son as her own.

After her death, he hadn't associated with women, save Margaret and Nanny.

His work had suffered since the situation with George and Eleanor arose. He'd made promises to the owners of three new estates being built within the Park walls. He sat at the desk and looked at the completed designs for each property. He'd already finished most of the work on each. For his own home, he'd chosen hearty grasses that wintered well for the lands bordering nearby properties. Evergreens edged the property lines and gave his house a natural appearance. He had relented, and come spring he would let the gardener plant perennials near the home. He was emphatic that no two of his designs were similar.

He sat at the worktable and stared out the window. "Damn you, George."

In the matter of a few hours, he'd come to covet his brother's fiancée. She was tall—taller than Ida—and slim with beautiful hands. She had blonde hair and cornflower-blue eyes. Eleanor was the complete opposite of Ida, who had been a brunette with brown eyes.

He left immediately and walked into town. He sent his grandmother a telegram informing her that Eleanor, the family friend from England, had arrived. He didn't add that she was inquiring about her fiancé. That would be obvious, and he didn't want that tidbit of gossip getting around town.

****

Eleanor followed Margaret back into the main hall. She grabbed her cape, gloves, and hat while the other woman took her travel case.

"Upstairs." Margaret glanced over her shoulder.

Eleanor slowly followed, trying to appreciate her surroundings. Questions swamped her, too many to get straight in her mind. At the top of the stairs, she stood in the main hallway. The same wood that covered the walls downstairs continued up here. The staircase chased the wall and continued up to another level. Margaret came to an intersection of sorts, and they stopped.

"The Mister's rooms are in there." Margaret pointed to the first door on the right and then across the hall to the left. "That's the nursery."

"Is that where Alfred stays?"

Margaret glanced over her shoulder. "You know about Alfred?"

"Yes, when I first arrived, he ran out the front door."

"I'll bet Nanny wasn't happy," Margaret said with a slight laugh. She continued down the hallway and pushed open the fourth door on the left. "This will be your suite."

"Suite?" Eleanor asked.

"Just a bedroom and sitting area."

Eleanor stood in the doorway, scanning the large bedroom. "It's beautiful. Who designed it?" She wanted to reach her fingers to the padded fabric walls. The soft greens were elegant, tasteful.

"There's a bathroom through here with the latest amenities," Margaret told her, pulling her back into the conversation.

Margaret pushed open the interior door and walked into a sparkling white room. She continued to a door on the other side. It led into another bedroom similar to but more masculine than the first one. Eleanor glanced around. The walls were covered in a comparable fabric, but the bold stripes were missing the floral pattern woven between the stripes in her room.

"The closets lining each side of the hall will hold your wardrobe," Margaret said.

"All right." Eleanor realized neither room contained a closet. This room had a desk between the front windows, several seating areas, and an armoire on the rear wall.

"When you and Mr. George marry, these will be your rooms while you're here."

"While we're here? I was under the impression this was to be our permanent home."

"I don't think the issue is settled. There were conversations before Mr. George left about you two moving north to his grandmother's house in Newport."

Margaret turned and walked back through the bath and into the bedroom. She put the bag beside a dressing table set between the two front windows. A vase of fresh-cut pink roses sat on the left side of the dressing table.

"The room is lovely." Eleanor saw her trunks were against the far wall, waiting to be unpacked. "Did Mrs. Crane design the rooms?"

Margaret turned to her. "I understand you have questions and you were expecting a different type of meeting. We're a casual household during the week when we don't have company. Why not settle in and then come down to supper?"

"Where?" Eleanor asked, her exasperation showing in her tone.

"Oh good gracious, I didn't realize the Mister didn't show you around. Downstairs, the third door to the rear. We have evening meal at seven."

"Thank you. You said this is a casual household. What does that mean here?"

"Generally, unless there are guests, we don't dress for supper. Occasionally, Mr. Phillip has his evening meal with me and my husband. Daniel is the caretaker and in charge of the horses. Sundays are more formal." Margaret picked up a pillow from a side chair, fluffed it, and placed it back on the chair. "There's a small glass breakfast room off the kitchen. That's where the Mister usually has his meals." She stopped and stared at Eleanor. "When was the last time you ate?"

"I'm sorry. I was listening, but there is so much to look at." Pulling herself from the side of the bed, she let her hand run across the beautifully carved wooden footboard. "You said to come down to the dining room. Does the household usually eat in the kitchen? That would be fine for me."

"Maybe when you're more settled. For tonight, meet Mr. Phillip in the dining room. Just relax, have a good meal, and let him explain the situation."

Margaret strode toward the hall door. "Tomorrow we'll unpack your trunks and get you settled. No need to change for tonight." She glanced around the room. "Laura will be your maid, and Sally is learning our routine. They are both still at the church."

"Thank you, Margaret." Eleanor choked back tears. It wouldn't do to let the housekeeper see her emotional over the situation.

"You're welcome. We'll have time tomorrow to get to know each other and for you to get to know the house."

Eleanor couldn't speak. A tear rolled down her cheek, but she didn't wipe it away, not wanting Margaret to see it. But she opened the door and left quietly.

They'd walked past a large wall clock in the outer hallway. It chimed six o'clock. Eleanor had an hour to pull herself together and meet the man who would determine her future. She cursed George. She had no idea who he was beyond the family name and the assurances that they would be compatible and that the future would be bright for the new couple.

"I'm not a bride-to-be. I'm an interloper." She let out the tears that had threatened to fall earlier. She dropped into a large chair under the front window and cried. She cried until her breath was shallow, her shoulders heaving. "This is more frightening than the idea of the commitment and the time on the ship." She stomped her foot. "Damn you, Father, for selling me off to the first family with a bit of cash to spare."

Standing, she took several deep breaths to calm herself. "No more now." She pulled a serviceable handkerchief from her travel bag. She looked out the window at a blanket of green grass; trees that had recently been planted, their leaves starting to turn color; and in the background, a mass of tall grasses she remembered from her times at the shore. She drew a deep breath and exhaled. "It would have been a beautiful view to see each day."

She moved before the dressing table and looked in the mirror. "Yes, this is not what you expected or were promised. Nothing ever is." She wiped her face and nose. "Now you make the best of the situation. If George comes back…" She took several deeper breaths and stood taller. "If George comes back, you'll meet, and only then can you know what might be. For now, they haven't turned me out."

She let out a sigh. When she woke and saw Phillip, she'd assumed he was George. He was handsome and tall with a short, dark beard. He had kind brown eyes. When he said he wasn't George, she had been instantly disappointed. She would have to be careful not to let her initial view of him become public. It wouldn't do for her to acknowledge that the first sight of this stranger had stirred her inside. She had watched his hands as he prepared the tea. Strong hands, she'd thought. She couldn't help but imagine their strength. She'd never felt such a longing, and now knowing this feeling was for the wrong man made her hesitant in all directions.

Eleanor pushed her shoulders back. "My gosh, look at my hair."

She sat before the mirror and coaxed her hair back into a style. "All your life you prided yourself on being confident and in control," she said to the face in the mirror. The journey had taken an unexpected turn, but she would bend with the curve. She was resilient if nothing else.

It was getting late. Margaret had told her not to dress for tonight. She brushed off the road dust from the hem of her skirt and straightened her collar. Three more deep breaths, and she walked to the hall door. "Damn you, George!"

She took her time walking to the staircase. Midway through the hall, she stopped to look over the railing down to the foyer. The side wall held the picture she'd briefly seen earlier. While she had no idea who the likeness belonged to, she'd decided he was a stern man, or at least he had been on the day the portrait was completed. The tapestry on the opposite wall was stunning, alive with color and the likenesses of deer and birds in the woodlands.

She could have a good life if she got to stay here at Crane House. Then reality struck. This wouldn't be her house. George was the younger brother. Phillip Crane was the lord of this manor. She had referred to the house as a stone castle, but he'd said it was a house.

Now she had to meet him for the evening meal. She wouldn't blame him for his immature, dandy brother, George.

Her booted feet echoed with each step she took across the slate foyer. Her footsteps sounded louder than they had this afternoon. She walked to the only open door and paused in the doorway of a lovely dining room. Margaret filled a water glass at the end of the long table.

"Come in, dear." She motioned Eleanor to the seat before her. "Mr. Phillip will be in shortly, and we'll get some hot food in you."

"Thank you, Margaret." Eleanor walked to the appointed chair and stood behind it. The table easily seated twelve, and a matching chair occupied each corner of the room.

Phillip entered from the side. She was struck by his good looks—rugged, not prissy and soft. His dark hair was brushed back, moisture clinging to the tips. In this light, his dark-brown eyes shone almost gold.

He held her chair as she sat. Eleanor watched every move he made. He hadn't changed but had rolled down his shirt sleeves and added a jacket.

"Thank you," she whispered. In the large room, her voice was almost lost.

He settled across from her at the far end of the table, and she put her napkin on her lap and waited for him to start a conversation.

Chapter Two

Phillip was beyond uncomfortable. Since his wife had passed away, women weren't important. Raising his son, finishing this home, and getting professional projects were all he thought of. Now this woman, the intended wife of his brother, distracted him to an uncomfortableness he'd long forgotten.

Margaret brought in the bowls of consommé and set one before each of them. Eleanor smiled her thanks, and Margaret left. Eleanor didn't dine until he lifted his spoon, the nonverbal cue to start eating. He ate several spoonfuls while watching her from under his lashes.

"This has a lovely taste," she remarked.

"Yes, Margaret is a good cook," he said after several seconds.

"If I'm to stay here for a while, I can help her."

"She does fine on her own and has two maids to help," he snapped. He put down his spoon. "I'm sorry, Eleanor. It seems we're both in an uncomfortable situation."

"Yes." She took another spoonful of the soup and set the spoon down. "Mr. Crane—"

"Phillip, please."

Margaret arrived and removed the soup bowls. Within moments, she returned with a large platter. Eleanor helped herself to a slice of venison and a boiled potato. Phillip watched every move her slender fingers made. When he'd taken his portion from the platter, Margaret placed it on the sideboard and left them alone. They ate several bites in silence, and Eleanor leaned back in her seat.

"The house is lovely. Did your wife design the interiors?"

"No. We were living in Newport when we decided to make our home here. We drew up plans, and I oversaw the building. While she was carrying Alfred, the travel back and forth became too much for her." He paused and drew a deep breath. "She never saw the project finished."

"I'm sorry. Your grandmother never wrote about her passing."

"Since you were supposed to marry my brother, it wasn't relevant. Once settled, you were to live in Newport with her."

"Newport? That was not in any of her correspondence either. She simply said I was to come here, be married, and start a new life. I suppose she wasn't very specific on purpose. It wouldn't matter to me. My father made it clear I was to follow orders and not embarrass the family."

"George took care of that for all of us. I sent a telegram to Grandmother this afternoon. We'll have her answer soon and can make plans for you accordingly."

"I see. George has left us all hanging," she whispered.

Phillip laughed aloud. "Yes, he has. Until we know more, try to settle in."

"Earlier you said nobody knew who I was. Will they assume I'm just a family friend visiting? May I walk outside tomorrow to see the town and the homes?"

"Yes, of course. We have bridle paths if you ride.

Some lovely shops too."

"Fresh air will clear my mind."

"Did you enjoy the voyage?"

"I did," she said.

He caught the hesitation in her tone but didn't interrupt her.

"I traveled as a companion to another woman your grandmother knows, a Mrs. Cornwell. Have you met her? She's a lovely woman." She pushed around the food on her plate. "At first the size of the ship was overwhelming but exciting. Once I wandered a bit, it became familiar. Actually, the ship was beautiful. The woodwork and furnishings were luxurious. Even my stateroom was well appointed."

Making polite conversation was difficult when his body overrode his common sense. He had no right to these thoughts about his brother's almost bride. He cleared his throat. "When winter comes, the pond freezes over and people skate. I'm hoping to teach Alfred this winter."

"You'd have to teach me too," she said with a smile. "I'm afraid I've never skated. But I do know how to ride a horse and a bicycle."

"Excellent. A lot of the ladies bicycle or walk through town."

"Mr. Crane…Phillip, if I meet anyone, how should I introduce myself?"

"There is a wedding tomorrow morning. You'll come. Margaret and I will introduce you as our guest from England, an acquaintance of my grandmother Agnes. She's been here several times and is known in town. Anyone who has spent time in Rhode Island knows her or knows of her."

Cheryl A. Cornell

"That might be best. When I leave, nobody will notice."

"You've already been noticed, Eleanor. When I sent the telegram this afternoon, several people mentioned my guest."

"Oh," she said. "Will that hurt your reputation in the town?"

"No. My explanation was accepted. It will be easier to introduce you tomorrow. Margaret will help."

As he said the words, Margaret came into the room and began clearing the plates.

"We were just talking about introducing Eleanor to the town tomorrow at the wedding."

"That will be fine," she said. "Would you like coffee here or in the parlor?"

"The parlor," he told her as she whisked away the used dishes. He stood and moved behind Eleanor's seat. "Shall we?"

"Yes, of course." She followed him into the hallway and through the second door after the entrance. "It's a lovely room." She turned several times to look around.

Margaret came in with a silver tray and laid it on a small table.

"Thank you, Margaret," Phillip said.

"You're welcome." She left without further conversation.

"Have a seat." He pointed to a club chair before the hearth with neatly stacked logs waiting for the strike of a match. It was still warm enough not to need a fire. He was careful not to waste firewood.

Phillip poured coffee into one of the cups. "Milk or sugar in your coffee?"

"A bit of sugar, please."

He used a teaspoon to add sugar to the liquid and handed her the cup and saucer. Then he helped himself to a cup, echoing her spoonful of sugar in his cup. "You take sugar in your coffee and your tea black."

"Actually, I generally put a little sugar in tea also, but this afternoon it was all so confusing, and I didn't want to be a pest."

He sat in the chair beside her, a small table separating them. This was better for him because in profile he couldn't see her piercing blue eyes. They sat in silence, staring at the logs and sipping the coffee.

"Margaret makes good coffee," Eleanor said.

"Yes, she does."

"When will I be able to get a newspaper? I should start looking for other situations."

"What if George comes back?"

"George! I won't marry him now. He sounds like a callous and irresponsible man. I have more respect for myself. I'll find a position in a shop or as a maid in the city."

"You'd rather work as a maid than marry George?" His opinion of her instantly rose. She didn't seem like a lady who expected to be coddled, but appearances could be deceiving.

"I don't see the alternatives. If I married him after all this, he'd walk all over me for the rest of my life. I had a vision of what marriage might be like, but chasing after a man who will only marry me for his family money wasn't in the vision. I suppose I read too much growing up. I was hoping for a romantic marriage."

Phillip laughed, knowing from experience romance didn't last. Then again, he hadn't married for love. His marriage had been an arrangement between families.

"You'd be disappointed going into marriage with any man thinking romance will last a lifetime. Everyday life will get in the way of romance."

"I understand the realities of marriage and the day-to-day responsibilities. It's just that I've met couples who keep their closeness alive long-term. But they start off filled with love and respect and, especially, compromise."

"That sounds very nice, but the realities of running a house and family take a lot of time and work. Soon, you'll both be busy and forget the small niceties and slights."

"Just to get through the day?"

"In a way. I suppose I'm not the one to give advice about romance. My marriage was arranged. I got lucky, and we found a compatible lifestyle."

"She wanted to leave Newport?" Eleanor sipped her coffee.

"She wanted to leave her overbearing family, just as I did. Moving here, we were going to start anew. Raise our children without our elders looking over our shoulders all the time, pushing in with their opinions and outdated mores." He turned and gave her a quick smile.

"I'm truly sorry. You should have had the chance to make a new life here in the home you both designed. With the beautiful child you created."

"Yes, we should have had the chance, but the decision was taken from us. Now I'm thankful to have the home and the child. Romance and women aren't in my purview any longer."

"I suppose I can't miss something I never had. My opinions were from an outsider's view when people are on their best behavior."

"Miss Sterling, you are the ultimate optimist."

"Not any longer," she said. She finished the coffee in her cup and, when he pointed to the pot, refused a refill. "Please call me Eleanor. I appreciate your kindness, but you don't need to babysit me." She stood and wandered the room from corner to corner.

"I don't have time to babysit an adult. You managed to get across the ocean. You'll find your way around the house and town."

"I'll do my best not to embarrass you or the family. I'm quite tired. Would you mind if I went up?"

"Not at all. I hadn't realized the time."

"I'm still on shipboard time. May I stop to talk to Margaret first?"

"Of course. She'll be better at giving you a rundown on the household."

"Thanks. May I take the coffee tray with me?"

"Margaret usually collects the tray."

"I understand, but I'd like to feel useful and find out more about the running of the household."

"Be my guest." He pointed to the tray. He put his empty cup and saucer on it, and she lifted it.

"One last thing. Is there a reading room or library in town?"

"Not yet. But there will be soon. You're welcome to borrow books from my office."

"Thank you. Good night." She raised the tray higher and left him sitting alone before the hearth.

Phillip was glad she was gone. He'd noticed her hands didn't shake. The china hadn't rattled on the tray as it would when Ida carried anything heavy. Even just a cup of tea or coffee would rattle.

Comparing the women was unfair. It wasn't fair to

Ida, Eleanor, or him. But he noted the difference. He couldn't think straight when Eleanor was nearby. Never once since he'd lost his wife had he thought to want another.

Upstairs in her room Eleanor lingered in the beautiful bathroom while washing up. She didn't unpack her trunks. Instead, she took out her dark-green skirt with the matching jacket and a white shirtwaist and hung them to let the wrinkles fall out. The white shirtwaist with green trim at the collar was in good condition and didn't need pressing.

She removed the pins from her hair and let it drape over her shoulders. She unpacked her personal-care items and placed them on the dressing table. Brushing out her hair felt wonderful. In the last years at home, her father had decided she didn't need the help of a maid to dress, so she'd learned how to get her corset on and off by herself. It wasn't easy, but it was a necessity.

After that, she carefully hung the travel suit in the bathroom, hoping the steam from tomorrow morning's bath would freshen it for another wearing. Her nightgown was clean and soft from the ship's laundry.

Eleanor pulled back the covers, dropped onto the bed, and reached to shut the kerosene light. Settled under the blanket, she scanned the room in ambient light. The moon and stars shone just outside the front window. The sight was lovely. Whoever got to use the bedchamber would be lucky. Unfortunately, she didn't think she would be the one.

As sleep overtook her, she was thankful for the reprieve from the new problems that would fill her future.

****

26

A knock on the door woke Eleanor to bright sunshine. "Come in," she said, confused. She pulled the blanket to her chin.

Margaret entered with a tray.

Eleanor pushed up against the headboard. The tea smelled wonderful. "Thank you. I would have come down to breakfast. I looked for you last night to ask about the household schedule."

"We'll work that out over the next days. For now, drink your tea and enjoy the marmalade on the toast. Our routine will go back to normal tomorrow. Laura and Sally are helping the bride dress."

"Thank you, Margaret. Mr. Crane…Phillip mentioned a wedding today."

"Yes, we'll all go. It will be a good time to introduce you to the community."

"I took out my green suit. I hope it's suitable for today."

"That looks fine. Will you need help dressing?"

"No, thank you. I should be able to manage."

"We'll leave at eleven. Now finish your breakfast and clean up. Meet us downstairs in the foyer, and we'll walk to church."

"All right. I'll bring the tray down with me before eleven."

Margaret nodded and left. Eleanor poured the thick brew into a cup and added a spoonful of sugar. It tasted wonderful. Though orange marmalade had never been her favorite, she wouldn't complain. She used it sparingly, but either the taste wasn't what she remembered or the person who'd made this was a much better cook.

She managed to get her hair in place and pulled

herself together without the help of a maid.

Dressed by ten, she went downstairs with the tray. The kitchen was empty. She washed and dried the dishes from her breakfast tray. She didn't want to open cabinets, so she put the clean items back on the tray for Margaret to put away.

While exploring the space, she found the small glass room at the far end of the kitchen that Margaret had mentioned yesterday.

Last night, Phillip had told her she could borrow books from his office. Since she hadn't been given the house tour yet, she wouldn't search on her own. She sat at the atrium table, watching the wildlife outside. The birds were beautiful, and the squirrels ran up the trees. Yesterday, she and Daniel had passed several pastures with animals beyond the fences, but she hadn't had time to ask him if they belonged to the Cranes or another family.

She helped herself to a cup of coffee from the pot still on the stove and studied life beyond the glass. A soft breeze rippled the leaves on the trees, and the tall grasses in the distance danced with motion. What would winter be like here? She rinsed her cup for a second time and replaced it on the tray. She carefully opened the rear door to admire the view. For the first of September, the weather was lovely, crisp and cool.

The lands seemed to go on forever, or for as far as she could see. She wondered how much of the land was Phillip's. When possible, she'd like to walk those fields and lose herself in the beauty and quiet.

The noise she heard from the rear of the house sounded like laughter. This morning, she noticed the kitchen door opened onto a large service porch. She stepped out and breathed in the fresh, cool air. Phillip came up with the young boy she'd seen yesterday on his shoulders. The familial connection was obvious. He stopped abruptly when he saw her.

"Good morning," she said.

"Morning." Phillip reached up and took his son from his shoulders. He bent down and whispered something to the boy.

Alfred took his hand and walked beside his father to her side.

"Eleanor, this is my son, Alfred."

"Hello, Alfred. We almost met yesterday."

The child glanced at her and back at his father. Then he stood straight and thrust his hand forward. "Nice…meet you," he mumbled.

She pumped his hand twice. "It's nice to meet you too. Is it cold outside?" she asked, seeing the child covered in several layers of clothing.

"Yep," he said, and Phillip tugged his hand. "Yes, ma'am."

Eleanor caught Phillip's slight smile confirming the child had answered correctly.

"Maybe, with your father's permission, someday we can venture outside, and you can show me around the gardens."

"As long as Nanny is with you," Phillip told her.

"Of course," she answered.

"We're going to get cleaned up for the ceremony. This will be Alfred's first time witnessing a wedding."

"How exciting. I haven't seen a wedding in a very long time."

Alfred stared at her, shuffling his feet.

"Go on now, upstairs," Phillip said. "Nanny will be

waiting. No arguing about your bath."

"Yes, sir." Alfred dropped his father's hand and bolted toward the entry.

"He is adorable," Eleanor said.

"Yes, when he's asleep. Come, we have time for a quick cup of coffee before we leave."

She walked behind him into the kitchen. He poured coffee into two cups and brought them to the table in the center of the kitchen where they'd had their tea yesterday.

He put the sugar bowl and a spoon before her. "Did you sleep well?" Instead of sitting across from her, he sat beside her with an empty seat between them so that they looked out the back door, not at each other.

"Yes, very well, thank you. The room is lovely." She fidgeted with her cup, brought it to her lips, but didn't drink. She searched for a safe topic of conversation. "Is there anyone in particular that is important to meet today?"

"A few people. I'll introduce you with a bit of their information."

"You mean like 'This is Mrs. So-and-So, the head of the choir'?"

"Or 'This is Mr. So-and-So. Don't turn your back on him. He may be in his eighties, but he still likes to pinch the ladies.'"

Eleanor burst out laughing, relieved Phillip would guide her. "Him, I'll watch out for. Who is the biggest gossip in town?"

"Right now we are still a small town. Most people here are kind and welcoming. What will happen when the rest of the residents move in over the next years remains to be seen."

"So be polite, but don't volunteer any real information?"

"Exactly. I've got to wash up, or we'll be late." He stood, put his cup and saucer in the sink, and left without another word.

Eleanor remained there in the light of the kitchen, letting her brain wander. She'd managed to get herself across the ocean and to upstate New York. She just had to make sure she wasn't caught staring at the master of the house. She had to keep reminding herself that she was supposed to be there for George.

But since George had run away, it wouldn't hurt to look at this man and wonder what it might feel like if he kissed her or touched her. While her thoughts were improper in all directions, seeing him, talking to him, created an unaccustomed rumbling heat inside. This was an attraction she would have to fight while she was here. Her future was uncertain. She couldn't bond with Phillip when she was to marry another or move on depending on circumstances.

****

Eleanor often wondered how a bride got ready for a morning wedding. Her preference would be in the afternoon, but some archaic law stated weddings couldn't bite into afternoon family time.

She and Phillip walked to church with Nanny and Albert. Phillip had cleaned up and wore a jacket over a clean shirt, vest, and tie. Nanny seemed like a no-nonsense woman who had a job to do, and keeping track of a precocious three-year-old child kept her busy.

Margaret and Daniel had gone ahead to help with any last-minute flower arrangements. Eleanor had met Margaret's husband, Daniel, briefly yesterday on the ride from the train station. He was in charge of the Crane house, lands, and animals. She'd seen him in passing before they left for the church. He'd been polite but preoccupied with getting ready for the ceremony.

The walk to church was pleasant. Eleanor smiled at those she passed, and Phillip introduced her to several others. When people learned her full name, they immediately associated her with the town's founder.

"Yes, we have a very distant familial connection," she said but quickly added, "I never had the pleasure of meeting him as I was born and raised in England. This is my first trip across the pond. I've been looking forward to meeting the rest of my long-lost family."

Most accepted her rehearsed statement, but she had no way of knowing what they thought behind her back with their whispers.

She thought the Crane home looked like a castle. The church near the center of town reminded her of a cathedral. It was a huge building with large leaded-glass windows that spread their colors on the walls, floors, and pews below. The patterns would change with the weather and time of day. She learned this was to be the first wedding in the new church.

Phillip guided her to a pew near the front while Nanny and Alfred took seats in the last pew. Eleanor assumed that if the child got cranky, they could make a quick escape without being noticed. Several other children were there with their nannies too. Just before the service started, Margaret and Daniel slid in beside Phillip from the far side.

"The flowers are lovely," Eleanor whispered to Phillip.

"Thank you. They're from my greenhouse."

"The ones on the altar and the nosegays on the pews?"

He nodded. "We have an organ on order and hope to have it installed by spring. The pews for the choir should be installed by the first of the year. The new candleholders should arrive soon."

The gentleman at the piano started playing, and the choir filed in and assembled before him. A large wooden cross stood in the center of a long wooden table before the back wall. Only candles lit the area. While the woodwork was stunning, the candleholders were small. She could only imagine what the permanent ones would look like.

All things to come, she decided. Would she be there long enough to see the finished church? She hoped she would. She couldn't help but wonder how the space would be decorated for Christmas. She released a deep sigh, acknowledging she wouldn't be the bride to experience the holiday season.

The groom walked to the front and stood with his back to the door. He ran his finger under his collar as if it were choking him. The pianist changed the song, and everyone stood. The bride came down the aisle, holding an older man's arm. She wore a beautiful pale-pink dress. She stared straight ahead. When she reached the waiting groom, both seemed to relax, large smiles on their lips.

They made a lovely couple, and both spoke their vows clearly. They didn't kiss at the altar. They walked back down the aisle, arm in arm, to the front doors where they waited to receive their guests. That was where they shared their first married kiss.

On the way out, Phillip introduced Eleanor to

everyone in turn. All she could do was smile politely. She'd never remember all their names. If she were to live here, to make a life here, eventually she would learn them.

Phillip had a prepared sentence. He nodded and said the person's name. "This is Eleanor Sterling, visiting from England. Our grandmothers are good friends."

She repeated their names and added something complimentary about the church or town. Some people asked uncomfortable questions about her being Phillip's fiancée. He and Margaret were quick to explain this was her first trip to America and they'd never met before. Nanny took Alfred home early.

The reception at the clubhouse was lovely. Cake, punch, and more introductions and questions. Again, she could only wonder what the people thought of her. She'd never know for sure. Their opinions didn't matter to her future.

She felt inundated with information. Most women just nodded, the men shook her hand, and a few women looked at her, a head-to-toe look.

"Have you met George?" one woman asked.

Another said, "Are you next to wed? I hear George is in the market for a wife."

She politely put them both off. "I'm just stopping to introduce myself before heading to Newport." She didn't give any time frame, saying only that this was a stop on her way north.

One woman had a younger daughter at her side. The mother glared at her with narrowed eyes.

The girl was obviously being positioned to become Phillip's next wife. Neither of these women seemed happy to meet her. She would ask Margaret later about their relationship and expectations.

"Alfred was very well behaved during the service," she whispered to Phillip.

"Yes, Nanny keeps him in line."

She understood she was the oddity of the group and everyone watched her, waiting for a mistake or faux pas. Smiling and nodding kept her from major errors. When the hour was up and the bride and groom had left, people filtered out. She hoped to get back to the Crane Castle before making a fool of herself.

A scowl crossed Phillip's features. From behind, she felt a stranger's hand on her shoulder. She turned quickly to see a slick-looking man leering at her.

"Miss Sterling, this is Mr. Deiden." Phillip sounded annoyed.

"Miss Sterling," he said with a slight bow. "I'm so pleased to meet you. I heard you were visiting." He gave her the once-over look she despised. "You're a guest of the Cranes'?"

"Yes."

"Just a guest, not a romantic interest?"

"No. I've just arrived in the States. I'm visiting with the family until the holidays when Grandmother Crane arrives."

"Wonderful. That means you're available for me to show you around the area. Maybe soon you'll allow me to show you New York City."

"No, thank you, Mr. Deiden. I've already spent time in the city before arriving at the Park. I've obligations not to be dismissed."

"I'm sure you could find some free time." His black eyes ogled her, reminding her of the men on the ship.

"No, thank you. As I've said, I have a full schedule

with the family, not to be ignored." She turned to leave, but he touched her shoulder a second time. She hoped the glaring look she gave him would dissuade his attention. She tried another tack. "Do you live here in the Park with your wife and family? I'd like to meet her."

He gave her a cynical laugh. "I've not fallen into the trap of marriage yet. I prefer to enjoy my bachelorhood a bit longer."

Phillip interceded. "Frederick is living in his parents' home."

"I much prefer the lifestyle of New York City. I weekend here."

"Enjoy your time in the city, Mr. Deiden." With determined steps, she moved away, but Deiden followed.

Phillip moved beside her. "Frederick, Miss Sterling has declined your invitation."

"Yes, she's a lovely addition to the town. I see your son is prospering."

He said the words as if the child were an inconvenience. She hadn't liked the look of him from the start. Now she decided he was just rude.

"Yes, Alfred is well."

"Good to hear. I was just telling Miss Sterling I could be her guide around town and maybe in New York City."

"Yes, and I heard her politely tell you her schedule was full."

"If she's family, then she should be free to see all men. It's not like she's a romantic interest, or am I wrong?"

"I've already declined your invitation, Mr. Deiden. While I appreciate the offer, I'm not interested in spending time with you."

"You have your answer, Deiden. I'll see you on the golf course." He offered Eleanor his arm, and she gently placed her hand on it and walked beside him to the other side of the room.

"He is awful," she whispered to Phillip as they made their way through the crowd.

When she began to believe she'd get through the day without any more issues, the snobbish mother she'd met outside the church all but dragged her daughter to Phillip's side.

"Mrs. Stevens, Miss Stevens," Eleanor said.

"Phillip, we were wondering if you will have time to have supper with us this Saturday."

"Thank you, Mrs. Stevens, but we already discussed your many invitations. I won't be able to join you anytime soon." He turned to leave, but the older woman grasped his arm.

"Don't think we all don't know about George leaving his fiancée without even meeting her. After seeing her, we know why. Taking this girl into your home will not fare well for your social life or business."

Phillip's expression faltered. Whether it was disgust or annoyance, Eleanor didn't miss the change.

"Miss Sterling's social standing is higher than yours, Mrs. Stevens." He paused, tightening his lips. "I've tried to be polite with your insistence and attitude, but that doesn't work, so I'll be blunt. I know how your deceased husband made his money. And everyone knows his death was at the hand of his lover's husband. You've been trying to maneuver me into marriage with your daughter, and it's not a prospect I'd look forward to or consider."

Mrs. Stevens exhaled a loud harrumph, and Phillip

winked at her daughter. She nodded and turned away.

"You should take her to find a husband someplace where her family's history isn't common knowledge," Phillip added.

"Well, I never," Mrs. Stevens started.

"Maybe if you had, your husband wouldn't have found solace with another woman."

Eleanor concentrated on not letting her jaw drop.

"Momma, please, may we go? Miss Sterling, I apologize for my mother's feeble attempt to find me a husband. One I don't want. Phillip and I have had this conversation several times over. Neither of us is looking toward a forced union." The daughter stood straight. "Come along, Mother. You've embarrassed all of us yet again. We'll discuss it when we're home." The young woman started walking. When her mother didn't follow, she paused. "Mother!"

The older woman turned with a huff and followed her.

"Are you sure you don't want her?" Eleanor asked Phillip. She tried to hold back a smile.

He directed her several steps toward the door. "Mrs. Stevens is looking for a bank account. Elizabeth and I have talked about this, and her goal is to turn eighteen and head out west. She'll start in San Francisco and explore from there. She wants to expand her musical talent, and I wholeheartedly hope she makes that happen." He grimaced. "As long as she takes her mother with her."

"Does my being here make the situation worse?"

"No. Mrs. Stevens assumes if she decrees something, everyone will fall in line."

"I hope Elizabeth becomes a musician known

worldwide for her music. Anyone who puts up with a mother like that deserves to get away."

"She'll go after the first of the year. The mother will go with her because she has no friends here and has already burned her bridges in Newport. She's a bitter woman."

"I'll say I agree with you there. Did she start this when your wife passed away?" Eleanor glanced around to make sure nobody could hear their conversation.

"No, she started talking of this when we were children. She'd go to my grandmother and tell her to keep me single until her daughter grew up to be my wife."

"What did your grandmother say?"

"About what you'd think. She said there is a large age gap between us, too much to be reasonable. That Elizabeth should be put in boarding school until she grows up. Mrs. Stevens didn't agree, and Elizabeth never got an education. When her husband was killed, she moved Elizabeth to the Park, hoping for another chance to marry her to…anyone."

"I feel sorry for Elizabeth."

"Don't. She remains quiet in public, but she has a plan. I just hope her mother goes with her. In reality, everyone in town hopes she'll leave."

"Tell me about the town, about the homes and residences." She was aware of being alone with Phillip and forced space between them as they walked.

She would linger in front of a house, and Phillip would tell her the family name and a bit about their history. "No two homes can look exactly the same. Exterior colors, gardens, and porch railings all have to have individual designs." He mentioned how the land looked before the homes were built and the reasons for lot sizes.

"Thankfully, you met most of the townsfolk, and the worst of them, today. Everyone is generally happy to be here in this new community for a fresh start. Mr. Stevens purchased the land while they were still living up north. He said he wanted to be closer to New York for business. Unfortunately, his business was another man's wife."

"Mr. Deiden is very determined in a glossy way."

"You're a lovely woman, Eleanor. You're free to get to know him if you'd like. Just don't tell Grandmother."

"I'll refrain from any further contact with him. He reminds me of the dandy men I met in the past." She stopped to admire a grand home on a hill. "The porch is lovely."

"Yes, this is one of the first homes to be completed." He told her the name of the family who lived there. "You said you've met men like Deiden in the past?"

"There were men similar to him on the ship. All puffed up and assuming women would swoon at their feet."

"And you didn't swoon," he kidded.

She smiled at his teasing her. "No. Mostly I glared at their advances, recoiled at their groping hands." She saw he was smiling back. "It's not funny, Phillip. It was gross and humiliating."

"How did you get away from them on the ship?"

"I asked the captain to keep them away from us at dinner. Mrs. Cornwell was very persuasive that I was promised and men's advances wouldn't be welcome at our table."

"Were you saving yourself for George?"

"No. George was just an idea, not real until we met.

And with the current situation, we won't meet. Those men on the ship had expectations I wasn't willing to fulfill." She turned and smiled at Phillip. "Just another reason the family called me a spinster, rude, and unfriendly."

"Is that who you truly are or who you've become to keep men away from you?"

"Those men deserved my disdain along with Mr. Deiden."

"You'd prefer to be alone?"

"Alone would be better than with the likes of those men." She paused as they walked through the stone pillars of the town proper. "The pillars are impressive."

He went on to tell her about the stone used in their construction. When the conversation stalled, he continued. "Who would you prefer to spend time with?"

"I'm not averse to spending time with you. I'm not sure how you feel about that situation. I understand it's forced because of George abandoning me."

"I'll look forward to time with you, even under the uncertain situation we're in now."

Eleanor took a deep breath. "Yes, the situation with George is uncertain. In my mind, there won't be a relationship with George. I deserve more from the man I'll marry."

"Yes, you do deserve more."

She stopped to admire the colors of the leaves turning on a tree bordering Phillip's property. She refrained from fanning her face with her hand at Phillip's comment of her deserving more. "Tell me about your business. I believe you're an architect?"

They walked slowly as she admired the greenery.

"Yes, I trained and oversaw the building of a few

homes in Newport. I also did the plans for my home. But I prefer to be a landscape architect."

"As long as you're happy," she mused.

She asked about his job, the houses, and the people who lived in them. Phillip stopped to scan the nearby land and homes. She needed to not consider this her home. She waited while he moved to the boundary planting and pulled a few stray weeds. He returned his attention to her, and she brought up a topic that was important to her.

"I'd like to ask a favor. I'd prefer to have meals downstairs and not in bed, although it was lovely. Last night's meal in the dining room was wonderful, but it's so much more work for Margaret. She mentioned you used to eat in the kitchen or the glass atrium to the side. May we continue to do that unless you're entertaining?"

"Of course."

"Thank you." They stood side by side, and she asked him what type of shrub encircled the space. He gave her the technical answer and then the common term. He also explained about the native grasses he'd planted to keep a natural look.

Phillip slowed his steps and cleared his throat as he surveyed the entrance to his home. "I got a telegram back from Agnes this morning. She wants you to stay here for a while. She's against sending you back to England. If you can be comfortable, I suggest we settle in and enjoy the holidays. Grandmother will be down before Thanksgiving and stay through the holidays. After the first of the year, the situation will become clear."

"Are you sure you want company for that long?"

"We should settle in and become a united front. Nobody changes Agnes's plans. She wants to meet you, and I'm to make you comfortable," he said.

"Just what you wanted—the houseguest who never leaves."

"I know I was rude yesterday when we talked in the kitchen. I didn't know how to tell you the truth without hurting your feelings. I felt honesty was the best way, even if it hurt."

"I appreciate the truth. I hadn't realized how uncomfortable you were being the bearer of such news."

"Then we have an understanding. We'll be fine."

"You aren't afraid of gossip from the people in town?"

"I think the biggest land mine was blown up today. Now when anyone asks, we can say you'll stay here for the holidays since Grandmother is coming down."

"I'd like to write a few notes. I'll use yesterday's date to thank Mrs. Cornwell. I'll draft one to my father to say I arrived and was welcomed."

"That might be best. I'm not sure if Grandmother plans on contacting your father again. I do know Mrs. Cornwell from Newport. She and Grandmother grew up together. They're lifelong friends, and the families were close."

"No matter what, Mrs. Cornwell deserves a thank-you note. Hopefully one to my family will keep them guessing." They were at the front door, and Eleanor stopped. "I'm a tad confused. May I ask about you calling Mrs. Crane, your grandmother, Agnes?"

Phillip paused with his hand at the doorknob and laughed. "I've been away from her influence for a long time. When she's here, we respect her with Grandmother. When she annoys me with her unsolicited influence, I refer to her as Agnes."

Eleanor smiled. "I understand. Back home we had several relatives who had similar influence. My brothers and I did the same thing, referring to them without their titles in private." She studied him in the midday light. "I'll get started on my notes this afternoon."

"That would make sense."

He opened the door and waited for her to enter. "If you'll excuse me, I have some work to catch up on in the greenhouse."

"You shouldn't feel obligated to entertain me. Last night you mentioned I might borrow some books."

"Yes, of course. Margaret will get you acquainted with the house and schedule today. I must be going."

He all but vaulted up the stairs, and she didn't see him again. Eleanor assumed he used the back staircase to leave.

Was he so uncomfortable with her presence he had to get away from her as quickly as possible? Of course, he had a business to run. And though it was best that they not spend a lot of time together, she was disappointed and confused.

Yes, she was disappointed about her almost husband running away. She'd thought it through last night and concluded that his running away was probably for the best. A man who wouldn't take responsibility seriously after making the agreement wasn't a man she wanted to deal with.

Her immediate quandary was her attraction to Phillip Crane. He didn't seem like a man who would want a houseguest with no predetermined end date. Yes, he was one of the most handsome men she'd ever seen, let alone met. His dark hair, beard, and tall, muscled frame were hard to ignore. His hands, large and work worn, intrigued her. She liked that he was tall. Most of the men she met were her height or only a bit taller. When she stood beside Phillip, she didn't have to slouch. She, too, was able to stand tall. Her mind kept returning to how his hands might feel against her skin.

She would have to be careful to keep her distance from him, or she might reach to touch the short, soft-looking beard that covered his face. Just the idea of being near him made her blush inside and out. Never had any man created this warmth within her. Now she understood what other women spoke about when they cooed over their mates. But he wasn't going to be her true mate.

Chapter Three

Upstairs after the wedding, Eleanor changed into a clean light-blue shirtwaist with a dark-blue skirt. Downstairs, she went to the kitchen and gently knocked on the door. She could hear several women talking about the wedding. She hoped Margaret had time to show her around the house, especially Phillip's office so she could borrow books.

"Come in, Eleanor." Margaret welcomed her. "This is Laura. She'll be your maid. This is Sally. She's training to be a maid."

Eleanor nodded hello to the women.

"Come," Margaret said. "I'll give you a tour of the house. The Mister said to make sure you knew where his office was so you could borrow books."

She left with Margaret, who pointed out closets, the office Phillip used, the sitting room, and the formal parlor where they'd had coffee last night. While they walked, Margaret filled her in on their daily routine. Upstairs, she was shown the nursery, although Alfred and his nanny were absent. She saw the other two guest rooms across from her suite. Margaret didn't show her inside Phillip's private rooms.

She told Eleanor there were two small guest rooms on the third floor, and she and Daniel had a bedroom and sitting room up on the third floor, which was accessed by the rear staircase. The maids shared a room across the hall from them. The other staff came in daily or several times a week to do the heavy work, such as scrubbing floors and cleaning windows and drapes. Eleanor would meet them in time. The housemaids did the daily dusting and straightening.

Downstairs, Margaret directed her to the office, a masculine room with windows overlooking the side yard. It was bright, and the walls had built-in bookshelves from ceiling to floor. They were filled with books. A large drafting table was centered on the back wall, and a partner's desk sat in the middle of the room. Several comfortable chairs were placed around the room as a counterpoint to the wooden stool at the drafting table and the high-back chairs on either side of the desk.

"On the walk back from the church, Mr. Crane said I could use his office to write letters and to borrow a few books." She wanted to reinforce she had Phillip's permission to use the room.

"There you go." Margaret pointed to the empty side of the double desk.

"Thanks. I'll just run up to my room and get my stationery."

"I'll call you for teatime."

They left the room together. Margaret headed toward the kitchen while Eleanor bounded upstairs.

Back in the large, masculine office, Eleanor started at the right of the doorway and began reading the titles.

"It would take me a lifetime to read all these," she said aloud. As soon as she said the words, she reminded herself this wasn't to be her home. She walked around the shelf-lined room and returned to the beginning. She chose a book on life in Newport, one on architecture, and a Dickens novel.

She sat at the huge desk with her private stationery and drafted carefully worded notes to be sent out the next day. The one to her father was basic. She'd loved the ship and was enjoying the train ride north. By making it sound as if she were still traveling, she avoided any information about George. The note to Mrs. Cornwell reiterated her pleasure at their time on the ship and assured her she was well on her way to her destination.

Both were required, but she didn't feel it necessary to tell either of the changes since the original arrangements were made. The last one was to George's grandmother. She thanked her for the trip and said she looked forward to meeting her. She didn't mention the missing groom-to-be. She wrote about the beauty of the home with its lovely turret and wood paneling. She added she was looking forward to exploring the lands and town where she temporarily resided.

She sealed the notes and left them on the corner of the desk. Later she'd take her stationery back to her room. She brought the books she'd chosen to the window seat. After settling on the cushioned seat, she scanned each book before deciding which to read first.

****

As Phillip washed up for tea, Margaret mentioned that Eleanor was in his office. He headed in that direction to tell her tea was ready and stopped short in the hallway. With a glance, he felt his stomach clench and his hands go sweaty. Eleanor was asleep on the bay window seat with books beside her and on her lap. Curiosity got the best of him, and he walked toward her. The one on her lap was a history of Newport. She must have fallen asleep while reading. He retraced his steps to the hall door.

He saw the neatly stacked letters on the corner of his desk. He stood in the doorway, staring at the woman. The sunlight brought out the golden highlights in her hair and the chiseled features of her face. He was surprised yet again that she was beautiful in her own way, one that ignited something deep within him. She had crossed an ocean and immediately had her future wiped away. Yet she'd never cried or cursed in front of him.

Seeing Eleanor reminded him that he'd accepted his arranged marriage to get away from Newport, as had Ida. She'd felt strangled by the rules of etiquette and had been looking for any valid excuse to move away. They'd had conversations before the marriage about just that. Neither had been looking to marry. They had both been looking to escape the family mores. Agnes had arranged the marriage of convenience, and they'd accepted the bargain to be free of Newport. He'd grown up with Agnes's meddling ways and agreed to take Ida as his bride.

Margaret bustled through the hallway, then paused. He turned to her and pointed to the sleeping woman.

She moved behind him and peered over his shoulder. "She is lovely."

"Yes. Too good for George," he mumbled. He realized he'd said it aloud and cleared his throat to defuse the comment. It wouldn't do him any good to have the maids talking behind his back that he was interested in his brother's fiancée.

"It looks like she got her notes written," Margaret said. "Should we wake her for tea or let her sleep?"

"You wake her." He tried to make his statement sound unimportant. "I'm going up to the nursery to get Alfred for tea." He left Margaret to rouse the sleeping

49

woman he was rapidly falling in lust with.

As he returned, Margaret and Eleanor left the office. He had Alfred's small hand in his and patiently waited while the child navigated the steps. In the parlor, he joined Eleanor for tea.

"Good afternoon, Phillip. Hello, Alfred," she said.

The child pulled away from him and, before Phillip could catch him, all but launched himself at the sofa and onto Eleanor's lap. "Hello."

"Hello, Alfred. It's nice to see you again."

Phillip was shocked to see his son so lively around this stranger. Alfred usually hid behind Nanny's skirts, but this woman made him smile. The two interacted and laughed together. This was a new side of his son and a different view into Eleanor's personality. To Phillip's knowledge, they'd only met briefly the day she arrived and had walked to church that morning for the wedding. But Nanny had held him tightly by the hand, walking several steps behind them.

"Alfred, we don't enter a room or introduce ourselves to strangers in that manner."

The boy turned and smiled at him. It was a smile he'd rarely seen. Then again, he didn't spend as much time with him as he'd like. But he had a budding business to oversee for their futures. After all, children were supposed to be raised by their nannies and only see their parents at teatime. He began to wonder if this was right for his son. Did he owe the child more of his time even if society dictated other rules? Or was this particular woman not the right nanny for his son?

Laughter interrupted his thoughts. Alfred sat beside Eleanor, and they talked animatedly.

"You don't have to play with him," Phillip said.

"We were discussing the alphabet."

"I don't know…all. She help me," Alfred piped up.

A deep-pink blush crept up Eleanor's cheeks. "I didn't mean to overreach."

"Numbers too," the child said with a wide smile.

"Yes, well, we'll decide that another time. After all, Eleanor is a guest, not your nanny." He glanced at her and back to his son. "Go along now. Margaret has your tea ready in the kitchen."

Alfred managed to get off the sofa with help from Eleanor. "Bye." He raced out of the room.

Phillip stayed in the doorway until the child reached the kitchen door. He entered the room, walked to the seat across from her, and waited while Eleanor poured tea for both of them.

"I'm sorry. I didn't mean to overstep. He was talking about his lessons. I didn't pry."

"I didn't think you did. I'm afraid Alfred has had a lighter hand than most children. With his mother passing and my work, Nanny has had too much free rein over him."

"That's what nannies are supposed to do. They raise the children and teach them."

He sat across from her and took his teacup. "I saw you managed to get your letters written. I'll get them mailed tomorrow."

"Thank you, but if you don't mind, I'd like to take them to the post myself. I'm used to taking morning walks, and it would familiarize me with the community and show people I'm just a guest. Unless you'd rather I not."

"I've told you I don't mind you walking the neighborhood. It's just that most of the time the maids do those errands."

"I understand. I don't want to make more work for Margaret."

"Walk to the post tomorrow." He paused to sip his tea but ignored the biscuits on the tea tray.

"It seems the more I try to help, the more nuisance I become."

"It's just the circumstances," he said. "I saw you chose a few books to read. Have you had time to do any reading?"

"I started on the history of Newport but will admit I dozed in the sun."

"Maybe you need something more to your interest."

"Yes, it was a bit…long-winded. The photos made it look lovely."

He watched her try not to laugh. "It's likely you'd learn more touring it in person rather than reading about the society."

"And their rules."

"Yes, the rules. We're much more relaxed here."

"For which I am greatly thankful." She resettled the books beside her. "I was raised with strict social rules. Some days I think I rebelled against them just because they were so strict. But I wasn't allowed to voice opinions. Even while my almost marriage was being arranged, I had no say. I wasn't informed until the deal was complete."

"That I can relate to. As I've mentioned, my marriage was arranged too." He stopped talking. He'd already revealed too much to this stranger. If she were to leave his home, which was the plan, he didn't want her to tell others about his disappointment with his wife or Ida's perceived disappointment with him from the comments he'd let slip.

"Would it upset the balance of the household if I spent time with your son? Maybe taking him on a walk into the backyard. May I read to him?" she asked. "Books of your choosing."

"I'll check what Nanny has been reading to him. As to taking him outside, I think the yard would be best until you get to know each other and you know your way around town."

"Of course." She glanced out the side window. "I'm not looking to take Nanny's place, just to be useful. I often read to my brothers and taught them their numbers when they were young."

"I got the impression your brothers were older."

"No, both are younger—one by three years and the other by five. But my nanny taught me to read early and encouraged me to get the boys interested in books."

"Did it work?" He leaned forward to refill his cup.

He lifted the pot, and she shook her head.

"It might have, but I was just a girl. Nobody in my family considered I had value beyond learning to be a hostess and wife someday. No one took me seriously. I can't tell you how many times a book was taken from my hands and replaced by sewing threads."

"And you don't like to sew?" he asked with a half laugh.

"I didn't mind the sewing, but I thought I could sew and read. Unfortunately, Father didn't think reading was worth the time. My brothers never wanted to read or study. The only reason they did was to beat out each other for the estate someday."

"Isn't the oldest the heir?"

"Most often, but Father has a way of using the heir

issue to pit them against each other." She leaned forward and put her cup back on the tray. "He felt they would take their studies seriously if there was an incentive attached."

"Did it work?"

She tilted her head to the side. "To a point. They've been in a lifelong struggle to persuade Father they would be the best to continue the estate once he passed."

"Has the issue been settled?"

"When they found out I was being sent away, they both seemed to relax. Knowing I wouldn't be a lifelong drain on their accounts and social lives eased them. I truthfully don't know what will happen."

She stood and walked to the doorway. "I'll return the books to their shelves on my way upstairs. I glanced through most of the book about Newport. I'd read something similar before I left home to familiarize myself with the region. I was unable to find much on the Park."

"It is a new community." He knew if he didn't continue their conversation, it would end. "What books interest you?"

"Too many," she said with a laugh. "I've read Brontë and Austen, but not in public. Father wouldn't allow that, so I read those in my room. Tolstoy's *War and Peace* took a while to get through. Dickens was a favorite. I did enjoy Alcott's *Little Women*, and I especially enjoyed *The Mysterious Key and What It Opened*. Just before I left, I borrowed a copy of Oscar Wilde's *The Picture of Dorian Gray*. That was an interesting book. I'd like to read it again one day. I rushed through it because it was borrowed."

"Seems you are well read, even if some of it

was…not for public consumption."

"I learned to get my sewing done early in the day so I could spend the afternoons and evenings reading in my room." She gave him a devilish grin. "Reasonably, I understand it was what society thought I should spend my time doing. But once you learn the basic stitches, how much time can any one person spend practicing them?" She shook her head. "I'm sorry. That was impertinent."

"You wanted to learn other things?"

"Yes, but I overstepped my place when I mentioned I wanted to learn more about planting the fields, rotating the crops, and learning the accounts."

"Which threatened your brothers, I assume?"

She tossed back her head and laughed—a full, hearty laugh. "Yes. If nothing else, it forced them to take the work of running the estate seriously." She hesitated and asked, "May I play the piano occasionally? I'll try to be respectful of Alfred's nap time."

"Of course you can play. I'm afraid to say it has sat there since we moved in. I never seem to find time to play."

"It was an acceptable form of instruction growing up. I'd like to practice occasionally."

"Let me know if it's out of tune, and I'll have someone come in and take care of it."

"Thank you."

Sally and Alfred approached. "Sorry to interrupt, sir. I'm about to take the young master back to the nursery," Sally said.

The child pushed past her and ran to his father.

"I'll take him up, Sally," Phillip said, and she turned and left.

"Alfred, it is time to head back to Nanny. What do you say?"

Alfred looked up at Eleanor. "Nice...see, ma'am." He gave an awkward bow.

"I hope to see you again, Alfred. Have a good night."

"See you at supper," Phillip said and took Alfred's hand.

He was thankful to be away from Eleanor. She was an interesting woman, one who wouldn't be appeased with embroidery samplers and sleeping the day away. While most women he'd known in his past were content to be waited on, Eleanor might take a different road. She talked a good line, but he had no idea if that was for show or if she truly felt disillusioned by her place in society.

She would be a dangerous woman indeed, at least to his quiet, staid life. She was becoming an irresistible impulse, one he'd have to resist.

Downstairs, he heard "Clair de lune" and paused to listen. She was good, perhaps a bit off key, but that wasn't her fault. Considering he hadn't touched the instrument in years, he couldn't complain. She had a light touch. He stood at the upper railing and listened to her play. He'd never heard music filter upstairs in this house. Now he acknowledged another thing missing from the home.

****

Eleanor was finding her way around the Park. Each morning after breakfast, she would wander through town, admiring the homes and gardens as she learned her way around. She'd found a smooth rhythm that didn't interrupt the household. She enjoyed the cool, brisk mornings and the red, yellow, and orange colors of the changing leaves.

Each morning, Laura would bring her a cup of coffee and help her with her hair and dressing. Having a second set of hands to help her with the daily dressing chores was a pleasure. She had breakfast downstairs and made a point of asking Margaret if she could be of any help. With the usual "No, thank you. Enjoy your day" answer, she grabbed her cape, gloves, and hat and began her walking tours.

She introduced herself with the same phrase. "I'm visiting with the Crane family until Grandmother comes for the holidays."

Apparently, the Crane name held some status. She'd been introduced as Eleanor Sterling at the wedding, and most people remembered her or her connection to the town's founding family. The actual connection had never been verified; her grandfather had used the name to further the family's social status.

She never mentioned that her side of the family was several times removed and had been left behind in England when the rest immigrated because their core values weren't similar. While her father was content to live off the family estate's income, he had no potential to strengthen it monetarily. Rather, they were left behind so as not to drain the family coffers.

Occasionally, she made a small purchase, but mostly, she admired the stock. One shop owner asked if she was related to Mrs. Cornwell. She was surprised they knew her companion from the trip from England to America, but she remembered that Mrs. Cornwell had grown up with Agnes and knew her well. Apparently, Grandmother Crane was in contact with most of the residents she'd known from Newport. Eleanor spoke mostly of the beautiful ship and the vastness of the ocean. She avoided any questions about her future in the Park.

After the first week, Phillip had offered her the use of his bicycle. That was one of the activities she'd enjoyed back home, and she had the proper riding outfit. She enjoyed the walks but more so the rides. She hoped no one in town would be horrified by her modified trousers originally designed for horseback riding. Her knee-high boots complemented the pants. The sturdy matching tweed jacket was shorter in the front and longer in the back for comfort.

She'd seen horses in the barn on one of her first walks but didn't dare breach the barn door without asking permission. And she hadn't asked Phillip about riding. Asking him to put aside his business to accompany her on a ride would be rude. Even if she wasn't to marry George, wanting to spend time with his brother was beyond unconventional. But did she care if she became unconventional? This was a new world for her. She was letting herself think beyond the agreement.

None of her concerns mattered. Gossip would abound because she was an oddity to the town. Staying with the widower Crane was obviously a topic of conversation. She hadn't forgotten the comments at the wedding.

She rode farther each day on the cycle and learned more about the streets and paths. For late September, the weather was still lovely, with crisp mornings, warm afternoons, and cool evenings. Some mornings, she sat by the pond. On cloudy days she visited the church to reflect on her unknown future. Her main wish was that she could somehow live in this beautiful place.

She was now an interloper in the family. Living with her father, she'd had little say in her future. Now she had none. In the afternoons, when she could find a newspaper, she would scour it for nanny or housekeeper positions. She'd found some, but Phillip suggested she wait until after the holidays before making permanent decisions.

In the last days over tea, they talked about the history of the United States. She hoped the questions she asked weren't too simple. She'd done some reading before she came, but sometimes she had questions her book didn't answer.

She asked Phillip to explain the Sherman Antitrust Act of 1890. He'd explained it in terms she understood, which led to other questions. She asked for clarification about their president, Grover Cleveland. She was from England, and Queen Victoria had been on the throne for decades. The short span of a four-year term was curious to her. Wouldn't longevity on the job be advantageous? And since he'd been president, why elect him a second time?

Phillip smiled and gave her basic answers. He started with political issues and moved on to the country being in flux. She reminded him she'd grown up with a monarchy.

"Did you see the World's Fair in Chicago a few years back?" she asked one afternoon as they sat on the front porch, enjoying their tea.

He shook his head. "Work on the house wasn't finished, and Alfred was just a year old. I didn't feel it right to leave him. The house needed to be overseen. I wouldn't have enjoyed the experience to the fullest. I was too wrapped up in my own problems and responsibilities."

"I'm sorry. I shouldn't have brought up the subject."

"It's fine, Eleanor. With time I've found perspective. I couldn't change the circumstances of Ida's death and just had to work through the tough spots. Having Margaret and Daniel here was a big help."

"They seem wonderful. Did you know them in Newport?"

"Daniel and Margaret were working on a neighboring property near Grandmother. The owners sold out to head west around the time I was relocating. We talked about them moving south. Both were anxious to leave Newport. The social rules affected them in different ways than me, but the constraints were there. Daniel is a good all-around outdoorsman. Margaret excels at keeping the house running, and you've eaten her meals. We came together at the right time to be advantageous for all."

"That sounds like it was a situation made to order."

"There was a bit of luck. And a bit of perseverance on all parts. It took a bit of time to get the household into the rhythm I was comfortable with." He smiled at a memory he didn't share.

"I think you complement each other."

"It helps that they both have a soft spot for Alfred."

"Who wouldn't? He's an amazing child."

Phillip waved to a passing couple. "Maybe I'll be able to take Alfred to the next world's fair. I believe the next one is in Brussels in two years. Then Paris in 1900." He glanced at her. "I spent a short time in Paris during my school years."

"I've never been. Was it wonderful, like the pictures portray?"

"The little I saw of it was magnificent. But I was young and didn't really appreciate my time there. I had classes to get through, and I spent most of my time with a stiff neck from looking up at the buildings."

She shared a laugh with him just as the postmaster walked by. They quieted until he passed.

"Did you ever see the queen?" he asked.

"No. I've been to London twice. I'm not sure she was in residence either time."

"Did you like London?"

"Yes. Of course, my trips were highly regimented by my mother at first and then an aunt who acted as chaperone." She shrugged. "Papa wasn't happy with my trips. He felt it was a waste of his money, especially since I was too young to be betrothed at the time."

They sat in silence for a while. She asked about a birdsong she was unfamiliar with. He pointed to a tree and gave her the name, and then he pointed to a different tree and bird and named them. She wasn't uncomfortable with the silence between them, the grasses and leaves rustling as background noise.

"Did you enjoy your time in New York City?" he asked.

"I loved the short time I spent in New York City with Mrs. Cornwell."

"I enjoy the occasional trip there. Mostly for business or household items. Some of the furniture in this house was manufactured in the city."

"I can only imagine how beautiful the house will be decorated for the holidays." She drew a deep breath. Would she see it decorated this year? "Thank you for talking with me."

They were quiet while they finished their afternoon

respite. She had to remind herself this was Phillip's home. She was just visiting, and this wouldn't be her home.

He would occasionally invite her to walk with him along the back acreage. Those were becoming her favorite times. He told her about his plans for the land, and she asked about his work. During those times, she asked about the new country around her.

He was quick to answer her questions about the history of her current surroundings. He gave her basic information on the strike in Pennsylvania with the Carnegie Steel Company. He mentioned the following strike in Buffalo, New York, with the Buffalo Creek Railroad when the company refused to obey new laws regarding work hours and increases in pay. He touched briefly on the panic the following year when the Philadelphia & Reading Railroad went bankrupt. He was quick to explain there was much more history he wasn't completely familiar with, like the miners' strike.

He suggested if she wanted more information, she might find details in the back issues of the New York newspapers.

"That would be interesting. Mrs. Cornwell told me I'd be welcome to stay with her anytime I was in the city."

He stiffened his posture. "Maybe later in your visit when you're a bit more settled."

He appeared to be uncomfortable with her mention of the trip, so she didn't press the issue. She had a hard time holding back her disappointment at his dismissal of her trip.

On other afternoons, they would walk around the town's main roads. Their discussions on literature were much more conducive to conversations. They were both familiar with Rudyard Kipling's *The Jungle Book* and Sir Arthur Conan Doyle's story of Sherlock Holmes.

****

On nice afternoons, she walked with Nanny and Alfred. She and Nanny didn't have much in common, and conversations were limited. But she was thankful to be outdoors. Occasionally, she would stay with Alfred while Nanny went to get his snack. They sat on a blanket in the backyard, and she went over his letters and numbers. Their times together ended with laughter and smiles.

This afternoon, Phillip watched them from the rear-porch overhang. When Nanny came to collect young Alfred, Phillip wandered into the yard. "You're very good with him."

"He's easy to be around." Her belly tightened, and that warmth she'd felt each time they were in the same area spread through her. But she couldn't get attached to Phillip. Her future was uncertain, and he was being gracious under the circumstances. Yet she had never known an attraction like this, had only read about it. Her frustration level rose every time she saw him, her body betraying longings she'd never known.

He reached a hand down to help her up. In that instant, she knew what she was experiencing wasn't just attraction. It was more. If she hadn't looked into his brown eyes, she would have been able to push aside the feelings. Now she couldn't.

He stared at her. She cleared her throat and gently took her hand from his. A red blush crept up his neck and across his cheeks. She knew he'd witnessed a similar heat overtake her face. Neither made a move to leave;

they stood rooted to the spot, gazing into each other's eyes. She should have walked away but didn't. Neither did he.

A door closed behind him, and Daniel exited what she called a workshop.

"Got the firewood stacked." He passed and continued toward the rear of the house.

Phillip gave him a wave of acknowledgment.

"Is that the shop next to the barn?" she asked.

He stepped back. "Part workshop and plant nursery."

"It's a big building," she managed, still staring.

"Yes, I do a lot of work in there, mainly starting seedlings and trying to cultivate different species from other areas."

"Someday I'd like to see your work." Embarrassed by her disclosure, she quickly reached down, picked up the blanket, and folded it. She gave him a curt nod and walked toward the house.

"See you at teatime," he called after her.

She paused, turned, and smiled at him. It took all her inner strength to stroll, not run, to the house.

Chapter Four

Phillip walked directly to his workshop, silently berating himself. He couldn't fall for her, George or not. He had a well-balanced life, and after Ida, he'd sworn off all women. Especially women who would think they could marry him and live happily ever after. No, he'd tried that, and it wasn't for him. While he'd eventually felt a true fondness for his wife, he wasn't a man who could summon love.

He'd seen relationships burn brightly and burn out just as quickly. Only hurt feelings were left behind. He'd had enough hurt to last a lifetime. Most importantly, he wouldn't let a woman get close to his son and then leave him heartbroken.

Seeing Eleanor with him in the yard this afternoon made him wonder if Ida would have sat on the lawn with her son. Would she have attempted to teach him letters and numbers or leave his education to nannies? Ida had been a product of the same social circle he was brought up in. She spent most afternoons lying on the "fainting sofa," too tired to do anything after spending the morning having breakfast in bed.

He remembered their first disagreement. He had simply asked, "What type of home would you like?"

"I don't know. You're the architect. You decide."

"But you're going to live there too. I'd like your input on the interiors, on the bedrooms."

"I don't care. I wouldn't know what to suggest." She waved her hand in dismissal.

He tried not to think about that time because the realization had hurt him deeply. She'd had no interest in the home they were to build together, and he wondered how much interest she would have had in raising the child they'd conceived. He'd had high hopes they might raise their children with love and laughter. Then he'd accepted she would leave child-rearing to nannies. He hadn't been able to disguise his disappointment, but he had pushed forward and designed the home he wanted to live in.

Would Eleanor one day fall into the same routine? Her being cut from a different cloth would be too good to be true. After all, she was technically from the Sterling family. They had the name and position. Even if Eleanor wasn't assuming she'd ever get their family estate in England, what would she do to get his estate and family holdings, both here and in Rhode Island?

A wave of revulsion washed over him at the idea that George might show up and marry her to get his inheritance. Could he let her marry George? She said she wouldn't marry him under any circumstances. That she deserved a husband who cared for her, not just for the finances she could secure.

Phillip grabbed his coat from the rack and walked out the back entrance toward a project he was pulling together for a neighbor. The plans were complete, but he needed a distraction. Above all, he had to keep these feelings private and not confess his newfound love for her.

"Oh God," he said aloud. "George, if I ever get my hands on you, I'll make you sorry you left. Sorry you left her without a word, sorry you left me in this situation, and sorry for coming back."

Out in the field he decided he'd skip tea today. Back in the workshop, he asked one of the workmen to head up to the kitchen and tell Maragaret not to wait for him. Then he lost himself in the rear of the workshop, hoping not to be found if anyone came looking for him.

Over their evening meal in the atrium, he and Eleanor were polite yet quiet. Gone were the easy conversational tones they had formed. Tonight, they were sullen.

Eleanor had apparently developed a similar notion. When he entered a room she was in, she went quiet, and she kept her distance from his son. That bothered him the most. He hadn't seen young Alfred as playful as he had been since she arrived.

Not for the first time in the last days, he questioned whether he wanted her to leave. Yet that was their predicament. This was his home and life, and her future lay elsewhere. Still, he'd only known her for a short time. After a month or two or a year or two, eventually the façade would fade. They were approaching the new century, and he couldn't keep up with the changes happening around him in the world. He had to assume the coming years would continue to change and at times confound him. The future would be easier to navigate without being responsible for a woman or wife.

****

Eleanor made a point of staying in her room more often when she thought Phillip would be in the house. She ventured down for meals and walks. She made sure he wasn't around when she wanted to exchange books from his collection. She practiced the piano after tea when she knew he'd be in his workshop. In town one afternoon, she purchased pencils with assorted lead colors and a pad of art paper.

On afternoons when she couldn't read anymore, she worked on her project for Alfred. She drew a zero on one page, a number one on the next, and continued until she hit nine. Then she chose different flowers she saw in the gardens and added the correct number of flowers to the corresponding number. She drew basic shapes and colored them in with the pencils. In the end, she'd made her own simple version of a primer for Alfred to learn his numbers. Depending how long she had to stay there, she would do something similar with letters.

On Sundays, they walked to church as a family unit. Unlike the wedding service, on Sundays they sat as a family, children included. She was surprised when Alfred crawled away from Nanny and pushed to sit beside her. He took her hand, and she didn't pull back, smiling at the child while singing the first hymn. At this point, rejecting him would have been more disruptive than accepting his attention, especially with most of the townspeople watching.

Halfway through the service, he became restless and Nanny took him home. Eleanor gave Albert a lot of credit for lasting that long on the wooden bench and remaining quiet. As she and Phillip walked home after the service, she brought up the subject in case it was a problem from his father's perspective.

"Were you bothered that Alfred moved to sit near me during the service?"

"I'm not sure what to think. Since you arrived, he's changed. He laughs and smiles more than ever. I've even heard him giggling at times. But he'll be disappointed when you leave." He glanced at her and back ahead.

"That's what I was worrying about. I'm becoming attached to him and don't want him to feel I abandoned him when I have to leave." She smiled at a shopkeeper and his wife she was beginning to know. "I also don't want to annoy Nanny."

"Some days I think Nanny was born annoyed, or at least it was a prerequisite for the job."

Eleanor burst out laughing, and Phillip laughed with her.

"I'm sorry, but your statement is accurate. Although giving credit where it's due, I think all nannies have that same attitude. Maybe they are trained to keep their charges in line. I remember my nanny without fondness."

"Mine was beyond strict. My mother was less strict. Agnes was the worst."

"She truly is the matriarch of the family."

"Yes. By necessity and by what she thinks society will accept."

Eleanor listened to the birdsongs as they walked. "By necessity?" she ventured to ask.

"In fairness to her, the family didn't make her a great match. My grandfather apparently liked to drink. He especially liked to gamble and wasn't good at it. She stepped in and took over the finances. Behind the scenes, of course. But from what I can gather, Grandfather was put on a budget. If she hadn't, he most likely would have gone through *her* family money quickly without question."

"Smart woman to stay behind the scenes and let him keep face in public."

"It was quite a change from what was expected, but she managed to keep the family together. No one dared talk about it in polite society, but Grandfather had an eye for the ladies too. She wasn't going to let him use her family funds to keep his mistresses."

"What is it about men and their mistresses? Really, if they're going to marry, why do they assume their wives will just accept their poor behavior?"

"I don't know. I married with the idea that we'd turn into a love match and neither would stray from our vows. I'll never know what might have happened."

"I'm sorry. I shouldn't have dragged up sad memories."

"It is reality. We were a match because we both felt strangled by Newport rules. We felt relocating here would give us a chance to draft our lives how we wanted."

"I'm sorry," she said again. "I've been told all my life I need to censor what I say aloud."

"How about we make a deal?" He glanced at her. "For the remainder of your time here, in private we speak our minds. In public we'll censor our words."

"That would be most appreciated."

"Fine. Although when you meet Grandmother, you'll note she feels she's lived long enough to be blunt, in private and public."

"It sounds like she's earned a bit of latitude."

"Say that after you've met her," he replied with a laugh.

She smiled. "I suppose with everything she's dealt with in her life, she's earned a bit of superiority. She hired Nanny, didn't she?"

"Yes, she did," he said. As they approached home, he cleared his throat and straightened his posture.

"I'll see you at lunch." She hurried inside, away

from Phillip and the casual conversation they were having.

****

The next few days went by with Phillip and Eleanor in an unspoken truce. Most afternoons, weather dependent, she sat on the back porch, carefully stitching initials and flowers on linen handkerchiefs as holiday presents for the maids. In her room in the evenings, she sketched pictures in charcoal and pastels. The first was for Grandmother Crane. It was her impression of her grandson Phillip and his son Alfred smiling together. The second was for Phillip. She chose the house as a backdrop and placed Alfred on his father's shoulders. Both wore wide smiles.

She still wanted to visit Mrs. Cornwell in New York City one more time before her life changed. She would send a brief telegram and ask when it would be convenient for a short visit. While she was there, she would look for the rest of the presents she had decided to give her temporary family. She'd buy a pipe for Daniel and a hatpin for Margaret. She'd already completed sets of three handkerchiefs—one set for each of the maids and a set for Nanny.

When she arrived in America, she'd spent a week with Mrs. Cornwell in New York City, settling from the journey and learning her way around. She and Mrs. Cornwell had passed several stores where she thought she could find a toy cart or preferably a toy train for Alfred and picture frames for the two drawings she'd done for presents. She remembered being in the yard with Alfred and hearing the train whistle in the distance, and she smiled. He'd exclaimed, "Train," and she'd told him he was correct.

She also wanted to order stationery for Mrs. Cornwell to be delivered as a gift after she'd left. Since they'd shopped together, she hadn't had a chance to make the purchase as a surprise. Having traveled across the pond with the woman, Eleanor knew writing letters was her daily joy. Mrs. Cornwell still had many friends and acquaintances and felt it was her duty to stay in touch.

The gifts were just tokens of thanks for their kindness while she was a forced visitor. She'd brought the plain handkerchiefs from home with the idea of practicing her stitches. She had been careful, and they would make nice thank-you gifts. The two pictures required a lot of time, but again, she'd brought most of her art supplies with her. Margaret's, Daniel's, and Mrs. Cornwell's were all small gifts she would purchase with the tiny savings she'd brought.

The frames would cost a little, but the expenditure was right to do since she was living in his home and, unfortunately, most likely in Grandmother's home eventually. She wanted to find a masculine frame for Phillip's drawing and a more feminine one for Mrs. Crane's picture. She had considered getting one for her wedding photo but decided to wait and see if there was a wedding. When boredom set in, she'd work on her gift ideas. A few days away from the house might do her some good.

The closer to the Thanksgiving holiday, the more fall decorations she saw. She would never forget the fond memories made during this trip. The orange and golds used in wreaths mimicked the changing leaves on the trees. Sometimes she felt melancholy, but that was due to her unsettled future. Christmas would be worse.

One afternoon, she'd left her number drawings on the office desk. She didn't dare share them with Alfred before getting his father's approval. Nanny would be another issue. Part of her job was teaching the child his numbers and letters. Eleanor believed it was a part of the job Nanny had let slide.

After supper, over coffee in the parlor, Phillip stared at her.

"Is something wrong?" she asked.

"I'm amazed at your artwork. I didn't know you had such talent."

"They're not a big deal. I figured they might help Alfred learn his numbers. If you're agreeable, I thought to do something similar with letters."

"It can't hurt. Nanny doesn't seem to be having much luck in that department, although she has the books to use."

"Will she be annoyed?"

"Most likely. But if it helps him learn, I frankly don't care."

"It's a good thing I'm not staying long term. I seem to annoy her because I exist. I wouldn't want her to think I'm trying to take her job."

"She gets paid to educate and watch over the child. She'll begrudgingly use them, but I think she'll make a point of saying they don't work."

"Maybe I could spend a few minutes in the afternoons with him when Nanny is at tea? If he seems to understand and learn from them, it would be silly to refuse to use them."

"Did you have a primer like this when you were a child?"

"No. I learned by default. Before my brothers were

born, my mother would read me stories in the afternoons when my nanny was on her break. My brothers had letter and number books, but I wasn't supposed to use them. Then again, nobody really kept a close eye on me, so I obviously did use them. I thought making the drawings fun with colors and shapes might help Alfred."

"Sally spells Nanny for an hour after lunch. Maybe that would be a good time to try. I'll tell Sally it's okay and not to mention it to Nanny unless she specifically asks."

"We could try that. Besides, I'll be gone in a short time, and he is your son. You make his educational decisions."

"One word of advice. Agnes will be here soon. I suggest you work with Alfred when she's napping in the afternoon too." He smiled at her.

Eleanor smiled back. "The time is going quickly."

"Yes, I agree. The last weeks went by better than I imagined. I dreaded having to tell you about George."

"Between us, I dreaded having to marry George." She didn't dare look at Phillip.

"Didn't you want to marry?"

"If I'd had a choice in the man, maybe. A total stranger who couldn't find a bride in his own country made me wonder. I was relieved when you said he'd run away."

"You know once you get to Newport after the holidays, Grandmother will have another candidate waiting for you."

"I'm wondering if after the holidays I might not move to New York City and take a job. Then I'd be responsible for myself, not a drain on your family."

"Good luck with that idea. I don't know what she

and your father have arranged."

"I'm an adult woman. I'll deal with my father. As long as he doesn't become responsible for me again, he won't care."

"Do you really believe that?"

"Absolutely. My mother passed away fifteen years ago. Since then, my father, much like your grandfather, has spent his time gambling and drinking. He was very relieved when your grandmother's letter arrived, although he wasn't forthcoming with the details. He didn't like my comments about how he spent the family money or how he was letting the estate go to ruin. And since I had no say in the running of it, my only ally was my younger brother. He saw the decay too, but he's not the heir apparent. We both assume under the current situation, there won't be much of an estate left for long."

"What will your brother do?"

"He's been scouting for a rich bride. It's the only way he'll ever succeed in life. He's very good with the law and would like to continue his education. He and Father were still in debate about his going to school when I left. I doubt Father will want to spend the money on his education."

"I hope he gets his education. That was one thing I did get, without question. Once the family realized I wanted a career, they were happy to send me to school. One less family member they eventually wouldn't have to subsidize."

They finished their coffee in silence. When she couldn't drink any more coffee, she excused herself. Sitting beside him was becoming difficult. Her desire to touch him deepened. She wouldn't put him in the awkward position of having to remind her he was not her intended.

The next days continued smoothly. Sally was content to give Alfred's care over to Eleanor each afternoon for an hour while she napped in the wing chair facing the fire. Alfred was quick to catch on with his learning. Eleanor was proud of him and made a point of telling Phillip of his progress over the afternoon tea.

"Once Grandmother comes, your afternoon teaching will be disrupted," he said.

"I understand," she said with a sigh. "At least you know he can easily learn. If his learning stalls when I'm gone, you'll know it's because Nanny isn't following through." She refolded her napkin in her lap. "I was thinking this afternoon, what if he tells Nanny or your grandmother about his newfound talents—"

"A smart nanny won't admit she hadn't been teaching him. She'll take all the praise."

"I'm glad you thought this through," she said, and they went their separate ways for the afternoon.

****

Thanksgiving was near, just a week away, and fall was in full color. Eleanor dreaded the holidays with more stilted conversations and endless cups of tea and evening card games. She wanted to see the holiday decorations in New York City. Mrs. Cornwell told her they were not to be missed. She especially didn't want to miss them this year because she had no idea where her future lay. She had no assurances she'd still be on the East Coast.

Agnes's coming sent the entire household into overdrive, just short of panic. Eleanor wouldn't overstep her position as a guest, but she would help when needed.

After supper Margaret asked Phillip if he wanted coffee in the parlor.

"Tonight, we'll stay here in the atrium. I need to go over the holiday plans with you and... Do you mind, Eleanor?"

"Of course not. I'd rather be part of the preparations than sit by and watch."

While they sat together, Margaret put fresh coffee before each of them. Daniel sat across from Eleanor, Phillip beside her. Margaret settled between them. They discussed town and social obligations in the coming weeks and the schedule to start decorating the foyer and the parlor for Christmas just after Thanksgiving. Eleanor had a few ideas but chose to hold back. This wasn't going to be her home. She shouldn't have a say. An hour later, they had set the plans.

"I'm excited about experiencing a genuine Thanksgiving. It will be my first," she said.

"I didn't think about the English not celebrating the holiday," Margaret said.

"We have harvest festivals around this time, but it isn't a true holiday." She drew a breath and continued. "While we're all together, Phillip, I'd like to head to New York for a visit with Mrs. Cornwell. I'll send her a telegram tomorrow and ask when she has a free afternoon. Is there anything you need for the holiday that I can bring back? I'd like to spend some time researching some of the historical issues we discussed a while back."

Silence, dead silence, was the answer. She glanced across at Daniel, but he tapped out his pipe. Phillip shuffled papers before him, head down. Margaret refilled coffee cups.

"What did I say wrong? Someone please tell me."

Phillip folded the papers before him. After a deep sigh, he said, "I don't know if that would be a good idea."

"Why? I managed to make it here from New York City. I should be able to retrace my steps and back."

"I don't have the flexibility to change my schedule right now," Phillip said, mainly to Margaret. "Maybe one of the maids, Sally?"

"Excuse me, but I'm not asking for a chaperone. Rather, I was carefully wording my plans. I'd like to get there and back before your grandmother arrives."

Phillip sprawled back into his seat. "One of Grandmother's letters mentioned she preferred you didn't travel alone...or anywhere really." He finally glanced at her.

Eleanor pushed back in her own seat. "I see. No, I don't. Almost by myself, I managed to get across an ocean with an elderly lady who is directionally challenged and doesn't like to be corrected. Is Grandmother afraid I'll bolt because of the situation with George?"

"Basically," Margaret said. "She mostly wanted to make sure you were safe."

"I see. And I appreciate her concern, but at my age, I'm capable of taking the train to an acquaintance's home I've already been to." She bit her bottom lip. "What if we just don't tell her until I'm back? When she sees I'm fine, her argument will be lessened, and I'll take all the blame. I'll say I didn't mention my plans until the morning I was leaving, after I'd already made the arrangements."

The three of them were quiet, none of them looking directly at her.

"I'm sorry, but I won't be held hostage, even in a beautiful home with friendly people, because your grandmother wants to control me. If I'm to have any relationship with her, she'll have to learn she chose an extremely outspoken and headstrong woman." Under her breath, she added, "She's already controlling my future. I have to have some say over my destiny."

"Maybe you could wait until she's here, and she could join you for the trip?" Margaret offered.

Eleanor was more confused than offended. "I'd like to spend a few days in the city holiday shopping with a friend. But if Agnes is tired from traveling, I couldn't go alone. That would be rude." She stood and took her empty cup to the sink, then turned and leaned against the cabinet. "Phillip, I doubt I'll have time to stop at the New York Free Circulating Library to study the newspaper back issues for the details on the historical issues we discussed."

Eleanor stayed quiet, debating her trip. She had to make a stab at her future independence, or she'd be lost to the family's strict social rules forever. She glanced at Phillip and tried to decipher his expression. He studied her from under his lashes. He looked directly at her, and she let out a breath she hadn't realized she was holding.

"Send your telegram. But please, Eleanor, make sure to be safe."

"I will. I'm not trying to unnerve the whole household. I just want to do a bit of shopping before the holidays. I did manage to do some solo traveling back home. I saw a few port towns on my own." She glanced at the stoic faces around her. "If I don't return, that would settle her problem with what to do with me."

She laughed, but none of the others laughed with her. "I'm sorry. That was flippant. But I will take the trip, and I'll be fine. I think it's unfair of her to make you all feel responsible for me. You've given me food, shelter, and friendship as a stranger in your home. My goodness, even Father didn't keep me on such tight strings."

She looked at each of them in turn. "Good night. I'll send my message in the morning and let you know when I'll be going. I'm sorry if this is uncomfortable for you all, but even I have to get out of this lovely castle on occasion." Under her breath, she said, "If it were going to be my home, that would be different. It's not." She dried her hands on the towel beside the sink. "Good night." She swept her skirt to the side, hoping not to trip on her way out with Phillip watching her intently.

Seeing this side of him, the cowering man who let his grandmother shake him... She definitely needed time away. While her first impression of him was as a strong, smart, virile man who just happened to be the most handsome man she'd ever seen, she couldn't let herself fall for any man who blindly followed the elders' rules without thought.

She was too annoyed to go to bed, so she went to the piano. She sat and played "Clair de lune." It didn't relieve her angst. Midsong, she switched to classical and tried to clear her mind. Half an hour later, she lapsed into a dark piece she'd learned years ago but only played when she was mad or angry. Pushing from the instrument, she felt better, lighter. She enjoyed playing and usually chose light pieces. Tonight, she wanted to soothe the mood she'd fallen into after being told not to leave the house. As she headed upstairs, she wondered if anyone else in the house had noticed the difference.

Upstairs, Eleanor had a mini fit of anger and resentment. If she'd been home in England, she would have walked out into the fields and screamed. After the newest decree from Agnes tonight, she didn't dare walk out to the fields and let the cool air take away her frustration. Here, she paced her room and mumbled about her frustration. She'd known what the arrangement was about and what was expected of her. But being ruled by a stranger in another state was beyond frustrating. On the trip over, she'd considered what her future husband's ideas of marriage might be, but she hadn't figured on having to appease his grandmother too.

She'd once read an article in a book she'd borrowed from her brother. The article defined true love as a question of wanting one's partner or wanting what was best for one's partner. Tonight, nobody had seemed to care what would be best for her. She was supposed to be a complacent partner. Again, she had a passing thought that she could leave and find a job, any job, after the first of the year just to get away from Agnes and the Crane family.

She would take her train trip to New York City and enjoy her time away. Deep inside, she wondered whether it would be the last trip she took on her own. She wanted a few days away from Phillip and Alfred. She was becoming attached to both.

Phillip was her main problem. In the short time she'd been at the Park, she'd become fond of him in all areas of life and love. He obviously had no use for her and tolerated her in his home. Her heart skipped a beat whenever she saw him with his son.

She was not looking forward to Newport. She liked this town and the lifestyle here. Finding a similar home in another strange place seemed impossible. It would help if she stopped imagining how he would touch her, love her. The smoldering looks she'd seen escape when he thought no one was watching were confusing. Why couldn't she have been promised to Phillip? That arrangement she could imagine.

"Curse you, George. Your greed set my world spinning with no direction."

She squared her shoulders. She'd had enough of a pity session. She was a strong woman with options. Whether Agnes realized it or not, Eleanor was not a fainthearted woman. Yes, women were supposed to defer to men, but she'd be damned if she'd give any person total control over her future or her body. She would listen to Grandmother's ideas for the future, but she would promote her options and opinions.

Leaving the entire Crane family might be her ultimate choice. She was educated and knew how society worked. Surely, she could become a nanny or lady's maid for a family in the city. America was a big place, and she wouldn't stay on the East Coast if the circumstances became uncomfortable.

"Agnes is just an older woman who assumes the world will stop moving at the sound of her raised voice," she whispered.

Well, she had a voice and an attitude. She would retain her ladylike persona, and she would continue to think before she spoke, making informed decisions about her future.

****

The next morning, Eleanor was up and dressed before Laura brought her coffee. She walked in the cold morning air and was at the telegram office as it opened. She sent her short request and walked home. She often walked past the meadow that housed the cattle, sheep, and hogs. Today, she climbed on the wooden fence and watched them for a long time. At least they weren't trying to control her future.

The rest of the morning, she sat on the back porch and pretended to read. While there, she saw a large black cat eyeing her from a distance. She'd seen the animal several times but knew not to approach him. She didn't know whether he was feral or a pet of the estate. Each time she saw him, he'd inched a bit closer. Yesterday, when she'd reached down and ruffled his ears, he sniffed at her skirt and rubbed his ears against her fingers.

Today, she looked at him and said, "You have pretty green eyes. Do you have a name?" She patted her lap and went back to her book, sneaking peeks from under her lashes to see what the animal would do. He paced and sniffed her skirt and, after circling once, jumped up and lay curled on her lap.

"Hello." She slowly reached to rub his ears.

The cat purred. They had passed the first hurdle. He stayed on her lap until Phillip came out of the shop building and the door slammed behind him. The cat stood, stretched, and jumped down out of sight. She couldn't read the expression on Phillip's face.

"Is there a problem with my petting the cat?" She no longer held her tongue as a good guest should. She wouldn't get answers if she didn't ask questions. She'd spent the last weeks in limbo with this situation created by others. From now on, she wanted a say in her future, especially since she'd had no say in this move.

Phillip shook his head and walked inside.

Chapter Five

Phillip sat on the back porch with a glass of whiskey. Seeing Eleanor's reaction to Grandmother's order restricting her from leaving the Park had been interesting. That was the first time he'd seen some true emotion from the woman. Finally away from her, he reiterated his need to put space between him and Eleanor. He wasn't looking for a wife. He'd already had one and wasn't thrilled with the experience.

Now, due to circumstances, by proxy, he'd become one of the demanding people controlling Eleanor's life. This wasn't a role he was comfortable with, and he didn't like the person the situation was turning him into.

His mind wandered, consumed with different scenarios of what their life together might have been. Ida had been chosen for him. After finishing school and spending several years as an apprentice, he'd returned to Newport with grand ideas. But his grandmother had had a different plan for him. Ida had already been in residence, waiting to meet her husband-to-be.

If he'd had more backbone, he might have fought the concept at least for a few years. But he needed a wife and family to be considered legitimate in society. He knew the family history and believed Agnes had tried to supersede family traits she found distasteful. Yes, her husband had been a gambler and womanizer, traits he'd not exhibited and hoped he'd never resort to.

His parents were more of a mystery. They had been killed in a boating accident when he was young, a preteen already away at school. He'd never heard stories about his parents being unhappy. Their marriage had been arranged. They had him and George and, in his mind, were just gone.

That was one reason he'd given Agnes a bit of latitude beyond being the woman who'd raised him—she'd never spoken ill of either of his parents. Then again, he hadn't asked about their relationship and didn't know what he would have been told if there had been issues. They were the people he had seen in silver photo frames on the piano in her parlor. He had snippets of memories. He remembered his father's love of sailing and his mother's laugh.

Eleanor seemed kind, and she held a classic beauty he'd seen during his travels in Europe. During those years away, he'd learned beauty could be fleeting, and behind closed doors, people revealed hints of their personalities they hid from the public. He wondered if her future would hold a peak-and-valley love or one that would grow slowly over time.

****

The next afternoon, Sally brought a telegram to Phillip. It was addressed to Eleanor, and he had Sally bring it directly to her. After all, it wasn't his mail or message, and she wasn't his wife or fiancée.

That evening, he came out of the shop and caught sight of her on the back porch with Cat sitting on her lap. He hadn't named the old mouser but had made sure the animal who lived in the workshop had water. Margaret would occasionally bring out scraps for him, but the cat mostly took care of his needs with the rodents he chased from the outer buildings. He also snacked on the feed for the livestock.

He'd never seen the cat friendly with anyone, nor had he known the cat was receptive to human interaction. But here he was, sprawled on Eleanor's lap. Until the day before, he hadn't known the cat interacted with anyone. The door shut behind him, and Cat startled on her lap, stood, and, after a moment of stretching, jumped down.

Eleanor brushed his fur from her skirt as Phillip walked past. "What's his name?"

He stopped at the kitchen door. "He doesn't have one. We refer to him as Cat. Usually, he's not friendly."

"He's sniffed at me a few times. Then he allowed me to pet him. Yesterday, he sniffed my skirt and jumped up."

She stared at him a moment too long, and he held her gaze for that moment.

"Is it a problem that I pet him?"

"No. I'm just surprised. He's never been social." He nodded and walked into the kitchen. He knew better than to stay there. Seeing her and not reaching to touch her became harder and harder. These feelings weren't conducive to a happy future for him or Eleanor.

****

Sally brought Eleanor a telegram from Mrs. Cornwell. Yes, Eleanor should come right away and stay as long as she liked. She'd thought to mention the telegram this afternoon, but Phillip had walked away after discussing Cat. During their evening meal, she told Phillip she would leave on the early train the next day and most likely stay two nights in the city before taking the train back. Her tone left no room for questions. She refused to be bullied and spoke clearly about her plans.

The next morning, she was downstairs early, her overnight bag packed. She had enough time for coffee in the kitchen with Daniel and Margaret. Phillip entered and offered to take her to the train in the cart. Daniel left to saddle the horse while they had their coffee.

Over coffee with Margaret and Phillip, she broached the thought she couldn't dismiss. "As we talked about the other night, please don't get involved with Agnes if she contacts you about this short trip. I'll deal with her wrath when I get back. I understand she will see my leaving as a sign of disrespect, and I will answer to her attitude." Margaret refilled her cup, and she smiled. "I'm not sure if you considered this, but we might be worrying for nothing. Mrs. Cornwell might have already sent a message about my visit."

"No matter what, she'll see this trip as a sign of disrespect," Margaret said.

"I understand, and I'll take the blame. This is my decision. As an adult, I'm going to take my last bit of freedom while I have it."

"What does that mean?" Phillip asked.

Eleanor hadn't expected him to comment. "It means my future is unsettled. Once Agnes arrives, we'll all know what she has in mind for me. I'm old enough to disagree with her if I don't like her scenario. I have a little money put aside, and I will move on if her plans don't suit me. I'll make it apparent this trip is my decision so she won't be angry with any of you. You simply have to say you told me of her requirements and I chose to change them."

"Oh dear," Margaret said.

Daniel came in the back door, brushing his hat on his pant leg. "All set to go." He poured himself a cup of coffee.

"Thank you, Daniel. I'm ready when you are, Phillip."

"I'll get my hat," he said and left the room.

"Is there anything you need or want me to bring back?"

"Just yourself in one piece." Margaret pulled a handkerchief from her apron pocket. She dabbed at a stray tear.

"Don't worry about me. I'm tougher than I look. I know when to keep my mouth closed and when to assert myself." Eleanor quickly hugged her and went to the foyer for her cape and bag. "I'll see you in a few days," she told her through the doorway.

"Eleanor, be safe," Daniel called after her.

"I will. No worrying about me. Daniel, you take care of Margaret."

"Always have, always will."

Outside, she bundled her skirt and climbed into the wagon while Phillip put her bag in the back.

"Do you need anything from the city?" she asked as they headed to the train.

"No, thank you."

They were silent for the rest of the trip. As they arrived, the train pulled into the station.

"Thank you for the ride." She climbed down from the wagon on her own, not waiting for Phillip to help.

He jumped out and grabbed her bag. They neared the train, and he handed the porter her bag. At the door, he discreetly pulled bills from his pocket.

"Thank you, Phillip, but I have my own money." She hesitated for only a second. "If Alfred notices I'm gone, please tell him I went to visit a friend and I'll be back soon." She walked to the open door the porter held and turned to wave at Phillip. For one quick moment, she thought she saw fear on his features. But that was ridiculous. He had no attachment to her and was probably wondering how he'd get out of trouble with his grandmother.

She enjoyed the train ride to the city. She would have a conversation with Mrs. Cornwell when she saw her. Had her host known about George while they were aboard the ship?

****

Eleanor arrived in New York later in the day and spent that afternoon with Mrs. Cornwell. The next full day, she invited Mrs. Cornwell to join her on her shopping excursion, but she was relieved when Mrs. Cornwell said she'd be staying home. She offered her maid as a companion, and Eleanor declined. They went over her purchases and the locations of shops where she would most likely find what she wanted.

Being on her own in a vibrant city was freeing and refreshing. She wasn't afraid to be alone. She relished not having to defer to another person.

After supper that night, Eleanor and Mrs. Cornwell enjoyed coffee in the parlor. When Eleanor had exhausted the details of her day, she paused to consider her next words.

"Mrs. Cornwell, were you aware of George's aversion to stability when we sailed?" On the ride to the city, she'd considered what information she wanted and the best way to get it from the older woman.

Mrs. Cornwell cleared her throat and gave her a half smile. "I wasn't sure of the…depth of his instability. I'm afraid he's disappointed you. I didn't know what would happen if you met in person."

Eleanor watched her for several seconds and let a laugh slip out. Yes, she could have been bitter. But that would shut down the conversation and information she wanted. "You knew I'd be disappointed when I arrived. Why didn't you tell me? It would have been much kinder."

"That wasn't my decision, dear. While I had my suspicions of George's commitment, I haven't seen him in years. He might have grown up and been ready to be responsible."

"Did Agnes have a backup plan for me?"

"Of course." Her lips spread into a full smile. "George was the fallback. Phillip was always the main purpose. Agnes felt you might complement Phillip and his life. She hoped you'd be kind to the child and be helpful in his work. That maybe if either you or he were interested, you might become a compatible wife."

"For Phillip?" Eleanor's voice cracked. Had she been so stupid these last weeks not to realize she was supposed to be with Phillip? "Did he know I was arranged for him?" She leaned forward in her seat. "Please tell me the truth. It matters to me."

"No, I don't believe he was aware of the swap Agnes had in mind. At least she didn't tell him outright. Since he knows her well, he might have wondered, but to my knowledge, he didn't ask."

Mrs. Cornwell nodded curtly and broke into enthusiastic laughter. "My dear, you don't question Agnes. She is the backbone of that family. And she raised those boys, so she's protective of them. She meant well, my dear. I only learned for sure since we've been home that George…chose to travel."

"Travel? From the sound of it, he all but ran for his life." Eleanor finally relaxed and enjoyed a laugh. "Seems Phillip and I were both misinformed."

"Don't be angry with Phillip. I'd consider he's a man with a lot of responsibilities. Romance and marriage weren't on his mind. Agnes wanted a second chance to get his life settled."

"I don't understand."

"She matched Phillip with Ida. Soon she realized they tolerated each other, but there wasn't a spark. Agnes hoped you might see a different side of him."

"Or he would be interested in me? And if not, she might drag George back to take me."

"She wasn't being cruel."

Eleanor exhaled a deep sigh. "No. Just manipulative."

"A lot of what I've said here tonight is speculation. I'll show you her letters, if you'd like."

"No, that won't be necessary. I do wish I'd known her game sooner." She sat back and considered how to deal with Grandmother when they met.

Not realizing she'd been caught in her own mind until the clock struck nine, she finally turned to Mrs. Cornwell. "Would you do me a favor? Please don't tell Agnes we had this conversation. I'd like some time to warn Phillip before she arrives."

"I won't tell her as long as you don't hold a grudge against me." She extended her hand to Eleanor.

Eleanor took her hand for a moment. "No grudges, but no more holding back important information. Thank you for letting me come to visit."

"You're welcome anytime." She hesitated and added, "My offer still stands. If things don't work out with Phillip, you'll always have a home here."

Eleanor nodded because the tears welling in her eyes kept her from producing words. She went to Mrs. Cornwell and hugged her. "Thank you. Although you might be sorry you offered me your protection. From what I'm learning about Agnes, you don't need her as an enemy."

They shared a laugh, and a sense of ease enveloped Eleanor, knowing the words of protection spoken on the ship were a true offer. With that subject finished, she discussed her travel plans for the next day.

Eleanor slid into bed, exhausted physically and emotionally. At least she had answers. She could keep the information to herself and let her time with Phillip progress naturally. But that wouldn't be natural because she knew the truth. Holding back the information would be selfish. It was better for him to hear it from her than have Mrs. Cornwell or Agnes tell him the truth and for him to find out she'd been told. No. When she returned home, before Agnes arrived, she'd tell him of the setup so he could make his own decisions about the future.

She spent a restless night considering her options. Morning came too soon with no definite answers. She'd been through the situation in all dimensions. They all led back to her wanting to explore a future with Phillip—one built on trust, not deception. Hopefully, tonight or tomorrow morning, she could get him alone for a few moments. Once he understood the situation, he could make informed decisions.

Would he see her as a potential mate? She hoped she and Phillip might confront Agnes together. She wondered how he would react to the situation. With several deep breaths, she accepted yet again that she didn't have much say. But once the holidays were over, she could start looking for a job in New York.

The trip had gone quickly, too quickly. She would have liked to have had a few more days. But the pressure of Agnes's decree weighed on her more than she was comfortable with. When she was told not to travel, her fantasy of an idyllic life rapidly died. So in her mind, she split the "error," as she decided to call it.

She would tell Agnes she made an error in interpreting her instructions and took the short trip to see Mrs. Cornwell. Depending on the lady's moods, she might add that she originally wanted to go for a week or two, but out of deference to Agnes, she only spent two nights and one full day in New York. The other two days were travel.

The ride back to the Park had her rethinking the new information. As a distraction, she drafted a short thank-you note to Mrs. Cornwell to be mailed the next day. Mostly, she had been wrapped up in her own thoughts. She had never liked confrontations, had been schooled to avoid them at all costs. But today, she was about to start a major one that would finally settle her future. Was she really attracted to Phillip, or was she looking for the easy answer? He wasn't an easy answer. Her reactions to him weren't for a home; her body and mind reacted to him as if he were a beau or her intended.

For once, she would like to make her own decisions about her future. She still would. Agnes might have set the field, but she and Phillip would have to play the game. She just had to inform him it was a game to Agnes and find out how he wanted to navigate the situation.

Chapter Six

Eleanor was thankful to see Daniel waiting at the station to take her home. Tuxedo Park wasn't home, but for the foreseeable future, it was her residence.

"Daniel, I didn't expect a ride. I was going to walk." She handed him her travel case.

"Margaret wouldn't hear of it. She's been on edge since you left. The sooner I get you back, the sooner she'll calm down." He tilted his head and eyed her. "You look...different, relaxed." He helped her up to the seat.

"Relieved," she said with a smile. As soon as she said the word, she knew it was wrong. She needed to talk to Phillip before divulging the information she'd discovered to the servants. But that was wrong. She didn't consider Margaret and Daniel servants, more the kind couple who kept the castle, the home, going. "I'm relieved to have gotten my holiday shopping done."

He turned the horse toward home in a slow gait. "As long as you're back safe." He lit his pipe, ending their conversation.

She took the hint and enjoyed the scenery. Once back at the house, she was surprised when Margaret grabbed her in a bear hug.

"Thank goodness you're home safe," she said.

"I didn't realize you were so uncomfortable with me going. I understood I went against Agnes's wishes. But I didn't realize how uncomfortable you and Daniel were."

"Or Phillip," Margaret said.

Eleanor followed her inside. She furrowed her brow but didn't question Margaret's comment.

"You're home now. That's all that matters."

Daniel came in with her travel case.

She thanked him, and he ascended the rear stairs and disappeared from sight.

"How is the rest of the household?" she asked.

"He'll be thankful you are home safe," Margaret told her. "Go on, wash up. We can have a quick cup of tea, and you can tell me about your trip."

The rooms upstairs looked the same, but Eleanor didn't feel the same. She felt freer. She hung up her cape and her traveling jacket and, after a quick washup and a bit of fixing her hair, joined Margaret for tea in the kitchen.

Telling Margaret about the shops, the decorations, and the holiday display windows was simple. She was excited to talk about her time in the city. She inquired about Alfred, and Margaret told her he'd asked for her. Margaret said Phillip mentioned she was visiting friends.

When tea was over, Margaret offered that Phillip was in the workshop. "Go and let him know you're home."

"Wouldn't Daniel have told him?"

"Probably. But once he sees you're all in one piece, he'll calm down too."

"He'll calm down?"

"Just go." Margaret shooed her out the back door.

When she left for the city, she'd been on edge about the circumstances. Going against Agnes's demands felt wrong, yet she needed to assert herself. If she were to have any future with Phillip, she didn't want to cower in fear of every time the woman spoke. Now she had to talk to Phillip and decide where her future lay.

The workshop building was much larger than she'd originally thought from her first short visit. She knocked lightly.

"Come in."

"Phillip, Margaret sent me out to show you I came back in one piece."

She took in the series of areas around her. The front area was what she would consider an office. The middle was set up as a workshop. Some flower and plant beds were raised; larger plants were in ground-level beds, and others were in containers and pots. The rear was a glassed-in greenhouse with small spots of green leaves peeking from the earth. "This is huge, much larger than I expected from my first visit."

"It expanded out of necessity once I started working here." He turned from the paper he was reading to look at her. "I have plans for several other greenhouses on the rear acreage. Hopefully, I'll get them built over the next few years."

"May I look at the plants?" she asked.

"Yes, of course." He stood and followed her as she wandered the rows of seedlings and older plants.

Some of the larger ones were wintering over in the warmth. She paused, and he told her the name of the flower she was unfamiliar with and where it would be planted. He leaned his hip on one of the benches, but she continued to wander.

"I never appreciated how much time and thought goes into a garden," she said. "I guess because I was never asked or asked the right questions. I was told to leave the workmen alone and go practice the piano or stitching."

"I never gave plants much thought until I went away to school. The grounds were a cornucopia of life I'd never thought about or experienced. It was my way of getting away from the schoolwork. I used to ask the gardeners about the plantings, and one day, one of them handed me a pair of clippers and told me to be productive while we talked. That was the best part of my education. Yes, I learned how to build strong structures, but I also learned about flowers, shrubs, and trees and what would keep them alive and thriving."

"It seems like you learned well." She headed down a different aisle. "What is this flower?"

"I won't give you the technical names unless you want to learn them."

"For now, just how to recognize them, please."

"This one is an oleander. It will grow large and wild if not trimmed, and they usually winter over without issues. I started these from cuttings a few months ago." He shrugged and continued. "I love my oleanders, but they are poisonous, so I never put them near homes. Only as colorful border plantings where they won't harm people or animals. They border my home too."

"What about this one?" She pointed to a flower in a different bed.

"That's a hydrangea, a summer plant that grows large if trimmed properly. But the flowers don't last in the cold." He gestured for her to move to a different area where flowers grew in all different colors and heights. "This is the hard part—keeping the flowers alive to be used in the house and church through the winter."

"I can pick out the roses along with the daisies. What is that one?"

Again, he provided the names of the unknown flowers. This was a subject she had no knowledge of but would like to learn. Would she have time to learn? The heat was so intense her shirtwaist stuck to her body. She refrained from pulling the material from her skin. The scents mingled to the point where she couldn't decipher one from another.

"They're beautiful, all of them. Now I understand why you spend so much time out here." She didn't add that she'd assumed he was hiding from her.

"Which do you like the most?"

"The lily of the valley and the gardenias. But I know gardenias don't last long."

"No, they don't, but they are beautiful."

She began to get anxious. The combined floral scents and the heat made her feel as if she were in a dream, a beautiful dream with a man she was falling in love with. Of course, he'd probably like to have a say in the matter, but her feelings were strong. She could only speculate on whether he had similar feelings. The next conversation would tell her what she needed to know. What she knew for sure was she couldn't project her feelings onto him. If he was interested, he'd let her know. After all, it was conventional for the man to state his feelings first. Yet she'd never be conventional, and she hoped Phillip wouldn't expect her to be. She walked back to the office area with him following to his desk. He sat and shuffled papers.

Eleanor refrained from primping her hair. The humidity would have the loose ends curling in different directions anyway. Knowing her attraction to him was most likely going to be quashed, she found it difficult to watch him. She assumed he didn't have any feelings for her, but a girl could dream. No, she reminded herself, dreaming was what got her in this situation. She felt the familiar burn on her cheeks as they reddened and gave away her thoughts. Focusing on his large, work-worn hands didn't help her composure. He turned away from her.

"Phillip, I'd like to talk to you. It's important."

"What do you need, Eleanor?"

"It's not what I need specifically," she started. "How is Alfred?"

"Confused that you were gone. I knew he was becoming attached to you, but I didn't realize just how much."

She caught the change of tone in his voice. "I'll try to keep my distance from him while I'm here. It's apparent you're not happy with my spending time with him." She didn't soften her annoyed tone.

He tossed the pages before him to the side. "I didn't mean it that way. I didn't expect him to notice your absence."

"Thank you," she answered with a sarcastic edge.

"I'm sorry, Eleanor. That's not what I meant. I'm just relieved you're back in one piece."

"Yes, I know. Agnes wouldn't be happy if I didn't return."

"Did you have thoughts of not returning?"

She paced the area before his desk and drew a deep breath before continuing. "Phillip, I'm going to be blunt, which you're aware polite women don't do. I have information to share with you, important information."

"Go ahead." He watched her intently.

"I had a long talk with Mrs. Cornwell. To get to the point, Agnes has been doing more than trying to marry off George. She brought me here to see if you'd be happy with me as a wife. Apparently, George was to be the fallback if you found me awful." The ache in her shoulders relaxed, and she released the breath she'd been holding.

"What?" He stood and paced the space behind his desk.

"Mrs. Cornwell swears she didn't know that was Agnes's main reason for bringing me here. In their correspondence since I arrived, Agnes mentioned she hoped I'd be a better choice for you than Ida was. She's felt bad that you two were not the match she'd hoped for."

He paused and shook his head. "I didn't know." He ran his fingers through his hair. "I should have thought more about her motives." He looked at her. "I'm sorry, Eleanor."

"Sorry I don't meet your standards for a second wife…or still sorry George left?"

"I'm sorry I didn't realize her ultimate motive."

"Yes, well, we have to decide how to handle her."

"Handle her?" He burst into a hearty laugh.

"Yes, what we want to tell her about her proposed plans for both of us."

"You've known about this longer. What did you decide?"

"I didn't decide anything. I only found out last night. I had to let you know what she had in mind so we could decide together what to tell her." She picked up a pencil from the desk and put it back. "I'm not sure I have a say in any situation. I'd like to be able to get some of my personal control back. What little I actually had. After all, I was brought over to be your bride or George's."

"Of course, you have a choice. I'm the one on the hot seat now."

"I didn't think you'd be happy, but I thought it was right to give you the information so you could make an informed decision."

"So we can make informed decisions." He dropped back into his chair and laughed.

"I'm happy I could give you a good laugh. Could you remember my future is still in flux?"

"I'm not laughing about us. I was thinking how we could get back at Grandmother for putting us both in this situation."

"How?"

He was still smiling. "Will your friend tell her she gave away the secret?"

"I asked her not to, but I'm not sure she'll keep her word. She's in an awkward position too." Eleanor sighed. "When is Agnes coming?"

"Tomorrow."

"Tomorrow! That doesn't give us much time to decide what to tell her." She picked up the pencil a second time, thought to break it in two, and gently replaced it on the desk.

"No, but hopefully, it means she'd miss a written letter unless your Mrs. Cornwell sent a telegram."

"I don't know if she would. She seemed sincere and relieved that I finally knew. That's why when I asked to come to the city for a visit, she wanted me there right away. I think her conscience was heavy."

"Agnes will arrive in time for tea, so we'd better decide what we want to tell her." He laughed a second time. He straightened the piles of papers on his desk. "I should have considered her ulterior motive."

"I was thinking about that on the way home. Do we have to tell her we know of her grand plan? What if we both continued to act unaware of her details?"

"Let me think about this for a while. We'll talk about the options after supper."

"All right," Eleanor agreed, "but until we decide, let's keep this between us. My trip seemed to weigh heavily on Margaret. She's also on edge with Agnes arriving tomorrow, which in turn, gets Daniel on edge."

"I should have realized sooner all the stress she's under. She'll be fine once Agnes arrives and gets out a few rude statements about the house and how it's kept. No matter what the situation, I'm sure she'll have a few cutting remarks meant to be polite but with rude undertones."

"Oh joy. Something else to look forward to."

He shook his head. She stood straight, uncomfortable with his newfound attitude about their situation.

Phillip glanced at her. "I'm sorry. I was just thinking how many times in my life I've had to do her bidding. I've decided I'm old enough to make decisions for myself."

"I suppose that means I'll be moving to Newport when she goes home. Or maybe I will find a job in the city and strike out on my own."

"Don't make any quick decisions, Eleanor. I'm trying to teach Agnes a lesson, not chase you away."

She gave him a quick nod. If she spoke, she was afraid her voice would give away her true feelings, feelings that he most likely would think were so outlandish he wouldn't consider them.

"I need some time to think this through. I'll see you

at supper." He continued to shuffle papers.

She turned on her heel and left. Quickly, because she was on the verge of tears. She couldn't let him know she was attracted to him and disappointed he didn't consider her wife material. After all, she was to marry his brother. He hadn't known the details until half an hour ago.

Inside, she headed to her room. She used the time until supper to unpack and hide the small gifts she'd bought in the city under the front window seat. She sat there, watching the leaves blow in the breeze.

****

Phillip couldn't believe what Eleanor had told him. After a moment to consider, he accepted it. His relationship with Agnes had been complicated…always. He remembered how strict she was when he was a child. She thought children were to be seen at teatime. That was all.

His mother had never been comfortable spending time with him and George when they were children. She consistently looked over her shoulder so as not to get caught by Agnes.

When his parents passed, he was thankful to have Agnes. By then he was older, but her rules were still strict. She allowed no back talk; his ideas had to be carefully worded, and the times to talk to her about them had to be carefully chosen. He learned to gauge her moods before bustling in and announcing an idea. He also learned early on that each person he came in contact with was a direct line back to Agnes. Good or bad, she'd always be informed about his daily activities.

After vacation and holiday breaks, he was glad to head back to boarding school. Not that the school wasn't strict, but with some distance, he finally got to see a side of life outside of her Newport home and social circle. The vastness of the outside world had made him study harder with the hope he'd be able to prosper in that larger world.

He sat back in his desk chair and propped his feet on the edge of the desk. "The old bat," he said and laughed heartily. Yes, she'd hatched another plan, and he had missed the signals.

Now he had to decide how to handle her and Eleanor. First, he had to accept that he'd been interested in Eleanor. Yes, he'd seen her blush and stammer when he was around. But that could be due to her inexperience with life. Could she actually be attracted to him?

He dropped his feet and stood. After locking up, he headed out to the barn. He loved his horses. Lately, he hadn't had time for them or a quick afternoon ride. He could change that.

He brushed the horse in the first stall. He used his pocketknife to slice an apple from the barrel by the door. He took the time to walk down the aisle, and after feeding the horses apple slices, he brushed and petted them. Even with Agnes in the house, he was going back to his old routine. An hour on horseback had always left him with a clear mind and an appreciation of his home and what he'd built.

None of that changed the fact that all hell was going to break loose. But he couldn't allow Agnes to rule his future again. He had decisions to make, and most of them included Eleanor. They would have to have a serious discussion soon. Tonight after supper, he'd sit her down and ask for her input on their futures.

****

The evening meal was over by the time Eleanor

filled in Phillip, Margaret, and Daniel about her trip to the city. She described the holiday store windows and some of the buildings she'd seen during her shopping expedition.

Over coffee, Phillip cleared his throat to get everyone's attention. "This is our last quiet meal. I'm going to miss our meals here in the atrium."

"I love the morning light coming through the windows while I linger over a second cup of coffee." Eleanor looked longingly around the area. "This has become one of my favorite places. I can see all the nature around us, the animals and the landscape."

"No more lingering," Margaret said after a protracted silence. "Tomorrow, Mrs. Crane will arrive, and all…will descend."

Daniel grunted. "I'll be outside most of the time," he said with a devilish smile. "She doesn't want to see or talk to me. I'm just a servant."

"No, you're not. You and Margaret are integral parts of this family and household. Agnes will have to adjust." Phillip sipped his coffee. "Unfortunately, we'll have to go back to suppers in the dining room. Afternoon tea will have to be in the parlor."

"What about lunch?" Eleanor asked.

"Agnes doesn't eat lunch. She has a large breakfast in bed and only comes down for tea. Of course, we'll have to dress for supper."

"Margaret, what can I do to help you while she's here?" Eleanor asked.

"Nothing. And I do mean nothing. If she sees you helping, she'll go on a tear about what servants are supposed to be doing and their responsibilities."

"It's back to reading in the window seat and more

embroidery," Eleanor groaned. "Will I be able to help with the holiday decorations, or is that forbidden too?"

"The groundsmen will come in on the Friday after Thanksgiving and do the majority of the setup. I'll try to let Alfred help decorate the actual tree, but only at the end when it's done. We'll save a few bows and ribbons for him to put on the lower branches."

Margaret topped off their coffee cups. "Once the tree is in place, you could help with some of the decorating. The workmen will bring the boxes of ornaments out of storage. Just don't let Agnes see you participating."

"What about help with the Thanksgiving meal?" Eleanor ventured.

"Most of the prep work is done. It would be best if you could help entertain Agnes to keep her out of the kitchen."

Another dead silence surrounded the table until Phillip laughed. "That won't happen. Agnes has never cooked a meal in her life, yet she continues to haunt the staff as if she were a trained chef."

"And the decorating?" Eleanor asked.

"She'll watch and give her opinion on how they are doing it wrong," Phillip said.

"I suppose she doesn't take afternoon naps." Eleanor hid her smile with her napkin. She would have to remember to keep such comments to herself.

"Unfortunately, no. Some days she'll retire to her room to write her letters, but she usually stays in the parlor or office. From there, she can keep an eye on the staff and how they run the house. And before you ask, she'll assume Alfred only comes down for a five-minute visit before tea. The rest of the time, she'll be annoyed if he's seen or heard."

"And I thought my nanny was tough." Eleanor brought her cup to the sink, rinsed it, and placed it on the side to dry.

"Eleanor, tomorrow morning, I'd like you to come with me," Phillip said. "We can take the horses and do a turn around the paths."

"I'd like that. I haven't ridden since I left England."

"Good. Can you be ready first thing?"

"Of course. I only need the coffee Laura brings me when she helps me dress. I brought my riding clothes. I'd like to get outside as much as possible before Agnes arrives...and while she's here."

He indicated his agreement with a slight smile. "We can discuss a few things during our ride."

She cleared her throat. "Would it be an issue for me to use a western saddle? I don't want your friends or neighbors to talk about how I ride."

"Not at all," Phillip said. "I'm surprised you've used a western saddle."

"Only when my brothers weren't around and there was no one to see me. I find it much more comfortable, and I have more control over the horse."

"I don't care who sees us riding. We'll talk tomorrow."

The group split up, and Phillip and Daniel headed outside. Eleanor stayed inside and helped Margaret with the dishes. The next weeks were going to be fraught with society's rules and old-fashioned ideals of life, ones Eleanor hated and had just begun to feel free of.

But she had some leverage left. She was eager to hear what Phillip had to say tomorrow morning. She assumed the horseback ride was for privacy to discuss

Agnes and her expectations. She would listen to his ideas and share a few of her own.

Tomorrow would be a long day, under inspection by Mrs. Crane. She reminded herself to call her that. It would be easy to slip and call her Agnes.

She was caught between fate and destiny. She'd always believed fate was the family she was born into. Destiny was who she chose to become. Now she was trapped between the two. She couldn't change the past, but she would seize control of her destiny.

Chapter Seven

The next morning, Eleanor rose early and dressed before Laura came in. She hoped Phillip would be too disgruntled to notice her male-oriented riding suit. She hated riding sidesaddle at home and, when not under the watchful eyes of her father, often rode through the estate straddling the horse. It wasn't ladylike but rather a small, nonverbal revolt against the rules. Today, she would ride freely. As long as they were home before Mrs. Crane arrived.

Downstairs, with her jacket and hat already on, she pulled on her gloves as she walked out the back door. Daniel brought around the two horses. Both were amazing animals. He lifted her onto the brown one while Phillip mounted the darker, almost black-colored, one.

"These are both Morgan horses, aren't they?" Eleanor asked.

"Yes. You're on Matilda, and this is Storm," Phillip said.

"They're both beautiful." She reached down and patted the horse's neck. "Where to?"

"I thought we'd take the outermost path to give you an idea of the size of the Park. On other trips, we can explore the inner paths."

"I'm just glad to be outside." She directed Matilda to follow Storm off the property and onto the path entrance. She studied the route so she wouldn't get lost in the future. Here all the trees looked similar.

Once they were away from prying eyes, Phillip turned to her. "You ready for a bit of speed?"

"Yes. We'll follow you." She gave Phillip the lead and goaded Matilda into a similar pace, following several feet behind him. When they were deeper onto the path, Eleanor shouted "Woo-hoo" and took the lead. She allowed her horse to follow the path.

For the first time since she found out about the arrangement, she felt relieved. She was outdoors with Phillip, the cold air was refreshing, and the colors of the turning leaves were stunning. When they paused at a clearing, she was almost breathless.

"This is amazing," she said. "The first part of the path was similar. Here the different trees are wonderful, and the air is clean and fresh." She didn't verbalize that she liked being secluded with him.

"Yes, it's a beautiful place. But I brought you here for a reason. We need to decide how to handle Agnes. Did you have any thoughts since we spoke yesterday?"

"I've been having thoughts since the beginning, some kinder than others. But I've had time to consider all this. What are your thoughts?" she asked. "You know her."

"I'd like to keep her off-center, as you suggested yesterday. Force her to reveal her plans, especially since George isn't here."

"Do you think she'll tell us the truth?" Eleanor asked while studying the trees and sky.

"Not at first. But she will eventually, which is where I need your help. After the weekend, I'd like you to start talking about going to the city for a job. Once she realizes you want to leave for a life of your own and you aren't keen to follow her to Newport, she might finally tell the truth—that she sent you here as a mate for me."

"Is that what you'd like me to do? Find employment in the city?" She hoped he didn't hear the tremor in her voice.

"No. I'd like you to stay here. I'd like us to get to know each other better, especially now I know I'm not stealing my brother's fiancée."

"Are you sure? You don't have to be responsible for me. I'm an adult and can find my way and a job. You shouldn't have to take me just because your grandmother had a plan. I'm sure you had plans too." She watched him for any indication of his feelings.

"Didn't you have plans?"

"Not ones I thought would come to fruition. Once the arrangement was struck, I was bundled off to be married without my wishes being considered or without even being consulted."

"What would you like to happen, Eleanor?"

"Now that I know the truth, I'd like to get to know you without the lies. But somehow, I don't think you were bargaining for a wife. You should be able to pick the woman you fall in love with, not take the family leftovers."

She wasn't prepared for him to burst out laughing. He pulled the reins of his horse and maneuvered close to her.

"I'm going to be honest, Eleanor. Since the day I found you asleep in the foyer, I was smitten. But you were supposed to be a sister-in-law. Now that I know your feelings on the topic, I'd like us to start over. Yes, I'm annoyed with Agnes. But I'm also attracted to you. The way you spend time with Alfred and are always offering to help." She opened her mouth to talk, but he put his hand up to quiet her. "I know about your helping Margaret and the maids. Moreover, I find that, beyond being beautiful, you are a smart woman. Any man would be proud to have you beside him. You have to decide if you'd be interested in getting to know me on a personal level or if you're not interested in me or having to contend with my son. We are a package deal."

"Yes, you are a package. But I don't want to be your partner by default. Just because I'm here doesn't mean you're obligated to marry me."

"I didn't say anything about being obligated. I'm asking if you're attracted to me."

"Yes, of course I'm interested." Heat rode up her throat to her cheeks. "I'm blushing just talking to you like this."

"Then I have a suggestion. We stick to the George-is-due-any-day story until Agnes finally gives up. In the meantime, I'd like us to get away from the house to have some private time to get to know each other. Walks, rides, skating. If anyone asks about our time away, we'll say I'm trying to keep you company until George arrives. We'll keep everyone guessing, especially Agnes."

"And Mrs. Stevens?" she questioned. With him so close, she struggled to keep the attraction to herself. She tightened her hands on the reins so she didn't reach out to touch him.

"There was never an attraction between me and Elizabeth. I've told you she has plans to move out west after the holidays."

Eleanor let out a heavy breath. "I'll admit I was jealous at the idea of you and Elizabeth." His smile immediately made her sorry she'd confessed. "I'm sorry

I told you."

"Don't be. I'm flattered. I did tell you at the beginning she wasn't a romantic interest."

"Yes, but that could have been for public consumption."

"We decided we would be honest in private. I am being honest."

"Then honestly, I'll admit I despise the little smirk on your lips at my confession." The horse shifted, and she resettled on the saddle. "Let's forget I mentioned her."

Phillip nodded. "However, in the spirit of being honest, when Frederick Deiden approached you at the wedding, I had an overwhelming feeling of jealousy."

"Did you?" She hoped it was the truth and he wasn't placating her.

"Yes. Uncalled for at the time because of George, but nonetheless, I was jealous."

"What if someone sees us together?" She glanced around the path and was thankful they were still alone.

"From the start, you were a guest for the holidays. Once Agnes gets here, that strengthens our story."

Eleanor stretched over the horse's neck while she rubbed her ears. "Am I truly the woman you want to get to know, possibly for the long term? Or is it just that I'm here and available? Most likely different from most women you meet."

He took several deep breaths, watching her. "If I'd never met you, I wouldn't know what I've been missing. Since I first saw your photograph, I was...intrigued. You were untouchable then because of George. The more time I've been around you, the more I want to get to know you better. Eleanor, you are the epitome of my dream woman. A woman I would have chosen for myself." He paused to study her. "Do you have an interest in me? I'd understand if you don't."

"I've already admitted I was interested in you. The day in the yard when you took my hand, my breath stopped. I am attracted to you in ways I can't comprehend. Just seeing you across the yard makes my belly burn. I see your large, work-worn hands, and my hands reach to touch you. I want to reach up and touch your beard. Is it soft or prickly? How would it feel to have you hold me? What would it be like if you kissed me?"

"Damn and hell, Eleanor. When you say things like that, I want to bundle you into my arms and kiss you until you tell me you'll love me, marry me, and stay with me forever. Here on this land in the home I've built."

Eleanor stared at him. "I've only known you a short time. How could you love me?"

"Crazy, isn't it? I knew when I found you napping under the staircase. I just knew. I sent up a prayer that George would come back immediately because I didn't want to suffer seeing you every day and not be able to touch you, talk to you, ask your opinion on important issues. Now I have a chance to do that, if you're not disgusted by my blunt words. We only have a short time before Agnes arrives. I need to know, between us, if you are interested in seeing if we're a fit." He drew a deep breath. "Is there any boyfriend or lover left behind?"

"No past men." She caught the quizzical look he shot her. "I was never presented to society. My father didn't think it was important. When he mentioned he didn't know what to do with a daughter, I didn't press the point. He was also very vocal about finances, so I didn't have a London presentation. He allowed me to attend a few local parties, but he became annoyed with those social situations and soon stopped me from attending."

"You didn't want to meet men outside your social group?"

"Too many unknowns. Father hated society functions and kept my mother from participating in most functions once they married. We only socialized with family and local neighbors." She glanced away and finally reestablished eye contact with him. "My social life didn't prosper with both my brothers' cruel gossip. I was too old, too bland, too critical for any man to want me."

"But they used you to foster their opportunities?"

"We went to church and local events. Father and the boys reinforced that I was boring, and they encouraged the idea that my past reputation was not friendly with boys or men."

"I must warn you, Eleanor, life here in the Park won't be anywhere near as exciting as Newport. We have a good life with friends and the community. But we don't throw fancy parties or balls."

"That's not the lifestyle I was hoping for."

"I don't want you to be disappointed later in life that you didn't have those experiences. Here, the most exciting parties are church socials."

"I've had enough experiences in society. I didn't ask for a fancy life."

"Will you be content with a country life?"

"I think country life suits both of us." She felt it was a genuine concern that he was warning or preparing her for their future. They were getting too serious, so she changed the subject. "It took a long time to have me foisted upon you."

"Let's put 'foisted' aside. I don't like that word between us."

"Would 'arrange' sound better?" Her horse took a step, and she retightened her grasp on the reins.

"We can make this about our arrangement or choose a different tack. What we choose for our future, between us, how we build life going forward together."

"That sounds wonderful but not realistic. We could work out that way, trying our best to make the match work."

"We both need to try our best to make this work. We both deserve a fresh start, regardless of how we came together."

"You're very sure of yourself." She smiled at him. "You may have to remind me occasionally." His smile made her feel as if they could have a future. "Interesting. You're asking me to see if we're a fit. On the boat, I didn't have a choice. I was literally shipped over because Agnes Crane offered my father money. I was bought and paid for, even if it was a somewhat unconventional bargain these days. I still had no say in the issue." She stopped to smile. "I think it would be wonderful to have a choice in my future. But I don't want you to go through with this plan if you feel obligated."

"I started out with a poor attitude because of the situation. Then I got mad because I knew I couldn't have you. This reprieve feels like a gift. If you think you could have feelings for me, will you stay and see if we fit together?"

"I'd like to try. But what about Agnes and the staff? Sometimes it seems like in that huge castle I'm never alone. Whether it's your house staff or the cleaning crew or even your landscapers, someone is always bustling around. I'm not complaining. I just can't figure out how we'll get some quiet private time to get to know each other."

"I understand there are a lot of people in and out, but that's necessary to maintain the house."

"I'm not complaining. I know what it takes to keep a castle running." She smoothed a strand of hair the wind had loosened. "It's quiet in the evening."

Their eyes locked, and neither she nor Phillip looked away. This close, he was more handsome than she'd thought. His dark-brown eyes glinted with gold in the natural light. Without overthinking the need or the want, she pulled off her glove and stroked his cheek.

"Your beard is soft," she whispered, continuing to stroke his cheek but not losing eye contact. "Is this okay?"

"Yes, it's wonderful, and I'm glad you made this first move." He reached his hand up to cover hers, took it in his palm, and brought it to his lips.

He kissed her hand, and her body reacted with a strange heat. "Phillip," she whispered, "are you sure you want to get to know me on this level?"

"Positive. Just give us a few weeks to see if we're compatible. Spend the holidays with us. After the first of the year, we can have a conversation and reevaluate our feelings." He released her hand, and she was instantly cold.

"Reevaluate our feelings?" She didn't conceal her smile. "What would you have felt if I was sent as your bride from the beginning?"

"Unknown," he said, watching her intently. "I'd

have been annoyed and resentful of Agnes meddling in my life again. She already married me off once. I always thought the second time I'd make my own choice, if there was a second time."

"And now she took that choice away from you again?"

Phillip pulled back and shifted on his saddle. "I'm trying very hard not to remember that detail. Yes, we've both been played and maneuvered. We have to decide if it matters in the long term."

The silence between them wasn't uncomfortable. Eleanor scanned the path around her, appreciating the myriad of colors of the leaves. Some clung to their branches, whereas others dangled in the light wind. She took a mental picture of the scene. Phillip relaxed back on the horse, his face turned up toward the sun.

"You are a truly handsome man, Phillip Crane."

"Thank you."

She was disappointed he didn't return the compliment. "I'd like a promise from you." She waited for him to look at her. "If we decide to try a clandestine romance, you have to be honest with me at the first of the year. If I'm not what you want, you must tell me the truth. I wouldn't want to spend the rest of my days knowing you stayed with me out of convenience and social constraints."

"I promise, Eleanor, but I want the same promise from you. Spending the next weeks together will let us get acquainted on a personal level, and you might decide I'm not the husband you want."

"You've got my head spinning. Husband? Do you really think you'd marry me?"

"Unless you turn into a shrew," he teased.

"Or you're a drunkard or gambler," she joked.

"But never a philanderer." His tone deepened. "If I marry again, it would be without other partners. No affairs, no mistresses."

"That's a given in my mind." Eleanor stared into the distance. "It would be wonderful if we were a match, a true match. The kind of couple who respects their mate in public and private. The couple that raises happy, polite, educated children. The couple who could laugh together, have private secrets. Nothing big or worrisome. Just an occasional look or touch that would let me know you appreciated me for who I am and the woman I'll grow into."

"We seem to be of similar minds on some of the important things for the future. There are others, but we'll have time to discuss them in the next weeks." He grasped her hand, squeezing it before bringing it back to his cheek.

"You are very sure of yourself. This is moving extremely fast. You only found out yesterday that Agnes maneuvered the situation."

"True, but from my first sight of you, with sleep in your eyes, I was lost. I realized you thought I was George, but the way you looked at me struck me deeply. I wondered what might have been if something like this happened." He gave her a sly smile. "I've been wondering about you, Eleanor, when I had no right to. Now I have the right, if you approve."

Eleanor moved her horse closer to his. With more courage than she thought possible, she slipped her hand from his to chase along his cheek and behind his head. He leaned forward and relaxed into her move. She kissed him. She'd actually taken a first kiss, relinquishing her grasp for a moment to watch his gaze. A second press of her lips to his, and Eleanor was lost. She wanted to do it again. She couldn't name the feeling; it was something she never could have dreamed of. But this feeling explained many things she'd seen in the past.

Her horse shifted and inched them apart. She froze, as a strange expression crossed his features. She read it as a devilish grin. If kissing him created that smile, she couldn't conceive the possibilities. The grin deepened as he reached his hand behind her head and gently pulled her closer.

Phillip kissed her, an adult kiss she hadn't experienced before. Want overrode all propriety, and she grasped the front of his jacket and tugged him close.

The kiss sealed her fate. The electric ripple that ran from his lips to hers opened a new world that was instantly addictive. Phillip drew back and looked at her. His grin gave her confidence in her femininity. A confidence she'd never felt or imagined she could feel.

The leaves suddenly rustled around them with a cold wind she was unable to ignore.

He smiled at her. "Did you feel that?"

"Yes. It felt like a cold fog surrounded us." Both horses took a few steps, obviously unsettled.

"Do you know what that means?" He smiled again, relaxing back on his horse.

"Agnes has arrived." She realized she'd said her thought out loud.

"Or she's well on her way." He looked at his pocket watch. "Unfortunately, it's time to head back."

She nudged her horse close to his. Since her future was unsure, she wanted one more kiss. She slid hands along his face, leaned in, and kissed him. Without hesitation, she took a second one.

He didn't let her go far. He wrapped his arms around her and pulled her as close as possible with them both on horseback. He was warm and strong. His kiss was an adult kiss, the second she'd experienced. Both from him. A blast of cool air enveloped them. He kissed her again.

He released his hold on her, and Eleanor drew him back. She replaced her hands around his neck. "I know my actions must seem scandalous. You need to realize I'm not a proper woman at times."

"My actions aren't proper either, and I don't care. When I close my eyes, I see your lovely blue eyes. How they watch me and make me feel young and vibrant again." He dropped his lips to hers and kissed her yet again. The cooling air and their horses' movements separated them.

"I definitely don't feel proper with you. When you look at me, I get a warmth inside. When you kiss me, you leave me tingling and wanton."

"Will it help if I take responsibility for being overbearing and starting the situation?"

Eleanor kissed his lips hard. "Yes, I'd feel better, but does it matter between us? Am I being naive? You are unlike any man I've ever met."

"That goes for me too. I've met a lot of women in my life, Eleanor. None of whom could ever contend with you. There is a stillness about you most of the time. Then I see you laughing with Alfred, and a softness, a kindness, overtakes you." He let out a deep breath. "When I kiss you, my body wants to betray me."

"Where does all this truth leave us?" She directed her horse to take a step backward.

The wind continued raining leaves down around

them. She resettled on her mount and pulled her jacket back into place. Her hair would have to wait to be repaired. Some ends always worked loose from her style. The wind made the situation worse, settling most of the length on her shoulders. She used her fingers to brush the hair from her forehead.

"No repairs here." She saw the same devilish smile on his lips that she was becoming familiar and comfortable with.

"I like it down even if it is unconventional."

"Only for you." She was becoming scandalous with him and didn't care.

He gave her a playful grin, and she maneuvered Matilda to take the lead on the path.

Back at the barn, Daniel took her reins. Phillip was beside her, his hands wrapped tightly around her waist, helping her down. She stared into the pools of chocolate she saw when she looked into his eyes. Whispering, she said, "No regrets."

"No regrets."

The heavy winds became persistent, almost taking her hat from her head.

"Agnes is definitely close."

She smiled at him and received that same grin she'd seen earlier. "Thank you for the ride," she said as she walked back toward the house.

Her actions weren't proper, and she'd have to remember her manners when others were around. This man was a romantic dream come true. She'd be disappointed if he didn't want her permanently, but she'd reluctantly go away. She would, however, leave educated in some of the ways of life she'd never imagined.

Later she would consider what would happen if he concluded she wasn't for him. She'd be crushed. But until then, she wasn't going to dissuade contact. Why deprive herself of a gift she might not be able to keep? She hoped what was happening was true and honest. When the moment came, she would make decisions for her future. Would she have the final say on that future? Could she make a choice that took her away from Phillip?

Deep inside, she felt being with Phillip was right. Of course, he might change his positions, but until he decided he didn't want her around him, she would spend as much time with him as possible.

Chapter Eight

Back at the house with the horses turned over to Daniel, Eleanor thanked Phillip a second time for the tour and shook free of the enticing look he gave her. Then she headed inside. Margaret was in the kitchen with several helpers she hadn't met.

"How was your ride? You have the blush of the cool day on your cheeks," Margaret said.

Eleanor didn't say it was because Phillip had kissed her. "It was lovely. The colors of the turning leaves along the path should be captured before they're all gone." She took off her hat and stuffed her gloves into it. She tried to repair her windblown hair.

"You should make those images into drawings," Margaret said as she motioned for one of the other women to fetch a bowl of dough from the sideboard.

"I'm not an artist." Having been told all her life that her drawings were useless, she automatically dismissed it as a nonissue.

"I've seen the drawings you did for Alfred. You don't give yourself much credit."

"They were just to pass the time." Since she'd made drawings as gifts for Phillip and Agnes, she'd wondered what they would think when they opened their presents. Some days, she thought her handcrafted gifts were a mistake, but on other days she stood fast. She wasn't rich. Giving something she had spent time on was instinctive to her.

Margaret vented her opinion as a harrumph. She pulled a tray from the far corner and placed it on the atrium table. She put Eleanor's jacket and hat on an empty seat. "Sit and eat. You don't want to meet grumpy Agnes with a headache or grumbling stomach. I'll get you some coffee."

Eleanor was hungry. She sat and pulled the cloth from the tray filled with sandwiches of ham on thick-cut bread. She reached for one and nibbled. Margaret came back with two cups of coffee.

Eleanor slid a second plate across the table to Margaret. "This is delicious, and you're right. I was hungry."

Margaret stood to grab a knife from the sideboard. She returned and cut one of the sandwiches in half. She ate a bite and stirred milk into her coffee. "About Mrs. Crane coming this afternoon." She paused to see who was within earshot. "Just be yourself, Eleanor. Daniel and I know the truth, and you and Phillip seem like a match. But you can't let her know that from the start. You two have to get to know each other and decide for yourselves."

Eleanor was surprised. "I didn't know you knew." She lifted her sandwich to her lips but didn't eat. "Does the staff know?"

"No, just Daniel and I. And Phillip didn't tell us. But we've dealt with her long enough to wonder if this wasn't her original thought."

"What do you think, Margaret? You know Phillip much better than I do. Would I be a good wife for him?"

"Only you two can decide that. But your morning rides while Agnes is in bed would be a good way to get some time from prying eyes."

"Would you be upset?" She felt her cheeks flush with color.

"Not at all. I'm just saying don't let the old lady rule your life or decisions. You are both adults, and you'll figure it out on your own." Margaret sipped her coffee.

"Thank you, Margaret." Eleanor finished her sandwich and the coffee in her cup. "I should go up and bathe. My hair is a disaster. It's going to be a long day."

"You have no idea." Margaret rolled her eyes. "Just be yourself and don't let her bully you. Polite is one thing, but sometimes the old broad needs a blatant reminder she doesn't rule you or this house."

Eleanor smiled and held back a laugh. "I'm thankful you and Daniel are here."

"Go on. Go get cleaned up for tea. Phillip will pick her up from the station soon."

She nodded and brought her empty cup to the sink. "Thank you for the lunch," she said, knowing the others in the kitchen were listening.

"I'll send Laura up in an hour to help you dress."

Eleanor collected her belongings and headed upstairs. No matter what happened, Margaret and Daniel were good people, and she liked getting to know them. With their help, the situation with Agnes might be easier. At least she had their blessings if she and Phillip got together.

She just had to get past the idea of Agnes meddling in her life, especially in Phillip's. Although that was why she was there, knowing they were both maneuvered into their current positions annoyed her. When she thought she was betrothed to George, she'd had no choice. Now, with Phillip, she wanted him to make his own decisions without further influence from Agnes. That probably wouldn't happen, but after their talk earlier today, she hoped he'd be strong and forthright when the time came to confront Agnes.

****

Eleanor dressed in her blue skirt with the white shirtwaist boasting matching blue trim. She'd chosen a book she thought Agnes would approve of, Louisa May Alcott's *The Mysterious Key and What It Opened*. She'd read it before and could carry on a conversation about the beginning of the story if necessary.

She couldn't concentrate on the book and soon heard noise coming up the road. The carriage was returning. She stood and smoothed her skirt, still clutching the book tightly. If she had something to hold, she wouldn't fidget. She'd summoned several versions of the older woman, and now she was about to meet her.

Moments later the sounds of hoofbeats and wooden carriage wheels on the road out front were an unmistakable confirmation of Agnes Crane's arrival from the train station. Margaret rushed to the front door. She had it open before the carriage stopped.

Eleanor stayed in the parlor doorway, book in hand, wondering what the next minutes would be like.

After her unsanctioned trip to the city and talk with Mrs. Cornwell, she felt lighter, freer, and almost positive about her future. Now the woman who had been pulling the strings of her life was about to reveal herself. Eleanor stood tall, proud, and determined not to be intimidated by her presence.

Cool air surrounded her, and she heard Margaret's voice.

"Welcome, Mrs. Crane. Your rooms are ready."

"Of course they're ready. You had weeks' notice." The elderly woman swept into the entrance, bringing the winds with her. She paused in the foyer and turned to look at Eleanor.

Whatever you do, don't curtsy. "Mrs. Crane, I'm Eleanor Sterling." She stepped forward and extended her hand.

"Of course, you're Eleanor. Who else would you be?" Agnes didn't reach to shake it. Instead, she turned to the pier mirror, unpinned her hat, and dropped it on the seat. Next came her gloves and her jacket. "Margaret, since it's so late in the afternoon, we'll have tea in the parlor now. Then I'll have time to rest before supper. Come along, Eleanor."

She passed Eleanor and gave her a once-over, a rude once-over like the one the uncouth Mr. Deiden had given her at the wedding. Eleanor drew a deep breath and walked into the room, into a glimpse of her future—good, bad, or different than she anticipated. Thankfully, Margaret was back quickly, and Eleanor heard Phillip speaking. Hopefully, he would join them. She stood tall, the book still in her hand. While Agnes took a turn around the room, she ran her fingers over shelves and photo frames to check for dust. Eleanor was so surprised she gasped.

Visually, Grandmother Crane was typical of what women her age gravitated toward. Her hair was swept up but not as high as the newer Gibson Girl style. Eleanor held back a smile, assuming no gray hair would dare invade her blonde hair. Then again, blonde hair usually camouflaged gray hair. Her dress was comparable to the fuller skirts and corseted tops that had been fashionable five years earlier. The bustle was what was worn today.

The fabric was heavy, meant for winter weather.

After a quick inspection of Eleanor's dress, Agnes strode toward the fireplace and dropped onto the blue brocade chair before the side window.

Margaret placed the tray on the small table before her. "Will there be anything else?"

"Make sure to send up tea to my maid while she unpacks."

"Of course, ma'am."

"Where is my grandson?" she asked as Margaret turned to leave.

Phillip appeared in the inner doorway. "I'm right here, Grandmother. Are you comfortable? Would you like the fire lit?" He didn't wait for an answer and turned to glance at Eleanor. "Come join us. I'm sure Grandmother has many questions for you, almost as many as you have for her." He stood half turned before the fireplace so nobody else saw him wink at her.

If she hadn't been so nervous, she might have laughed. "Yes, of course." She skirted behind Agnes's chair and took the window seat. She placed the book beside her.

Phillip took the upholstered seat across from Agnes. "Shall I pour?"

"No, thank you. I was taught from a young age how to pour tea and make a guest comfortable." Eleanor winked at him, knowing Agnes couldn't see. "Mrs. Crane, lemon or milk?"

"Lemon." It was a stark answer, as if Eleanor's not knowing how the stranger liked her tea were an affront to humankind.

Eleanor held her breath until she had served each person. Thankfully, her hands hadn't shaken, and she didn't drop anything. This woman made her nervous, which was the game she would play until Eleanor chose to change the dynamic. Not now. The woman had just arrived. They had time to unravel her lies.

"For future reference, how do you prefer your coffee?" she asked Agnes.

"Light and sweet" was another short answer.

"Every person should know how to serve tea and coffee, according to my nanny," Eleanor told them.

Agnes exhaled a harrumph and turned to stare at Phillip, ignoring the comment. "Tell me about the trip to New York to visit Mrs. Cornwell, Eleanor."

She didn't gasp at the statement. Mrs. Cornwell would have notified Agnes of their time together. "I had a lovely trip. The weather was cool but not cold, and all the holiday decorations were magical. It was nice to see Mrs. Cornwell home and settled."

Phillip cleared his throat, which Eleanor assumed was an attempt to interrupt the line of questioning.

"And you were told I left specific orders for you to stay here at the house?" Agnes asked.

Eleanor lifted her chin and looked at Agnes. "Yes, Phillip and Margaret were very careful to let me know your preferences. Since George hadn't arrived, I chose to use the time to take care of a few errands before he comes."

"That doesn't answer why you went when you were specifically told not to."

Eleanor was grateful the woman didn't use a cane. She was sure Agnes would thump it on the floor to punctuate her words. "I went because I'm an adult woman capable of riding the train and getting through the city on my own. I made a point of getting through those errands to be here to meet you upon your arrival."

"But you still went." Agnes glared at her and set her cup down. The china rattled with the force.

"Yes, I went. If George had been here as promised, I would have asked him to escort me. Since you'd been traveling, I had to wonder how tired you'd be, and I didn't want to force you to make yet another trip."

Phillip sat back with his left ankle crossed over his right knee. Eleanor glanced at him but couldn't keep his gaze, afraid she'd lose her composure and laugh aloud. Considering the scowl on her face, Agnes wasn't used to getting this type of answer.

"Once more, why did you go when you knew I didn't want you to leave?"

"I went because I wanted to." Eleanor brought her tea to her lips and sipped. "If you're up to it, Mrs. Cornwell would like you to spend a few days in the city with her."

"You seem to have become a world traveler in the last weeks."

Agnes sounded aggravated. Good. That was what she hoped for. "I learned how to read a map and train schedule years ago. Common sense goes a long way in navigating new places."

Agnes cast her a critical look, her nose scrunched, her eyes half closed, and her forehead wrinkled. "Enough. We'll continue our conversation over supper."

"Not this conversation. You asked, and I answered. There will be plenty of subjects to discuss over supper in the next weeks. My first one will be when is my fiancé due to get here?"

Agnes stood. Phillip rose and extended his arm to his grandmother. Eleanor remained seated, sipping her tea.

"We won't change for supper. It's been an exhausting day," Agnes decreed as she and Phillip left the room.

Eleanor refused to let the older lady get to her. She'd learned at a young age to be polite but not to let anyone walk over her, especially brothers and people who thought they could rule her with money or a rude word.

"Have a good rest, Grandmother. We'll see you for supper," Phillip said from the hallway.

By then, Eleanor had picked up the book and pretended to be reading. After a few minutes, she put the book aside, loaded the cups on the tray, and headed toward the kitchen. Daniel met her at the doorway and took the tray from her.

Phillip sat in the breakfast room, a large smile on his lips. Eleanor dropped into the chair across from him while Margaret put a plate of biscuits and four cups before them. She poured fresh tea for them, and she and Daniel settled in around them.

"How badly did I annoy her and ruin my reputation?" Eleanor asked. "How mad is she that you let me go? Surely, she will assume my attitudes are because of poor breeding. She'll be rethinking the agreement right about now."

"Yes, she will," Phillip said with a full smile. He let out a light laugh, and Daniel laughed with him. Even Margaret seemed to bite back a smile.

"Go on and laugh. I'd better start looking for a job after the first of the year, or sooner if she really doesn't want me around."

Phillip sobered. "We have an agreement that I expect you to adhere to. As for Agnes, she'll calm down now she knows you won't let her walk over you."

"This whole situation has my stomach knotted. I'm generally not a rude person, and if I am, I usually keep it behind closed doors. I don't know what came over me that I spoke to her like that." She picked up her tea and drank a bit, appreciating the taste. "I'll have to apologize to her tonight."

"Oh no, you won't!" Margaret said. "You said nothing wrong, and you were honest. She doesn't deserve an apology."

"A bit blunt, but it was worth it to hear her tone change." Daniel stood, took a few of the biscuits from the plate, and left.

"She'll mellow after resting. Besides, unless she's ready to reveal her plan tonight, she'll have to be careful." Phillip selected a biscuit from the plate and ate it in two bites.

"I'm not sure I can keep up the animosity," Eleanor told him.

"Things will settle down. Better she knows up front you won't cower from her rudeness."

"I hope you're right." She considered taking a biscuit but changed her mind. "I'm going for a walk. Margaret, do you need help with supper?"

"No, we're all set. Get some fresh air but be back in time to wash up."

She ran up the back stairs and retrieved her coat. Outside, the temperature had dropped. She smiled. Was it the climate here in late November? Or had Agnes's arrival brought the chill? At least she was outside.

Their evening meal went by with terse comments from Agnes. Nothing seemed good enough for her. The food, the room, the service. Eleanor was thankful Agnes decided to skip coffee in the parlor and had it served upstairs so she could rest.

****

Phillip sat behind his desk in the workshop the evening after Thanksgiving. He hadn't been thrilled with the holiday. But then, except for his son and Eleanor, he wasn't thrilled with much of anything lately. The weather had turned colder, and the prospect of Agnes in residence for six weeks was not conducive to a cheery season.

He was thankful Agnes stayed in her room until teatime on most days—unless she was bored. Then she wandered the house, annoying the staff with her comments and disapproving suggestions. On Sunday, she would attend church with them and make a point of renewing friendships with others who had relocated from Rhode Island.

He'd originally thought to have Alfred join them for the Thanksgiving meal but was now glad he reconsidered. She'd seen the child from a distance yesterday when he was downstairs for tea, and turned away from him. Phillip had Nanny quickly take him from the room. He decided not to subject Alfred to a formal meeting, especially when the household was so tense. No matter what they did or said, everyone was wrong. Agnes had definite ideas about the world, how homes should be run, and how people should behave.

Most memories of his childhood were difficult in all aspects. His mother would stop in to see him and his brother every morning. The household was quiet that part of day, and their time with her was usually uninterrupted.

Teatime was tense. He and George were dressed in

their finest and expected to behave correctly. There were only questions about their lessons, no laughter, and after harsh critiques of their replies, they were swept away from the adults. He had vivid memories of Agnes berating his mother when he or George answered incorrectly or misbehaved.

When he was a child, holidays were uncomfortable. Agnes would question him and George about their studies, as she did at teatimes, always finding fault with their answers, never offering a "good job" or "well done." Alfred was still too young for that kind of criticism, but Phillip had promised himself his home would be filled with joyful memories.

The only time he remembered his parents smiling and laughing was on weekends when they would take him and George to the beach or out sailing.

He'd never found solace or enjoyment in sailing after his parents' accident. He'd been taught the process of the winds, the sails, and maneuvering the craft on high seas or with no wind. But after their accident, he'd lost interest in boats or the ocean.

He stood and wandered farther into the shop area, surveying his plants and picking the stray weed. This year's holiday had been sullen. No one had smiled, and conversations had been stilted. He'd experienced stress long forgotten. He'd never seen Eleanor so quiet, her words censored, her posture board straight. Although the meal was delicious, nobody had seemed to enjoy a bite. He considered ending Agnes's visit early. Could he pack her up and send her home if her attitude didn't change, especially toward Alfred?

The days would be very long with his grandmother in the house. He was used to steeling himself against her rude comments and interruptions, but he worried about how Eleanor would fare. After all, her life had been uprooted for a reason that didn't exist. He sent up a silent prayer that the chaos of finishing the decorating would go smoothly.

He didn't sleep well that night. Thoughts of Eleanor swam through his mind. He had high hopes for the future if she was beside him.

****

Eleanor did her best to forget Thanksgiving Day. Agnes had made it difficult to exist in her presence, let alone to enjoy the excellent meal Margaret prepared. She'd managed to stay in her room until her presence was required. When she found Margaret alone later that evening, she'd made a point of telling her the meal was delicious.

In her room after the tense day, she knew she didn't want her home to experience that stress. If she and Phillip were to marry, they would have to come to terms with how their household was run. From her perspective, it wasn't with Agnes in charge.

Today, the house was abuzz all day with a crew bringing in the Christmas tree. They set it in the foyer, where it could be appreciated by anyone in the main area of the house. They also hung greens around doorways and fireplaces on the main level.

Agnes skipped afternoon tea downstairs because of the flurry of activity. That evening before supper, she requested to see "the child." Phillip told her Alfred would be asleep by now and waking him would change the boy's schedule. She didn't care.

Nanny had brought Alfred downstairs to see the tree and decorations at the usual teatime. Phillip had seemed happy the child was so pleased. Alfred was animated and had a hundred questions, most of which were answered. He'd been told over the next few days more decorations would be going up and he could help at that time. A few questions were left open ended, such as when he'd get presents.

As the three of them waited in the parlor, Nanny brought Alfred down. Eleanor was uncomfortable in the formal dress she had changed into according to Agnes's requirements. That meant several more hours of formal dress, formal posture, and censoring her thoughts. She'd run her finger under the collar of her dress several times, feeling strangled by the high-necked material.

Alfred had been woken from a sound sleep. Once he awoke, he wanted to see each room's decorations. At one point, he pulled away from his father's hand and ran between the rooms, delighting in each new view.

Agnes's annoyance was apparent from her muttered comments about the boy having no manners. Nanny took him back to the nursery, and Phillip opened a bottle of wine. He handed around a glass to each woman and poured one for himself. He sat on a sofa across from his grandmother. Eleanor was glad to be sitting on the window seat to the side, not directly across from Agnes, and waited for him to start the conversation.

"Supper will be ready soon," he said.

"I'm not impressed with the child." Agnes took a sip of her wine. "Too unruly. You have to get Nanny to train him better."

"He's a lovely child," Eleanor said. "He's smart and loving. If you'd seen him this afternoon and his fascination with the decorations, you'd think differently."

"Don't let him fool you, Eleanor. All children his age learn early how to make adults think they're adorable. They can smile and be charming when they are constantly watched. But don't let him sidetrack you. When he's not being overseen, he'll show his true personality." Agnes looked at her through lidded eyes.

Agnes's comments riled up Eleanor, which was probably what the woman intended. She would take a different tack. "You'll have to remind me of that when George and I start our family."

"I've told you once. Remember it because I won't spend my days educating you on how to be a parent." She put her glass on the side table with a thud and stood. "Supper should be ready. It's after seven. Or doesn't the household run on a schedule?" she said, walking toward the dining room. Phillip joined her, and Eleanor trailed behind.

When they were seated, Margaret brought out the soup and placed it on the sideboard. She filled the bowls and set one before each person, then hurried out. Eleanor struggled to get down a few spoonfuls of the liquid. The taste was enticing, but her stomach was unsettled. She was annoyed with Agnes. One side of her knew not to get involved. The other side wanted to stand up for the child. They ate the rest of the meal in silence.

Back in the parlor, they waited for Margaret to bring in the coffee. Agnes began another tirade about Alfred's behavior, noting she would send another nanny when she got home. Then she insinuated that maybe it would be better if the child were raised in Newport, where she could keep a closer eye on him.

That was when Eleanor had had enough. "I'd think you'd realize waking the child from a deep sleep would create an issue. If you'd come down this afternoon, you would have seen the wonder in his eyes when he saw the decorations. Maybe tomorrow before tea he'll behave to your liking." She realized what she'd said aloud and instantly offered to pour the coffee.

Phillip thanked her with a nod as he accepted his cup. "Grandmother, Alfred is my son and will reside here in the Park with me. The choice of his nanny is my concern. As Eleanor stated, your request to see him altered his schedule. Tomorrow will be better."

"That's ridiculous. Children have to learn to adapt to their elders."

"Older children, yes. At Alfred's age, I won't berate him for acting out. He's not a trained circus animal who performs on cue."

Eleanor had to look away. She bit the inside of her lip to keep from laughing.

"Well, I never. I raised you and your brother with manners and schedules. You both turned out fine."

"Nanny raised me, and whether you believe it or not, I did turn out well. As to George, I'd say we have differing opinions on his childhood and the adult he grew into."

"He was younger than you when you lost your parents. It was important he be given some time to adjust."

"Adjust? Is that what we're calling his behavior now? He's adjusting to being an adult?"

"We're talking about raising your child," she said, her tone deep.

"Yes, Alfred is my son, and I take responsibility for his future. We may not do things as you did, but he's generally a happy child, healthy and inquisitive. I won't change that for anyone who can't see the possibilities before him." Phillip put his cup aside. "In five years, the new century will be here, and his life will be totally different from our current life."

"Not if you don't allow it. Maybe it's time to think about boarding school. Next year he'll be old enough."

Eleanor choked on her coffee at the suggestion and knew they watched her. "Sorry, I swallowed wrong."

"Agnes, my son is only three." Phillip spoke up. "I respectfully disagree. I'm not sending him to boarding school, and I flatly refuse to allow you to raise him in Newport."

"That's enough. I didn't come here to be berated." She rose and placed her cup aside. "I'll see you for tea tomorrow. Maybe by then you can corral the child to be better behaved."

"Good night, Mrs. Crane." Eleanor collected the cups and saucers from the table and set them on the tray. She wanted another cup of coffee but wouldn't dare ask while Agnes was there.

Phillip followed Agnes to the doorway and slowly walked her to the staircase. He called up to her maid, and the slight woman appeared at the top of the stairs and made her way down to meet them.

"Good night, Grandmother. I'll see you tomorrow afternoon," he said.

Agnes took her maid's arm and trudged upstairs. She mumbled under her breath about Alfred's behavior.

Eleanor watched from the parlor doorway. "I'd like fresh coffee. How about you?"

"Yes, please." He took the tray and walked to the kitchen. Only Margaret and Daniel were in there; the rest of the servants had scattered.

"I have fresh ready," Margaret said.

"Yes, please." Phillip laid the tray beside the sink.

Eleanor followed behind him and smiled at the sight of the table in the atrium. She headed to her normal seat and all but dropped onto it. The other three filed in around her, Margaret filling waiting cups. A deafening silence hung between them, and then Phillip laughed. Eleanor laughed too, and soon all four of them were laughing.

"I needed to laugh. She is a woman with strong opinions," Eleanor said.

"That's a polite way of saying she's rude and overbearing." Phillip looked at Margaret and Daniel. "I wish you could have seen the look on her face when Eleanor mentioned George's name."

"How long do you think she'll keep up the charade?" Daniel asked.

"I don't know. Until I lose my composure," Phillip said.

"I apologize. My comments didn't help her mood," Eleanor admitted.

"That's because you caught her off guard. Reminding her of the ruse to get you here and put us both through her hoops was unexpected. I knew I was annoyed with her, but controlling that annoyance won't last long. I'll wind up saying something that lets her know we're onto her setup," Phillip said.

Eleanor sipped her coffee. "She kept that smug look on her face, scanning me like I was a horse she was considering buying."

Daniel laughed aloud. "I've been on the receiving end of that look."

"Anyone who has met her has been on the receiving

end of her critical look. She assumes she'll intimidate everyone, and then nobody will go against her wishes," Phillip added.

"I grew up with aunts and uncles who gave us similar looks, like we didn't deserve to breathe the air they did. Unfortunately, my father didn't stop them. He allowed them to belittle us and our dreams if they didn't concur with theirs." Eleanor shifted in her seat. "I'll get my attitude right."

"Don't go changing your attitudes, Eleanor. I like you just as you are. Changing to please her will only make matters worse. I'm fine with your attitudes. Remember what she's done to both of us. I'm thankful she brought you to my home, but she doesn't run this household." Phillip drank his coffee.

"Yes, but I don't want to be angry with her forever. If she hadn't made the arrangement, I'd never have met any of you." She glanced at Phillip. "I'm thankful to have met all of you."

"Things will settle down soon. She'll start reminding everyone in town who she is and expect the proper social niceties."

"Why does she assume she has all the pull and authority?"

"Because she has the money, Eleanor." Margaret lifted the coffee pot, but they declined refills. "She forgets Phillip doesn't need her financial help. If she can't rule him with finances, she'll belittle his home and family to get her point across."

"What is her point, then?"

Phillip stood and dropped his hand on Eleanor's shoulder. With a light squeeze, he said, "That she is the matriarch of the family and should be respected. But when she can't get respect, she uses her money to remind everyone of her superiority. Unfortunately for her, I'm beyond needing her financial help and will raise my child as I see fit as well as run my home to my liking."

Margaret smiled. "Until recently, nobody dared go against her rules. Phillip has made a home here without her influence. She doesn't like not being in control."

"I understand not being in control of…anything. I wasn't in control of my life back home, and now I'm still at her beck and call."

"Not for long. Her façade will fade when she realizes we know her plans." Phillip squeezed her shoulder a second time.

"Do you think she spoke to Mrs. Cornwell before she arrived?" Margaret asked.

"I'd be surprised if she didn't. Remember she knew Eleanor went to New York and we didn't tell her."

"You're right of course. It's going to be a long six weeks to the first of the year." Eleanor stood and headed outside to the back porch.

A few minutes later, Phillip came out and dropped a shawl around her shoulders. "Don't stay out too late. It's colder than you think." He brushed a lock of hair from her forehead. He held her gaze longer than needed.

The instant he touched her, her stomach flipped. Just a slight touch turned her emotions on end. "I'll be in soon. I just needed some fresh air."

"Will you meet me tomorrow morning around ten for another ride?" he asked.

"Yes, I'd like that."

"Good night, Eleanor. Get some sleep."

"Good night, Phillip." She was a tad sorry that she hadn't asked him to stay or that he didn't suggest it. But they had a date for a ride tomorrow morning. She heard dishes rattle from the kitchen behind her and smiled. His leaving her alone was right. While she trusted Margaret and Daniel, she had to be cautious with Laura and Sally. They didn't need to know her business. Neither did Nanny, Agnes, or Agnes's maid, Greta.

Chapter Nine

The next day Eleanor and Phillip rode out on a different path. Unfortunately, this path was more popular, and they passed many people. She'd already met some of them, but others she hadn't seen before. As expected, Phillip introduced her as Eleanor Sterling, a guest of his grandmother's, who was visiting until the first of the year. Most people were polite, some friendly, and others wary of her presence and Phillip's explanation.

Their ride back was less populated. This path was wider, and they rode side by side.

"I'm sorry the path was so busy this morning," Phillip said. "I suppose most people are out before it gets too cold."

"I'll take the cold. It's the ice from Agnes that frankly…"

"Go on. Please finish your thought."

"Frankly, she annoys me in all directions. I expected her to be harsh and derisive, but she is just contemptuous." She tried to curb her ire.

"Go ahead, Eleanor. Let it out. Say what you want to." Phillip's lips spread into a small smile.

"I found her waking Alfred at her whim, regardless of his schedule, irresponsible. As she is so quick to tell me, she raised children. She should know better." She slowed and took several deep breaths. "I understand he is your son and I have no right to comment on how you raise him, but to listen to her tirade about his behavior was awful. I hope Nanny got him upstairs and out of hearing range before she launched into her monologue." She guided her horse first on the narrowing path and waited until he caught up. "If you laugh at me, Phillip…"

Before she could continue, he leaned toward her and wrapped his hand around the back of her neck. With a slight shift in the saddle, his body was close enough for his lips to cover hers. She was surprised but didn't pull away. Rather, she leaned in, using her hand on his chest to steady herself for another. His kisses made her feel alive in new ways, and Agnes was forgotten. When he paused and drew back, she studied him. She leaned in again and kissed him. In the distance she heard voices. She pulled away quickly so they wouldn't be seen.

"I wasn't laughing at you, but I was smiling. I'll admit it. I like and appreciate how you consider Alfred's needs."

"He can't fend for himself," she whispered.

The voices that broke them apart grew faint. Several moments passed, and they didn't meet anyone on the path.

"I know how that feels. He doesn't deserve to be pigeonholed because of his age."

"Is that how you see me raising him?"

"No, oh no. When he sees you, his little brown eyes light up, like you're a present every day. I understand you have a business and castle to maintain, but he does enjoy his time with you." The horse moved, and she held his gaze. "It's not my place, but I would be upset if you let Agnes raise him."

"Not to worry, Eleanor. I meant what I said

yesterday. He is my son and will grow up here, with me."

"I do hope so, Phillip."

He guided his horse ahead of hers. Seconds later, another rider approached. Phillip made a quick introduction, and the man rode on.

He waited while she caught up to him, and then turned back to her. This time the press of his lips was quick and hard. "You make me think of things I've long ago forgotten. Some I only wondered about, but you make me feel alive. I've been stagnating for three years. Eleanor Sterling. Thank you for waking me up. I'll be eternally grateful for myself and for Alfred."

"I've woken you up?" She bit her bottom lip to suppress a smile.

"Yes, and I'm thankful. I'd forgotten to appreciate the small things, including my son. It isn't possible to forget about you. Eleanor, you are the Christmas gift I hadn't thought to ask for."

"That's lovely, an unasked-for gift. Will we get complacent with time?"

"Not if we don't let it happen. As long as we remember to appreciate each other." He watched her intently. "My thoughts of you override my work and common sense."

She felt the heat rise on her cheeks. She now recognized it as arousal. "Is that so bad?"

"No, it's not. In fact, I'm enjoying it immensely." He winked at her. "I know we said we'd wait to talk about the future, but in just this short time, I feel as though my initial decisions are solid."

"What decisions?" She finally turned to see the path and trees around them.

"The ones that will embarrass you and make your

cheeks redden again."

She looked at him, confused, then realized he was speaking about their compatibility. "Yes, I'll admit I'm attracted to you. I don't understand all the feelings, but when you kiss me like you did just now, I feel as if we're on page one of a very long book that we'll write together."

"That's a beautiful analogy, Eleanor. Thank you for considering we'd have a fulfilling future. When we spoke last time, it was all so confusing. But pushing Agnes and her plan aside, I'm attracted to you in ways I've never been attracted to any other woman."

She inhaled the cool air as she listened to his words.

"I've never felt like this, even with Ida. You give me hope, Eleanor. Please don't take that away from me."

"You confuse and embarrass me at times, Phillip. But you are the first man, or person for that matter, that I dare speak my mind to unfiltered. Because of the situation, we've been up front about the future. Can I assume my personality doesn't offend you?"

"In private, I want you to always be yourself—inquisitive, indignant, and honest. In public, we'll both have to remember we're on show."

"Thank you for allowing me to spend time with you outside the castle."

"House," he reminded her.

"In the beginning, I wondered if I'd ever see you again. I was afraid George would show up and we'd leave. I'm glad that he ran from responsibility. Now we have some time together. But I will warn you, Phillip, somewhere along the line we're going to get caught in a compromising position."

"I do hope so." He leaned back on his mount and

smiled at the sky.

"I do understand your references, Phillip. Just because I've never indulged in them doesn't mean I'm completely naïve."

"Would you like to indulge in some of them with me?"

"I've been thinking on it, and I'll let you know when I decide to throw all caution to the wind and let you love me."

"No, Eleanor. Caution to the wind, yes, but not just me loving you. You loving me back. Loving each other where no embarrassment exists. Where you know you can trust me with your secrets and well-being and I can trust you."

"That sounds wonderful, but I still have to wonder what else will befall us before the first of the year."

"Until that time…" Phillip grasped her by the shoulder.

This kiss was soft at first, sensual and filled with longing. Then it deepened. She tugged the lapels of his jacket to hold him to her. For long seconds, she found heaven, literally and metaphorically. These feelings were wonderful, and she understood that they were a gift in some sense, that she might not feel the same with a different man kissing her. At the thought, she pulled back and straightened her hat.

"You goad me toward behavior I know isn't proper, let alone conventional."

"You have to decide if you want to be conventional the rest of your life. Or behind closed doors, do you long to be the woman you hide, the woman you were taught not to let act or speak? She's the woman I want to live with, the one who won't be submissive…outside the bedroom."

Eleanor felt her chest, neck, and face redden, but she didn't look away. "Submission in the bedroom works both ways, Phillip. Are you willing to give me equal time in charge?"

Now his cheeks reddened. "I'll have to think on that. It never crossed my mind."

"Something to think about for the future. It might be interesting." She grasped the reins, and the horse began a slow walk toward town. She was glad Phillip was behind her—he couldn't see her smile. He hadn't expected her to turn the tables on him. But now he was thinking about it, and so was she. She'd never been brazen, and it gave her an unexpected thrill.

Back home, she thanked Phillip for the ride and tour of the path and headed inside to wash up and change for tea. A large crew of men continued wrapping evergreen boughs everywhere. In the parlor, maids decorated a small tree. Red ribbons folded into bows hung everywhere. The center chandelier wasn't left alone. A man on a tall ladder strung evergreen boughs with ribbons attached to them. Even the banister was wrapped. The fresh scent was everywhere.

After spending several minutes leaning on the upper railing, watching the process, Eleanor remembered Agnes. She would not approve of her riding clothes in the house or…anywhere. In her room, she cleaned up and changed into her blue skirt and solid light-blue shirtwaist. She sat in the chair by the window and let her mind wander about trusting this man with her most embarrassing and untutored ways. Would he be annoyed with her inexperience, or would he see her as an asset? Time would tell. For now, she closed her eyes and savored the wonderful thoughts of how he'd touch her, love her, and how she'd reciprocate.

While Nanny was on her break, Eleanor took Alfred into the office and showed him how to glue interlocking strips of colored paper into long lengths. The fire burned brightly before them. She sat on the carpet beside him, enjoying his innocent pleasure in the process.

When they used all the paper she had, she carried the paper lengths into the hallway and helped him drape some of them over the lower branches of the tree. He seemed delighted to have helped, clapping as they finished, his smile wide. Eleanor didn't realize Phillip had come in and observed from the hall doorway.

"That's wonderful, Alfred." He walked toward them.

"El'nor helped," the child said.

"Did you say 'thank you'?"

"Yes, Alfred was very polite." She helped him straighten a paper length that had fallen off a branch.

Phillip swept the child up into his arms and helped him place the last of the decorations on the upper branches. She stood back, watching father and son accomplish the task. She'd never had her father's attention when she was young or when she was an adult. The simple act had Alfred and Phillip smiling. They stood back, and Alfred clapped his hands again.

"A job well done." Phillip kissed his son's cheek and set him down. "Nanny will be wondering where you've gone to."

Within a moment, Nanny appeared at the kitchen doorway. She took his hand and headed back to the nursery.

"Thank you, El'nor," Phillip teased, using his son's

abbreviation of her name. "It was kind to spend time with him."

"It was my pleasure. He's very smart, Phillip. Once you show him what to do, he can follow along without much supervision."

"I'm sure there was more to it, but he was delighted with the attention and the lesson." He walked toward her and reached his hand to hers. She gave him her hand, and they walked side by side into the parlor.

Agnes came from the office and paused in the doorway. She seemed irritated, and Eleanor braced for another round of insults and lectures.

"Good afternoon, Agnes," Eleanor said.

"Not so much." Agnes took her preferred seat and waited, none too patiently, until Margaret brought in the tea tray and, when they were all served, scurried from the room. "Do you think your attention to Alfred is proper?" She looked at Eleanor.

"Excuse me?" Eleanor said. What had she done that wasn't proper?

"Sitting on the floor with him isn't ladylike."

"I didn't think anyone was around." She sipped her tea to avoid further comment.

"There are always staff around. You should know that."

"I do, but it was easier to do the project on the floor at his level than to make him sit at the table."

"You shouldn't be doing projects with him at all."

Eleanor glanced at Phillip.

"I respectfully disagree. If Eleanor is willing to spend time teaching him and he enjoys the time, what's the harm?" he asked.

"It's not proper. That's what nannies are for."

Agnes's tone was adamant.

"Please don't blame Nanny. I was the one who decided on the project. It was my choice to spend the time with him."

Agnes grumbled and held her cup out for Phillip to refill. When the cup was full, she nodded. "I still don't like it."

"Then don't spy on anyone. Did you let Eleanor know she was being watched, or did you slink away once you saw Alfred enjoying time with her?"

"I don't slink, Phillip."

"Did you notice he was happy?"

"He's a child. He should be told when he's happy."

Eleanor coughed at the comment. "Excuse me?"

"Yes, I remember you telling me and George when we were supposed to be happy. Frankly, it annoyed me when you did."

"Yes, you weren't a happy child."

"Leaving my childhood aside, I'm always happy when I see my son smiling and laughing."

"He needs a stronger hand," Agnes said, dropping her hand heavily on the arm of her seat.

"I'll decide how strong a hand he gets, Grandmother."

Eleanor wanted to run from the room. "It was my fault. *I* invited him to work with me. I didn't consider you'd find it so improper."

"I do, but since it's done, let's forget it. Just don't do it again, Eleanor."

She placed her cup on the side table and stood. "I can't promise not to spend time with the child, Agnes. I'll make sure you're not lurking in doorways before I do projects on the floor with him." She grasped the side of her skirt. "If you'll excuse me, I have things to do this afternoon. I'll see you both at supper."

She refused to turn around and strode directly upstairs. In her room, she sat before the mirror, staring at the woman who looked back at her.

"I don't care who she is. I'll not let her berate Alfred for being happy." She grabbed her wrap and headed down the back staircase and directly out the kitchen door to the rear porch. She sat quietly, taking controlled breaths. Cat jumped up beside her and nudged her hand.

"I'm sorry, boy. I was distracted." She reached to pet him, and soon he curled up on her lap and accepted the soothing strokes she made along his back. "I'll tell you one thing, Cat. If that angry lady thinks she can rule this household too, I'm going to have a few things to say, and they won't be conventional from a young lady." She stopped petting him, and he nudged her again. "I wonder what supper conversation will be."

"Most likely, she'll tell us all about the social season in Newport and what we missed."

She sensed Phillip was near but hadn't seen him.

He stepped closer and leaned on the back of her bench. "Whenever she feels she's been bested or reprimanded, she always defaults to the 'season' I missed and all the people I could have met."

"Do you want to meet more young ladies…people?"

"No. I've made my decisions about ladies. I have no use for another."

Her cheeks heated, and she laughed aloud. "Let's hope she's not standing behind the door listening to us."

"Agreed."

"See you at supper," she said.

Phillip strode toward his shop.

Eleanor wasn't sure if the silence at the supper table was better than having Agnes berate them.

The next day, they woke to a cold rain, and there would be no horseback rides. She went down to breakfast and afterward returned to her room where she sat under the window to work with her watercolors. All she could hope was that by staying out of the way, she'd not bother anyone...or at least Agnes.

Hearing how the woman talked about her grandson and great-grandson infuriated her. How dare she waltz in and assume everything would be done to her liking and perfection level? Thankfully, if things worked out with Phillip, they'd reside in the Park. If for some unknown reason, he changed his mind and wanted to move to Newport, she would have to consider changing the direction of her future. She still had choices, but Phillip would be her first.

****

On the Sunday after Thanksgiving, the household awoke early and headed to church. Eleanor was surprised Agnes wanted to walk. Although she'd hoped to make the walk alone, that was fine with her. Nanny took Alfred. Margaret, Daniel, and the maids made up their own line while she, Phillip, and Agnes walked together.

November had gotten colder in the last days, much colder. She couldn't decide if it was because fall was turning to winter or if some of it was due to Agnes's attitude. It didn't matter. They were out of the house and away from the daily routine. Since Agnes's arrival, nothing anyone did was proper or correct. From the way the house was run to the Christmas decorations, no one could please her.

With the church in sight, Alfred pulled from Nanny

and ran to Eleanor's side.

"El'nor." He reached for her hand.

She glanced at Phillip, and he nodded. She held Alfred's small hand in hers and listened to his animated ideas of the service. She diplomatically slowed her steps to match the child's, letting Agnes and Phillip walk ahead. During the walk, she reinforced his numbers and letters.

Agnes commented loudly that it was Nanny's responsibility to teach him to count and read and to take him to church. Eleanor slowed their pace a second time so Alfred wouldn't hear her running commentary on how to raise the boy. When they reached the church steps, he paused and gave her a low bow. His cap fell off.

She picked it up and plopped it back on his head. "Thank you for escorting me, Alfred."

"Wel'come," he said, and Nanny all but swept him inside.

She and Phillip waited while Agnes acknowledged everyone she came in contact with. Most had left Newport long ago.

The service was similar to the ones Eleanor had experienced in the last weeks and ones she'd grown up with. She didn't need the hymnal for the words. Her voice was strong and the words memorized.

Leaving church took forever. Agnes had to stop and converse with everyone. Not just a pleasantry in passing but in conversations. If the weather hadn't been so brisk, they might have been there much longer. When Agnes invited several of the women over for tea on different afternoons, Eleanor stilled. That would mean she'd have to participate.

"Eleanor will be available to help decorate the

church during the holiday week," Agnes said in a loud voice.

None of the ladies listening mentioned she'd already volunteered. She'd get to know some of the ladies in the community better, but she had no idea how Agnes would account for George. It wasn't her problem.

The rest of the household had gone ahead while Agnes had her conversations. On their walk home, she wasn't surprised to hear Agnes complaining. Again.

"Eleanor, you're spending too much time with the child."

"Did you expect me to ignore him or decline his invitation?"

"You're overstepping your place with him. Especially since you'll be leaving soon for Newport."

"I was under the impression we were waiting for George to arrive." The look Agnes shot her would have had a lesser woman shrinking back. Eleanor straightened her posture, waiting for her answer.

"Newport will be better for you after the first of the year."

"He's stood me up here. What makes you think Newport will be better after the holidays? Do you have information you're not sharing? How do you know he won't do the same in Rhode Island?"

"There will be other men to introduce you to up there. Men of upstanding families whose histories and pedigrees I know."

Eleanor stopped walking. "Did you ever think George would show up here to meet me?"

"I'm just considering them as a backup plan if George disappoints me and decides his life will go in a different direction."

"Disappoints you? I'm going to start thinking long and hard about where I want to go after the first. Mrs. Cornwell has offered me a room if I want to stay in the city."

Agnes expressed her dissatisfaction with a harrumph. "You won't be happy there."

"I enjoyed my time there last week. I believe I could build a life there. I'm educated. I could become a nanny or a librarian or even do accounting work to pay my way." She was on thin ice with her comments, but she'd had enough of Agnes's superior tone.

"I brought you here. I'm responsible for you, and you'll go where I see fit."

They were almost home, and Eleanor wouldn't give Agnes a way out. "While I appreciate your kindness, Agnes—" She paused, using the woman's first name to make a point. "—I will accept Phillip's hospitality until the first of the year and decide my future."

"I never expected you to be so insolent."

"I'm an adult woman, Agnes. Maybe you should talk to George about insolence." She drew a deep breath. "If you hadn't raised him to be a feckless man, none of us would be in this situation."

At the house, Alfred played on the front lawn under the watchful eye of Nanny. He called to her, and she swept her skirt to the side and passed Agnes without another word. She stayed with him, picking up leaves and asking him about the colors. When she had her temper in control, she joined Agnes and Phillip in the foyer just in time to hear them talking.

"I didn't expect her to be so snippy. Better George isn't coming," Agnes said to Phillip.

Phillip helped Agnes with her coat. "George isn't

coming? What do you know that I don't?"

"We'll discuss it later."

Eleanor stood beside the pier mirror to take off her gloves, hat, and cape. She didn't hold her tongue. "Agnes—"

"You should be thankful I brought you here. George or not, you'll be comfortable here."

"Phillip and his staff have gone out of their way to make me comfortable, but this isn't my home. It seems you knew George wouldn't be here. I need to make a future for myself."

"Don't go rushing into important decisions."

"This will be my decision, Agnes. I can be self-sufficient, and I'll find other options for my future, especially since it seems you lied about George wanting a wife."

"You'll stay here until I decide different. I'm responsible for you. I brought you here. Things will work out." She primped her hair and turned from the mirror. "George may still show up."

"No." Eleanor squared her shoulders and drew a breath. "Even if he shows up, I won't marry him. I don't know him, and his behavior proved to me I don't want to get to know him or marry him. He is disrespectful beyond anything I've ever known. His not showing up was unacceptable in itself, but he didn't even send a letter of explanation."

She took another deep breath. "I didn't want this arranged marriage. You are well aware the money you offered my father was the catalyst or I'd still be in England. George jilted me, and that tells me a lot about how you raised an immature and weak man who is still a boy. And since we're on the subject of you raising

George, I find it hypocritical for you to tell Phillip how to raise his son."

"Well, I never," Agnes said.

"And you shouldn't again." Eleanor snatched up her outer clothes. Phillip had apparently left the foyer sometime during her conversation with Agnes. "I'll see you at tea," she said over her shoulder as an afterthought.

"Young lady, I didn't dismiss you," Agnes said loudly.

Eleanor waited but didn't turn to face her. "Yes?"

"You don't know the intricate nature of the situation."

At that comment, Eleanor turned to watch Agnes. "What I know is that you coddled and indulged him all his life. Considering he'd only come back for the money, he'd be better off not tied down to any woman. He'll cheat and betray me or any other spouse arranged for him."

She paused for effect. Since she'd gone this far, she would finish her thoughts, not knowing if she'd ever get the chance to speak her opinions again. "I'm disappointed in him but thankful for the reprieve. You, madam, are worse. You knew how he'd react, yet you still made the arrangement that sent him running for parts unknown. I came here in good faith, but apparently you knew there would be issues. Now you think you can manage me like you tried to manage George. Unfortunately for you, I won't be maneuvered to your liking." She chose her words carefully before continuing. "You should contact my father for a refund of your purchase price as it seems I've disappointed you too." Eleanor walked toward the kitchen, refusing to give Agnes a chance to respond.

Phillip met her in the kitchen doorway. She pressed her hand to her throat, trying to calm her breathing. While she'd managed to tell Agnes her true thoughts, she was shaking. He smiled at her, and she relaxed.

"Well done, Eleanor."

"I've never spoken to anyone in that tone, especially an elder."

"It was well deserved. Few people ever tell her the truth, or at least to her face."

He smiled, and she felt her belly heat. She held back a laugh, knowing Agnes was still within earshot. Eventually, they both laughed aloud.

Eleanor sobered. "Phillip, please don't let her browbeat Alfred. I wouldn't want to see him turn into another George."

"You truly care about him, don't you?"

"Yes. He's intelligent and quick to learn. Don't let anyone tell him different."

"Not to worry. It's easy to acknowledge her opinions, but that doesn't mean I follow her wishes. Remember I grew up with her. I swore if I had my own children, I would raise them differently. That's why my home is outside the town limits. Yes, we're involved in the town, but we have some separation from them and their influences."

"It sounds like you thought this out carefully."

"I had a long time to consider my options and always knew I'd take my inheritance and make it what I wanted for me and my family."

In the distance, Agnes called for her maid, her voice echoing.

"I'm glad you did." Eleanor winked at him and rushed through the kitchen to the back porch. She tried to relax in the shade and welcomed Cat beside her, stroking his ears. He circled twice and lodged himself onto her lap.

Chapter Ten

Phillip dreaded afternoon tea with Agnes. After her post-church conversation with Eleanor, he worried about the two women being in the same space. But if Eleanor was to stay with him, she'd have to learn to stand up to Agnes or be walked over for the rest of her life. He didn't want that for him, Alfred, or the children they might have.

"Hello," he said as he entered the parlor. Eleanor put aside the book she'd been reading. Agnes followed him in just as Margaret laid out tea. When they were settled with cups before them, they sat in an awkward silence.

"We've heard the telephone lines will be coming soon, maybe next year," he offered as a diversion and conversation starter.

"If you'd pushed harder, they would have already been installed," Agnes commented. "It's the same with electricity. If you'd been more demonstrative, you might have it now."

"Both were beyond my position," he said, his voice tight with the tension he felt.

"He seems to be doing well without it for now. The kerosene lighting is more than adequate," Eleanor said. "With the turn of the century coming soon, there will be many changes."

"Eleanor," Agnes said as she placed her cup on the table. "Did you know Phillip had the opportunity to build

Cheryl A. Cornell

his home within the city walls but chose not to?"

"No, I wasn't aware."

Phillip was thankful she didn't let on he'd mentioned it to her during their ride.

"The land was part of the original family parcel. When the plans were being finalized, he pulled his acreage. Wanted to be separate from the town. What a mistake." Agnes vented with a loud harrumph.

"Grandmother, I've explained this to you many times. I wanted my home and family to have their own space. I'm part of the community, have full rights to all the facilities. By separating, I'm able to keep my business and greenhouses going without restrictions."

Agnes waved her hand at him. "No matter, it's too late to go back."

"Yes, thankfully, it is." He put his cup down. "If you'll excuse me, I'd like to spend time with Alfred." He didn't wait for a response but rather fled the room with measured steps. He left Eleanor to take the brunt of his grandmother's mood. He would apologize later.

****

The next afternoon, Phillip guided Alfred on his pony, showing him how to hold the reins. He gripped the back of his jacket just in case the boy slipped. He was thrilled the child enjoyed the process, and Alfred's little laugh was contagious. He had to treasure these moments, as his young son was growing quickly. He wanted him to have fond memories of their time together while teaching him not to be afraid of the animal.

The wind strengthened, and he saw Nanny heading toward them. He turned the pony in the direction of the barn. Once there, he lifted the boy off its back and gave him a hug. "You did well today, Alfred. Almost as if you'd been riding all your life."

The boy smiled.

Phillip hoped he'd know it was a compliment even at his young age. Putting him down, he added, "Off to Nanny now. It's teatime."

His son looked to Nanny and back to him, then he ran off and met her halfway to the house. Phillip hadn't realized Eleanor was in the shadow of the porch.

"I hope you don't mind me watching. I love his laugh. He makes me think the situation will all work out."

"It will, eventually. Walk with me?"

"Of course." She fell into step with him as he headed toward the back acreage.

"I'm proud of you, Eleanor. Yesterday, you stood up to Agnes and told her your truth. I can't imagine many people have tried or succeeded."

"I hope I haven't gone too far. After last night's mute meal, I'm not sure where I stand with her, but I hope to not have to confront her again."

While they walked, Phillip pointed out several areas of plants she wasn't familiar with. When they came to a muddy spot, he clutched her by the waist and lifted her over the puddle. He put her down but kept her in his grasp. She didn't pull away. Rather, she stretched her arms around his neck. Leaning down and pressing his lips to hers was simple, but noise in the distance had them pulling apart. They changed directions to a different plot of wintered flowers, and he explained what he hoped would grow there again this spring.

"I had no idea how much acreage you had here."

"Enough, as I keep telling Agnes. Within the town limits, the parcels are much smaller. I would have had to build the greenhouses elsewhere. That would mean traveling to work and losing control of the surrounding areas, besides the extra costs."

"It makes sense to me to be separate. As you mentioned, you have full access to the amenities."

Phillip laughed. "Without their prying eyes and tongues."

"Do you think the townspeople talk about us?"

"Possibly, but not to worry. They don't matter to us in the long run. Their strict rules, outdated ideas of what life should be, annoy me. I don't want Alfred growing up constrained by strangers."

"That's the best gift you could give a child."

"You're the best gift I could receive, my Christmas bride."

"Christmas bride." She smiled at him. "I thought we decided to talk after the first of the year."

"I know that's what we said, but it's a long way off. Christmas will be better."

"What will Agnes say?"

"Let's not tell her until it's done."

He laughed with her, and they continued their walk through the fields. He accompanied her back to the house. She sat on the rear porch with a book she kept tucked under a pillow. Glancing back, he noted Cat was heading toward her. He shook his head and smiled. The damn cat never gave anyone the time of day, yet when she came outside, he was drawn to her. As were he and Alfred.

In the greenhouse, he meandered along the rows of tables and held a running commentary with himself. Knowing he was alone, he spoke low, as if the seedlings would respond.

"I have a decision to make and quick. I promised Eleanor I'd give her until the first of the year to decide our future. I know this is all happening fast and I've been lonely at times. I didn't acknowledge that until I met Eleanor. I don't want her just for company for me and Alfred. I have true feelings for her.

"She's a hard woman to resist. She's resilient and brave, outspoken, and kind to pets and children."

He moved to a different table of seedlings, where he paused to pull any tiny weeds that dared poke through the dirt. "It's her damn blue eyes and golden hair that attract me to her." He imagined lacing his fingers through her silky locks and drawing her to him for intimate times.

"I have to accept she'll be a challenge to me and most likely me to her. I can only hope it will open doors I've not experienced in the past. Ida had been quiet and shy around me. Damn, I like that Eleanor challenges me.

"Since Agnes arrived, the household has been tense. It reminds me of growing up with her in Newport. Even her maid carries a look of panic whenever I see her." He remembered how nothing in the household was correct. How she thought they needed to be more conventional.

He closed down the greenhouse and walked out to the barn to check on the horses. He grabbed several apples from a barrel near the door and took his penknife from his pocket. He sliced one in half and fed it to the horse in the first stable. He repeated the process by rote while his mind wandered.

He had decisions to make. Decisions that had to be made quickly. Seeing Eleanor stand up to Agnes told him he was right about her and possibly the future they could have together. Resisting the automatic reach to touch her was getting too hard. Her independent nature and staunch beliefs attracted him, especially when he saw how she protected Alfred.

Later that night after supper, instead of sitting in the parlor playing cards with Agnes, he'd invite her for an evening walk. She'd spent most evenings playing card games with Agnes and played secondhand hostess to her afternoon tea parties with the local ladies. Agnes be damned.

Yes, they were decisions she had to make, but he wanted her to have all the facts, not just suppositions. Only then, if she chose to leave him, would he be able to deal with the loss.

****

After supper, Phillip asked Eleanor to walk with him before it became too cold for an evening stroll. "It's a full moon tonight," he said by way of explanation.

Agnes raised her brow in disapproval, but he quickly added she was welcome to come. He knew she hated the cold. He ushered Eleanor to the hall and waited impatiently while she ran upstairs for her coat and gloves. He was pulling on his coat when she returned. He wanted them out of Agnes's reach and supervision. They walked side by side to the field away from meddlesome eyes and ears.

"I know this is unconventional, but I needed to speak with you alone."

"Is there a problem, Phillip? Have you decided my speaking bluntly to Agnes was rude?"

"No. But with the days passing quickly, I'm afraid I'll lose my opportunity."

"Go on," she said, looking quizzically at him in the moonlight.

"You're beautiful in this light." He reached to stroke her cheek.

"Thank you," she whispered.

"I know we talked about getting to know each other, and I promised to give us time to get to know each other. But in the last week, things have changed."

"What changed, Phillip?"

"I have. I would like you to seriously consider marrying me. Becoming my wife and helping to raise Alfred. I'd like to know the household is in good hands."

"Your household is in good hands. Margaret is wonderful at running the home."

"Yes, but she's not you. And seeing you each day makes me want you for my own."

"Because I'm a good deal, paid for, and conveniently installed here already." She gave him a teasing smile.

"My good luck," he told her. "I want you for myself in all ways, as husband and wife. In public and private. Waiting until the new year for your decision is a waste of time." He took her hand. "I understand this is fast, but will you consider this a marriage proposal?"

"Yes, it is fast. Yes, I agree I'm falling in love with you too. But…"

"Talk to me, Eleanor." He drew her into the circle of his arms.

"What if we're not compatible?"

"I can only tell you my version of marriage is forever. Yes, we'll argue and bicker. And hopefully laugh and smile and make memories with our children. If we want this to be a strong marriage, we'll work through the problems. We'll make the important decisions together."

"This all sounds so easy, too perfect. I've no experience to draw on. I need some time to think through this."

"Are you skeptical of marriage or marriage to me? Or is it Alfred?"

"No, I love Alfred. And I'm falling in love with you. But there is one thing that annoys me." She pulled from his grasp and walked a few feet away, staring at the night sky.

"Of course, we'll annoy each other on occasion. Sometimes on purpose and sometime not. But with time, we'll work through those issues, become stronger. I'm not saying it will always be easy. Being an adult isn't easy, but we can be there for each other to lean on. Talk to me, Eleanor. It's the only way this can work. Is it George, or would you like to be courted by other men? I don't want you to look back and wonder what you missed out on by not spending time with other men." He gave her his best smile. "Not that I'm asking you to meet others."

"I've met enough men in my life—good, bad, and cynical. I was stuck in many situations where men made assumptions and I had to correct them." She glanced at him and laughed aloud. "I had to punch one in the stomach to get him away, but that was when I was ten."

He laughed at her statement.

"There were many men on the ship who seemed to think I was available, and I had to deter their advances. Some took the hint easily, while others weren't happy when I talked to the first officer and asked them to keep us separated. The way they looked at me and watched my every move was revolting, as if I were chattel. Even with Mrs. Cornwell beside me, some were relentless."

"But you knew your own mind. Were you keeping them away because of George?"

"No, between us, George was a faint concept. And once we were on the ship, Mrs. Cornwell told me if I didn't want to marry George, I could always stay with her. That was a relief. To know I had an out if George wasn't what he was represented to be was a godsend. It took the pressure off me. She said she would talk to Agnes if that happened and shelter me."

"Do I make you feel like chattel? Are my advances unwanted?"

"Of course not. You've known from the first time we rode the trails I was interested in you...and before too." She looked at him intently. "You're different, Phillip. I'm afraid if we were to marry, we might end up resenting each other because of the situation."

"That would only happen if we let it." He tipped her chin up to meet his lips. This kiss was different. Intense and erotic. Eleanor melted against his body.

When he finally pulled back, she smiled at him. "What if I disappoint you as a wife?"

"We'll learn our way together, as long as we're honest with each other." He kissed her again, nipping at her bottom lip. "Give us thirty or forty years to get to know each other and then decide."

"I've never felt like this before. I don't know how to process it. I know I've been sheltered, but wanting you the way I do is... I can't rationalize it."

"That's called lust, Eleanor. With time, we'll learn to enjoy and satisfy each other."

"You won't mind teaching me?" Eleanor wrapped her hands behind his neck.

"That is a husband's honor."

This kiss was different yet again. His hand slid up to cup her breast. She moaned at his touch and, in a bold move, dropped her hand to his thigh. He groaned, and she turned away.

"Oh, Phillip." She turned back to him and, smiling, slipped her arms around his neck again.

He instantly grasped her by the waist and drew her closer.

"It will upset me that Agnes will get what she wants, what she set up for us."

"Does it truly matter?"

"Only that she'll lord it over us for the rest of her life."

"Only as much as we allow. We have to keep our perspective on the future. Our lives, marriage, and home will run the way we're comfortable with. We'll soon be in the new century, and many things will change. We'll experience them together and make decisions about our future together."

He kissed her again. She inched back to look at him, but she didn't leave his embrace.

"I hope you mean those words because I plan to hold you to them for the rest of our lives," she said.

"I do mean them, Eleanor, with all my heart. Ida was an arrangement, and we liked each other, but it was never love. It never felt like this. This is love."

"Do you think Alfred will accept me as a stepmother?"

"He already knows you and likes you. More importantly, he trusts you. I see how he gravitates to you. In his young life, he's only known Nanny as a female influence. Do you see raising him an issue?"

"I'd be proud to be his governess or guardian,

whatever word you choose to use."

"Eventually, I think it should be *mother*, but that will come with time. I want us to be a true family unit."

"How about we let him decide what to call me when he gets older?"

"That I can agree with."

"This is all so fast. What if we have another child?"

"I'll be happy with any children we have. I want them to be healthy and have you as their main influence. I want us to be a family."

"What will we tell Agnes?"

He laughed aloud. "Nothing. We can let her stew a bit, but eventually she'll see we're right together, if she hasn't already."

"Our own home and family. I never thought I'd find true love. That's what I feel, Phillip. That this is true love."

"I knew it was true love the day I found you asleep on the bench under the stairs." He gave her a full hug, dragging her against his body. "Let's make this a happy home, Eleanor."

"Here, on this land in our own castle?" Her lips spread into a smile.

"House…" He kissed her again.

"Home. Our stone home," she whispered and kissed him back. "With you as my Christmas husband."

****

One day slipped into another. She and Phillip spent most mornings together. They rode horses and bicycles and took long walks alone. Occasionally, they'd be seen by other townspeople and learned not to care. The time was swiftly coming when everything would be revealed to Agnes.

Eleanor kept busy practicing the piano, reading, and spending afternoons with Alfred when Agnes napped. She read on the back porch in the late mornings, Cat curled up on her lap. When she had no excuse, she spent evenings playing cards with Agnes. She quickly learned that Agnes was not a gracious loser, and on occasion she lost the game on purpose. From her perspective, Agnes's afternoon teas were a success, but she never received a verbal confirmation from her.

Whenever possible, she rode the trails around the Park on her favorite horse, sometimes alone but better times with Phillip. She enjoyed walking beside him and Alfred while Alfred practiced balancing on his pony around the house grounds.

Against Agnes's wishes, she and Phillip took young Alfred on a train ride. It was the most fun she'd had since Agnes arrived. Alfred loved the motion and changing scenery. He especially liked the whistle, which he made a point of imitating whenever possible.

As Christmas approached, Agnes complained less. Phillip was open with the occasional brush of Eleanor's shoulder or his hand touching hers when they were alone. She and Phillip often talked of the holiday plans. At times, his eyes sparkled in the light.

Sometimes when he was near, she could picture their wedding, their future, their children. She could picture the church draped in evergreens with candlelight reflecting the stained glass. Other times the vision evaporated, and she became sad. Then she would see Phillip or Alfred, and her hopes were renewed.

Agnes gave up berating her when she spent time in the kitchen baking with Margaret. They made cakes and cookies to take to the church and for their neighbors.

Eleanor learned to smile and do what she wanted.

One afternoon, Agnes stood in the kitchen doorway, watching and listening to Eleanor, Margaret, and the maids laugh over childhood stories. Eleanor knew another lecture was coming. At supper that night, it began.

"Eleanor, you must be careful what you say to and in front of the help. It's not good to mix with them." Agnes took another spoonful of her soup.

"I understand your point, but surely stories of holidays from our youths can't hurt. Besides, I always felt being kind to the staff helped insure their loyalty."

"I don't like it," Agnes told her, raising her voice. "Phillip, you shouldn't allow it either. You were brought up better."

"Yes, Grandmother. But your household was different, and twenty years have passed since I lived with you. With being away at school and moving here, I'm much more relaxed."

"I don't like relaxed!"

"Then go back to Newport."

It was a blatant statement, and he didn't lose eye contact with her. Eleanor was proud of his resolve.

The color drained from Agnes's cheeks as she put her spoon down. "You are rude."

"Yes, I apologize. But sometimes it's the only way to make you listen to me. Under my roof, we do things differently."

Her displeasure was punctuated with a harrumph. "In my day…"

"Yes, but we're not in your day." Phillip took several measured breaths, stood, and walked to his grandmother. He leaned down and kissed her cheek, then strode back to his seat. "The soup tonight is delicious, don't you agree?"

Agnes ignored his comment.

Later in the parlor for coffee, they were quiet, and Agnes retired to her room early. Eleanor moved to the piano. She hoped Agnes would hear her notes and not scold her for spending time alone with Phillip. She practiced "Silent Night," "O Holy Night," and "The First Noel" carols. She sang the words in whispered tones, not wanting anyone to hear her, even Phillip.

The next afternoon at tea, Phillip announced the three of them were heading to New York City to visit with Mrs. Cornwell and do some holiday shopping. He had arranged for dinner reservations on the second night. They would leave the day after tomorrow and spend two nights. It was a statement, not a request. To finish the topic, he told Agnes that Mrs. Cornwell was to spend the week between Christmas and New Year's with them. If she chose, Agnes could stay in the city for the days before and come back with her.

"Thank you, Phillip. That sounds like a lovely trip. I'd like to spend a little more time in the city before life changes." Eleanor smiled at him and didn't care if Agnes watched.

"Hopefully, the weather will hold out. It will be cold, but we'll all enjoy the difference in scenery. Besides, I want to order a few things for the house."

"This is short notice," Agnes proclaimed.

"Just tell your maid, Greta. I'm sure she'll be able to have you packed and ready. Mrs. Cornwell knows you'll bring your maid, so I don't see any issues."

Eleanor hid her smile with her napkin.

"Good night, ladies. I want to check a few things in

the greenhouse before turning in." He left them alone.

Eleanor was suddenly anxious to get to her piano practice. She fled the table as soon as was polite and kept herself busy until Agnes went up. Witnessing Phillip handle Agnes was interesting and reassuring. He would take charge of future issues with her. While calm, he quietly let her know it was his house and he'd make the decisions.

****

The following afternoon, Eleanor bundled up and walked into the town, appreciating the decorations and fresh air. Christmas was in full regalia. Homes were decorated as well as storefronts and common buildings. Wreaths, garlands, and stars were all around. The town smelled of spices and gingerbread. The whole area glistened with holiday magic.

Everyone she met or came in contact with was in a good mood. They passed pleasantries beyond just a nod. She'd spent many an afternoon in the church with her thoughts since arriving in the Park. The interiors looked magnificent, aglow with candlelight, flowers, and ribbons. Some days, she would sit quietly in the back, listening to the choir practice their carols. When they sang "Away in a Manger" or "We Three Kings," she held back tears. On other days when the church was empty, she would sit and ponder her future with Phillip and Alfred, maybe someday another child. At times she feared her future with Phillip was only a dream, but seeing him made her believe it could be real. She cherished those moments.

She could think straight when she was alone. Her quiet thoughts reinforced her feelings for Phillip. Marrying him wasn't just a solution to her future. She had fallen in love with the man. She loved how he moved, how his brown hair fluttered in the wind. How he laughed with her and Alfred, especially when he taught Alfred to ride the pony. Away from others, mainly Agnes, he was relaxed.

She found a bench beside the lake and sat enjoying private time away from the house. She decided the tears that fell down her cheeks were from the cold, not from fear.

"May I join you?" Phillip moved to sit next to her.

"Of course." She tucked her dress closer to her so he had room to join her. "I'm happy to see you."

He handed her his handkerchief. While she blotted her cheeks, they were silent. She didn't object to his arm reaching behind her.

"How can I help? Are you having second thoughts about spending your life with me?"

"No help needed. I was appreciating such a beautiful place. Had I known you and this place were waiting for me, I would have enjoyed the journey much more."

He drew his arm back and straightened, turning to watch her. "I have to remember we're in public. It's taking all my strength not to touch you. Your hair, your cheek…"

"Nobody is stopping you from touching me," she said with a smile. She hoped he'd understand her invitation.

He resettled his arm around her, laughing lightly. "We can have a good time together, Eleanor."

"I'm counting on that. We deserve to have a close private life."

"A close private life. Is that what we're calling our soon-to-be marriage?"

She felt the heat traveling up her neck and landing on her cheeks. "I want us to enjoy each other. Isn't that what a marriage is supposed to encompass?"

"In my mind, yes, but we both know not every couple is comfortable with each other."

"I'm glad we have a moment alone. I'd like to get your opinion on a few things."

"What's on your mind?"

"You've been married. I'm sure you're aware of the important issues beyond the physical."

"Don't discount the physical."

He gave her the smile that made her burn inside, and she reached her gloved hand to his cheek.

His eyes closed at her move. "Talk to me, Eleanor."

"I feel we'll be compatible in that area. For me, true compatibility comes with a profound sense of safety, and I don't mean just financial security."

"Go on," he prompted.

"There will be conflict between us at times. I hope we'll learn how to negotiate those conflicts and manage them before they become major issues."

"We've talked about public and private moments. What has you on edge?"

"I suppose this all seems so idyllic now. I'm afraid once we're married, everyday life will come between us. We talked about that too, but the conversation is different from the reality."

"We'll learn from our arguments and fights. As you pointed out, negotiating is key. What brought this to mind?"

"I was thinking about my parents' marriage. I don't want to spend my life being told what to do, say, and act without some discussion."

His lips spread into a wide smile. When she pulled from his grasp, he gently pulled her back to him. "If you hadn't noticed already, you are a confident woman. No man, even your husband, will stand a change of bowling you over with convention."

She glanced at him, wanting and needing his reassurance.

"Eleanor, we won't have their marriage or anything like it. This is America. We are very different from our parents. Hell, look how far I came from Agnes's way of life and thinking."

"There are other things we need to bring to this union. Affection doesn't seem to be an issue. So far, I feel we've been honest with each other. I wouldn't want that to change."

"Neither would I. There is also compassion and consistency."

"Along with loyalty and flexibility," she added.

"Yes, and respect goes both ways. We will learn to adapt to each other's ways."

"I do respect you, Phillip. I hope my curiosity won't embarrass you, especially when it comes to…private times."

"We talked about learning what each other likes and doesn't. It can be exciting to love another person, Eleanor. All the talk nannies and parents force us to believe will become insignificant in our relationship. What we decide together will be right for us. Nobody has a right to know who we are behind closed doors."

"I hope you don't forget that in time when you're bored with me. I will make an effort to be a good wife. That's my commitment to you and to Alfred."

"Somehow, I think Agnes has become a flea in your

ear. How about this? From now on, she can prattle on about whatever she wants or considers proper. Nobody could stop her if they tried. But we make our own way, our own decisions."

"I suppose I sound childish, but there are so many unknowns from my perspective."

"Life is full of unknowns—some good, some horrible. We weather them together, in our way."

"Thank you, Phillip. My parents weren't a good match, and their arguing often left me wondering what would happen in my future relationships. Because Mother passed away, I've no idea if they would have worked it all out. I do know they came to harbor great disrespect for one another. I couldn't stand it if you came to despise me in any way."

"When I look into your cornflower-blue eyes, I melt inside, Eleanor. I could never despise you in any way. Of course, we'll argue, but we'll work through the issues. That's the only way long term." He squeezed her shoulder. "I'll make you a deal. If I'm being a boor or rude, you just have to put some distance between us. That will be our way to defuse bad situations. After a bit, we'll come back together and talk out the issues, work through them."

"That sounds efficient." She smiled and then laughed. "I've got one more thought, that our commitment to each other will force us to be kind and respectful."

"Is that what you want all the time? Kindness and respect?"

Her cheeks heated with embarrassment. "Of course, most of the time, except behind closed doors…"

He laughed aloud. "Forget New Year's Eve. Marry

me tomorrow, and we can start enjoying each other right away."

"A compromise? Christmas is two weeks away. You mentioned I could be your Christmas present. We could be a Christmas bride and groom. We could be each other's present." Eleanor smiled at him, a new confident smile.

"Tomorrow too soon?" he jested. "Okay, Christmas Eve. How does that sound?"

"Two weeks isn't too long. Besides"—she snuggled close to him—"I like the idea you want me…and we won't forget our anniversary." She glanced over her shoulder and didn't see anyone. Her hand slid across his knee.

He squeezed her shoulder and sighed. "We're definitely going to have a bright future."

If the wind hadn't picked up, she would have liked to stay there longer, but the cold became biting, penetrating her outer layers. They walked home, hand in hand.

"My Christmas bride," he whispered, raising her hand to his lips.

"My Christmas groom," she whispered back.

Chapter Eleven

Supper that evening wasn't quite so sullen. Phillip was glad he'd made arrangements to go to the city. He'd thought to slip away on his own to choose Eleanor's ring, but he wanted them to have a special time before the holidays. After all, they hadn't dated. His instant attraction for her overwhelmed him at times. He was speeding things along, but his feelings wouldn't change, and he wanted to be able to touch her openly. To love her in private in ways he never found with Ida. Yes, his imagination was swirling, and from the little contact they'd had, he imagined Eleanor would be adventurous with him.

After supper, he found her on the front porch and dropped a shawl over her shoulders, though she wore a coat.

"It is a beautiful night," he said. "The wind has died out since this afternoon."

"Yes, it is. Thank you for the extra warmth."

"You're welcome. Do you mind me springing the trip on you without conferring with you?"

"Not this time. It's still your household."

"But next time I'll include you in the decisions. I'd like us to slip away for a few hours one morning."

"Something specific?"

"Yes, I'd like you to be with me to pick out your wedding ring." He stepped next to her, his body close, his hands on her shoulders. "Is that okay with you, or would you rather it be a surprise?"

"I'd like to have a say, especially if I'm to wear it the rest of my life."

"That's what I assumed, but I'm trying to remember to include you in decisions instead of making decrees."

"Thank you. If we're to marry and join our lives, I'd appreciate being included." She started to turn in his arms, but he lightly pressed her shoulders.

"I don't know who is still awake inside."

"Of course. It's been interesting to see how you avoid confrontation with Agnes."

"My parents' relationship was much more relaxed, even in Newport. They always seemed annoyed with social conventions. I'd like us to stray from convention when possible. After all, in a short time we'll be in the new century. I say we make our own rules, especially in private."

"I would like that too. If you hadn't already realized, I'm not a conventional woman, no matter what the circumstances were that brought me to you. Mrs. Cornwell didn't mind us making this trip with little notice?"

Again, he squeezed her shoulders. "She's not as conventional as we might assume. And she seemed very pleased that we're forming plans for the future."

"Phillip, you told her?" This time she did turn into the circle of his arms.

He held her tight. "Why not? Mrs. Cornwell was aware of Agnes's plans for us. And it will be good for her to be with friends for the holidays…and our wedding."

"Our wedding," she whispered.

"I was hoping to announce our engagement the Sunday we get back from the city. Christmas Eve is the following Sunday. Would you like that, or am I pushing you faster than you're prepared to go?"

"I'd like us to be together in all ways. Becoming your wife on Christmas Eve sounds perfect. We'll start the new year as husband and wife. That seems fitting too."

****

Their train ride to the city had gone smoothly. Laura, Eleanor's maid, and Greta, Agnes's maid, conversed throughout the ride. They both seemed happy to be away from the house and routines. These few days would give them a respite from their usual duties.

When they arrived at Mrs. Cornwell's, she was openly glad to see them. She greeted Agnes with a kiss on both cheeks. Eleanor, she pulled in for a hug and more kisses. "My dear, your gift arrived yesterday. The stationery is lovely and is appreciated."

"I'm glad you liked it."

Mrs. Cornwell stood before Phillip and smiled. Then she hugged him. Her butler took their coats and escorted the maids upstairs while they settled in the parlor before supper.

"No need to change for supper," she told them when they were seated with a cup of tea before them. "I'm sure Phillip wants to show Eleanor the city at night." She winked at him.

"A wonderful idea, Mrs. Cornwell."

Agnes harrumphed.

"Since we're all here in private"—Phillip glanced from his grandmother to Eleanor and back to Agnes—"it would have been nice to know Eleanor was to be my bride. I'm not sure why you both thought to confuse her with thoughts of George." He waited while the women looked at each other.

"If she'd come here as your bride and you two didn't have a connection, it would have been difficult for everyone involved." Agnes brought her cup to her lips. "Besides, an old lady can still meddle and have a bit of say in her grandson's life. Remember I didn't make such a good match for you with Ida."

He sat forward. "I didn't know you understood the situation."

"At first, I didn't. But when Ida was staying with me and you were down here building the house, she confided she'd not been as receptive to you as she might have been. Apparently, there was another young man she was interested in, but he wasn't ready to marry. She was a few years older than you, dear. Ida felt your match to her might be her last chance."

He shook his head in disbelief. "You knew all along?"

"Not until near the end," she admitted. "She knew she wasn't going to live long. She always said she was delicate and was thankful Alfred was healthy, but she hoped to never have to carry another child. And she knew your longing to have a large family."

"No, she wasn't happy carrying Alfred. But knowing she'd hoped he would have been fathered by another man explains a lot about her attitudes." Again, he shook his head. "Why not tell me sooner?"

"I told you when the time was right. Much earlier, you might not have accepted the truth."

"Agnes, I'd like to shake you," he said. Finally, he laughed. "But since you brought Eleanor to me, I'll let it go. Mrs. Cornwell, were you aware of the situation?"

"Most of it. Agnes and I grew up together. We've been friends for many years. It was natural for her to confide in me. Last spring I stayed with Eleanor's aunt in London. When I met Eleanor, I felt she was right for you. Both of you have an unconventional air about you. A much better match, I'd agree."

"Mrs. Cornwell, had you informed me, or at least given me a hint as to the future, I might have been a much better companion on the journey over. I know I was quite tense and unappreciative of your company," Eleanor said.

"You were a pleasant companion, my dear. And I didn't want to get your hopes up if you and Phillip took one look at each other and despised the idea of a future together."

Mrs. Cornwell smiled, and Phillip couldn't be mad at the kindly woman.

"Agnes had told me her feelings about her match for you and Ida long ago. Once I met Eleanor, I mentioned her to Agnes in a letter."

"So you sent my photo to Agnes?" Eleanor asked.

"Yes, after a return letter," Mrs. Cornwell confirmed. "Your aunt was happy to give me the photo. She understood your father wasn't looking to make a match for you. Rather, to keep you there as a spinster to run his home."

"I didn't think Auntie understood," Eleanor whispered.

"She did. She knew you'd never get away from his grasp without intervention."

"I'll have to write her and thank her for her insight," she said.

"Just don't let your father know she was involved," Agnes added.

"No, of course not."

"Phillip, if you two met and didn't like each other, nothing was lost. I would have taken Eleanor back to Newport and made a match for her there. Since you two have come to an arrangement, I see no harm done." Agnes sipped her tea.

"And Agnes had warned me not to elaborate." Mrs. Cornwell glanced at Eleanor.

Agnes, on the other hand, wore a grin that Phillip knew meant she'd bested him. He hated her smug grins.

The clock struck four. "Phillip, why not take Eleanor for a walk around the neighborhood before supper? It will give Agnes and me some time to catch up," Mrs. Cornwell suggested.

Eleanor laughed. "Are we being dismissed?" She stood and placed her cup on the tea tray.

"It seems we are." Phillip, too, put his cup on the tray.

"Be back before seven," Mrs. Cornwell added. "Pull the bell so the butler can get your coats."

Outside, wrapped for a winter walk, they strolled several blocks before Eleanor turned to Phillip. "I didn't expect them to concede so quickly."

"Technically, they didn't. By my bringing us here to Mrs. Cornwell's, well, they couldn't keep up the charade much longer. Are you still annoyed with them?"

"I'd like to be, but since we don't seem to despise each other, I'll let it go. It won't do us any good to hold on to a mood."

"Agreed. We can save it for when Agnes really annoys us in the future." He took her hand as they wandered the blocks and admired the decorations. "Tomorrow morning, we'll shop for your ring."

"Will you wear a wedding ring?"

"Yes, in public. But you must understand when I'm working it might become a hazard. Jewelry has a tendency to get caught on tools outdoors and in the workshop."

"I understand. But in public, I'd like anyone who sees you to understand you're not available."

"Agreed." They crossed onto the next block and continued in silence except for discussing specific decorations and bits of architecture they liked or didn't like.

****

The next morning, Phillip took Eleanor to a jewelry store. She'd never seen so much beautiful jewelry— rings, necklaces, and bracelets. They wandered among the cases, each pointing out something they liked.

"What rings do you like?" he asked.

"There are too many to decide. Maybe a slim platinum band," she said, not wanting to seem greedy.

"No stones?"

"Aren't they expensive?" she whispered while scanning the shimmering options.

"This is a once-in-a-lifetime purchase for us, Eleanor. I plan to do this once. Please be honest."

She smiled, gave him her opinion, and let him decide. "Did you ever hear the stories about stones being related to birthdays? That the color would reflect the dates?"

"I've heard about it, but not enough to make any decisions. Would you like colored stones?"

"When are your and Alfred's birthdays?"

"We were both born in July. What about you?"

"April," she said.

"Diamonds are the birthstone for April, and rubies are for July," the salesman said with a wink at Phillip. He moved down to another case and brought out a tray of rings with colored stones in them. Without much conversation, he took one with a large diamond in the center.

Eleanor shook her head. It was too large. After several options, she spied one she liked. "May I see that one?"

He took the ring from the tray and handed it to her. It was a platinum band with a round-shaped diamond in the center. A circle of smaller diamonds surrounded it like a halo.

She slipped it on her finger and admired it. "It's beautiful. It reminds me of a flower."

Phillip squeezed her arm. "Price isn't a problem, Eleanor. I want you to pick what you'll love wearing...forever."

Looking at the ring again, she gave it back to the man behind the counter. "It's beautiful, but I think it's too much for our lifestyle."

The gentlemen handed it back to her. "Might you try it back on for size?"

When she did, the ring fit as if it had been made especially for her. After realizing she'd admired it for too long, she handed it back. "May we see some bands?" She moved to another display.

With Phillip beside her, they agreed on simple platinum bands. After he had his finger sized, he walked away with the man to complete the sale. She wandered around the store while he took care of the purchase.

Phillip joined her, and they headed outside. They paused along the store's wall to be out of the pedestrian traffic, and he asked her, "Will you be content with the plain band? Please be honest."

"I think the band is beautiful, especially since you'll wear the matching one…when you're not working."

"What about the diamond ring?"

Her cheeks heated, and she turned to look in the display window. "It's beautiful but too expensive. I'm sure there are other things at the house to spend that money on."

His laughing at her wasn't the reaction she expected. "Don't make fun of me, Phillip. Would you rather I spent money indiscriminately without knowing the details of your finances?"

"No, and I shouldn't have laughed. We'll have a conversation about money when we get home. For now, let's just enjoy our time here. The rings will be sized and ready to be picked up before we leave for home." He slipped his arm around her shoulders. "Where would you like to go next? Dress shopping?"

"I thought I'd wear a dress I brought with me. It's not a true wedding dress, but it's white with light-blue trim. I ordered it for the local season before I heard about the move. When I learned I was to be married upon my arrival, I talked to the dressmaker. We made a few changes. It's not an elaborate gown, but I think it's beautiful."

"If you're comfortable with the dress, I'm sure I'll love it too. This is our real wedding. I just didn't want you being disappointed years from now that you didn't have a proper wedding dress. But since we're here, you should pick up whatever you think you'll need for the winter."

"I purchased a few winter things before the trip, and I'd rather walk around Central Park. Last time I was here, I was alone and only walked the outer path near Mrs. Cornwell's home. Can we walk through the zoo?"

"Of course." Phillip tucked her against his body, and they wandered toward the park. They stopped to admire the decorations in the shop windows.

"Next year we could bring Alfred to see the decorations. He'll be old enough to appreciate the displays."

Eleanor agreed, and he smiled.

They fell into a companionable silence as they walked the path. Phillip would stop and admire some of the planting beds, telling her about the individual plants and flowers. While visiting the zoo, they resolved to bring Alfred back in the spring. Then they took a short tour of the Art Museum of New York City.

Eleanor was thrilled with the art works. "These are stunning," she told Phillip. "I've never seen so much amazing art in one place." She and Phillip discussed a few each of them preferred and concluded they would need longer to truly discover the wonder of the paintings.

"Maybe when we bring Alfred to the zoo in the spring."

"Zoo in the morning with Alfred and the museum for our afternoon when he's napping."

"That would be lovely," she told him.

On the way back to the house, they stopped in a sweet shop and picked up licorice for Alfred and chocolate cream candy for the staff.

Back at Mrs. Cornwell's home, they had time for tea and to relax and change for their evening meal. Phillip took them to a famous steak house for supper. Eleanor tried not to seem awestruck by the restaurant but couldn't help but marvel at the room. Their meal was delicious, and they all smiled and laughed. Eleanor decided Agnes's meddling wasn't important any longer. Of course, the champagne Phillip ordered helped ease the conversation.

After their meal, they walked down to the Ladies' Mile. The window decorations were beautiful, especially the ones at a big department store. Thirteen window scenes depicted children's stories.

"These decorations are amazing. Next year we must bring Alfred to see them," Eleanor said.

"That would be wonderful," Mrs. Cornwell told her. "Of course, you'll stay with me."

"Thank you," Phillip answered. "That's a lovely invitation. We discussed bringing Alfred to the city to see the zoo in the spring."

"You'll stay with me whenever you are in the city. You'll always be welcome."

"I appreciate that, Mrs. Cornwell. We may just accept and take you up on your offer," Eleanor answered.

"If you remember, he's a spirited child." Phillip smiled.

"All children are spirited. That's what nannies are for," Mrs. Cornwell said. She and Agnes walked to the next window.

The rest of the evening, they strolled along the main streets and admired the decorations.

At home, they gathered for a late cup of coffee before retiring. Mrs. Cornwell accepted Phillip's invitation to join them for the holidays sooner than originally discussed. She signaled to her maid, giving instructions for their trip the next day.

When the ladies retired for the night, Phillip took Eleanor to a local restaurant, where they danced to the small band. Being in his arms reinforced her decisions were right.

The next morning, Phillip slipped out early while the ladies were having breakfast, but he was back in time to collect them and make their train home. Eleanor wondered if he was picking up their wedding rings but didn't ask. Their time in the city was over, and they headed to the train station. She looked forward to getting home. Being away, she realized how much she missed Alfred, Margaret, and Daniel and the house.

She couldn't remember when she'd smiled as much as she had in the last few days. She enjoyed the ladies' tales of their younger times in Newport.

****

Once back at the Park, life got busy. Besides the holidays, they had two guests to keep occupied. Phillip was openly thankful Mrs. Cornwell had come home with them. She was a good companion to Agnes.

Agnes had stopped berating him about the running of the house and his son's behavior.

Since their return from the city, Eleanor seemed at ease working with Margaret in her role of soon-to-be wife. She was careful to voice her opinions on certain things, such as the wedding details and more importantly, Alfred, in private.

Margaret and Daniel seemed to feel more secure in their roles at the home too. He heard more laughter around the house, especially from the kitchen when Agnes wasn't around. Even the maids were more at ease. Only Greta, Agnes's maid, still seemed pensive. Then again, she'd have to return to Newport with the woman.

Phillip managed to get stolen moments with Eleanor. She'd wander into the workshop and kiss him for no reason. They made a point of going riding on the mornings when they could get away. Those times alone on the paths, they discussed their future and the future of the world around them.

Phillip asked whether Eleanor could live in the country full time or did she want to take a house in the city. She seemed aghast at the idea, her hands tightening on the reins. They slowed the horses to talk.

"No, I'd prefer to live here in our castle. It would be nice to occasionally go to the city for shopping or a show, but the sheer amount of people makes me uneasy. If you don't mind, I'd like to live here. I don't think I'd mind trips or vacations, but I'd want the Park to remain our home. This is where you have your business. This is where Alfred has grown up so far. In a short time, he'll be going to the Park school. I'd like him to have this as the castle he remembers when he's older."

"Stone house," he reminded her. The sun was visible through the trees, the leaves long gone from their summer growth. "What do you think of our winter path?"

"Castle or house, it will be our home," she said with a smile. "I like the path both ways. Without the leaves, we can see who's coming if I want to kiss you."

He didn't wait. He moved his mount closer and drew her to him. Their kiss was a renewal of the passion he felt. After several more, he released her from his hold and straightened on his horse. He watched as she pulled her jacket into place and smoothed her hair from her face.

"Okay, Eleanor. Unless you change your mind,

we'll live here and travel occasionally. We can deal with changes down the road."

"One thing"—she kept direct eye contact—"I don't want to spend too much time with Agnes in Newport. I understand she's your relative, but I can't imagine living with her for long periods of time. We seem to have struck a truce, but it won't last long."

"Agreed. An occasional visit to Newport for the beach but in small bits of time."

"One other thing."

Her hesitation was palpable, and he drew a deep breath, waiting for her to continue.

"While we've never met, I'd prefer not to spend a lot of time with George. I know he's your brother, but I don't want to make any of us uncomfortable. We don't know what Agnes told him. I feel bad remembering all the things I said about him early on."

"You were reacting to what you were told. In reality, he's always been a mendacious child, and he grew up to be a worse man."

"The information did make him seem irresponsible."

"Actually, I think Agnes mentioned you in passing, hoping he'd go away. It's no secret among the family he had no ambition to marry or take on a profession for money."

"How does he think he'll live?"

"Probably off the kindness of rich women."

"Which I am not." She shook her head.

"Agnes probably told him he'd be responsible for your support too. That surely would have sent him running."

"So she chased him away?"

"That's my best guess. If he'd stayed, no matter how much he liked you, he would have made excuses. Since he's my brother, I can say this. He's very much like my grandfather. Gambling, drink, and women are his forte."

"So he'll come back once we're married and in need of money. Will he assume you'll help finance him?"

"He knows better than to expect me to help him with money. We were both left a similar inheritance from our parents. I don't know how much of his he's gone through, but when I married Ida, he made references to living with us. Ones I shut down immediately. He understands I won't be his meal ticket." He reached for her hand to reassure her. "He'll milk Grandmother for all he can get and eventually sweet-talk some rich young woman into marrying him. When her money runs out or she objects to him using her for her money, he'll move on."

"What if he shows up unannounced?"

"I'll pay his train fare to Newport, back to Agnes. And I'll buy the ticket, not give him the money."

"Thank you for understanding." She reached her arms up around his neck and kissed him full on the lips, a hard smack of skin to skin. She let go of him, and he wrapped his arm around her waist and drew her back for several more long, erotic kisses.

When he released her, she used her hand to fan her cheeks. "Phillip, I suppose we can't go against convention and kiss at the altar after we're married. It would seem scandalous to…everyone."

"How about when we walk down the aisle, we can stop and kiss before we leave the church?" He gave her his devilish smile. He noted her neck and cheeks blushed pink. "That seems like a reasonable compromise."

When she smiled, he knew his decisions were right for both of them. "I'll have the vicar announce our engagement on Sunday before Christmas Eve. We'll get married the afternoon of Christmas Eve. Do you have any objections?"

"None, except for Elizabeth Stevens. I hope she doesn't think we're doing it to slight her."

"Her mother will, but Elizabeth will understand."

"What about the wedding?" She stroked his cheek.

"When you touch me like that, Eleanor, I see a flash of excitement in your blue eyes."

"I'd think you'd want me to be excited," she told him.

"Absolutely. As to the wedding, I think we should get married in church and invite the congregation back to the house for a glass of punch and a slice of cake. I want everyone to see you as my wife and Alfred's mother, as the new mistress of Crane House." He studied her. "Could you be ready for a one o'clock ceremony? Then we can have the evening to ourselves."

"Almost alone," she teased.

"Agnes and Mrs. Cornwell will have a glass of wine with us after supper and diplomatically retire early."

"I'd like that. We can attend Christmas service as husband, wife, and son."

"I like the idea of you already considering us a family."

"Would you be upset if I admitted when I first arrived, I dreamed of becoming your wife? And meeting Alfred, who wouldn't want to be in his life?" She let out a sigh. "I never could have imagined it would work out for us. I'm truly thankful for all the changes."

"I've been thinking about marrying you since I first

saw you asleep on the bench under the stairs."

"That bench is my lucky spot in the house."

"Agreed," he told her. The wind picked up, and the horses shifted. "We should get back before it gets too cold."

Eleanor pulled the reins and guided her horse back toward home. He followed close behind, enjoying the view. After handing over the reins to Daniel, they walked toward the house.

"I should have asked sooner, Eleanor. Would you like to wait until your father and brothers can travel to be here for the ceremony?"

"No. He didn't think to consider me when he made the arrangement with Agnes. And I don't want to wait months for him to arrive. If he did come, it would be another distraction. He can choose to travel to see us in the spring, if he's so inclined. It would be the same if my brothers came." She glanced down, but Phillip lifted her chin. "If Father comes here and sees what you've built, I'm afraid he'll want money. He's taken enough from Agnes."

"As long as you won't be disappointed your family isn't here."

"I'll draft a letter to my father to be sent at the first of the year. No disappointment. This is our fresh start. We consider our feelings first. You and Alfred are my family."

"I'm going to love being married to you."

"I should hope so," she said with a glint in her eyes.

"Just remember one thing always, Eleanor. I do love you in a way I never knew was possible to love any woman."

"I love you too, Phillip. As I never considered I

could love any man."

"Let's keep it that way. You and me, always."

"And Alfred too," she added. She hugged him tightly for long moments. When she drew back, she stared at him. "Crane Castle," she whispered and laughed. "I think that would be lovely for our wedding and our future. Will the wedding on Christmas Eve be too much work for Margaret?"

"She'll bring in a few extra hands to help her through the week, and some of the ladies from church will offer to help. The community always helps with all occasions, good and bad. I'll tell her tonight to start planning. Once everyone in town knows we're to wed, they'll all offer their assistance."

"Besides loving you and Alfred, I'm going to love being a part of the community." She smiled at him. "I suppose everyone will talk that they were right to assume we were to be betrothed when I arrived."

"Of course they'll talk, but it will be good gossip. That they met you and knew we were a match."

"This is all so quick, but a good quick. I don't think I could stand a long engagement. Being so close to you and not being able to touch you."

"You, my dear Eleanor, are an irresistible impulse to me, one not resisted."

She grinned at him. "I like being an irresistible impulse…but only to you."

"Always, only ours."

Her expression changed, her brow furrowing. "What will you tell Alfred? How will you tell him?"

"I don't see it being a problem. We can just say we're getting married and now you'll live with us always. That he's a lucky child to have such a warm and welcoming woman to help guide him to the future."

Chapter Twelve

The week sped by. Mrs. Cornwell was a godsend for keeping Agnes from being too cranky. Eleanor wore her good blue suit to church on the Sunday their Christmas Eve marriage would be announced.

Before the start of the service, Phillip pulled her aside. "I spoke to Elizabeth earlier. She knows about our announcement and marriage."

"Is she upset?"

"No, she's fine. Her mother, on the other hand, will be highly annoyed." His smile defused her concern for the other woman.

"Thank you for telling her in advance."

"It is my pleasure to announce Phillip Crane and Eleanor Sterling will marry on Christmas Eve at one p.m.," the officiant said after the service. "Everyone is invited back to the Crane house for refreshments. The Christmas Eve service will go on as scheduled at nine p.m. There will be a town holiday celebration on Christmas Day afternoon at the clubhouse."

The announcement went over with ease. Only Mrs. Stevens retained her continual pinched expression and voiced several loud harrumphs. The rest of the congregation gave their congratulations and offers of help to get ready.

Phillip waited until the crowd settled. "There will be an afternoon reception on New Year's Day at the clubhouse as usual," he added.

As they exited the church, Elizabeth made a production of grasping Eleanor by the shoulders and kissing each of her cheeks. "I'm so happy for both of you. It's apparent to everyone that you are perfect for each other."

"Thank you, Elizabeth. I appreciate you understanding." In a louder voice, she said, "I'll look forward to seeing you on the day. Of course, you'll bring your mother."

Both women glanced at Mrs. Stevens, whose expression looked as if she'd just bitten into a lemon.

Elizabeth reached up and kissed Phillip's cheek. "I'm happy for both of you. I'll make sure Mother doesn't make a scene." She moved away, and the next person congratulated them.

Most of the women offered their help where needed. Getting out of the church took a few minutes, especially since Agnes seemed to be holding court yet again.

Eleanor stood beside Phillip, accepting congratulations and waiting for Agnes and Mrs. Cornwell to finish their conversations. A light snow fell as they waited. It coated the entire church and grounds.

"It's beautiful," Eleanor told him.

"Yes, it is, but you're more beautiful." His arm encircled her waist.

She didn't care who saw the moment of affection. After all, they had just announced their upcoming marriage.

That afternoon, he gathered the older ladies, the staff, and Alfred in the foyer. Before the Christmas tree, he got down on one knee and officially proposed to Eleanor.

"With the help of my meddling grandmother, I've fallen in love with this blue-eyed beauty with flaxen hair. With her smile and loving attitude toward me, Alfred, this house, and everyone who lives here. Even the townspeople know she belongs here. Eleanor, will you marry me, be a mother to Alfred, and make us a home here?"

Tears filled her eyes, and she took a second to savor the moment. "Yes, of course, I'll be proud to be your wife and Alfred's mother."

Before Phillip could open the ring box, Alfred moved beside her and took her hand. "Does this mean I can keep you?"

"Yes, always." She lifted him onto her hip and kissed his cheek. She looked down at Phillip. When he opened the box, she couldn't hold back the tears. All she could do was whisper, "Phillip, it's beautiful."

He took the diamond ring surrounded by rubies and slid it onto her finger.

"Thank you. Rubies for July."

He stood and kissed her lips. With Alfred between them, they had a family hug. One by one, the rest of the staff moved forward to congratulate them.

Mrs. Cornwell took Eleanor's hand in hers and smiled. "It's lovely. I wish you both much happiness."

"Thank you," Eleanor said and kissed her cheeks. "Thank you for being a part of my extended American family."

Alfred was finished with hugs and kisses and squirmed to get down. He ran to the tree, watching the bows and ribbons glisten in the afternoon light. Nanny gave them a slight smile and made her way to Alfred's side.

Agnes slowly walked to them. "I'm very happy for you both."

"Thank you, Grandmother. But no more meddling," Phillip said with a laugh.

She reached for Eleanor's hand and inspected the ring. "You did good, boy." In an unexpected show of emotion, she hugged Eleanor and then Phillip. She turned away to dab at the tears in the corners of her eyes. "Engagement aside, are we going to have tea this afternoon?"

As if on cue, Margaret announced tea was served.

****

The next days hurried by. With the help of Laura and Sally, Eleanor made sure the dress she'd brought with her was fitted and pressed to perfection. On Thursday afternoon, she was thankful to have a few minutes alone. Someone knocked on her bedroom door, and Agnes entered with a package. She handed it to Eleanor and took the chair under the window. Eleanor unwrapped it and found a lovely embroidered floor-length veil.

"It's beautiful." She brought it to her head and viewed it in the mirror.

"Ida wore her mother's veil. That's the veil Phillip's mother wore when she married his father. They had a wonderful marriage, and I hope you do too."

Eleanor walked to the dress hanging on the back of the bathroom door. "It's as if they were purchased together. Thank you, Mrs. Crane."

"You're welcome. I'm very happy for you and Phillip. I hope you've forgiven me for the little charade that brought you here."

"Of course. At first, I wasn't happy with the situation, but that was more due to my father's actions than yours. Once here, I couldn't deny my attraction for Phillip. I knew instantly no matter who George was as a man, I couldn't have married him. If the situation had worked out differently, I would have left for a job in the city."

"I'm delighted it worked out for both of you." She stood and headed to the hall door. "I'll expect more great-grandchildren…soon."

Eleanor blushed and smiled.

"Come along, it's teatime."

"I'll be right there." She paused and held the veil to the dress once more, admiring them together. She still wasn't completely sure how she'd gotten so lucky.

Someone knocked on her door again, and she realized she'd been daydreaming. "I'll be down shortly."

The door opened, and Mrs. Cornwell peeked in. "May I come in?"

"Of course." Eleanor spied the package she held.

"I wanted to catch you alone. I didn't want to embarrass you."

"Please, come have a seat." Eleanor pointed to the chair under the window.

Mrs. Cornwell crossed the room. She stopped and looked at the dress and the veil now hanging alongside it. "It's beautiful, Eleanor. You'll make a stunning bride." She handed her the package and took the comfortable seat under the window. "It's for your wedding night. I know your mother passed a long time ago. Every woman should have a lovely nightgown."

Eleanor pulled the ribbon from the tissue and lifted out the two pieces of gossamer fabric with lace trim. It was a gown with a matching robe. "It's beautiful. I've never owned anything so pretty." She was thankful the maids weren't in the room.

"Now you do, and when you wear it for Phillip, he will appreciate you even more."

"Thank you, Mrs. Cornwell. It's a lovely gift. I'm afraid I never considered buying anything like this for myself." She knew her cheeks flushed with an embarrassed heat. "I suppose my flannel sleep dresses aren't honeymoon-worthy."

"At least not for the first night."

They both laughed. Eleanor held it up against her body.

"My dear, do you have any questions about the wedding night?"

Eleanor felt her whole body heat yet again, felt the heat rise from her chest, over her throat, and land on her cheeks. "Before I left England, our housekeeper had a talk with me. She went over the basics. Some I'd heard of, and some not. But she was kind to take the time. I believe I'm somewhat prepared and hope Phillip will understand his guidance will go a long way to making both of us enjoy our time together."

"Fine. If you ever have any questions you don't want to ask your husband, by all means come to me. I was married for thirty years." She looked around the room, as if to confirm they were alone. "It can be wonderful with the right partner. I was lucky. We loved each other and enjoyed ourselves. Remember a sense of humor will go a long way toward smoothing out difficult issues."

Eleanor put the lace set on the bed and walked to hug the older woman. "I appreciate the gown, but I value our friendship more." The hug ended with both of them dabbing at escaped tears.

"Phillip is a good man. Learn to talk with him, to tell him your fears and accept his. It will all work out in time. You both deserve to be happy." She straightened her skirt. "Come along. Everyone will be waiting for tea…and you know how Agnes hates to be kept waiting." They walked down the stairs, arm in arm.

Later, alone in her room, Eleanor started to get butterflies in her stomach. She wasn't anxious about marrying Phillip. She worried more about the physical side she had no experience with. She hoped he'd remember she was untutored in all the ways of love. Yes, they'd touched and kissed, and he always left her with a longing ache.

While she wouldn't admit it to Mrs. Cornwell, she'd borrowed her brother's book on the subject. That had been an eye-opener, and unfortunately, she hadn't dared ask a friend or the housekeeper about some of the more embarrassing and confusing details.

She wanted to please Phillip and hoped once they were alone, she'd relax and they would enjoy each other. After all, wasn't that what they'd told each other? That in private they wanted a relationship that was honest and enjoyable for both of them in all ways. She remembered how soft his beard was to her cheek and hoped it would feel the same…all over.

****

The next days went by with strangers in the house. Eleanor knew some of them by sight but not by name. Wandering into the kitchen, she saw the beautiful cake Margaret was making for her and Phillip's reception.

"Margaret, it's beautiful. Thank you for everything. I know this is a lot of work, but I'm thrilled."

"You're welcome. Now go and relax. I've got

enough hands in here. Rest while you can."

Margaret shooed her from the room, and she headed to the parlor for tea. After tea, Phillip asked her to join him for a walk before it got too cold. Outside, she felt renewed. The cold forced her to think straight. They wandered toward the rear acreage, and he finally spoke.

"Are you having second thoughts? I know this is quick and I pushed for the wedding. I'm wondering if you just said yes to please me."

"Yes, I want to please you, but I didn't want a long engagement. It seems when you know something is right, there is no reason to wait. Our whole relationship has been unconventional. Why should we start now?" She paused and watched him. "Unless you're having second thoughts?"

"Not at all. I just want to make sure you aren't feeling pressured."

"I appreciate you thinking about this. I do have one issue." She glanced around her to buy time with her words.

"Go ahead. We're supposed to be honest with each other."

"It's just... I have no experience...running the household, being a mother, and especially being a wife."

He dropped his arm around her shoulders, pulling her tight. "We'll build this relationship together. I'll try my best to answer any questions you'll have, and we'll figure out the rest along the way."

"As long as we decide together and don't let others influence us." She tried to hold back her smile, but her lips curled up, letting it come forward.

He laughed with her. "Agnes has done the last of her meddling."

"I hope so. I don't want to seem unappreciative, but I'd like us to raise Alfred according to our values."

"Agreed. Agnes can voice her opinions in limited amounts outside of his hearing, but that's all they are. Her opinions. We make the decisions about our children without her meddling."

"And the wedding night?"

"We'll find our way together, Eleanor. If you don't like something or want to try it again, you just have to tell me." He glanced at her. "So far, I don't think you'll have trouble expressing your opinions."

"You may be sorry you said that someday."

"No, I won't. I just want us to be honest." Phillip pulled her into the circle of his arms and kissed her full out without hesitation. She kissed him back without reservations.

****

Christmas Eve day dawned bright and cool. It was a perfect day to get married. Eleanor had never had so many people fussing around her. Sally was there with coffee and toasted bread, all but forcing her to get something into her stomach so she wouldn't faint.

Laura helped with her hair while Sally made sure every detail of the dress was right. She was glad she'd stuck with the dress she'd brought with her. It wasn't a traditional wedding gown, but she liked it because it didn't have a tight neckline. Rather, the back of the dress had a high collar that dipped slightly in the front to a small, rounded neckline. The bodice was pleated with blue trim the same color as her eyes. The rear bustle swept into a short train, the material pleated and accented with more blue trim. The sleeves were long but not tight, which allowed her to move easily. Wearing Phillip's mother's veil completed the look.

Before she had time to think, she was getting dressed. Someone knocked on the door.

Margaret entered with two wrapped packages. "The Mister sent me up with these."

Eleanor carefully pulled back the tissue from the smaller package to find a coronet of gardenias and lily of the valley. It was beautiful. The second package, the larger one, was a bouquet of the same flowers with rows of ivy trailing down. She brought the bouquet to her nose, enjoying the scent of the delicate flowers. She turned to Margaret. "Please thank Phillip for me."

Margaret smiled and slipped from the room. She wished she had more time to appreciate all the amazing things that were happening, but the time had come to head to the church. The maids gave her a moment alone to catch her breath. When she came downstairs, Daniel was standing at the front door, and Margaret and Sally waited alongside him.

They rode with her to the church and made sure everything was in place before they opened the church's inner doors.

Eleanor turned to Margaret. "Thank you for everything."

"You're welcome. Make it a good life. You both deserve to be happy."

"I'll do my best." She drew a deep breath and nodded she was ready.

Margaret slipped inside, and soon the music began. The inner doors opened, and Eleanor stood to look at the altar. The ladies had decorated it with poinsettias, ribbons, and bows. The candles burned brightly. The sun reflected the colors of the stained-glass windows around the room.

She looked ahead. Phillip waited for her to meet him. He was the most handsome man she'd ever seen, and he was going to be her husband. He stood tall in a dark-blue frock coat, his gold watch chain glinting against the blue of his vest. He smiled at her, and the nerves she'd felt all morning disappeared.

Slowly, to take in the moments, she walked up the aisle toward him. Alfred stood beside him in short white pants with a white jacket. His little vest was the same dark-blue color as his father's suit.

Agnes and Mrs. Cornwell were in the front row, and Margaret, Daniel, along with the maids and Nanny were in the second. She couldn't believe how many people had come out to join them. She caught sight of Elizabeth in the middle row, and they smiled at each other. Mrs. Stevens's expression held a permanent scowl.

Alfred glanced her way and tugged at his father's coat. "El'nor is pretty." His voice echoed loudly.

"Yes, she is, son." Phillip grasped his son's hand and turned back to watch her walk to him.

She could never have believed this was how her life would work out. The entire time she was traveling to America, she had been angst ridden, heading to a marriage she didn't want or ask for. Now those days faded as she approached her soon-to-be husband. His smile gave her the courage to continue toward him.

When she was almost to him, he walked to her and grasped her hand to make those last steps together. They reached the altar, and Nanny took Alfred's hand.

"Thank you for the flowers. You knew they were my favorites," Eleanor said.

"You're welcome. You are stunning. How did I get

so lucky?" He brought her hand to his lips and kissed it lightly. "Together we chose our path, Eleanor. You've made me very happy."

The officiant cleared his throat to get their attention as they stared at each other. They said their vows with clear voices and exchanged wedding bands. Eleanor had never been so happy.

With the service completed, they held hands, walking toward the door. Outside was bright and clear. The light shimmered against her dress and hair.

"You are stunning, Mrs. Crane. Almost ethereal," he told her.

"It's the lighting," she teased. "You are a handsome man, Mr. Crane. I'm glad you'll wear the wedding band in public. It will gently remind any lady who has desires for you that you are taken, that you are my husband." With that, she leaned up and kissed him on the lips.

Phillip wrapped his arm around her waist and brought her against his body. His kiss was a little more daring, but she didn't care. She enjoyed the moment. When he pulled back, the congregation was staring at them.

They greeted each person in turn and reminded everyone about the reception back at the house. Once there, a photographer took their pictures in front of the Christmas tree as a couple and with Alfred completing the family. Eleanor called the older ladies and staff forward to be included.

****

Phillip stood in the doorway to the parlor, a glass of punch in his hand. It had been a long day, and he was tired. Eleanor would be tired too. She greeted the guests, smiled, and accepted congratulations. Agnes held court in the main room, sitting regally in a wingback chair before the window. The church pianist was kind enough to return to the house. Phillip danced with his new wife in the foyer several times. With an audience, they were socially correct, not how he'd wanted to dance with her. He would have to wait until tonight to hold her close.

He had spent a long time trying to deflect his feelings for her. He'd never forget his first sight of the woman asleep in the foyer. She was lovely with golden hair. It was in fashion to gravitate toward brunettes, but this blonde-haired woman took his breath away. When he'd seen her blue eyes, he was stunned and disappointed. After all, at that point he'd thought he was having carnal thoughts about his brother's soon-to-be wife.

Thankfully, Agnes's meddling ways had brought Eleanor to him. The first weeks had been tough for both of them. She was inexperienced and had been unhappy about the forced marriage to a stranger in a foreign land. He still remembered the horror and relief she'd showed when he told her the intended groom had fled.

Those weeks had wreaked havoc on his easygoing life. Yet at every turn, she'd surprised him, especially how she interacted with Alfred. Seeing his son's acceptance of the stranger made him realize how much the child missed a woman's influence, this woman's influence.

When she was around, he felt renewed and vibrant. When they talked alone, he stared at her. She was a stunning woman who didn't seem to know her own beauty or worth. Now she was his bride, and he'd do anything to keep her happy. He was lucky she liked living in the Park. She was making friends with the older ladies of the congregation and was mindful of other people's feelings.

His first marriage had been a convenience for children and companionship. When he lost Ida, he'd sworn he'd never marry again. After all, he had an heir, his home, and his business. Until he'd seen and met Eleanor. That had been when it struck him what had been missing from his life and first marriage.

Someone went to shake his hand, and he roused himself. He'd been daydreaming. But why not? This beautiful woman had just married him. All he could hope was they be compatible long term. She glanced across the room at him and smiled. He was beginning to know that smile and what it might hold for them after the company left. He reached a hand to her, and she joined him, clasping her hand in his.

As he showed guests out, she slipped from his side. A moment of panic set in, and then he saw she held Alfred in front of the Christmas tree, pointing out ornaments and flowers. The move to envelope her within his arms was becoming automatic. He swept them into a light waltz. He couldn't remember when he'd felt this content. His son's giggle warmed him. Had he ever felt so complete? This was a feeling he never wanted to forget.

With their company gone, he retired to the parlor with Eleanor, Mrs. Cornwell, and his grandmother, and they had a simple supper of sandwiches and coffee. They ate slices of the cake Margaret had made. They all agreed it was a masterpiece of flavor and baking.

He invited the ladies to the parlor and handed around glasses of wine. His toast was simple. "To my wife."

They toasted, and Eleanor added her own thoughts.

"To my husband who wasn't supposed to be. I'm a lucky woman to have fallen in love with him and him with me. And to Agnes, for her meddling ways that brought us together."

He glanced around the room as they sipped. This was his family. His grandmother smiled at him, and he winked at her. They'd found their truce.

Phillip was getting frustrated with the company around them. They would all go to the evening service. He wished they could skip the choral service, but that was unacceptable. After all, the entire community had turned out to wish them well. They agreed earlier that Eleanor would take off the veil and coronet of flowers but wear the white dress to the service tonight. He would wear the suit he married her in. Nanny changed Alfred into long pants. The child probably wouldn't stay awake for the whole service, but it didn't matter.

Halfway through the choral service, Alfred fell asleep with his head in Phillip's lap. When Nanny moved to take him home, Phillip shook his head. Yes, the child would be off schedule tomorrow, but this was a day to celebrate.

Once home, Nanny attended to Alfred, and the adults, including Margaret and Daniel, gathered in the parlor.

Phillip handed around glasses of port. His toast was the same as earlier in the day. "To my wife."

Eleanor added her own toast, similar to her previous one. "To my husband who wasn't supposed to be. I'm a lucky woman to have fallen in love with him and he with me." Then she added, "To Agnes, for her meddling ways that brought us together."

They laughed and sipped their drinks.

"I think that should remain our Christmas toast."

Everyone around them agreed with a "Hear! Hear!" and drank again.

When he was trying to figure out how to get them to retire for the night so he could have private time with Eleanor, Margaret and Daniel excused themselves and both ladies stood. As if on cue, Mrs. Cornwell and Agnes kissed him and Eleanor and again wished them a happy life and family.

Finally, they were alone. He swept her into his arms and danced her around the foyer, music not needed. She melted against him, and he knew his life had turned for the better. With Eleanor beside him, they would build a life in her stone home.

She rested her head on his shoulder. "Thank you for marrying me, Mr. Crane."

"Thank you for marrying me, Mrs. Crane." This kiss was private. "Merry Christmas, Eleanor."

"Merry Christmas, Phillip."

He didn't know how long they danced in the foyer, but when she drew back and reached for his hand, he gave it willingly and followed her up the stairs to their new beginning. Tonight, she didn't need Sally or Laura to help her undress. It would be his honor to help her.

****

On Christmas morning, they couldn't escape the required pleasantries even though he and Eleanor would have preferred to stay in bed, alone for private time. Eleanor dressed in a light-blue dress. Phillip gave Alfred a few small toys to keep him occupied while the adults gathered for coffee and a light breakfast before church. He understood it would be obvious to anyone who looked that their wedding night had been a success.

The morning was crisp and cool, and walking to church left them chilled. Inside, the church glowed with candlelight.

When the service ended, they headed home for Christmas supper. Afterward they handed out gifts. Phillip had purchased tokens for the staff—a box of candy with a small cash gift. Margaret and Daniel were each given a gift—tobacco for Daniel and a scarf Eleanor had helped him pick out for Margaret—along with tickets for an early spring vacation to visit a friend up north.

He and Eleanor had purchased silk scarves for Agnes and Mrs. Cornwell along with train tickets for each of them to visit later in the new year. When he finished, Eleanor stood and distributed her gifts to the staff. She gave the hand-embroidered handkerchiefs to the maids and Nanny. Margaret was thrilled with her hatpin, and Daniel nodded his thanks at receiving his new pipe.

She had a framed watercolor of her New York City home for Mrs. Cornwell, who was surprised that Eleanor had done the fine work. Agnes seemed delighted with the drawing of Phillip and his son. She was also surprised by Eleanor's artistic talent.

Phillip was amazed as he opened his present. He marveled at the framed drawing of him with his son on his shoulders, walking the field behind the house. He tugged her onto his lap and hugged her. "This is wonderful, Eleanor. You even managed to capture a little bit of mischief on his expression. I love this and will keep it always." He wiped a stray tear from his cheek.

He handed Eleanor a box from a fancy New York dress shop but cautioned her the contents might embarrass her. She smiled and slowly took off the cover. Inside was a light-blue nightgown and robe. While she showed the ladies the gown, she didn't pull it out from the box.

"It's beautiful, Phillip." Their kiss wasn't for public consumption, but they kissed anyway.

One more gift remained on the table. Eleanor called Alfred into the room and handed him the package. She dropped down to his level. "Merry Christmas, Alfred." Then she kissed his forehead.

He looked to her for permission.

"Go ahead and open it."

He pulled the paper from it and smiled. "It's a train! El'nor, thank you." He ran to his father to show him the present. "Choo choo." He imitated the whistle sound.

"Did you say thank you to Eleanor?" Phillip asked.

"Yes, he did," she offered as she stood beside them.

Alfred soon disappeared into the foyer, his whistle noise fading. Soon he was back with them, the whistle noise increasing. They managed to wrangle it from his little fist while he napped before the fire in the parlor.

They enjoyed a light meal and retired to the parlor afterward. Even Agnes didn't comment when Alfred was allowed at the table for a short time. He ate a few bites and was excused to play in the foyer. When it became too quiet, Phillip found him asleep yet again on the floor near the tree with his new toy train in his little hand. Nanny arrived and took him upstairs.

The staff gathered in the kitchen for their meal, while the core family group walked to the meeting house for the planned afternoon drink. Phillip realized he now had a core family, including Mrs. Cornwell. He would have preferred to stay home but understood it was necessary, especially since the whole congregation had supported them. Agnes commented about skipping the drink, but Eleanor spoke up.

"I understand we're all tired. But it would be impolite to skip the celebration, especially after everyone has been so kind to Phillip and me."

"Eleanor is right. It would be easy to nap before the fire, but it wouldn't be socially acceptable. Would it, Grandmother?"

Eleanor laughed openly, and finally Agnes laughed too.

Epilogue

Christmas Eve, One Year Later

Eleanor stood in the foyer and admired the Christmas tree. This year's tree seemed larger and more impressive than last year's. She waited for Agnes and Mrs. Cornwell to come down for an early supper. These days she was tired but exhilarated. Thankful for her husband, home, and family.

Margaret and Daniel were well ensconced in their positions and more like family than employees. They'd also been helpful with getting her settled in as the mistress of Crane House—or Crane Castle, as she still referred to it in private with Phillip. She'd come to love this little town and most of the people who lived there. Yes, some jealousy from the younger women in town and the occasional whisper reminded her they all assumed she'd arrived as Phillip's fiancée. None of the talk mattered to her, as she technically did arrive as his bride-to-be. Never did they discuss that outside of their home.

She was thankful Elizabeth and Mrs. Stevens had left for the West Coast shortly after the first of the year. She hoped Elizabeth would find success with her music and Mrs. Stevens wouldn't chase away possible male companions for Elizabeth.

Now a year later, she still hadn't met George and wasn't unhappy about that issue. During the summer,

Agnes received a letter saying he'd met a young woman out west and was happily married. Through gossip, they'd learned the bride's father was a prosperous banker. Apparently, he kept a watchful eye on George and how he spent his wife's money. Eleanor occasionally wondered what would happen when he left her for a better bank account, but that wasn't for her to worry about. Phillip reminded her he wasn't their problem.

Alfred was growing tall and strong like his father. He seemed to have a knack with animals and continually brought home stray kittens he found on the back acreage or the Park while walking with Nanny. Once Phillip convinced him they had to live in the barn, he accepted his responsibility to keep them fed and groomed. Even old Cat, who had once been disagreeable, became social with the other pets and household members.

Never could she have imagined on the voyage over where this new life would take her. While her initial introduction into the Crane family was stilted, she and Phillip had long left that behind. Occasionally, they teased Agnes about her meddling, but it was in good fun, not in anger.

Their first anniversary had come quickly. She and Phillip shared much laughter and love between them. When they discovered in the spring the baby was on the way, they'd had several private conversations about not meddling in their adult children's futures, or at least restraining themselves unless it was absolutely necessary for their health and well-being.

When she'd been anxious about the physical side of their marriage, Phillip easily guided and reassured her. She also knew at times she all but shocked him with her needs and wants. He'd told her they needed to talk over things, and she made a point of doing just that, at least in private. Which led them to where they were tonight.

Upstairs, one-month-old Lily was securely tucked in for the night in the nursery. Alfred had taken to becoming her protector too. Lily was named for Eleanor's favorite flower, lily of the valley. Thankfully, their original nanny had received a better offer from a couple in New York City and moved on in February. Together, she and Phillip, along with some references from Mrs. Cornwell, had found an older woman who fit their family situation much better. She was strict but was quick to give hugs and praise when warranted.

Alfred was beginning to read and knew his numbers and letters. This nanny was teaching him to write. He would tell anyone who would listen it would be his job to teach his sister to read and write when the time came. He'd begun sitting beside Eleanor at the piano and now recognized notes and picked out his scales.

During the summer, even Agnes had been impressed with Alfred's learning ability. She never admitted the original nanny she'd chosen was a poor fit, but it didn't matter to Phillip or Eleanor. All that did matter was that the child was healthy and prospering.

Tonight before the tree, Eleanor sent up several prayers for her good fortune in finding a man who respected and understood her. Who loved her in all phases—good, cranky, outspoken, and loving. She and Phillip still quipped when she called their house a castle. He was quick to remind her it was a house. She was quick to add it was their home.

Phillip joined her before the tree. He wrapped his arm around her shoulders and pulled her close. "How do you feel?"

"Hungry," she teased. "The ladies should be down soon."

"Did I ever thank you for marrying me, for being a mother to our son, and for giving me our daughter?"

"Maybe once or twice. Have I ever thanked you for marrying me, for letting me become Alfred's mother, and for giving me Lily?"

"Maybe once or twice." He pulled her into his arms for a passionate kiss. Their moment was interrupted by Agnes clearing her throat from the top of the stairs.

"That's enough, you two," she said good-naturedly. "It's time to eat. And we all know if we don't feed Eleanor, she'll get cranky."

Mrs. Cornwell was beside her as they descended the stairs, both of them laughing. "Of course she's hungry. What with that baby upstairs taking all her energy."

"She'll need food to get through the service tonight," Agnes added.

The ladies paused beside Eleanor and Phillip.

"It's a lovely tree," Mrs. Cornwell said.

"I'm surprised it's still standing with Alfred's running around," Agnes added. She laughed at her own words.

"We'll be right in." Phillip pulled Eleanor back into the circle of his arms and continued the kiss that had been interrupted. "You've made me a happy man, Eleanor."

"You've made me a happy woman, Phillip, in all ways." She winked at him, and he blushed. "Merry Christmas, Mr. Crane, and happy anniversary."

"Merry Christmas, Mrs. Crane, and happy anniversary."

She took his hand and walked beside him into the dining room, into their futures.

A word about the author...

Having been born and raised on Long Island, New York, my husband and I were both eager to leave the urban lifestyle behind us and explore our futures. With his encouragement, I'm living my dream of writing romance novels full time. Our new rural setting allows us time to enjoy each other and leaves me guiltless hours in my imagination indulging my other passions.

Alexi smiles, reaches over, and pulls open the book to reveal a charcoal sketch of a roughly drawn cityscape. Tall towers loom large in the distance as the scene reveals a bustling street populated with darkly shaded figures.

Emma leans forward, reaching out to touch the page, eyes wide. Her fingers trace the lines of black and grey with something approaching affection.

"This one, it speaks to you, yes?" Alexi asks, eyes suddenly alight.

She stares at the page. "Yes…I've been here before, in…"

"In dream," Alexi says, nodding.

"Yes," she answers distractedly.

Emma turns the page, revealing a second cityscape drawn in heavy colours. The same dark towers fill the skies, surrounded by red-brick buildings, bustling city streets, and crimson dust. Again and again, she turns the page, running her fingers over each picture, eyes wide with wonder.

"It's…it's like someone is pulling the pictures right out of my head."

Alexi nods. "You remember, yes? The dreams?"

Emma looks up from the page. "Yes. I remember. I remember it all. The smell of spices in the air, and roasting meat. I remember the dust in my eyes and grit in my mouth. I remember the feel of people pushing past me, the sounds and smells of animals everywhere. I remember it all like it happened yesterday."

Alexi pulls a small writing pad from his jacket and begins scribbling. "And when was it being? Your dream of red city?"

"A week ago. That's why I answered your ad. I came on it by pure chance and…"

"And dreaming before the last week? When was it you last be dreaming of red city?"

"I…I don't know. Maybe a month or two. I've only dreamt of the place half a dozen times over the past few years, but each time it's so vivid. It leaves me disoriented when I wake up, like I'm not really sure where I am. I had to take the day off work after the last dream."

Alexi writes furiously. "When you are dreaming, are you recognize anything similar to this world?"

"I…I'm sorry I don't understand."

He waves his hand around, indicating the surrounds of the diner. "This place. Are you recognize anything in the red city which is not from that place? Anything which is not belong?"

"You mean, like an iPhone or a car or something?"

He nods.

"No, not that I can remember. Nothing like that. Just the city."

"And you are meeting anyone in this dream place? You are talking to anyone, anyone that you know?"

"No. No, I don't think so."

Alexi nods. "No friend or father or something like that? No one you know from this world?"

Emma pauses, eyes narrowing. "What do you mean by *this* world? Look, can you tell me what this dream is about or are you just going to keep asking questions? I came here because your ad said you'd have answers."

Alexi holds up a hand, continuing to scribble furious notes for a few moments while Emma waits impatiently, her eyes returning to the sketch book and an image of a city wall pitted with age and lined with mismatched hovels at the base. After a few moments Alexi finishes his writing, places the pad and pen on the table, and points to the picture lying in front of Emma.

"This place is…is being not just imagination. Is *real* place, in world of dreams and imagines, but is also *real* like me and you." He thumps his knuckle against the tabletop. "Real like this. Some people, only a few people, can dream of red city. Is always the same. Dream is real, is vivid. People waking up next morning and not knowing where they are. Feels like they really are being in that place, the red city. You see, yes?"

"And you've met a lot of other people that have dreamt of this place?"

He shakes his head. "Ten years, I have searched for peoples who go to red city. Ten years and I speak with three hundred twenty peoples, maybe more even than this."

Alexi holds up his hands, dropping three fingers from his right hand. "Seven peoples have been to red city. Alexi confirm it. Only seven from three hundred twenty. Is only very small number of people who see city and remember. The rest are only waste of time."

"That's where these drawings are from? People describing their dreams?"

He nods.

"What does it all mean then? Where is this place, really I mean?"

Alexi shrugs, smiling. "Ten years I search for the red city and I not finding out. Only little pieces of puzzle Alexi can find, but not enough. But I tell you what I know, and you let me draw your dream, yes?"

"Yes. Of course. Just tell me for God's sake."

"Good. Good."

Alexi opens his pad toward the back and starts sketching out a series of shapes. "Is map of city," he explains. "Very rough and not so complete, good to start. City is somewhere in place of dreaming, but not like dreams. City is solid, is real. Perhaps is another dimension? Perhaps another consciousness? Nobody is knowing. But is real and some few peoples can go there in dreaming."

He slides the pad across to Emma, motioning toward the centre of the map.

"This one, in middle, is tall towers. Is four or maybe five towers, but never being less or more than this. Towers are to be seen by every persons who go to city. Always in background, the towers. Always dark and tall and also make feelings of badness inside. You feel it yes, when you look at towers?"

Emma's eyes return to the cityscape sketch. "Yes, I feel it. My whole gut tightens when I look at them."

Alexi nods. "Is the same with all peoples who go to red city. Everybody is scared of tall towers. Everybody don't like to looking at them."

He jabs excitedly at the lower right quadrant of the circular map. "Look here, this one is like temple or parliament. Sometimes, the ones that go to dream city end up here. They are seeing priests or something, walking in and out. Dressing in red robes and looking very official."

Alexi points to another portion of the map. "Here, I talk to man who finding himself stuck in this place. He run into religious cult, or somethings like that. Like monks from old time, with robes and, this thing."

Alexi squashes his lips with the fingers of his right hand, miming the working of a needle with his other hand.

"They sew up their lips?" Emma asks.

"Yes, yes. He sees them with sewn-up lips. And walking slowly around red city, like this."

He mimes a monk walking about with a dour expression. "Nobody is knowing what they are doing, but five out of seven sees them."

Alexi smiles. "The man who is getting stuck here—" He jabs the map. "He getting stuck with the monks, so he can't see much of the city. They just keep him in their house and feed him. Others see them walking in city, in other places. But he is just getting stuck."

He looks expectantly at Emma. "Did you see monk with sewing up lips?"

She shrugs. "Sorry, no it doesn't ring a bell."

"No matter, no matter. Is okay. Alexi is just happy to be meeting another one who dreams of red city. It much to excitement. Now, back to map. Many other things I could show you, but here is most interesting things."

He marks several points throughout the map with an asterisk, mumbling while he works. "Here, over there, and this one here too. All of these places are being where the dreamer has to seeing the running suit."

Emma looks at him blankly.

"The running suit, the casuals for exercising."

"I'm sorry, I don't know what you mean. A tracksuit?"

Alexi claps his hands together. "Yes, yes, the tracksuit. This is the one, yes."

"I still don't under…"

"Only a little of the seven who dreaming of red city see this one, but occasionally they see man or woman in…"

"A tracksuit?"

"Yes, yes, tracksuit. Is spring up from the city because, is peculiar, yes? It does not fit with red city, these people being dressed in tracksuit."

"Wait, you're saying there are people in there dressed in normal tracksuits, like what you'd see in a gym?"

He nods furiously. "Yes. They are being entirely out of place! Always running or hiding. Always stick out from background. One even talk to the dreamer. Normal, everyday words like we using now."

"So where are they from? The people with the tracksuits?"

He shrugs. "Nobody is knowing. I tell all the dreamers I meeting to please talk to tracksuit peoples if you see them again. But nobody sees them in a long time, and so I know very little. Perhaps is…"

He stops short, his eyes drawn to the front door of the diner where movement precedes the jingling of a series of bells at the top of the doorway. Alexi's eyes widen, prompting Emma to turn around. Standing in the doorway is the oddest pair she has ever seen. A seven-foot giant with impossibly broad shoulders and a face carved of dull flint stands at twice the height of his diminutive companion, a ginger-haired dwarf wearing a three-piece suit and sporting a silver cane. The little man's eyes lock in on Alexi instantly, and he walks at a casual pace toward the booth, while the hulking brute stays by the door, wearing an inscrutable expression.

Alexi surreptitiously closes the book of sketches and his writing pad, sliding both beneath the table and out of view. He becomes visibly agitated, eyes darting to-and-fro as though considering a rapid exit. Emma follows his eyes to the doorway.

"Who are they?" she whispers.

"I not know," Alexi hisses. "Say nothing about red city, yes?"

She nods, just as the ginger-haired dwarf comes into view. The little man grins widely, speaking in a sonorous tone. "Doctor Alexi Ivanov, I presume," he says as a statement rather than a question.

"And the lovely Emma Graceworth," he says, bowing slightly.

Before either of the pair can break free from their stunned silence, the suited figure thrusts his walking stick with frightful speed into Emma's leg, following up the gesture with a second blow at Alexi's ankle, before either can react. Emma feels a sharp sting, followed by a sensation of numbness as the world rapidly begins falling away. Alexi struggles to stand, clutching at his sketchbooks as he stumbles to the floor. He flails about, eyes wild with fear.

"Mr. Fern," says the dwarf, brushing distractedly at his coat jacket. "Would you be so kind as to escort our guests to the trunk?"

***

Two figures stand in front of a two-way mirror, watching Alexi squirm in a nondescript metal chair at the centre of the interrogation cell. Both men are of short stature. Both are dressed in immaculate three-piece suits. Both are shadowed by giants, looming from the rear corners of the room.

"He's done some good work," Flax says, leafing through the doctor's confiscated volume. "There's a lot of garbage in here, but some of it is on point."

Giant nods. "The question is whether it's in our best interest to let him run about as he has been or bring him into the fold. Some men are devils when consumed by the hunt but grow flaccid once the object of their desire is attained. Perhaps it would be better to set him loose, confiscate his work, and thus fan the flames of his passion?"

Flax shrugs. "On the other hand, letting him know what's really going on might allow him to ask some far more important questions than he is currently asking."

The two are silent for a moment, caught in reflection.

"What of our enemy?" Giant askes. "Are they aware of Dr. Ivanov's work?"

Flax shakes his head. "Not that we can see. We're not tracking all of Eva's agents, though, so there might be one or two who have eyes on him. Honestly though, all of this seems relatively harmless. I doubt they'd see him as a threat."

"True, but sooner or later they may learn that we've been using the good doctor as a recruiter. Seven people in ten years is nothing to write home about, but five of those have been in the last two years and, as you know, the numbers are increasing."

"We could always pull back on recruitment. Just take a few of the ones that come to Ivanov?" Flax offers.

Giant shakes his head. "We cannot afford to risk losing even one soldier. War is almost upon us, and we need every recruit we can gather. Even those who can't fight offer invaluable information and can scout for use in and around Rust."

"So, what do we do with the doctor then?"

Giant considers the question, stroking his chin as he watches Ivanov squirming in place. "We let him go. Take a few pages from his books. Just those that are nearest the mark. Keep tabs on him and be sure he knows of the girl's absence. See that additional funds come his way. An anonymous benefactor perhaps, a relative of one of our older recruits?"

"Very good. I'll drop him somewhere just outside town."

Rust Fairy-tale by Doan Trang

3. Journal Entry: Julius Mann, March 12

Dr. Ivanov has returned to us a changed man. His meeting with Emma Graceworth brought about some unexpected results. For three days upon his return, the doctor locked himself in his room and refused to speak with me or anyone else on the team. We were at the point of bringing in outside help when he finally emerged, blurry-eyed and with a fistful of hand-drawn notes.

He recounted to us the story of his abduction, of the strange pair who had accosted him and Emma Graceworth at the diner. They had asked him no questions and had kept him in isolation for only a few hours before releasing him again. His captors had also torn several pages from his notebook, pages which, we were now informed, he had spent the past few days meticulously re-creating.

There was more than a little concern that Dr. Ivanov had suffered a breakdown of some sort, that the whole abduction story was a fabrication. We were, however, able to recover footage from one of the security cameras the doctor had set up at the diner, which corroborated at least part of his story.

After a time, once the doctor had showered, eaten, and slept, we were able to speak in more detail about his experiences. He has become convinced that there is far more at stake than we had first supposed. Whether a government agency or some other organization, he believes that at least one or possibly multiple groups know of the existence of the red city and have a vested interest in protecting its identity.

One great mystery which has perplexed our team seems to have been resolved. Successful candidates who we are able to meet with, and who confirm the existence of the red city, are rarely seen after our initial meetings. They seem to move overseas or take obscure job postings. Given the timings involved we hadn't really made any connection to this gentle vanishing and their initial meetings with Dr. Ivanov. Only this year has he started to suspect some kind of causal connection between the candidates meeting with us (and discussing their dream encounters) and their disappearances. The primary reason why serious suspicions hadn't been raised earlier is that family and friends of the candidates seemed to have had perfectly reasonable (and consistent) rationales for the sudden disappearance of the candidates in question. There was no sign of worry and apparently no loss of contact. When we tried to follow up with past candidates, however, we invariably met with failure.

Dr. Ivanov has become convinced that the same organization which accosted Emma and him have been snatching past candidates away shortly after his meeting with them. Note that none of the unsuccessful candidates have disappeared. The mentally unstable and non-remarkable dreamers seem to go on with their lives as normal; only those who dream of the red city vanish.

I had worried that this experience would cause the doctor to falter in our objectives, but the opposite appears to be true. He now demonstrates a renewed vigour for the project. His abduction seems to have confirmed that a great deal of our work is on track. He has redirected our efforts to focus our attention on three primary aspects of the city (which correspond to those pages torn from his workbook):

- The Five Sisters—those dark towers which stand at the heart of the city,
- The tracksuit-wearing figures (typically younger adults) that seem to pop up here and there throughout the city, sometimes interacting with the dreamer,
- A figure that has only been mentioned once, via the memory of a scrap of graffiti on one of the city walls which read, *"all hail the Shackled Man."*

4. The Mancer-Machinist

During daylight hours he assumes a mild-mannered affectation; clothed in a dull grey suit and tie, frequently seen shuffling through the halls of *Unidex Consolidated*, heavily laden with manila folders stuffed with asset and liability ledgers, invoices, statements, and innumerable pieces of accounting paraphernalia.

Kelvin is neither the best nor the worst actuary at Unidex Consolidated. His primary asset is that of being unremarkable in a department that excels at the dull and uninteresting.

He sits at a nondescript cubicle for 8.5 hours each day, toiling quietly away upon a landscape of neatly formatted spreadsheets. He breaks for yogurt at 10 a.m., for cheese and ham on rye at 12:30, and a banana at 2:30 before heading home at 5:30 p.m. with the great unwashed on the subway.

He greets Maggie with a bland smile, enjoys a meal of pork and potatoes, watches two hours of television, and kisses his wife good night.

"Don't stay up too late," she warns, knowing too well that her plea will go unnoticed.

He nods, smiles, heads down to the basement, and give up his daylight self in favour of an alternate persona…the *Mancer-Machinist*.

Amber light hangs thickly in the red-bricked basement, giving shadows a sinister air. Kelvin walks to a small metal locker and dons the thin leather apron hanging inside. The act of pulling tight leather ties serves to reorient his mind to the task at hand; the first step in his nightly ritual of transcendence. He slips off his shoes and walks to the wooden table at the far corner of the room. Within a few minutes he has flicked requisite switches, twisted dials, arranged tools and gadgets in precise order, and slipped on the pair of multi-lens goggles that aid in the more precise tasks of his trade.

He slides a small, well-worn wooden box from a secluded niche in the red-brick wall and pulls out the bronze cube from within. The device whirs and whines, vibrating sporadically in response to his touch, and Kelvin feels his heartbeat flutter in anticipation. With the greatest of care, he pulls miniature pliers from a leather sheath and sets to work, tweaking a filament here, a cog there. He works with the expert grace of an obsessive genius, fine-tuning the device, which continues to vibrate and hum in response to his delicate touch.

After an hour or so of work, Kelvin lifts the metal device and places it on a small pedestal to one side of the room. A large mirror hangs on the wall directly behind the pedestal, reflecting the sharp edges of the device with soft amber light. Kelvin pulls off his goggles, letting them dangle by leather chords below his neck. He breathes deeply, staring into the rippling surface of the mirror.

A dozen times now he has stood thus, on the cusp of that great beyond which separates the waking world from that other realm; a world of monstrous potentiality, where the banal is twisted into something profound and potent. That self-same potency is the opiate for which Kelvin's soul aches, the drug which brings intolerable mental anguish to each moment he is forced to live away from the mirror, the machine, the severed membrane between worlds.

The online communities and shadowed chat rooms from which he previously drew solace no longer feed his soul sufficiently. He has outgrown the petty ramblings of those who seek to dip their toe into the red river. Likewise, he is now wary of the darker, more insidious intelligences at work throughout the internet hub which proselytizes for the red city and its crimson surrounds. Whether driven by other mancers such as himself, or something more dangerous, he has determined that it is no longer safe to share his etheric advances with the internet.

With a long exhalation, the Mancer-Machinist places his thumb and forefinger on both hands to either side of the whirring device into which his keen mind has been poured. There is a sharp click, followed by a stab of pain at the pads of his fingers where shallow needles penetrate the skin with blistering speed, pressing through calloused skin with frightful ease. Blood trickles down the shallow bronze grooves cut into the outer framework of the device, edging slowly toward the centre of the whirring mechanism at the heart of the machine. Kelvin closes his eyes briefly.

It was his blood which served as key and catalyst for the device, discovered by happy accident one night in June. For years without joy, he toiled with the device, pressing theory into practice and wrestling with unyielding objects of wood and steel, chemical and electric current. For ten years this secretive alchemy reaped no serviceable fruit. Always something was missing, something arcane and essential. Robbed of innumerable hours of sleep and sick with failure, the erstwhile Kelvin cut his right index finger in a fortuitous moment of carelessness. Blood trickled into the workings of his device, bringing life to this latest incarnation, and transforming the hapless actuary into the Mancer-Machinist for the first time.

Kelvin bites down against the pain, holding the device tightly against the pedestal as it bucks and jostles against his grip. The spinning metallic spindles at the heart of the object begin to glow with an unnatural crimson light, and the basement fills with the sound of rushing wind, interspersed with a noise like the eerie crackling of a bonfire.

The Mancer-Machinist holds his eyes open, staring at the centre of the mirror while the air around him is filled with a deafening cacophony that presses against his skull like a pair of gigantic hands crushing a pumpkin. Blood trickles from his nostrils, weeps from his ears while the device continues its disturbing dance. The pain is excruciating, but only serves to sharpen the Mancer-Machinist's resolve.

There is a sensation of liminal trespass, of pressing beyond the bounds of what is permitted. The Mancer-Machinist can feel the unfathomable attention of dark forces coming into focus as the device does its transgressive work. He can sense the dark machinations of monstrous beings rumbling in the space between that which *is* and which *might be*—a growing pressure that threatens to unravel both mind and matter.

At the climax of the ritual, the mirror cracks, a jagged edge opening up from the top left corner and running diagonally to the mirror's bottom edge. The crack widens, slowly expanding to reveal a dark crimson space somewhere beyond. Kelvin's lips twist upward in a smile as a portal opens before him, opening out into a curious netherworld draped in blood and darkness.

The roaring of the wind falls into the background, and Kelvin's senses suddenly clear. He begins to see clearly through to the other side of the mirror. A familiar sight emerges, dark red-brick walls cracked with age, a series of distant sculptures, twisted human forms dancing in silent agony. It is a room which Kelvin has visited several times previously, the abode of a nameless demon with whom the actuary has conversed from time to time.

Kelvin waits patiently, biding his time in the hope that the demon will appear. At first the majestic creature had been incensed at Kelvin's intrusion, but over time he had come to welcome the would-be Mancer's visitations. While the demon revealed little of his own origins, nor the world into which Kelvin's mirror now peered, he showed great interest in Kelvin's world and the possibility of effecting a crossing from one locale to the other.

A figure emerges, dark and powerful but ill-defined. It stares through the cracked mirror at the Mancer-Machinist with eyes that seem to glow with crimson light. The demon is cloaked, broad-shouldered and wearing metallic affectations which reflect dull light from that other dimension. The Mancer-Machinist shivers with a mix of pain and anticipation.

"Greetings, Mancer," the figure behind the cracked mirror growls, his voice hard-edged and surrounded by trailing whispers. "It has been too long since we last spoke."

The Mancer-Machinist nods, attempting to show deference. "My apologies. I was…detained."

"My Mistress grows impatient," the dark figure behind the mirror says. "We must affect a crossing soon, lest her ire be tempted."

"Yes, yes I know. I have what you asked for. It's here, in my pocket." The Mancer-Machinist raises one hand from the gateway device, shakily pulling a small vial from his pocket and holding it before the mirror. His body shakes with pain and there is blood leaking from his nose, but the Mancer-Machinist remains resolute.

"It took a great deal of effort to bring this to you," he says, voice trembling. "I have transgressed many of the laws of my people in order to procure this gift."

He holds the vial shakily. It's thick, darkly crimson contents ooze with sinister intent inside the vial. He keeps his eyes on the mirror, not wishing to catch sight of the object he holds and risk the memory of its forging.

"Well enough," the demon says, extending a hand. "Pass it to me and our bargain is struck."

The Mancer-Machinist hesitates. "And you will give me what I wish? If I hand this over to you, I'll get everything I've asked for?"

The demon nods. "And more besides, Mancer. You will be hailed a champion among my people. You will be rewarded beyond what you have asked, for your service to the Red Queen and her city."

The Mancer-Machinist grits his teeth against a sudden rush of pain as the demon reaches through the void, toward the vial. His body shakes violently, but he holds fast to both gateway device and vial, pressing his will against the pain of his flesh.

"You promise?" he asks, eyes beginning to loll with delirium. "I will have eternal life?"

Dark fingers, charred with fire and shedding dust-coloured vapor, reach through the mirror and clasp the vial. Smoke swirls about the room. The demon roars in agony, his extended limb igniting in a burst of violent amber flame. The Mancer-Machinist, too, cries out and, for a moment, two worlds are connected in agony. There is a crack in the cosmos, felt at the very foundations of existence. Two worlds shift, ever so slightly, and the mirror between them breaks.

***

They find Kelvin's corpse frozen in an absurdly grandiose pose; fingers outstretched toward the shattered remnants of an old mirror. Fire has scoured the basement, reaching upward to devour most of the house and those within it, yet Kelvin himself remains oddly untouched by the flames. His face sits in a rictus of agony, and blood runs from eyes, ears, and nose, like a stigmata parody.

It is a paramedic who makes the first error, reaching out to touch the corpse. Blood and muscle, bone and sinew, all that the Mancer-Machinist was falls to dust in an instant. The remains are studied at length by the brightest minds of a generation, but they yield no secrets and raise only troubling questions. Alien elements are found among the actuary's ashes, and there is an anomaly of impossible dimensions among the remains of Kelvin's house.

A small sliver of darkness, through which a blackened hand reaches, still clutches at the remnants of a broken vial. The breach spews strange radiation and whispers of dark and interminable intelligences from the space between dream and reality. An entire block of houses is relocated, so that ground zero can be quarantined and studied at length. The portal in miniature, with its demonic appendage, resists all attempts at comprehension, yet the continuous study of every conceivable reading does prove one troublesome fact. The portal grows, each year no more than a millimetre. And each year, the tormented machinations from the darkness within grow more and more vivid.

These are the details which are kept from the press and the general public. But the bodies found buried in Kelvin's back yard do not lay undisturbed for long. Nor do the horrific devices he has engineered in other hidden rooms branching off from the basement. All told, the diminutive actuary had killed thirteen people. He had taken blood and organs and manipulated their substance by chemical and mechanical means. He had reduced thirteen innocent dead to a single vial of dark fluid, whose remnants can still be seen within the crushed and blackened hand from the void.

5. Faith, Hell, and the She Devil

Dear Dr. Alexi Ivanov,

It has been some time since I last wrote, but I want you to know that I've made some progress lately in our work. I've managed to track down a genuine instance of *Traumwelt* crossover, in a somewhat curious subject. A young preacher who calls himself Jackson Spark (I tried to track down his real name, but he's done a fair job of wiping out all traces of his old life) has begun to make a name for himself here in the south. He's gone from nothing to the number one televangelist slot here on the East Coast in just a couple of years. This sudden rise in reputation is based primarily on an alleged vision of hell.

Now, I know what you'll say to that, but I'd ask you to forestall judgement until you've read the full transcript below. The transcript has been taken from a meeting I attended a week ago in a large auditorium. I've typed his words directly from a recording, but I must confess fixing the odd grammatical error here and there. I don't doubt that you will still catch the essence of what he's getting at.

I'd ask you to pay particular attention to his description of the devil (indeed, how can you miss it!). There's no doubt that his vision is in fact a crossing and that the devil he constantly refers to is none other than our illusive RQ. That's what strikes me as odd about his story (which has undoubtedly been embellished over the past few years). This is a man who claims to have been in the presence of the RQ herself and, if there is even an ounce of truth to his claim, this is unprecedented. I don't want to overstate the matter, but this could be our first close-up perspective of RQ, and if so, then some frightening possibilities and questions arise.

You'll have to forgive the casual sexism and hubris in the text that follows. Like many of his ilk, he is a somewhat self-obsessed character with more than a dab of religious megalomania thrown into the mix. Nonetheless, I hope you will see through this, to the heart of the message. These are exciting times, Dr. Ivanov, and if this man's claims can be substantiated, we are one step closer to tangible proof of the existence of both the *Traumwelt* and the red city.

Yours,

Julius Mann

Transcript: Jackson Spark 12 November, Glasshouse Theatre 19:00

I hear a lot of preachers talk about faith. You gotta have faith that the Lord hears your prayers. You gotta believe in your heart that you're gonna win through your time of trial and tribulation. You gotta have faith that all things work together for good, for those that love the Lord. Now I ain't saying that you don't need faith, brothers and sisters. Faith'll move mountains. It'll turn the tide on any battle and win the day every time, sure and true. But there are times, dear people, when faith just isn't needed. An apple falls from a tree, you don't need faith to tell you it's gonna hit the ground. It's there, plain and simple, right in front of you.

Now we preachers are known for fire and brimstone, telling folks about the fire that waits for the unrepentant. It might not be considered proper in this day and age, but the truth is the truth no matter what century you live in, amen?

[applause]

So, I'm a preacher and I ain't gonna shy away from tellin' it like it is. We're gonna talk about hell, brothers and sisters. We're gonna talk about the devil and her minions, and we're gonna talk plain and simple because the hour is short and the time is now and we can't afford to put this off for even a second.

I spoke about faith just now, about times when you don't need it. So, let me set the record straight and drop a powerful knowledge on you, brothers and sisters. I believe in salvation. I believe in the judgement and I believe in redemption and salvation through our Lord and Saviour, Jesus Christ. But I don't need faith to believe in hell. Because I've been to hell, brothers and sisters. I have had a visitation, a vision. For three days and three nights, like our blessed Lord, I was transported to the pit of hell and tormented by the devil and her angels!

[applause]

There, I said it again. Did you catch it? I said *her*, brothers and sisters. I said *her* and not *his*. Because the truth that the devil has kept hidden from you all these years is that she can take many forms. The devil might take the form of a needle in your arm, or sexual temptation, or the homosexual man spreading his perversion. But the devil I saw, brothers and sisters, was no man.

Now, before this story is told, I need to set the record straight a little. See the word devil, in the original Hebrew is the word *sa'tan*. And that word doesn't mean a man, or a fallen angel, it means adversary, pure and simple. It means the one who opposes God and all his goodness. It means the enemy, and, brothers and sisters, there ain't nothing in the good book that says the adversary can't be a woman!

Now I'm not talkin' about women like there's something wrong with being a lady. Goodness no. The Lord loves women and children. Men, our job is to look out for our women, to put our arm around them and keep them close. Our women are treasures that we gotta look after, bless God!

No, all I'm sayin' is that the devil can take many forms, and the devil I saw in hell was a woman.

It was two years ago now. I was a youth Pastor down in the Valley, working nine to five at the local diner while I finished my studies. I was working hard during the day and studyin' at night and, let me tell you brothers and sisters, I might have many gifts, but studyin' ain't one of them. It was hard work, but I gave it my best because I believe that if a man says he's gonna serve God, it's his duty to learn all he can about the good book and…well, I won't go on. Suffice it to say that I was tired and worn out.

After a late service one night, I headed home and was about to hit the bed when I felt the Spirit move within me. The Spirit impressed on me a mighty powerful need to pray. Now I was tired, brothers and sisters, bone tired and wantin' sleep like a starvin' man wants food. But I dragged myself down to my knees and prayed, waiting for the Spirit to give me some guidance.

Then, something happened. I can't rightly say what, because it all happened too fast. There was a light, a kind of blinding brightness just like old Paul on the road to Damascus. Then, I was pulled into darkness, I felt my body transported somewhere. I heard the rushing of a great wind and I was filled with terror. I'm not ashamed to admit it, brothers and sisters. I was scared beyond words. You ever wonder why every time an angel appears to someone in the good book it always says they were fearful? Well, I can tell you, when you come face to face with the supernatural, it'll scare the livin' heck out of you, yes sir.

Well I opened my eyes a while later and found myself lying in the dirt, surrounded on all sides by red dirt and stone and a desert that ran as far as the eye could see. Now if there was fire and brimstone I might have known where I was right away. But it took me some time for the realization to really sink in. Don't get me wrong, it was hot, hot and dry and desolate. My body ached as well, like someone had taken to me with a switch. I tried to stand, but it took me a little while to find my feet. Now I walked, brothers and sisters. I walked for more miles than I can count, and the sun beat down on my head. I was thirsty and bone tired and aching all over. It wasn't until at least a few hours had gone by that I saw something in the distance that promised refuge. I saw a city, big and old and real run down. It was red, like everything in hell, and, had I known what awaited me within the devil's palace, I would have turned away and ran as far and long as my legs would take me.

Now the devil ain't no fool, and there ain't no warnin' signs in hell. No sir, you just gotta keep on keepin' on, while your body's achin' from the heat and the dust and the pain of all that walkin'.

As I walked closer to that big ol' city, I saw towers reachin' out to the sky like the hand of God, only I knew in my gut that it weren't the hand of our Lord; not in that place. No sir, that was the hand of the devil, sure enough, all bony and black and reaching out to pull folks down from the world above into hell for all eternity. I walked on and started to see folks here and there. Small homes and farms, only they were filled with rotten crops, and the people were all hollow eyed and in a power of torment. I tell you brothers and sisters, I've seen pain in my life, but this was a whole lotta somethin' else entirely. These folks were rotten inside and out, just like the land of hell itself.

Nothin' grew there in that red desert. Nothin'. There were no trees or grass, no rivers or lakes. Why this ol' place was just as far as you could get from the blessed Garden of Eden. Just a barren wasteland and this evil city, risin' up like Sodom and Gomorrah.

Well now, I weren't exactly in my right frame of mind after all those miles walking in the baking heat. So, I walked right into the jaws of that cruel city, lookin' for water and something to ease my pain.

Now, don't get me wrong folks, I was never alone in this place of torment. Even there, in the depths of that place, I could feel his mercy [points upwards]. I could feel the Spirit within, givin' me strength. I need for you all to understand that now, before I keep tellin' this here story. Because things get a little nasty from here on, and I need you to understand that the Lord sent me to this place to teach me something. He took me to hell to show me what awaits the sinner and the unfaithful. That's a hard lesson to learn, but I am humbled that the Lord chose me to learn it.

I won't lie to ya' now. It weren't no walk in the park. It weren't no picnic, and that's for sure. I was scared. I cried out to the Lord. I cried out and asked the Lord to deliver me from the pit. But even with all that, I knew that my time in hell was only a short while. I knew that my Lord would take me from that place and restore me.

Now…where was I? Gotta get back on track, 'cause I get all riled up when I gets to talkin' about this. It still hits me right here [taps his chest].

Well, I walked into the jaws of hell and found a city of lost souls. Don't let anyone tell you that there's plenty of room there in hell. It might be big enough to fit all the sinners, but I tell you, when I walked into that city, I could barely move without some lost soul crashin' into me. Thousands, millions of lost souls, all filled with sorrow and hate and hopelessness, all wanderin' aimlessly around that red city. It was a city without hope, without joy or happiness. I tell ya' brothers and sisters, this was like…I suppose kind of an anti-Zion, if you catch my meaning. It was the opposite of the heavenly city. All cramped and hot and filled with lost souls. But those lost souls weren't the worst of it. No, not by a long shot.

I must have wandered through that wretched city for a day or more before the devil's agents found me. Now I'm not talkin' pitchforks and horns, like you see in those old-time paintings, no sir. These were big ol' boys with faces like men, eyes of fire, filled with hate. They dragged me through the city, took me to a deep dark dungeon, and strapped me down upon a metal table.

Now, I gotta warn you folks, things get a bit nasty from here on in, so I'll spare you the gruesome details. The only one that wins from that kind of thing is the devil herself and her kind, so I won't dwell on the details. Suffice it to say that demons worked a powerful torment on my body and soul. I felt such pain as I've never felt before or since, an unholy kind of pain that tears at a man's spirit. I'm not ashamed to admit that I cried out, like our Lord in the garden. I cried out that the Father would take the cup from me. It's true. And then, right when it was more than I could bear, the devil herself appeared.

Now, I didn't recognize her to begin with, and maybe that's half her trick. We know that the devil is a prince of lies, we know that Lucifer was the most cunning of all the angels, and there's no reason to think that changed after the fall. I gotta be honest, though, brothers and sisters, the devil right up and took me by surprise. I never expected her to be a woman, to be clothed in womanly form. There were no horns, no red skin or any of the things you'd expect. She was a woman, beautiful by all accounts, but you could see the cruelty in her eyes. There was something else in there as well, a burning like all the fires of hell were trapped there in her eyes.

Once the demons had done their work, the devil herself spoke to me. Now, I can't recall the words, but I'm reminded of our Lord's temptation. She promised me the world, if I would only forsake the Lord. She promised that my torment would be ended if I just turned my back on the Lord Jesus Christ. Can you believe it?

Now, I'm not a special kinda strong or anything like that. Whatever strength I have comes from the Lord anyhow, so I ain't takin' any credit. Right there, in my deepest, darkest hour, I felt the Spirit rise in me and resist the devil's words. I refused her temptation and let the Spirit fill me with divine strength. Right there, that's when the Lord reached down with his own hand and pulled me from that place.

[applause]

So, let me tell you folks, I've felt the fire and lived through the flame. I've been tested and, by the grace of God, prevailed. And I'm here to tell you tonight that hell is real, the devil is real, and she is gunnin' for you folks. Temptation lies around every corner and we've gotta clothe ourselves in the armour of the Spirit and fight the good fight. Time's a wastin', folks. We gotta get out there and tell people. No more pussyfootin' around, we gotta tell folks the truth, that hell is real and waitin' for all those who don't accept Christ as their Lord and saviour.

[applause]

Now, in a moment folks, we're gonna bring the band back up here and worship some more, see if we can't raise the roof in this place and touch the heavens. Meanwhile, I want to encourage you all, if you want to hear more about this vision of hell, head on down to the foyer after the service tonight and grab yourself a copy of my book, *Hell is Real*. I encourage you to buy a few copies. Give them to your neighbours, your family, friends.

In the book I go through my experiences in a lot more detail than I can right now. And, I'll be honest, the Spirit was writin' through me when I wrote that book. You can feel the power of the message when you read it. There's plenty of scripture in there, so I encourage you to use the book as an outreach tool. Give a copy to your workmate, your unsaved friend or relative. It really will change their lives. And, hey, buy yourself five copies of the book and the sixth copy is free, so there's a bargain for you.

[applause]

Amen, amen. Well hallelujah, let's sing.

THE RED QUEEN

6. Sandman

Seven a.m. and I'm halfway through a shitty cup of espresso when old Bill calls me into his office. I slide into the ripped-up leather chair opposite his desk and take another sip of coffee.

"Any good?" Bill asks.

I shake my head. "Fucking terrible."

He smiles, then tosses a manila folder across his desk.

"What's this?" I ask, picking up the file and leafing through it.

"Court ruling just came through on the Ghost. All unsolved missing person cases which fit the profile are now classified as suspected murders, making our mysterious spectre the number one serial killer in our patch."

I throw old Bill my favourite *you're shitting me* look, and he grins back at me. "Like I said, Murphy, the ruling was handed down this morning. The DA's managed to convince the courts that our Ghost is the real deal, and now it's your job to hunt the bastard down and get some closure on this whole saga."

"Jesus, Bill, just how many fucking missing person cases are you sticking me with?"

He shrugs.

"I'm giving you a team for this one. Gonzalez, Pike, and Rickman. You take point and you run the team. Just get me some bodies, or at the very least, some answers. Everyone's watching us on this, Murph, so make it quick."

"Can I finish my coffee first?"

"Do it walkin', Murphy," he says, turning his attention back to his laptop. "It was all well and good when these were just hippies and drifters, but there's a Senator's kid involved now, so we need this thing shut down asap, one way or another."

A number of smart-ass remarks cycle through my head, but I ditch them all and head out of Bill's office. The manila folder in my hand feels like the proverbial millstone around my neck. This kind of missing person's shit never ends cleanly and screwing up a case involving a Senator's baby girl is a sure-fire way to end up flushing your career down the shitter.

The three stooges are waiting for me when I get to my desk. I can't help the sport's commentator in me from coming out when I see them. *Gonzalez, the fiery Argentinian... Pike, the wiry Brit with a head like a spoiled cabbage and a heart of gold... Rickman, the plucky little stalwart who clashes heads with every prick in the precinct and managed to come out on top despite her size and gender.*

I call them into the war room and throw the remainder of my coffee in the trash. I'm gonna need something much stronger before the day is out.

A series of nods and winks are exchanged as the three take their seats around a large rectangular table. I throw open the folder.

"Take a good long look, boys and girls," I offer, moving over to the murder board and picking up a whiteboard marker. "It seems that one of us unfortunates has caused offence to the powers that be, and someone upstairs has taken it upon themselves to take a shit on our heads."

Pike titters, while the other two start dividing run sheets and photos from the folder.

"As you know, Senator Greyson's youngest has been reported missing and no ransom demands have been forthcoming. In another era, that might be seen as par for the course for an eighteen-year-old trust fund princess with a silver spoon wedged firmly up her ass. But this is *not* the good old days, and it seems that the most viable explanation for the princess's absence is not an impromptu trip to the Bahamas with some preppie, ascot-wearing, hyphenated last name, twenty-year-old fuck with the keys to daddy's yacht and a pocket full of ecstasy. No friends, we live in a different time where such simple answers are behind us. It seems that the good Senator is convinced that the G-Line Ghost is responsible."

I hold up a hand, stopping the interruptions before they start.

"Now you're all passable detectives, so I know what you're thinking. Firstly, as his name suggests, the Ghost is nothing more than a boogie man the press has used to connect the dots on a spate of missing persons reports over the past few months. There's no solid evidence that he exists, or that any of these cases are connected. Secondly, even if he were real, the Ghost reportedly abducts his victims from the subway, close to the G-Line to be precise. The chances of Princess Greyson wandering around the filthy underbelly of the city with the great unwashed are slim. But I need you to put all that logic behind you, ladies and gents, because we are officially on the clock on this one. We have three days to find ourselves a Ghost and come up with some answers, or we can all look forward to a fulfilling career as traffic wardens."

Pike raises his hand, speaking before I've even acknowledged him. "Since when does Homicide work the missing persons cases, Gov? Fuckin' unprecedented, is that."

"Since five minutes ago, Pike. Now keep your trap shut and let me finish my rant."

Rickman doesn't bother raising her hand. "I gather Missing Persons is gonna take on some of our workload then?"

"That's a good point there, Gov," Pike adds. "Don't seem fair, us cleaning up their mess and doin' our own shit as well."

I slam my hands down on the desk, just loud enough to get their attention. "Look, I don't know what gave you the impression that this was a discussion, but it isn't. The gods have fucking spoken and now it's time to get to work. We've got three days to come up with answers and we're gonna be watched like a hawk on this one, so unbunch your panties and get to it."

I jab a finger at Pike. "Head down to the subway and start squeezing your CIs. Offer them whatever you need to offer to get information and find me anything you can on this Ghost."

I turn to Rickman and Gonzalez. "You two run these missing cases and try to find me some connections. Speak to families and friends and see if we can't find some common ground somewhere. And Gonzalez, for the time being you can shelve your usual suave gigolo, granny-fucker routine, okay. I don't need you sticking your Mexican pecker inside any of our grieving mothers, got it?"

I get a round of meagre agreement.

"Our line to the press is that we are working a series of leads, and any updates will be provided by myself at scheduled press conferences. I don't want any of you even thinking about the press, let alone talking to any reporters no matter how nice a pair of tits they're sporting. I'm looking at you, Gonzalez!"

The Argentinian grins.

"Bring everything in here and keep off the radio and your mobiles unless it's urgent. If we need to, we can ring in a couple of uniforms to handle some canvassing, but I don't want them knowing about the murder angle on this. Just tell them we're helping out our friends from Missing Persons tidy up the books for the quarter. I'll cover whatever overtime you want for the next few days, and we'll get a couple of cots set up in here in case anyone wants a kip."

I lean in, trying for the last time to impress the importance of the case on the three veterans. "You're permitted to shower, shit, and shave, but other than that, there's no downtime on this one, ladies and gents. Get it done and get it done quick."

Pike raises his hand, this time waiting for permission. I shake my head. "No, Pike, for the hundredth fucking time, titty bars and all-you-can-eat buffets aren't counted as legitimate business expenses, no matter how often you ask."

He frowns, shrugs, and then heads off.

***

"Speak."

Rickman opens her notepad. Her eyes are bloodshot, hair frizzy at the edges. "Total of thirty-three missing persons, twenty could have been snatched from somewhere near G-Line stops. The others either don't take the train or were too far away."

She scans the notepad. "No real connection between the victims… timing is about one per day. No ransom demands. There are ten drifters, and the rest are all average Joes, except for Julia Greyson of course."

I turn to Pike, whose peppery stubble is starting to run wild across his gaunt face.

"Sweet pile of fuck all, Gov," he says, scratching at his chin. "Been through every CI and subway rat I can find, and nothing comes up. It's like you said, Gov, there is no Ghost. Just a fucking coincidence."

I shake my head. "We can't afford coincidences. And I'm starting to think there's more here than what we're seeing, just by the sheer numbers. Thirty-three people; even for this city, that's extreme."

"People trafficking?" Rickman offers.

I consider it. "The victims are too varied. Some old, some young. Only a couple of foreigners in the group too, so I doubt the Russians would be involved. They normally stick to anything they can sell for sex. No, we have to stay on the Ghost theory. Where's Gonzalez?"

"Subway," Rickman says. "Running down a possible lead in one of the old lines. He's got the rail authority opening up all the old tunnels so he can check it out."

My phone chooses precisely that moment to start ringing. It's Gonzalez.

I pick up.

"Speak."

The sound of heavy breathing, scuffling sounds echoing off hard surfaces.

"Gonzalez?"

More noise, like the chattering of inhuman teeth, the sound of laboured breath increasing.

"Gonzalez, what the fuck is—"

A gunshot peels through the speaker, cutting into my ear drum just before the connection cuts out.

"Fuck!"

I hit redial, start heading to the door, motioning to Rickman. "You know where he is?"

She nods, concern written across her face.

"Take us there now and get some uniforms over there."

The office phone rings, but Gonzalez doesn't pick up. Rickman slips on her jacket, and the three of us head out of the office at a jog. We take an unmarked sedan, and Rickman slips on the lights and siren. I dial Gonzalez again as the car charges out of the parking lot, wheels smoking. No one answers.

"Fucking fuck!" I turn to Rickman. "He had people with him, yeah?"

She nods, bracing herself against the pressure as she pulls the car sharply around the bend. "Couple of boys from the rail authority. He had to get City Council permission to get down there so plenty of people know about it."

"Probably just shooting at a fuckin' rat," Pike offers, checking the ammo in his Glock and holstering the weapon while the car rolls left and right. He leans forward from the back seat and picks up the radio mic, starts calling for backup.

I call Gonzalez again. I get no response. It only takes a few minutes to reach the closest subway. We bail out of the car and head down the stairs, following Rickman as she darts through the crowd with the directional sense of a basset hound. At the far end of the north platform, a pimple-faced kid in a high-vis jacket stands guard by a metal door. Rickman flashes her badge and pushes her way past. I follow behind as Pike gives the bemused guard instructions.

A tunnel lined with metal pipes and concrete walls runs for a few hundred feet, then ducks left and then right. We follow Rickman through the tunnel at a run, flashlights bobbing up and down. I try Gonzalez's number again. No luck.

"Should be through here," Rickman says, pulling out her weapon and kicking open a metal door.

We head through, checking the angles with Pike at the rear. We enter a large tunnel which is partially lit by a series of sparsely placed fluorescent lights hanging from the roof. Rough stones crunch under foot and we follow a pair of old train tracks toward a vacant platform to the left.

"There, on the track," Rickman says, starting to run. "Jesus, oh fucking Jesus. It's Gonzalez."

He's lying on his back, staring up into nothing with glassy eyes. Rickman checks his pulse, leans down to check if he's breathing while Pike and I clear the scene. There's nothing but empty space all around us. The platform is empty, its stairs gated and locked shut.

"He's breathing," Rickman says, slapping the fallen detective on one cheek. "Gonzalez, can you hear me? It's Rickman. Can you hear me?"

Nothing. He lies in silence, staring into space.

"I'll check further ahead," Pike says, walking on through the tunnel with flashlight and weapon drawn.

From the other end of the tunnel, I hear uniforms and EMTs making their way toward us. I give Rickman the nod, and she gets to work while I take a closer look at Gonzalez. The greasy bastard looks completely vacant, like nobody's home. His breathing and pulse are steady, and there are no signs of physical injury that I can see.

When the paramedics arrive, they find a small puncture on the side of Gonzalez's neck. I ask them if they've got any idea what he was hit with but get the usual *you'll have to wait and see* bullshit.

Gonzalez's phone is lying on the ground a few feet away. I pick it up with a tissue and stuff it carefully into a zip lock bag. Not the worst start to an investigation but fucking close to it.

***

The sun has set somewhere outside, and I'm sitting in Bill's office, having had the shit torn out of me for the last half an hour. The old boy looks at me, and I can read the frustration on his face. He wants to lay into me again, but he also knows it won't make a difference. What's done is done, and, whether he admits it or not, there wasn't a damned thing any of us could have done to anticipate what happened to Gonzalez.

"I'm bringing in outside help," he says flatly. "A specialist."

That piques my interest. "What kind of specialist exactly? The feds? A consultant? Just who exactly has the requisite experience to deal with this kind of shit?"

Before Bill can answer the question, it dawns on me. "Oh no, Bill. No, Bill, fucking no."

He shakes his head. "It's out of my hands. The decision has already been made."

"He's a fucking loon!"

"He gets results, and that's all that matters at the moment."

"So, you want us to hunt a fucking psycho magician or whatever the hell the Ghost is by bringing a lunatic?"

Bill spins on his heels, glaring at me, fury boiling just beneath the surface. "Look, I don't have a choice, okay! Do I want this psycho in my precinct? Of course, I fucking don't, but you lost a detective in the first twenty-four hours of your investigation. I've been ordered to bring Holden in, and that's what I've done. Now work with him and get this shit done!"

Detective Nick Holden is waiting for me in the war room, dressed just as I expect, in a pair of tattered cargo shorts and a cheesy Hawaiian shirt. He smiles when I walk into the room, hands me a slip of paper which says, in no uncertain terms, that he is expected to run lead on this investigation. I crumple the piece of paper between my fingers and drop it to the floor, trying my hardest not to look like I want to punch the guy in the neck.

"Frizzy and Pip have filled me in on where you're up to," Holden says without preamble. "Good work if you ask me, but I think you're gonna need to broaden your search a little."

I feel my jaw clench. "What exactly do you mean by *broaden*?"

He smiles. "I mean you gotta start talking to kooks and whackos, simple as that. Hell of a lot goes on in this city that regular folk don't know about. You gotta know who to ask."

I'm about to offer a sharp reply when he holds up a hand and throws a manila folder in my direction. "I'm not saying you guys have to actually go and do that. It's already been done."

I open the folder and start reading sketchy details about a European-looking gent named Klaus Hudermen. He has an evil scientist vibe, but there is no concrete lead that I can see, just scraps of hearsay and second-hand accounts. The photo of Klaus is badly blurred and looks to have come off a subway camera.

"Okay, Holden, what the fuck am I looking at here?"

He pulls a Snickers bar from his pocket and peels back the wrapper like it's a banana. "You're looking at the Ghost, friend. Ghost of the B-line or whatever. That's your guy right there."

"G-Line," Rickman corrects, rolling her eyes.

"That's the one," Holden says, pointing the Snickers bar at her.

"This is the guy?" I ask, shaking my head and leafing through the notes in the folder. "Honestly, Holden, you've got fuck all here. You can't expect me to believe that he's our perp."

Holden holds the Snickers up to his nose and sniffs it, long and hard. Then, he re-wraps it and shoves it back into his pocket without taking a bite. He closes his eyes for a few seconds, then turns back to me.

"Didn't say anything about murder, did I?"

"What?"

"They're not dead. He drugs his victims, much like your Detective Gonzalez, and takes them to his lair, but he doesn't kill them. At least, he hasn't yet, I don't think."

As one, Rickman and Pike turn their heads to me, wearing a mixture of bemusement and anger.

"So, let me get this straight." I hand the folder to Rickman. "You've got a bunch of half-assed, second-hand accounts and one grimy photo, and that leads you to the incontrovertible conclusion that this Klaus Huderman is our Ghost? Not only that, but you've also managed to confirm that he hasn't killed anyone, but just abducts them for some reason?"

Holden nods, and there's not a trace of irony in the gesture.

"Just where the fuck do you get off?" I feel my cheeks start to redden. "We've been working this case twenty-four seven, piecing together first-hand statements and hard data, and you come waltzing in here—"

He holds up a hand to pull me up short and, for a brief moment, I picture my fist slamming into his bastard face.

"I said I don't *think* he's killed anyone yet. That may change now that your detective Gonzalez has given him a scare. So, we need to move quickly."

With that, he heads out the door, leaving the three of us standing there, holding our frustration and anger. A moment later, he ducks his head back in the room.

"In case I haven't made it clear," he says, "you should all come with me."

"Where to?" I hiss between gritted teeth.

"We're going to have a chat with Mr. Klaus Huderman."

***

Despite our protests, Holden has us pile into his beat-up old Bedford van. The thing coughs and splutters like an asthmatic with bronchitis and leaves a trail of thick black smoke from its exhaust, announcing our presence with the occasional backfire. Pike sits up front while Rickman and I are stashed in the back of the van. She leans forward, concern heavy on her face.

"What's the deal with this guy, Murph?"

I shrug. "He's a fucking lunatic, that's what. Some kind of specialist inspector for the Feds who works all the whacky cases. I had a run-in with him a few years back."

"What kind of wacky cases?"

I shoot her a dead stare. "Vampires, werewolves, zombies, fucking ghosts, you name it. Anything too kooky for real police to take seriously, this guy gets the case. Not just for our precinct though. He's worked with the Feds here and overseas. The guy's a fucking legend. That's why the bastards have brought him in on this. It's just his kind of gig."

"Yeah, but is he any good?"

It takes me a few moments to respond. "He's a fucking disgrace to the force. But, yeah, he gets results. Wish I could say otherwise, but he has a habit of solving these kinds of weird cases."

She nods. "Okay then, what's the deal with the Snickers?"

"Lactose intolerant," I explain. "Little perv gets off on smelling shit he can't eat. First thing he orders at a restaurant is a chocolate milkshake. Fucker doesn't drink it through, he just sits there sniffing it all night."

"And what's the deal with the eye?" Rickman asks.

I shake my head. "Some kind of accident with new experimental contact lenses, or something like that. I only heard about it second-hand. Holden thinks the lens lets him see into, I dunno, the spirit world or whatever. Says it helps him."

"Makes him look like David Bowie's special cousin," Rickman says, without humour.

We pull into a subway entrance, and Holden leads us down to the nearest platform. He heads to the far end of the station, near a pair of trash cans and a broken vending machine. It's only as we get closer that I make out the rough shape of a hobo sitting beside one of the trash cans. The guy is little more than a collection of rags and discarded plastic bags. He smells like a sewer, but Holden doesn't seem to notice. He heads up to the guy and kicks him lightly with one boot.

"Need your help, Guardian," Holden says, giving the hobo a second kick.

The bundle of fetid rags stirs. A face appears, and the garbage pile starts to rearrange itself into a roughly human shape. Beneath tattered rags a grimy, scarred face looks at Holden with something like hatred.

"We're looking for the Ghost, the one that's been taking people from all over the city and stashing them. We know he's somewhere down here, so we need to know where."

The hobo's eyes turn toward me, flickering to Pike and Rickman, then back to Holden. Despite myself, I feel a momentary flutter of fear at the hobo's unnerving glance. There's something alien about it, something unnatural. Twenty years I've been in this business, and I've come face to face with a whole lot of nasty in that time, but something about this guy has my stomach doing the twist.

When the hobo speaks, it's with a voice far deeper and smoother than I expect, as if someone else's voice is being channelled through a speaker around the guy's neck.

"And what price do you pay for such information, mortal?"

Without batting an eyelid, Holden pulls something from his pocket and tosses it to the hobo. A grime-covered hand shoots out from the pile of rags with impossible speed, clutching the object out of the air. The hobo inspects it closely, and I lean forward to get a better look.

"Fuck's sakes!" Pike blurts. "It's a fucking toe."

I turn to Holden, but he ignores me. The hobo inspects the severed big toe with interest, eventually slipping it back into his rag pile and nodding at Holden.

"Follow the access path left of the eighth junction box. Beware subterfuge, he is not defenceless."

Holden smiles. "One more question. If this guy's some kind of body-snatching bastard, why haven't you lads done anything to stop him? Isn't the whole snatch-and-grab thing a disturbance in the force or whatever? That's usually the kind of shit you boys are interested in."

The hobo moves slowly, devolving into his former state without a word. Holden turns to me.

"Okay, we need to get to the eighth junction box. Not sure what we'll find, so keep your weapons ready and eyes open."

He moves to the edge of the platform, jumps down and heads off into the tunnel.

"Wait, you can't just…" Rickman calls out.

"Don't waste your breath," I say. "Just get support down here quick and see if we can shut down this line for the next few hours. For fuck's sakes, this is a live subway."

Rickman nods and rushes off, already dialling on her phone while Pike and I follow after the Hawaiian-shirt-wearing buffoon.

"You see that fucking toe?" Pike asks.

"Yeah, I saw it."

"A fucking toe, Gov. A toe!"

"Just keep your eyes open and try not to shoot Holden in the ass, no matter how tempting it is."

We follow Holden through the tunnel, then through a locked doorway to a small corridor which leads south. Fluorescent lights flicker above us as we follow Holden further and further through a maze of corridors. As we reach a crossway, he stops in front of a large metal grid to the side on the right wall. Holden grabs the grate and wrenches it free. There's a hole, a tunnel leading down into dark earth, with a makeshift wooden ladder.

"Don't know why the press went with 'Ghost,'" Holden says, sliding down into the hole. "I'd have thought Moleman would be more appropriate."

We follow the hole down into a long earthen tunnel, lit with amber lights cut into the wall. The ground is squelchy underfoot, and there's a scent of ash in the air. The tunnel twists and turns, heading steadily downward. After a few minutes we come to a small corridor that opens out into a larger room. The walls and floor are covered with some kind of clay brick, and there are old fashioned lamps hanging from the ceiling, filling the room with weak amber light. Wooden crates and boxes are stacked around the room, as well as pieces of scrap metal and heaps of odds and ends.

Holden waves us over to a door at one end of the chamber. Weapons ready, we move in close, just as Rickman and half a dozen uniforms come up behind us. I turn, motioning for them to keep quiet while Holden opens the door.

The smell of acrid rot hits us immediately, bringing bile to the back of our throats. One of the uniforms vomits, earning himself a withering glare from Rickman. Holden pushes the door right open and heads through at a crouch. It's only then that I realize the stupid bastard doesn't even have his weapon un-holstered. He's holding something outstretched in his right hand. I can't see what it is, but I know it's not a gun.

We head into the room, fanning out and checking the angles for signs of movement.

"He's gone," Holden says, standing to full height.

I motion for the others to sweep the room. It's larger than the previous chamber, and its walls are lined with floor-to-ceiling bookcases filled with books. At the centre of the curious library are twelve stainless steel beds, each with a body lying still, with various tubes and wires heading off from their bodies in all directions. There are odd devices hooked up to the bodies, strange mechanical things with amber light valves, pumps, pistons and various clockwork contraptions. It's a steampunk wet dream, wrapped up in a fucking nightmare.

"They're still alive," Holden says, "though I don't recommend unplugging them. Not without a mop and bucket."

I head to the nearest victim, a middle-aged man with thin wisps of hair on his head and liver spots on his arms and legs. He's naked except for a small towel over his genitals. Tubes are sticking out of both arms and legs, and there are wires and electrodes connected to his chest and head. A quick check tells me that his pulse and breathing are relatively strong. Rickman moves up beside me, pulling a wad of papers from her jacket. She riffles through them, settling on one and thrusting it in my direction.

"Derrek Howel," she says. "Went missing a month back."

I take the run sheet and examine the picture of Derrek that was. Take away the tubes and wires, add a little more blubber and some colour and he's a dead ringer.

"I'll check the others," Rickman says.

I nod, lost in my own thoughts.

***

The underground chamber, it turns out, can be accessed via three tunnels that all lead out to the subway. Apart from the main chamber and entryway, we find half a dozen smaller rooms; a modest kitchen, workshop, living quarters, and several storerooms. The Forensics team is set loose to try and make sense of the contraptions to which the kidnap victims have been attached. They make little progress with the medical equipment and even less with the bizarre contraption in one small room at the back of the burrow.

The machine looks like the offspring of a union between a pipe organ and a satellite from the 60s. It's powered by some kind of coke-driven boiler; a steam powered monstrosity that the brightest minds in the precinct can't figure out.

Once I've had just about all I can take of that underground hell, I move back above ground and find my team gathered by a hotdog stand.

"So, what's the deal, boss?" Rickman asks, with Pikeman devouring a hotdog to her left.

I shake my head. "No fucking idea. They didn't find any more bodies, so we're still missing Greyson and the rest."

"What about the Ghost?" Pike spits between mouthfuls.

"A loon, judging by all the shit we found. Guy's cracked. Forensics can't make head or tails of what he was doing to the victims, or what that big fucking machine was all about. I think he's just a psycho with a bent mushroom and too much time on his hands."

Rickman frowns. "A loon with a lot of cash."

I nod. "And the resources to snatch thirty odd people without us getting a whiff of it."

"What about the magic man?" Pike asks, pointing his half-eaten hotdog at Holden, who is talking to a reporter a few feet away.

I shrug. "Honestly I don't know. Haven't had a chance to talk to him since he found the place. No fucking idea how he managed to pull this one off or where he gets his information from."

"Some kind of hobo, toe swapping scheme," Rickman says, showing a rare smile.

A uniform arrives and hands me a thick, black coffee. I give him a nod and bury myself in it.

"Head's up, Gov," Pike says, a moment before Holden slides into view.

Holden orders two dogs with the lot and starts devouring the first while most of the contents of the second start dripping down his other hand.

"Okay, Holden, what's next?" I ask, dreading the answer.

He takes another mouthful before replying. "We've got bods combing the underground looking for tunnels, so it's only a matter of time before we find the other nests."

"Nests?"

"Two or three, I'd expect. This bastard's careful. Doesn't want to keep all his eggs in one basket."

"Okay, so what's his play then? I take it you're not buying the whole psychotic loner bit?"

He shakes his head. "He's got help, and this isn't a simple case of one man with a bent brain. Shit, they never are. There's organization here, and intent. They're trying to do something extraordinary."

"What?"

He shrugs. "Can't really say. The boys at the Bureau don't like it when I give away state secrets. All I'll say is that I've seen equipment like that before. I worked a case a few years back with some nutsack in the burbs who was building a magic portal in his basement. The guy was two pickles short of a Big Mac, but he was one of those idiot savant types; a real nutbag genius. Turned out there was a whole pack of nerdlings all chatting online. Some kind of *Dungeons and Dragons* thing gone bad. Most of these guys were harmless, but this fucker had carved up a pile of bodies and buried them in his backyard. Then he turns on his magic fucking portal and burns his house down with the wife and kid asleep upstairs. There's something about our little Ghost nest that rings a lot of bells, you know what I mean?"

I nod.

"Question," Pike chimes in.

"Shoot," Holden fires back.

"Okay, don't take this the wrong way, chief, but where the fuck did you get that toe?"

Holden grins. "Swiped it from a morgue on my way over here. Took it off one of the bodies on their way to the burner, figured it might come in handy."

He pulls something from his pocket and shows it to Pike. It's a zip lock back just big enough to hold a pair of severed toes that are already starting to blacken. I stop sipping my coffee and feel my stomach lurch a little.

"Watchers use this kind of shit for currency," Holden explains, "so I keep a couple of the fuckers on me at all times. Never know when you're gonna need to bargain with the guardians of the old world."

About a thousand questions start jumping round my head, but that part of me that's had twenty years on the job takes over, putting the questions to the slam before they get out of my mouth. I hold up a hand, stopping Pike midway through whatever he's about to ask.

"Okay, let's put a fucking cork in the crazy for a few minutes shall we, ladies and gents? Remember it's our asses on the line for this one, so how about we get back to the case and the question of how we're going to track down our Ghost."

Holden polishes off his first dog and starts greedily devouring the second. We sit there watching him like a trio of tourists watching a snake eat a possum. Not for the first time, I think about how rewarding it would feel to slam my fists into that smug ugly face of his. I'd lose my badge, probably end up selling vacuum cleaners door to door, but it would almost be worth it.

Something beeps nearby and, like trained dogs, we all check our phones. All of us except Holden. He just keeps right on eating. The beep chirps a second time and Holden drops his hotdog, twists, and pulls something I haven't seen in thirty years out of his pocket.

"Holy shit!" Pike offers, his face split by an impossibly wide grin.

"Tell me you're not looking at a pager?" I ask, already knowing the answer.

Holden shrugs, reads the message off the top of the pager and starts walking off toward his van.

"Let's mount up, cowboys. Looks like we've got ourselves a lead."

***

The pager leads Holden to another of the homeless bums that seem to comprise his CI network. There's another exchange of toes, and we're led down a series of subway tunnels to an abandoned sewer outlet. There's an old control room and a small bathroom in the sewer maintenance facility. Behind a row of long abandoned lockers, we find another burrow leading downward.

To my surprise, Holden pulls a Magnum .45 from somewhere and gives us the hush hush sign as he starts climbing down into the hole. All the banter has gone, and there's a severity to his expression which I haven't seen before. Low and behold, somewhere beneath that ridiculous exterior there lurks an actual officer of the law.

After a few steps through the earthen tunnel, it's clear that this is not like the last nest we entered. There's a tang of blood in the air and rot coming from further down the tunnel. Holden is cautious. Stopping every few steps to examine the wall or floor. He says nothing, motions us forward slowly. We head down a steady slope, the tunnel lit by the same mysterious amber lights as the other nest. Water starts to pool at our feet, though it smells suspiciously unlike water.

We reach a metal doorway, and Holden opens it gingerly after a lengthy inspection. The door is pitted with rust and grime and there's water running constantly down one side of its length. I'm just about through the doorway when a scream cuts through the air. My heart starts thudding and I move ahead, ready to run. Holden motions for us to stay in place. In the dim amber light of the tunnel, there's something dark and dangerous in his eyes.

He puts a finger to his lips, turns, and continues to walk slowly through the tunnel. A second scream hits us like a screwdriver through the ear. Pike and Rickman are twitching, looking back and forth between Holden and I, begging for permission to run ahead

After an agony of moments, we reach another door, and Holden begins his painstaking inspection. The screams continue, followed by panting and other sounds that fire the imagination with ghastly images. It's the scream of a young woman, and I'm praying with every fibre of my being that the scream doesn't belong to Julia Greyson.

Finally, Holden opens the door and moves through. We follow after, guns at the ready. We enter a huge domed chamber with walls and ceilings lined with copper panels that reflect the light in ever increasing shades of orange and red. There are bodies strapped to metal tables, tubes attached to the same strange medical contraptions we saw at the other nest. These bodies are bloodied and battered. Some have cuts and abrasions; others are missing limbs and organs. There's a horrific stench in the chamber which threatens to involuntarily empty my stomach.

We follow Holden through the grotesque carnival of victims. Rickman checks one of them in passing. Alive. It seems that they're all alive, but in varying degrees of wholeness. The scream hits us again, and I look toward the far end of the chamber where a figure in a tracksuit is fiddling with a mammoth contraption of pipes and wires, cogs and wheels. The thing looks like a Harley that's been turned inside out and grafted with a pipe organ and a steam locomotive. It hisses and spins, wheels and cogs grinding softly.

We head closer and I strain to see. There's someone strapped to the front of the machine, arms and legs splayed like the Vitruvian Man. It's a young woman, naked, wounded. Each time the guy in the tracksuit does something to the levers and mechanisms of the machine, she lets out a screech of pain. Her body shudders, and trails of blood run down from her ears and eyes, carving a crimson path across her naked flesh.

I'm about to put an end to the scene when Holden stands, heads toward the tracksuit torturer with his Magnum ready.

"Police!" Holden calls out. "Police with very big guns!"

The guy in the tracksuit spins around slowly, screwing up his face as though he hasn't understood. He's a thin man with gaunt features and an Eastern European look.

"Get your ass on the ground and hold your hands behind your back," Holden goes on as the rest of us fan around him.

Tracksuit smiles, leans over to flick a lever on the machine, and, just like that, the lights go out.

"Fuck," says Pike, fumbling with his flashlight.

Images flash before my eyes as I fumble for my torch. The machine is still clunking along, the woman is still screaming, but I can't get a look at the freak in the tracksuit.

"Left!"

"Right!"

Rickman and Pike call out their directions, spreading to the left and right in a practiced pattern, scouring the room with flashlights. I resist the urge to go and get the tortured woman, moving back into the darkness and keeping my flashlight locked dead ahead. Holden vanishes from view, not bothering with his own flashlight. There's a sound of scuffling. A gunshot, followed by shouting. Then the lights come back on, and I see Holden standing by the machine, with the guy in the tracksuit thrashing about on the floor holding his left foot.

As if to top off the most disturbing case I ever witnessed, Holden takes a moment to pull something from his pocket. He unwraps the Snickers, takes a long, perverted sniff, and then puts it back in place, wearing a stupid grin.

We get the girl down from the machine. She's delirious, shaking with shock. It's not Julia Greyson, and I feel a strange mix of relief and anguish at that fact. Pike and Rickman call in the scene and start looking at the rest of the victims. I move to Holden and the tracksuit. He's still wearing a stupid grin when I get to him.

"Oh, you're gonna love this one, fella," he says, grabbing the tracksuit by the scruff of the neck and shoving him hard to the ground.

The guy squirms and starts rambling in a language I can't understand.

"Pull back his shirt," Holden says, "and get ready to have your mind blown!"

I do as he says, tearing through the thin fabric to reveal a gruesome tattoo which almost takes up the whole of the guy's back. It's in the style of an ancient mask, some god or demon from legend. Dark eyes and a heavy brow are complemented by a toothy snarl which is more animal than man. I look up at Holden.

He grins. "Just keep lookin," he says, reaching down and prodding the tattoo square in the left eye.

The tattoo face recoils, squinting at Holden's intrusion and screwing itself up. From somewhere nearby a deep, raspy voice bellows in time with the movement of the tattoo face.

"Fucking quit it!"

I look up at Holden.

He grins.

I puke.

***

After a few hours and a few shots of whiskey, I join Holden in an interrogation room. He's got the tracksuit guy spun around and strapped to a chair, his back bare and the gruesome tattoo snarling at us. I've stood in this room a thousand times, grilled a thousand different suspects from petty crooks to big time mobsters. For the first time since I was a rookie, I haven't the faintest clue how to proceed. For once, I'm happy for Holden to take the lead.

He sits on a chair opposite the tattoo and pours himself a glass of whiskey from a small hip flask. He takes a sip, lets out a big breath and just stares at the tattoo for a few minutes. Neither of them says anything. I can smell the whiff of hard liquor as it drifts through the room, and my mouth starts to water. I'm not a heavy drinker myself, but the last couple of days might change that.

"You're new," Holden says, without warning. "I mean, I've met the Strect and half a dozen Shadowmancers, a few Thaumadren, and the odd Spectral. Hell, I'm on a first-name basis with the Watchers, but you're something different. Some kind of inky vampire, I'm guessing. You hijack your victim's skin and once you've settled in you start to control their actions, yeah? Who was this kid anyway, some street urchin, the local tough guy who went into the wrong tattoo parlour and literally got himself some wicked ink?"

The tattoo blinks, still snarling. It looks up at Holden with something close to pure hatred.

"A man can live only once," the tattoo growls, "and when one's work takes longer than a single lifetime, one must improvise."

Holden nods. "Yeah, I hear ya. The whole mortal coil shit is a real stick up the ass."

The tattoo scowls, grinding inky teeth.

"Look," Holden goes on, "you might as well tell us the whole story, fella. That fine young cannibal you've got yourself printed on is going to be tried for abduction, mutilation, and attempted murder among other things. He'll be sent to the big house for the rest of his life, however long that may be, but that's not the end of the story for you, I'm afraid. See, I'm gonna arrange for a friend of mine to do a little ink work before you get transferred out of here. Nothing too complex, just scrubbing out a mouth, a couple of eyes, maybe make the design a little more impressionistic."

The expression on the tattoo's face turns from outright rage to something more uncertain.

"Thing is, this friend of mine isn't your regular tattoo artist. He specializes in…shall we say, the more exotic types of body art. I don't know for sure, but I'm reasonably confident that he won't have a problem making some changes with whatever magic ink you used to graft yourself onto the young lad's back. So, I've got some questions that need answering, and I figure, if you tell us what we want to know, I might be persuaded to call off my artist friend."

The tattooed face runs through a flurry of emotions, settling back to its natural demonic snarl. It seems to settle itself.

"Ask your questions."

Holden grins. "Okay, let's start with this. Who the fuck are you, and how the fuck did you end up tattooed to this guy's back?"

The tattoo pauses, arranging its thoughts. "I was sent here many years ago, through a tear in the fabric between worlds. It was a different time, and such things sometimes occurred. Through the Clockmaker's genius I was able to affect a crossing into this place. As I passed through the way between worlds, however, my wits were addled.

"When I arrived in the waking world, I could remember nothing of my former life, nor my mission. It took a great many years and almost a whole lifetime to come to my senses, by which time I was too frail to continue my Mistress's work. Thus, with much of my thaumaturgical knowledge returned to me, I set about a plan to prolong my life long enough to finish the work set for me. It was by happenstance and luck that I came upon the notion of the tattooed visage you see before you. I enlisted the help of a trusted associate and set about a work of profound transmogrification, worked upon my own psyche.

"The endeavour took ten years to complete, and it was only through the diligence of my associate—who, in return I had gifted many thaumaturgical secrets which he employed for substantial financial gain— that the translation was able to be completed. We found a young lad by the docks, and I was tattooed upon his skin for a paltry sum. It took a further five years for me to master the art of somatic manipulation. Five years of petty thuggery and manual drudgery before I could wrest my host out of his monotony and manage complete control over his faculties. I was, in effect, reborn."

"And your associate?" Holden asks.

"Long dead and gone. Endowed with obscene wealth, he lived a luxurious life until his dying day, but I no longer had contact with the man once our work was completed. In time, I was able to affect a second crossing to the young specimen whose back I now inhabit. Full somatic control was much easier to implement, given my previous experience. Thus, I have spent several lifetimes setting about the work for which my Mistress had sent me. This world is a primitive, backwards place, so it took quite a while for the—"

The door to the interrogation room slams open and the captain walks in, looking like he's just sat on a cactus. He doesn't even see the tattoo face as he enters, just starts barking orders.

"Okay, son, sorry about this but we've been kicked off the case. They found Miss Greyson a few minutes ago and she's in sound health, so our job is done. I need you to finish up here immediately and get cracking on a report so we can close this down."

I hold up my hand. "Hold on Bill, we haven't finished—"

"Out of my hands," the Captain blurts, a little too fast. "The whole case is going over to the Feds and we've been ordered to take our hands off. That means *now*, people, so let's get cracking. The Feds will handle things from here."

Holden spins in his chair. "Captain, I should remind you that I'm not—"

"Not under my jurisdiction, yes, I know, Holden, but I just got off the phone with one Special Agent Rook and he is pulling you from the case immediately. Wants you in Washington for a new case, asap."

After a brief moment of confused hesitation, I follow Holden out of the room. As we head through the door, I catch sight of a dwarf in a three-piece suit, walking with a silver cane in front of a mammoth guy with a shaved head. The little guy nods to us as he passes and then heads into the interrogation room with Man-mountain following behind.

The captain leads us to his office and has us sit down. He explains that he's been ordered to hand over all case materials to the feds and that we're all off the case effective immediately. I press him on just how the hell something like this would happen and he starts sweating. Says he's got a call from the Superintendent himself and that the Secretary of Defense is involved.

"Look, boys, I know this bites hard, and I don't like to be the one to say you have to suck lemons, but I honestly don't have a choice on this one. Shit, I've never heard the Superintendent so riled up."

Holden nods. "Figured we'd have a little longer before they shut it down. Should have guessed."

***

An hour later and we're sitting at a café outside the station, Holden staring into his milkshake, me nursing an Irish coffee. In this moment, I'm too pissed at the system to hold any grudges against Holden and his Hawaiian-shirt-wearing, big-toe-toting, milkshake-staring insanity. In this moment, we're just a couple of cops who've been shafted by a bunch of assholes somewhere high enough up the ladder to control the weather.

"Isn't the first time this has happened," Holden says, still staring at his milkshake. "To be honest, I'm not even that surprised. It's just, to find something like that...it's incredible and we had him right there, talking."

I nod, take a sip of coffee. Then Holden does something I've never seen before. With a deep sigh, he picks up the milkshake and drinks. Downs the whole thing in a few seconds and then leans back in the seat patting his belly, a wide grin on his face.

I'm about to say something when he holds up a hand. "I know, I'll pay for it in a few minutes. Sometimes, though, you've just gotta bite the bullet."

"Was it good?"

He turns to me, still wearing a milk moustache and not bothering to wipe it off. He grins. "Never quite lives up to the expectation, but yeah, that was pretty fucking fantastic."

Even as he says the words, his smile falters and he grabs at his stomach.

"How long have you got before…"

He shrugs. "Ten minutes. Maybe less."

I take another swig of coffee and catch sight of something big and ugly out of the corner of my eye. A huge, suited thug and the dwarf in the three-piece are heading our way. It strikes me again just how big the brute with the shaved head is, but as they draw near, it's the other man that captures my full attention.

"Gentlemen," he says in a cultured British accent far too deep and rich for someone that small. "I'd like to thank you for your cooperation with this investigation. I understand how frustrating it can be to have your prize snatched away at the last minute like that."

Holden snarls, but I can't tell whether it's because of what the guy said or the work that milkshake is presently doing to his gut.

"Much of our work is highly classified, you understand, so I can't reveal much of it. However, seeing as you have already spoken to the Ethermancer and given that your efforts halted such profoundly abhorrent activities, I feel it is only fair to fill you in on some of the missing pieces."

Holden stands, holding his stomach and grimacing.

"You're leaving us, Agent Holden?" Giant asks.

Holden shrugs.

"I have a pressing appointment with the shitter. I figure Rook will fill me in on what I need to know."

Giant nods. "Indeed. Stirling work, as always, Agent Holden."

I watch Holden walk off and start slowly making the connections. *Agent*? So, Holden has moved up in the world it seems?

"Well, Detective, it seems that you and I are afforded a brief opportunity to chat."

He offers a hand and I shake it.

"Director King," he says, "though I tend to go by Giant. I am aware of the irony, of course."

The big brute behind him pulls out a chair and Giant sits down, handing his walking stick to Man-mountain. He pauses for a few seconds, gathers his thoughts.

"Now, where to begin? The man you apprehended is not local to this area, as you have undoubtedly guessed. I will not insult your intelligence by suggesting that what you have seen in that interrogation room is some kind of ruse or trickery. He is indeed a tattoo of sorts who inhabits and manipulates the host upon which he is situated.

"In his own vernacular, the so-called Ghost is a highly skilled Ethermancer—that is, someone skilled in the art of etheric manipulation. To simplify this, you may think of it as a kind of thaumaturgy or, to be more reductive and somewhat vulgar, *magic*. He comes from another realm, which it would do no good to discuss here as there is simply too much ground to cover and we will stray into classified paths very quickly.

"Suffice it to say that his sole purpose in our world is to create a portal or gateway back to his own world. He does not work alone but is part of a network of sycophants who serve a single mistress—and once again, I can give no more details. The method your Ghost was attempting to use in his quest to open a portal was the extraction of certain etheric essences from the human body and the application and amplification of those essences via the rather convoluted machinery you saw in his lair. It was for this purpose that the Ghost abducted so many poor souls."

I move to speak, but he holds up a hand and I stop short.

"Please, no questions. I have but a little time and should not strictly be discussing these matters with you. I have little more to say in any case. It remains for me to thank you once more for your efforts and to tell you that you have stopped something far more dangerous than you could ever know. You will have a great many questions, no doubt. But I urge you to put those aside and return to your normal life. Forget what you have seen here, and it will go well with you. Of course—" He pulls a card from his pocket and drops it onto the tabletop. "—there is another possibility. If you are not averse to working in areas which are somewhat less than conventional, we can always use a skilled operator such as yourself."

He stands, and the big man moves his chair aside.

"Not sure this type of thing sits well with me," I offer, honestly.

Giant nods. "True, our line of work is not for everyone. Holden has a unique mindset which makes him ideally suited to it."

"He's a grade-A loon," I say, "but you can't argue with his results."

Giant smiles a little. "True enough. Well, the choice is yours, of course. If you would like to pursue this line of work, contact the name on the card. If not, simply forget what you have seen and return to your usual work. Please bear in mind, though, that failure to keep the details of this case to yourself will bring swift consequences."

I nod. "Kind of figured that would be the case. I'll make sure the team keeps a tight lip."

"Excellent," he moves off, throwing me a casual wave as he leaves. "Farewell then, Detective."

***

A day later and the three of us are standing around Rodriguez's bed at St Margret's. Rickman is wearing a rare smile, and Pike is picking his way through the box of chocolates by Rodriguez's bed. The man himself is awake and alert. Doctors say he'll be fine to leave in a few days.

"They still dunno what it was that freak stuck me with," he says, rubbing at the small scar on his neck. "Man, it sent me on a trip though, you know. Like, crazy shit, you know?"

His eyes glaze over a little.

"It was like I was in a crazy dream…but it was too real, like I was really there…this big red city…"

7. The Couch

Tuesday March 2 / 3:00pm / Session 1

"It always starts the same way. I'm standing outside a huge gateway with a wall running around to either side. It's made of iron and clay bricks or maybe some kind of stone. Covered in red dust like everything in the city is. There are metal spikes on the top of the wall, but they look old and rusted out. The whole place is super old and worn-down. Almost falling apart in some places. I usually start off outside the walls in the outer part of the city. Kind of like slums, I guess."

"Describe how you feel when you first appear in this city."

"How I feel? That's kind of changed over time. I didn't really feel afraid the first time I went there. Just curious mostly. Like when you go traveling and you hit a new city. You're kind of just taking it all in, but you're also a little wary because it's all new and different."

"So, you felt largely at ease?"

"Yeah, I suppose so. In the beginning at least. There was just so much to see. So many people too. I kind of didn't have time to think about it first up. Just got caught up with the crowd and let it take me around the place. People shouting and shoving shit in front of my face. The whole place stank of spices and fruit mixed with cow shit. Thing is, I could actually smell it all. Like, it smelled real, you know?"

"And what of the people in this strange place? Do they interact with you in any way?"

"I can touch them, if that's what you mean, yeah. Well, they are usually doing most of the touching if you get my meaning. I mean, you ever been to India? It's like some of those markets in India, just packed full of people all crammed in against each other. The whole place felt so real. It wasn't like any dream I've had before. Most of my dreams are just the usual thing, you know, like forgetting to wear pants or handing in an essay late and getting reamed by the lecturer, that kind of thing."

"Anxiety dreams."

"Yeah, totally. I also get a lot of just boring ones that don't have any real meaning. Just stuff that happened at college the day before, or food. I get a hell of a lot of food dreams. Not like I'm a patty in a burger or anything, just dreams about all different kinds of food, and the odd sex dream too. Oh, I forgot the main thing! The city is completely red. Not like red like a tomato, but like an orange-red kind of colour. It's like red dust is everywhere in the air, all over the place. The buildings are mostly made of the same stuff as well. Damn, I can't believe I forgot that. It's like the main thing about the dream. Just red everywhere."

"You mentioned that you were not afraid initially. I gather that started to change as the dreams progressed?"

"It's kind of hard to explain. For a while, I was just too smashed to think anything was wrong. Just figured it was a normal dream like any other. A bit weird, but maybe I just ate some bad pizza or something. Dream kept coming back, though, and I kept popping up in the same place. It was all the same, but there were some differences too. Like I never really saw the same people. Except for some of the people selling fruit and shit in the markets. The other people, though, were all different. Some of them were a little freaky too."

"Freaky?"

"Just weird tattoos and piercings and shit. And, I dunno, the way they dressed. Some had strange masks. It was kind of like a carnival or something like that."

"And this began to frighten you as the dreams progressed?"

"Yeah, I guess so. I think it was all a bit overwhelming, you know?"

"Was there something specific about the city that made you feel afraid, or do you think this is more of a general anxiety caused by being thrust into such a vast crowd?"

"It's hard to explain, doc. I just started getting really scared that I was trapped. After the first few times, I figured out that I was dreaming. It felt like one of those lucid dreams where you can control what you're doing. Once I figured that out, I started to feel like maybe I wasn't going to wake up again. Felt like something was trying to keep me there, in the city. Freaky, I know, but it feels really real each time I end up there. I wander around for hours, trying to figure out a way to get back. It really freaks me out, doc. Just when I feel like I'm never gonna get out of that place, I wake up. Happens the same way each time."

***

Preliminary Notes:
Subject experiences a variety of lucid dreams which allows a limited degree of autonomy within the boundaries of a recurring geographical setting; a "red city" with medieval themes.

Subject feels anxiety at the prospect of being trapped in this dream world. Anxiety increases to climax shortly before waking.

Frequency of dreams has increased over the past few months.

No changes in work or social life in the past year which might explain dream anxiety. No deaths in the family or other obvious triggers. Subject is in third year of an education degree, stable relationship with a long-term girlfriend.

Suggest brief childhood regression to look for signs of a trigger earlier in the subject's life.

Tuesday March 9 / 3:00pm / Session 2
"Something's different, doc. It's hard to describe. I went to the city like normal, and it was all like I remembered. Same smells and same people; all of it was the same. Like the last few times, I realize that I'm dreaming and start freaking out. I try to find a way out of the city, and the anxiety starts getting to me. That's usually when I wake up. Only this time it was different. This time I just blacked out. I was still in the city somehow, but I wasn't awake. Like I said, it's hard to describe. I just remember being there but also not being awake. Or, maybe I was awake, but just surrounded by blackness? I woke up with a bastard of a headache and a big gap in my memory."

"And this is markedly different to the other occasions when you've experienced the dream?"

"Hell yeah. I can normally remember everything. Like, really clearly. Not this time though. Just a couple of minutes and then it all goes black. I know I was still in there though; still stuck in that city. I've tried really thinking about it, but when I try to remember what happened, I feel kind of terrified. Feels like something has been scrubbed from my memory, and when I try to get to it, I freak the hell out. The other dreams I could cope with. After I wake up, things go back to normal after a couple of hours. After this latest one, though, I feel anxious all the time. I got stuck in the elevator on the way up here. Had to have an old lady talk me off of it."

"I see. Well, for the human mind, trauma is trauma. It doesn't typically differentiate between the real and the imagined. Both evince the same effects upon stress levels, emotional and physiological responses, and so on. So, if you've imagined something terrifying, it's reasonable to assume that your body would undergo the same kinds of reactions as real, tangible danger. Anxiety is a perfectly normal result of such trauma."

"But what does it all mean though? Why can't I remember any of it?"

"Selective amnesia is the psyche's way of protecting itself. If you have dreamt something profoundly traumatic, your mind won't let you face that trauma head on. It's far more likely to subvert or twist that traumatic event into something unrecognizable. Your red city, for instance, may be your psyche's way of protecting itself against a real or imagined trauma. There may be something in your past which has triggered a connection to the present, and these dreams are your mind's attempt to cover over the painful reality of that central trauma."

"Okay, but why the sudden blackout? I mean, I can remember right up to a point, and then it just goes black."

"It might be best to think of this as a protective mechanism. It's the mind's way of protecting itself, changing the story you might say. Only, on this occasion the trauma is so vivid that your mind has simply blacked out the episode all together."

"Okay, doc, so what do I do?"

"Well, that's the question, isn't it? To put it bluntly, we need to uncover that which is hidden. We need to uncover the trauma at the centre of your dream anxiety and *name* it. We need to give it an identity, and by naming the trauma we can better understand it and, ultimately, master it. This won't be a simple or short process, but I can assure you that I've taken a great many patients through this process, and the results are overwhelmingly positive."

"Right, okay. Well let's do it then, I guess."

"Now, normally we would start with childhood, but I think it best to begin with your most recent dream as that is causing the most trouble. To uncover the trauma, which is driving your dream angst, we need to uncover that part of the dream which your psyche has chosen to keep hidden. There are a few ways we could do this, however, I'd suggest we attempt a mild form of hypnosis. It's a perfectly safe way to explore your dream world and perhaps uncover some aspects of that world which are hidden for the moment. I'll be with you throughout the session, and you should be able to explore the darkened regions of the dream without the same fear or emotive potency."

"So, it's safe then? I'm not gonna get stuck in there or anything?"

"It's perfectly safe and, no, you're not going to get stuck anywhere. You'll be here with me the whole time, and you won't actually be dreaming, per se. Think of it as a little journey through some of the rooms of your mind. We're going to walk through those rooms together with a torch to see what is causing you such anxiety, that's all. I'll just bring you into a shallow meditative state, and we'll go for a stroll through this red city of yours. How does that sound?"

"Okay. But you'll pull me out if shit starts getting too nasty, yeah?"

"Indeed, I will. If things move beyond mild discomfort, I'll simply wake you from the meditative state and we can move on to a different activity for a while."

"All right. Let's do it then, I suppose."

"Just lay back and relax. I'm going to twirl this medallion in front of your eyes for a while, and I want you to concentrate on the way it spins to and fro. Just concentrate on the spinning and on the image of the butterfly that seems to flap its wings as the medallion spins. That's it…spinning to and fro…breathe deeply."

"…"

"Now, I want you to enter a light, meditative sleep, but you'll still be able to hear my voice and talk to me while you're sleeping. I want you to take me to this city, guide me through it step by step. Just describe what you see and hear as you walk through."

"…"

"Jason?"

"…mmm…"

"Okay, Jason, I want you to take me to the red city and walk me through your dream nice and slowly, okay. You are my eyes and ears in there, so you must describe everything just as clearly as you can. Do you understand?"

"…okay…"

"Good. Now, where are you presently?"

"I'm at the city gate. There are people everywhere and they look funny. It's like a medieval fair. There's a guy trying to sell something to me, a clay pot or something. He's shoving it in my face, but I don't have any money."

"Good, good Jason, now let's start moving through the city, shall we? You can leave the pot seller behind now."

"Okay. I'm walking through the gate. It's huge. This whole place smells like animal shit. It's very crowded. There are animals and people everywhere."

"Describe these animals to me, Jason."

"That one's kind of like a sheep, but it's neck is way too long. There's a fox with two tails and a bunch of goats, but their faces are all weird."

"Okay, let's keep walking shall we, Jason."

"Okay. I'm moving through the street, toward the market. It's super dusty. I can feel it all in my hair and my mouth. Shit, there's that guy again."

"What guy?"

"The guy. The beggar. I've seen him before. Big fat bastard and I don't think he's got any clothes, but the fat is covering up his junk. He sits there painting with his toes. I think he's too fat to stand up."

"Why don't you go and take a closer look, Jason? Describe to me what you see."

"Okay. I'm walking closer. Damn, he smells horrible. He's painting… oh…it's the city. He's painting little pictures of the city on some kind of clay plate. He's using his toes to paint. Looks pretty good for someone with… Oh fuck!"

"What is it, Jason?"

"Shit! Damn, I forgot. The other guy's just turned and given me the stink eye. Shit, he's got a mean look to him."

"What other guy, Jason?"

"The fat guy. The beggar, he's like, joined at the back with a scrawny dude that looks like his nose has fallen off. They're like Siamese twins, or whatever, but joined right down the back. It's like one guy's sucked all the life out of the other one. Like the fat guy is using all the nutrients and the skeleton guy is just hanging on."

"Okay, Jason, why don't we move on? Unless there's anything else you'd like to explore with the beggar?"

"Yeah, no, let's keep going. The guy's still giving me the stink eye anyway. Creepy fucker. Okay, so I'm walking again up through a really narrow street. There are people everywhere, and they smell like they've been swimming in pig shit. Some kind of noise coming from around the corner, like bells or something like that. Not sure what it is, but everyone is running fast to get to it."

"Let's follow the bells, Jason, see where they lead."

"Okay, it's... There's some kind of other market. Yeah, it's just a market. They're selling fish and bread and a bunch of other stuff. The bell is still ringing but I can't see anything yet... Oh shit."

"What is it?"

"Bell just stopped ringing and... I dunno, I'm standing next to some kind of wagon. There's a..."

"Jason?"

"..."

"Jason, what's going on?"

"I dunno... It's just black. Someone is pushing me, and I can't see anything."

"Who are you with?"

"Can't see, he's got a bag over my head. Must be big though. I think... he's carrying me over his shoulders."

"Where is the man taking you?"

"..."

"Jason?"

"..."

"Jason, where are you now?"

"Okay, the bag just came off...there's... I'm lying on something, like I'm standing up, but they've got me strapped to a rack or a metal bed. I'm somewhere dark... There's a little bit of light but not much... Smells like chemicals and...my hands are strapped down... I can't... Oh, Jesus!"

"What is it, Jason, what do you see?"

"Jesus Fuck! Fucking fuck! FUCK!"

"Tell me what you're seeing, Jason. You're perfectly safe. Just describe—"

"FUCK! I can't fucking.... Fuck, get it away from me you... FUCK!"

"Okay, breathe deeply, Jason. I'm going to click my fingers three times and then you're going to slowly wake up from your dream. You'll feel peaceful and calm, and you'll join me in my office, okay?"

click click click

"Jason? Are you okay? How do you feel?"

Notes:

Subject is experiencing heightened anxiety due to traumatic nature of the red city dream. Conducted mild hypnosis on subject and moved through dream in order to locate traumatic core. Subject was abducted within the dream and woke to something too profoundly confronting to describe.

Subject emerged from hypnosis with mild loss of memory. Subject had no ability to recall the events which had transpired in the session. It is as if the central trauma of the dream has brought about an amnesia that moves beyond the dream itself and into the real world. Subject remembers walking through the door for our appointment but can recall nothing past this point.

Next steps are to attempt a dream walk-through a second time but record the results. I will also bring the case to Dr. Reichmacher for a second opinion.

Thursday March 11 / 10:00am / Session 3 [Emergency Session]
"I feel like I'm losing my shit. I keep... I keep seeing stuff. This guy was following me. A guy in a hoodie, but I couldn't see his face. Just his eyes; they were glowing red, and I could feel them staring into me."

"You saw this figure following you in the street?"

"Not just in the street. I see it sometimes reflected in glass or in the mirror. He's just standing behind me, staring at me."

"Do you recognize the figure?"

"No. I can remember seeing him anywhere before. Doc, you gotta help me, man. I'm freaking the fuck out. Everywhere I go I see this guy. It's like he wants something from me. Like he's got unfinished business. Maybe some kind of ghost haunting deal? Jesus, listen to me. I'm losing my mind here, doc. It's freaking Kelly out too. I try to keep it under control, but it just hits me every now and then. I'm not sleeping either. Too damned afraid. Jesus, I pissed myself the other day just thinking about it. But I can't even remember what I'm so afraid of."

"Okay, let's discuss this figure you keep seeing."

"I can't... No, no, no. Just... I can't face it again, doc. You've just gotta help me... I can't..."

Notes:
Subject attended emergency session in an extreme state of anxiety. Symptoms include lack of sleep, hallucinations, mild somatic symptoms (rash, itchiness, etc.), and terror-induced urination. Subject was unable to

continue session due to subject falling into a mild catatonic state brought on by preliminary discussion of hallucinations experienced as a result of repetitive dream anxiety. Subject taken to St. Hellen's to undergo observation.

Raised case with Dr. Reichmacher and discussed rapid decline in subject's mental stability. Very few similar accounts could be found, other than those which involve significant drug usage.

Tuesday March 16 / 3:00pm / Session 4
Notes:
Subject failed to attend scheduled session. After initial overnight observation at St. Hellen's, subject's catatonic state receded. Subject was able to make contact via phone and arrange a follow-up appointment, however, subject has not attended.

No response to follow-up phone call.

Thursday March 18 / Journal Entry
I have chosen to record these details in my own journal rather than the official file notes due to the frankly bizarre nature of what I am about to write. Never in all my years have I encountered such a perplexing and unsatisfactorily concluded case. The young man who came to me only a few short weeks ago seemed well-adjusted, bright, and in good physical health. His only complaint was the suffering of a reoccurring dream which seemed to be producing mild anxiety.

In a remarkably short timeframe (I'm unsure whether the subject's rapid descent might have been exacerbated by therapy itself, though one certainly hopes not) the subject developed excessive, debilitating symptoms which seemed to manifest around a central amnesia. During a limited hypnosis session, I was able to guide the subject through the dream world with remarkable clarity, until the subject (i.e. the subject's dream-self) was apprehended by some agency or other. While further events were shrouded in ambiguity, I get the sense of some kind of traumatic scene played out within the dream—a scene so vivid that the subject's mind has interpreted this as real, experienced trauma, and has thus set about defending itself by means of a profound amnesia.

As with other such traumas, in this case the buried memories have found their way to the surface by means of a series of escalating symptoms. What is significant about these symptoms is their rapidity of development. Symptoms that would usually develop over weeks and months appeared to spring up almost overnight, and in clusters (both psychological and somatic).

A more profound and puzzling aspect to the case was the subject's sudden disappearance. Family members and friends alike were unable to supply any reasonable explanation for the absence. The young man in question did not live alone, but with several other students. After his admission to St. Hellen's on my recommendation, the subject's girlfriend insisted on staying with him, sleeping on a mattress on the floor in the subject's room (the subject's family feared suicide, though the subject never voiced an inclination toward self-harm). According to the subject's girlfriend, the young man went to sleep in his usual manner and was simply not there the following morning. The door to the bedroom had been locked on the girlfriend's insistence, and none of the others in the house heard the young man leave the premises. Likewise, there are security cameras in the entryway to the apartment which, I am reliably informed, showed no sign of the subject exiting the premises.

Despite these profound oddities, an exhaustive search was undertaken by friends, relatives, and the local authorities, but to no avail. No trace of the young man could be found.

I confess, I have no answers to this problem. I am perplexed beyond reason, and my confusion has been exacerbated by a case I discovered this past week in a pile of old papers in my study. Penned by an obscure practitioner from the 1970s (a Dr. Fillstrum who practised in Vienna at the time) the paper outlines a case wherein a young woman has a reoccurring dream of a "red city." The dream seems to haunt the young lady, and, over a period of weeks, symptoms begin to develop (anxiety, rashes, hallucinations—not dissimilar to those of my vanishing subject). Fillstrum attempted to regress the young lady but found nothing of consequence. Her dreams became more and more vivid, though, to the point where she could no longer separate dream from reality.

After several months, the young woman simply disappeared—vanished from her bed without a trace. The good doctor made a point of emphasizing that the young woman was staying with her family, who insisted that the house was locked up tight for the entire night.

I have no idea how to proceed from here, nor whether I should even attempt to pursue these mysteries any further. All of this can be explained by simple coincidence, of course. A little forgetfulness here and there, a smattering of exaggeration; it can all be explained away quite reasonably. Yet there is an eerie air of veracity to Fillstrum's tale which corresponds too closely to my own experiences. I am left with only questions.

Is there something to this red city? Does it reflect some deep anxiety within our collective unconsciousness? Are there other cases of dream related disappearances?

More troubling than any of this, is my latest experience. It is perhaps due to the long hours I have spent devoted to thought about the red city and these vanishing subjects. It is perhaps due to my own stress levels and the pressures of an unforgiving vocation.

Last night I had a dream. I woke in a city, red-walled and crumbling.

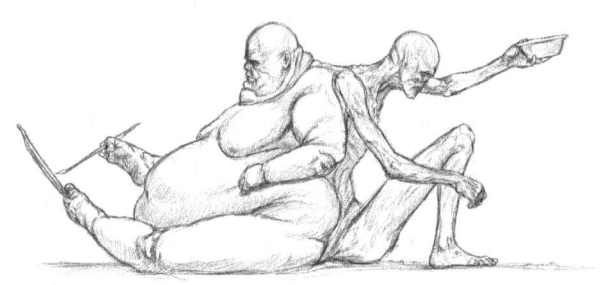

TWINNED BEGGAR

8. Idleskein

The young witch stands above a pitted gravestone, fingers twisted into arcane forms while she recites the careful Latin phrases used to invoke ancient power. The moon reaches its apex, and she twists her fingers in intricate patterns above a bronze bowl sitting on the gravestone, its contents glimmering in the moonlight.

The smell of rotten meat and pungent herbs hits her from below, bringing bile to the back of her throat. She forces back the urge to vomit.

Tonight. It must be tonight.

"It won't work, you know," someone says from behind her.

The voice cuts like a blade, dashing the young witch's concentration and setting her heart into a gallop. She breathes deeply, resisting the urge to turn around.

"Is that right?" she asks, her hands suddenly shaking.

"Yeah, you've got way too much Nightshadow in there. You might get a little bit of a light show and maybe a tremor or two, but you're not gonna raise good old gran from the dead with that little number."

She spins to see a raven-haired woman in tight leather grinning broadly from her perch above a neighbouring gravestone. Without preamble, the woman slips off the stone and walks casually toward her, holding out a hand.

"My name's Jade," the woman says.

"Willow," the young witch replies warily, shaking hands with the older woman.

"Jesus, Willow, your heart is beating like crazy. It's okay, you can relax. I was the same when I tried my first spell. Almost peed my pants when something actually happened."

Willow frowns. "You're…"

"Of the craft," Jade says, nodding. "Twenty years this spring. It's been in my family for generations."

She raises her hands and spins slowly. "Every once in a while, I come back to my old stomping ground, for nostalgic reasons. I must tell you, I didn't expect to meet a budding witch out here on a Thursday night."

Willow opens her mouth, but no reply is forthcoming. Jade draws closer, lifting a hand to trace the line of Willow's vibrant red hair as it trails across her cheek.

"You remind me of myself when I was a girl," Jade says. "So pretty, and so naive."

Willow opens her mouth to reply, but Jade cuts her off with a casual flick of her wrist.

"Look, no pressure, but if you want to know more about this—want to know how the craft really works—come by The Stray Cat around eight tomorrow night. I'll introduce you to the other girls and we'll have some food, it'll be fun."

She smiles with something approaching seduction, winks, and then turns and strolls off into the night, her hips swaying hypnotically. Willow watches her go, feeling the warmth in her chest start to abate. She turns around to the bowl of herbs and mystical titbits and backhands it onto the grass. Jade had been wrong, of course. She wasn't trying to raise her grandma from the grave, or even bring back a pet cat. Nor was this Willow's first spell. This was merely the latest in a series of mystical experiments, born from a few scraps of paper saved from a tragic fire years earlier. The spells were incomplete, she knew, but something inside drove her to find their full meaning.

The particular spell Willow had been working on this night was intended to bring life to the dying, rather than raise the dead. She had selected a wilting rose for the attempt, which now lay in a sorry state atop the grave. Willow smiled, thinking how ironic it would have been if the spell had actually raised someone from the dead.

The following night saw Willow reluctantly in attendance at The Stray Cat, a bar on the outskirts of town and apparent hangout for a circle of witches who shared a penchant for leather jackets and Appletinis. In the nights that followed, Willow came to know Jade and her cadre. Married to money and with far too much time on their hands, the world of magic served primarily as a convenient distraction for the would-be witches. Yet, for all this, there was power within the group, if somewhat lacklustre.

Under Jade's guidance, Willow became more effective at the construction and execution of minor spells. The other women were astounded by how quickly the new member of their circle was able to learn new skills, showering praise on Willow as though she were a puppy or a team mascot.

She endured the incessant blather of the witches, listening to their prattle about upcoming trips to the Hamptons, a husband's well-deserved promotion, and banal gossip about this or that acquaintance. Willow smiled and played the good little meek girl, gaining what experience she could and enduring the idiot attentions of these women that she despised.

After three months, Willow had decided that she could learn no more from Jade and her leather-clad coven. They had helped her focus her power, but the grand sum of their efforts was a simple spell which addled the memories of a well-built bartender with which the cadre had become infatuated. Willow craved more than parlour tricks and base manipulations. There was something *real* here, lying beneath the surface, and she was determined to get to the heart of it.

On the night when she planned to make her break, a new figure emerged from the fray, forever altering the trajectory of Willow's life.

***

"Bullshit!"

The word comes from a shadowed corner of the bar where a slim figure sits hunched above a glass of beer. As one, the women turn, staring daggers. Willow squints, trying to make out the scrawny figure sitting in the corner.

"When we want your opinion, we'll ask for it," Jade says, acid dripping from her tongue.

Through the shadowed corner, Willow makes out a pair of dark eyes staring from beneath a tattered, wide-brimmed hat. The man speaks in the raspy tone of a long-time smoker, as though each word has to squeeze through tattered lungs and a shredded larynx to be freed. The withered man seems to be addressing her directly.

"You can waste your time with this gaggle of simpletons if you wish," he says, lifting his drink and taking a small sip, "but you'll never learn anything worth knowing, and you'll never get answers to the questions that are clawing at your mind."

A series of hissed breaths and profanities surround the coven. Jade puts a hand on Willow's shoulder. "Just ignore him, sweetie, he's harmless."

"Who is he?" Willow asks.

Jade waves a hand dismissively. "Just a tramp, darling. Nothing to worry about. He's not right in the head, that one. Calls himself *Idol-skin* if you can believe it."

Moira, another of the cadre, leans in conspiratorially. "They say he turned up here twenty years ago. Walked into this pub covered in dirt and blood and completely naked. He was ranting and raving and the police had to lock him up. I think he ended up doing a stint in Hillview for a few years, but they released him, and now he just wanders around begging for money and talking nonsense."

The sharp sound of scraping wood cuts through the air. The coven turns as one to see the tramp standing at full height, brushing at the lapels of his tattered jacket with exaggerated import. He wears the dishevelled remnants of a three-piece suit, complemented with a pair of old sandals and a dark, wide brimmed hat that droops with age and lethargy.

"These others are nothing," he says in his gravelly tone, "but you, my dear, have something about you. You see it, don't you? You see through the vain concoctions and pretence? You know that there is more to this than mere chicanery and self-obsession."

He takes a step forward, walking with far more poise than a man in this state should be able to manage.

"Oh, go back to your corner, won't you," Jade spits.

"Ignore the words," Idleskein says, lifting a hand and making it into a bony fist. "The words are nonsense. What matters is intent, clarity of mind, and the mancer's gift, of course."

He continues to walk, taking a series of slow deliberate steps. Jade stands, moving to intercept but, at the moment the tramp opens his fist she and the other witches fall to the ground in gruesome unison, their bodies suddenly limp.

"The blood," Idleskein continues, still walking toward Willow, "is where the greatest power lies, but there are a great many hazards which follow the use of such mancery."

Willow turns to the fallen woman, panic clawing at her.

"Fret not," the hobo says, drawing Willow's attention with a voice that seems to radiate power and authority. Within moments she is face to face with the man, feeling his hands on her shoulders, staring into cold, dark eyes. "They will sleep for a time and wake with no memory of what has passed."

It's only then that Willow realizes everyone in the bar has keeled over. She's standing alone, staring into the eyes of a dishevelled madman and unable to look away. Somewhere deep inside, in the part of her which aches for real magic, for real power, a spark ignites once more.

***

In years to come it will be that moment back at The Stray Cat—with Jade and her fellow wannabe witches lying unconscious and the madman standing in front of her—that will stand as the defining point of Willow's life. Intrigued by the man who called himself *Idleskein*—a name whose meaning she would never come to fully understand—Willow follows him out of the bar and to an abandoned hovel on the outskirts of town. In the coming days and nights, he teaches her about a form of magic which is both powerful and terrifying. Idleskein's words are opaque and infuriatingly philosophical, yet Willow perseveres with his odd lessons, knowing that her power grows greater with each lesson learned.

The mancer's art, Idleskein informs her, revolves around the manipulation of the ether—that invisible bond which unites all matter and determines the form and shape of all things. Her mind calls back to basic biology and her earliest knowledge of DNA. In Willow's mind, the principles are similar—Idleskein's magic is simply the manipulation of some kind of cosmic DNA. It is a real-time twisting of the things that currently *are* into things that *might be*.

She learns that the words and symbols Jade and her coven held so dear were of little value to real etheric manipulation. Knowledge, will, and the gift of ethermancy, as Idleskein calls it, are what truly matters where magic is concerned.

Within weeks, Willow is bending the very fabric of inanimate objects; transforming green grass into red nettles, warping solid metal, and causing shadows to dance and become solid. With each lesson her body aches, her mind reels, yet her hunger for more is ravenous.

"It is with blood that true ethermancy is most effective," Idleskein insists. "The ether is bound more tightly with the blood of the living than any other substance. It is, shall we say, *charged* with life, and that combustive element gives blood its etheric vitality."

With this and many more increasingly obscure lessons, the hobo wizard instructs Willow, day by day. She finds herself growing more powerful, despite her inability to grasp the intricacies of his lessons. It is as though his words themselves are spells which wrap themselves around her mind and unlock her potential.

Of the man himself, she learns little. Each day he is dressed in the same tattered suit, reeking of alcohol and tobacco and looking thinner and more unwell each time she sees him. Yet, despite his physical degradation, his spirit seems roused. With each new lesson and each new success, he grows more animated, more excitable.

After several weeks of intense work and great progress, the strange tutor begins to unveil a little of his true self. Willow learns that he is not of this world, but of another place where ethermancy is common, yet outlawed by those in power. The world of his origin is a harsh, unforgiving land, filled with grief and misfortune. Yet, as he opens up to her, Willow sees the longing in his eyes, to return to the dry crimson deserts of his homeland.

"There is a means," he explains one day, "a means of affecting a return to the Traumwelt, to my beloved city. It is a dangerous thing, and I have little time left to attempt it. Yet, perhaps with your help, I might achieve that which I desire."

As the lessons continue, Willow begins to see the world around her in fluid terms. She sees not only the *actual*, but also the *possible*, and her abilities grow so profoundly that such possibilities are no longer beyond her. The penultimate lesson which Idleskein teaches takes Willow beyond the realm of traditional sorcery to a place reserved for story and legend.

A small cat, hit by a car and long dead, is placed before her while Idleskein watches from the shadows close by. Already, she can see the weaving of etheric strands which might bring back the feline traveller. She works quickly, exercising her will upon the lifeless corpse, making connections of etheric energy, transmogrifying base substances and infusing life where degeneration has set it. It takes an hour of her will, but the time passes for Willow in a matter of moments. When she is done, the cat wakes, darts off into the corner of the room and sets about calmly preening itself as though such cleaning is the most sensible response to sudden resurrection.

With that single act, Willow has become something more than a mere tinkerer in magic. Willow has become an ethermancer.

***

"The food, the porridge you've been feeding me. There's something in it, isn't there?"

The hobo wizard nods. "An accelerant to your abilities. A necessary factor."

"What is it though? If I stop eating your food, will the magic fade away?"

He shakes his head, smiles crookedly. "You are an ethermancer now, child. That which has grown within you cannot be undone. The gifts you have fought to apprehend are yours to keep. I urge you to eat but a little longer, that you may help me in my quest to return to my homeland. But once my quest is ended, you will go on as you are now, a mancer in your own right."

Trust has grown between them, built over months of discovery and etheric development. Yet, even so, Willow can't help the feeling that she is being manipulated in some way. There is more to all of this than what Idleskein is willing to speak of—other, perhaps darker, motives at play. In the coming days she begins to squirrel away a part of herself; to sequester some small part of will and emotional investment, away from the wizard and his plans. A small reservoir of etheric energy is stored somewhere within her mind, somewhere separate from the daily exercises and experiments Idleskein takes her through. It is a small thing at first, a simple, protective mechanism. But it grows steadily.

Three months pass after the resurrection of the cat, and Willow's abilities grow exponentially. Idleskein begins to reveal a little more of his plan to return to the Traumwelt. He takes her to an abandoned cabin in nearby scrubland, to a bunker hidden beneath the shack, a sizable room furnished with a variety of surprising amenities. At one end of the bunker is a small chamber with a large, ornately framed mirror against the wall. A series of clockwork mechanisms and steam-powered contraptions are hooked up to the mirror, powered by a small boiler in a lower room within the bunker.

The hobo wizard explains that one cannot simply open a portal to the Traumwelt, that the usual method of transgress is solely via dreams and is rarely predictable or guaranteed. He explains that some people are naturally susceptible to travel between realms and that a very few are able to affect a permanent crossing, however, such crossings are entirely without the volition of the dreamer and are simply a matter of chance.

"Through the application of what we might term *science*, though of an entirely different order to that practiced in this world, we may be able to artificially engender an opening to the Traumwelt. It will take considerable etheric intent to open such a portal, but such force is insufficient to maintain a crossing. These devices you see before you are intended to stabilize the path between worlds, to ensure a degree of safe trespass."

Idleskein goes on to inform Willow that there are grave dangers to such a crossing, and a significant price must be paid for the privilege. Beings of terrible power inhabit the way between worlds. They are, according to the wizard, capricious and jealous of their territory. To attempt a crossing by the simple use of ethermancy would be akin to lighting a beacon to these intra-worldly deities—blood in the water.

In front of the large mirror, Willow notes, is a peculiar clockwork mechanism attached to a plain wooden chair. The mechanism appears to fit itself to a subject's head, some kind of clockwork-powered helmet, whose purpose she can only guess at. When she asks Idleskein of the device's purpose he is sketchy and distracted in his reply.

"For one to cross, another must stay behind," he says, wringing his hands distractedly. "While I move beyond this world, you must remain to keep the portal open. The device will serve to keep us connected for those few moments as I traverse the way between worlds."

With a level of animation she has not witnessed in the man previously, Idleskein sets about stoking the boiler and setting the machinery to action.

The portal machine stutters to life, gears and cogs whirring slowly at first until a smooth rhythm is reached. For some minutes, Idleskein works a series of dials and levers to the side of the mirror device, tweaking settings with the manic focus of a mad scientist. His eyes are wide and filled with zeal as he goes about his work.

"We will attempt a crossing this very night," he says excitedly. "I have taught you all that I can, and you have sufficient knowledge to set out upon your own path."

Willow frowns. "So that's it? That's all there is?"

"No, child. There is far more, but alas, I cannot teach it. I must return to my native land or risk withering to dust and ash. If I do not affect a crossing this night, I may not have another chance."

"Okay, so what the hell do I do then? I mean, I've learned a lot. I can even bring back the dead, if the circumstances are right. But what do I do with that? I can't go public and, from what you've already told me, it's not likely I'll be able to find many other ethermancers on this planet."

He smiles, putting a bony hand to her shoulder. "We must all choose our own path, child. Have I ever led you to believe anything different? Still, there is one last gift I intend to give you."

He moves to the far end of the main bunker, leading Willow to a large wooden trunk filled to the brim with neatly bundled stacks of hundred-dollar bills. Willow's eyes try to dislodge themselves from their sockets.

"What the hell? There must be millions in there?"

Idleskein nods.

Willow bends down to pick up a stack of hundred-dollar bills, not quite believing what she's seeing. "I don't understand? All this time you've been walking around looking like something someone has scraped of their shoe, and you've got millions of dollars just sitting here? You couldn't even have spent a little money on some clean clothes?"

He laughs and, for the first time she can remember, seems genuinely happy. "I have no need of money," he says, closing the chest. "I seek only to return to the red city. So, I leave this to you, a final gift of thanks for your aid."

The gift throws Willow off balance. As Idleskein sets about making final preparations to the machines, her mind keeps returning to the pile of cash at the other end of the bunker—a fortune, *her* fortune. It wasn't a life purpose, but it would certainly help her get started.

"You will need to channel pure etheric energy toward the mirror," the wizard says, directing Willow to sit in the chair and attaching the clockwork mechanism to her head. "You need not perform a specific task, simply direct your power to the mirror, and I will do the rest." He straps her into the chair so gently that she misses seeing the bronze barbs attached to the wrist straps and clockwork helmet. The small metal barbs prick her skin a little, but there is only minimal discomfort.

"One final thing," Idleskein says, "there must be blood to open the portal. Both yours and mine, though only a little, I assure you."

As he speaks, he runs a crooked nail down the palm of his right hand and cuts into the flesh, leaving a bright crimson mark. He moves to the clockwork machine and drips a few drops of blood into a small metal receptacle to one side of the helmet contraption.

Idleskein instructs Willow to begin channelling etheric energy, and she does as he asks. The power comes quickly and in far greater potency than she has previously been able to muster. Indigo strands of etheric energy are wrenched from her body, absorbed into the shimmering surface of the mirror. Idleskein tweaks a few settings on the machine, then bows to her, a curiously formal farewell.

"Goodbye, dearest Willow. I thank you for your sacrifice."

As he turns to walk through the mirror, there is a hard edge to his smile. His eyes show the slight edges of what might be disdain or distaste. Momentary panic sets in as Willow watches the wizard move through the mirror and into the murky purple light beyond. Something grabs at her wrists, ankles and neck. Invisible teeth bite as one, cutting through flesh and sucking at her blood with vampiric brutality. The pain is blinding and instant. Willow feels as though she is being flayed alive, stripped of every ounce of vitality. The clockwork machine drains her blood with cruel efficiency, while etheric power still pours from Willow's body in great gushes. She screams, but the breath is taken from her, and no sound escapes her lips.

All at once, she sees the mirror device as it truly is; not a portal between worlds, not an amplifier of etheric power, but a snare, a vampiric pump to drain her life-force. That small inkling of deception she had sensed in Idleskein blooms into monstrous proportion. All of the hours spent learning magic, the weeks and months of practice and gruelling work, it had all been for one horrifically banal purpose. She was no ethermancer, no grand magician or dark witch. She was a battery, pure and simple.

In the moments before the last embers of life are drained from her body, Willow sees a vague image open up at the centre of the mirror. Murky, and warped by etheric forces, an image emerges of a gaunt figure in a tattered suite standing in a red desert. In her final moment, she imagines the figure bowing, a wicked grin on his sallow face.

***

Time bleeds, melds, warps.

Etheric power swirls, invasive and insistent.

Flesh and blood are infused, charged with etheric force.

Willow that was, is no more, yet some part remains. The part that she had cunningly squirrelled away survives the tumult and emerges in the aftermath. She remembers herself but is no longer bound to the fleshly vehicle of her former self.

She is reborn, transformed by the flow of etheric force and the thaumaturgic serendipity of circumstance.

I feel it, the power coursing through every fibre and sinew... I am...I was, Willow... I live...and yet all is made new... I see with eyes that are not my own... I feel more than the senses of my flesh... I am infinitely more and somewhat less than I was... I am...

Ethera.

9. Excerpt from "Tritease on Rust and her Surrounding Hamlets"

Built upon the fabric of dreams, its landscape responds to the etheric cognition of those living in the waking world. Consider the largest and most profoundly imagined cities of the waking world, such as New York, Beijing, London. These "real" cities have their doppelgangers in the Traumwelt, cities founded on the raw fabric of dreams.

When New York sleeps, and many of its inhabitants play out dream scenarios among the streets, byways, and apartments of that great city, so the Traumwelt's shadowy representation of New York grows more substantial in form. Conversely, when the people of New York wake, its cousin in the Traumwelt grows ill-defined, warped by its lack of concrete substance.

So it is that the towns, hamlets, and cities of the Traumwelt ebb and flow with the nightly dream patterns of those who live in the waking world. Where one is night, the other is filled with substance and veracity, and conversely, where one is day, the other is made monstrous—a twisted facsimile of the original, fraught with insubstantiality.

Only Rust resists the flux of which the Traumwelt is comprised, held fast by the resolve of the Red Queen and bound inextricably to her etheric aura. The growth and distortions of that great city are of a far more organic order, decay mixed with the tidal movements of its inhabitants.

Over the centuries, that same solidity has begun to stretch out, like the roots of a tree, spreading to other cities and hamlets throughout the Traumwelt with the diaspora of demigods (such as the Clockwork God and his followers). Such reluctant permanence has made possible the migration of peoples, the rise of mercantile industries and the emergence of lesser principalities. Yet, for all their growth and development, it is to Rust alone that dreamers are drawn—pulled by some ineffable etheric force through the portal of dreams into the crimson land.

There are, it is said, vast swaths of land to the north and southeast of the red city which sit in a state of minimal flux—great cities which cling to the fabric of the dreamworld, borrowing their solidity from the Red Queen and her fellow demigods. The dispossessed and disenfranchised have begun a migration of sorts to these semi-stable lands, moving in such numbers that entire societies have emerged in these regions, each with their own hamlets, rulers, and politics.

While little is known of the Shackled Man prior to his emergence as leader of the rebellion, it is believed that he spent a great deal of time wandering these semi-permanent lands, gaining a name for himself as a feared mercenary in the region. Over a decade or so, the fabled Shadowfang and her shackled benefactor began to stake their claim over the red wastes—guns for hire in a lawless expanse of cruelty and desperation. The ebb and flow of power in those lands was guided on a knife edge held by the Shackled Man.

More impressive perhaps than his mercenary endeavours, is the stand at Baronsville—a small hamlet of no more than two or three hundred souls, beset by shadowspawn and very nearly wiped from the map. Again, little has survived to outline the details of what transpired at Baronsville. We have but scraps of information and a highly inflated oral tradition to rely on. Whatever the truth of the matter, we can say with confidence that Baronsville does indeed exist to this day due to the deadly arts of a pair of assassin/mercenaries—a tall gunslinger with a broken shackle on each wrist and a young girl with fierce eyes and deadly skill with a rifle.

One final locale which deserves mention is the expansive caverns of the Underwood. Sitting some few dozen feet below the great Salt Sea (a vast wasteland of shimmering salt crystal found north and east of the red city—a flat expanse devoid of life and water) the Underwood forms its own peculiar cosmos, replete with all manner of animal life and more than a few indigenous inhabitants of the hunter gatherer ilk. Richly furnished with hardy flora, the Underwood has long been pillaged for its wood and water, though the countless years of thievery have left barely a mark on the region, so vast and unyielding is its scope.

- The Chronicler

Rust City by Karthik Arvind Kumar

The Fleshworks by Karthik Arvind Kumar

10. The Script Rebellion

Litmus Shule sits despondently above his apparatus, his many digits plying their trade along the complex, interlocking network of pulleys, levers, and buttons which comprise the mechanical heart of the Litmus Inkery. Established years earlier, the inkery had come to occupy pride of place among the many and varied artisan stalls and curiosities that lined the streets and byways of the trade district, clinging to the city's arteries like food sticking to the gullet of a dying behemoth.

Litmus himself had founded the Inkery a decade or so after he arrived upon the crimson shore. Torn from his old life by a cruel twist of fate, the little man's ineluctable optimism had driven him to build a home and business for himself amid the alien spires and dusty streets of Rust. Gifted at the calligrapher's art, Litmus Shule had quickly distinguished himself among the lesser artisans and scribesmen of the city, producing inks and parchments of such distinguished quality that his work eventually piqued the interest of the city's ruling bureaucracy; the Administratum.

Weighty commissions began to flow in his direction during those early years, such that he was forced to expand his enterprise and take on a small but dedicated workforce to meet the sudden demands of Rust's considerable bureaucracy. It was at the height of his success that Litmus

Shule chanced upon a young woman from the old country who had only recently set foot upon the crimson streets of the red city; she was brought to Rust by the unconscious byways of the dream and its dreamer.

Litmus had taken to the woman with unbridled affection, welcoming her into his house and providing for her needs during the early days of her transition. She was an auburn beauty with sharp features and pale skin, alone and fearful of the bustling metropolis in which she suddenly found herself. Months passed, and Ellie grew to love her benefactor; the slim, middle-aged calligrapher whose inkery had grown successful despite the harsh and unyielding nature of the red city and its inhabitants.

Five quick years passed. Five years of hard work and the inestimable pleasure of love's embrace. The two lovers worked side by side, Litmus teaching the young woman his intricate trade day by day. Ellie took to the work with abandon, applying her own skill with needle and thread to such effect that Litmus was able to move beyond the production of loosely grouped parchments, toward bound volumes which gave off a distinguished air of permanence.

But Ellie's work with stitch-craft was far surpassed by her gift with quill and parchment. Where Litmus wrote with rare skill and precision, Ellie's work was of an entirely different order altogether. Words, letters, symbols all danced upon the page, mesmerized by her gentle touch. She wrote with speed and accuracy, that much was true, but there was more of the artist than the clerk in Ellie's writing. Each ending was made with a gentle flourish, each pause with subtlety and grace. Where emphasis was needed, her strokes grew thicker, more insistent. Where cunning was required, each letter took on the guile of a fox. The quill danced in her hand as though thrilling to her very touch, and she drew illuminations of such staggering beauty that the godling prince Salik himself had begun to show interest in the work emanating from the Litmus Inkery.

It was there, amid his pride at her skill and accomplishment, that Litmus first felt the inkling of dread which would grow to become his constant companion. In the years he had lived in the red city, he had seen much and heard more. Long nights spent at the local Brewhouse, exchanging rumours and peddling gossip with the regulars, had furnished Litmus with a troubling picture of the wider city and its inhabitants.

Rumours held that the city was filled with cutthroats and informants who spied upon the citizenry and were ever watchful for signs of perceived dissent or disloyalty. Shopkeepers had been dragged from their homes by black-hooded figures and never seen again. Businesses had been burnt to the ground, property seized, and market stalls closed indefinitely, all on the word of the Red Queen's spies, or at the behest of the Administratum priests who governed the city and its outlying territories.

Litmus had asked again and again, what crime had these men and women committed, but only rumour and myth could be heard in reply. *She is a jealous ruler*, some offered. *She abhors beauty in all its forms and cannot abide the success of others.* On and on the rumours broiled, and Litmus's view of the city grew darker, even as his business bloomed under the tender touch of his beloved Ellie.

Then came the day when the Red Guard marched down the stone thoroughfare outside of Litmus's inkery. A dozen red cloaks led by a tall, remade figure with mechanical protuberances jutting out at shoulder and back, bristling beneath a long, crimson cloak. While guardsmen waited outside, the hulking Sergeant entered the inkery, stooping beneath the front doorway with a grimace.

His face was hard as granite, made fierce by the long scar leading downwards from a silver orb where the man's left eye should have been. The soldier introduced himself as Ogden Blint, Sergeant of the Red Guard and special emissary to the Red Court. Litmus had been out on an errand during the visit, so it was left to Ellie to greet the sergeant with her usual good nature.

Blint had commissioned an urgent script and demanded that the work be carried out immediately, and in his presence. Ellie had protested of course, but the Sergeant would not be put off and, reluctantly, Ellie was forced to acquiesce. She penned the script in front of the guardsman, writing with her usual grace and superior skill. Thus, it took only a few seconds to seal her fate.

Litmus had returned to his inkery a little later in the day to find his neighbours distraught and angry. Helmat, the stone worker, was sitting with a bloodied nose upon the street, surrounded by a dozen others from nearby stalls and businesses. With eyes filled with sorrow, the burly stone worker informed Litmus that the Red Guard had stolen his beloved, without reason or recompense. Litmus had charged into the inkery, finding only the brief script his beloved had sketched and a small wooden token, painted red and bearing the seal of the Administratum.

In the days that followed, Litmus had petitioned the Administratum courts for Ellie's release. His endless pleas were met with flat responses. Ellie had been taken for the "illegal employment of mancery, plied with paper and ink in strict defiance of the Queen's edict." She had been stolen away for breaching the standing prohibition against unauthorized uses of ethermancy within the red city and no petition, bribe, or plea would bring about her release.

The taking of Ellie Shule had been a public spectacle. She had not been silenced in the night by the Warmaster's Butchers or accosted while at market by militiamen. No, the red priests intended to make a point, and they had used Ellie to do just that. Litmus did not believe for a moment that the blood priests cared about Ellie's gift. Nor did he suppose that the Red Queen herself would even know of Ellie's supposed crime. Ellie had simply been caught up in the larger game of propaganda and bureaucracy— waged between agents of the Red Queen and those voices of discontent that seemed to grow louder with each passing year.

For weeks on end Litmus had argued with the Red Priests, insisting that his beloved knew no mancery, that the charge was unfounded. As the days passed, however, Litmus's mood soured, and he grew reflective and morose. He recalled with painful fondness the subtle dancing of Ellie's hands as she put quill to paper—the extraordinary skill with which she illuminated text with subtle reds and yellows, gold and silver, exquisitely rendering each page with apparent ease. After long hours of introspection, he supposed that there was something of mancery in Ellie's art. Perhaps, what he had seen as a singular gift was the subtle manipulation of etheric forces? He doubted Ellie herself would have known what she was doing. Nor would she or Litmus have known that such subtle and harmless manipulations of the ether were forbidden among the Red Queen's subjects.

Gradually, the calligrapher's despair bloomed into a dark anger. He spent endless nights interrogating each acquaintance, each friend and colleague, searching for some scrap or sign of betrayal. Which of them had slain his beloved with their wicked slander? Who had betrayed the calligrapher and his love, and what was the price for their betrayal? Someone had spoken with the Red Guard. Someone had betrayed Ellie and condemned her to the Red Queen's cruel service for the rest of her days. A rival calligrapher perhaps, some upstart from King's Gate or the Fens?

He would not see his love again; Litmus knew all too well. Rumours and wild speculation both agreed that, once charged and apprehended, no one left the Queen's service. At least, not without passing through the fleshworks and emerging as something horrifically new.

***

After the initial months of rage and helplessness, Litmus set upon a new course of action. Gradually he began to trust again, surrounding himself with like-minded souls who had lost loved ones or been afflicted by the Queen's justice in some fashion. His every spare moment, his every coin was spent in search of information, some news of his beloved or detail about the inner workings of the Queen's court. He paid well for information and soon gained a reputation among several disreputable elements of the city.

Each scrap of information he wrote down for posterity, hiding volumes of gathered intelligence in a hidden storeroom nestled within the inkery basement. Over time, he began supplementing his income by selling information and not merely buying it. Litmus grew shrewd in his dealings with friends and foes alike; working in secret beyond the eyes and ears of those who could betray his cause. He gathered to himself a society of trustworthy scoundrels—bakers and stone workers, millers and thieves, cutthroats and artisans from across the length and breadth of the red city.

Newcomers to the society were tested rigorously, their loyalty purged by fire and tribulation before entry would be granted. Loyal lieutenants gathered around the erstwhile calligrapher, carrying out acts of miniature rebellion, bolstering discontent among the masses, and frustrating the Queen's justice wherever it could be done at minimal risk. There were no meetings, nor gatherings of any size that could court the attention of the Queen's informants. Information was passed by word of mouth or via a series of scripts, penned in ink of such temporary constitution that it would vanish irrevocably after the passing of a single day. By such measures *The Scripts*, as they had become known, avoided the watchful eye of the Red Guard and the Administratum both.

Two years passed, and Litmus's love for Ellie continued to stoke the fire in his gut. She was alive, he knew, and working in the Red Queen's service, among one of the many and varied clerk's offices at the Administratum.

If rumour held, the clerks and scribes of that office were occupied day and night with the copying of arcane manuscripts, etheric symbols, and the minutiae of innumerable detestable experimentations. Ellie, whose gift for calligraphy had seemed so singular to Litmus, was merely one of a hundred such gifted individuals, shackled to hardwood desks and forced to ply their art without freedom or creativity.

The scales were lifted from Litmus's eyes, and he began to see the red city as it truly was. Not as the haphazard accumulation of displaced peoples, working toward a tolerable existence in a harsh and unyielding land. The city was more than clay and dust, more than ramshackle buildings, gutter rot, coal and fire and steam. All of its multifarious life, its manufactured goods, its libraries and temples and sewers and slums; all were cogs in a single great machine.

Just as arms and fingers grasp at root and flesh and blood and fruit, to deliver sustenance to the body. Just as each limb and thought and organ works to feed a singular brain, so all of the parts of the great red city worked to feed the Red Queen and her cruel ambitions.

The farms and granaries, fields and orchards to the fertile west of the city produced an abundance of food, whose bulk was stripped bare as the great cargo trains move through the upper citadel, lavishing gifts upon the disinterested nobility and those petty barons who had elevated themselves by dint of mercantile cunning and thievery. Vast quantities of food were channelled to slaves who worked the quarries, mines, offices, metalsmiths, and even the fleshworks. The Red Guard took their share, of course, leaving little more than scraps for the vast underclasses who occupied the bulk of the city and its outlying regions.

Gigantic works of wood and metal were built and transported beyond the city and into the great Shadowlands to the west, where the Red Queen housed her most closely guarded secrets. There, among the broiling storm clouds and shadowed valleys, the toil of a thousand citizens birthed something monstrous, which had been crafted from the mind of their inscrutable sovereign. Countless of the Red Queen's subjects died in service to this unknown goal—toiling from dusk till dawn at mill wheel or anvil, bellows or boiler, cart or carrion pit.

Litmus saw that his own work—the work of which he had been so proud only a few short years earlier—had done nothing more than serve the Red

Queen's mad scheme. Every chit and scribble, every ledger and record which had come from the Litmus Inkery served to grease the wheels of the great machine. Mercantile deals were notarized, city ordinances recorded and disseminated to the populace, invitations for grand balls were printed and issued, and all ultimately in the service of the Red Queen and her godling madness.

His precious Ellie had been reduced to one more cog in the great machine—spinning endlessly without hope or meaningful purpose. She would work all the days of her life at quill and parchment, until her fingers wore through to the bone and her heart failed. Then, Litmus knew, they would toss her aside like a broken cog and put another in her place.

He felt enraged at the indignity, the callous wastefulness of such a grand, mechanised bureaucracy. But more than this—more than the indignity and injustice—was the fact that this price of countless lives was given in service to an unknown goal. None knew why they worked, nor what their lives of service purchased. Perhaps, if some grand ideal or goal was made known to the people of Rust—perhaps then, they would give their life freely, or at least without resentment?

∗∗∗

Litmus walks at pace through the crooked streets. The stench of roasting meat mingled with effluent and the ever-present dank of the Fens clogs his nostrils, bringing up bile as he negotiates the haphazard shacks and piled heaps of detritus that constitute the building blocks of the southern Fens. Something skitters past his leg, and the calligrapher feels his heart skip. He freezes in place, clutching at the knife strapped inside his jacket. He catches sight of a scrawny figure darting through the debris, its mangy hide red with welts and pathetic tufts of fur. Litmus takes a deep breath.

Stray dogs and beasts of more questionable heritage roam free during the night hours, scavenging for food with wary eyes and pricked-up ears. They are withered, gaunt looking things, surviving off what little they can snatch from the miserable inhabitants of the slums of the lower city, ever wary of themselves becoming a meal.

His heart still racing, Litmus continues on through the streets. Here and there, through crooked slats of wood or scraps of metal, he feels distrustful eyes glaring from the shadows. He is a trespasser in this hive of despair, an unwelcome external presence amid the sprawling slumlands of the south.

The crowded streets broaden suddenly, opening out into a large courtyard which is curiously free of debris. Dull white cobblestones gleam beneath the crimson moonlight, newly swept and polished, giving the courtyard an eerie, surreal texture. At the far end of the square a large, rounded building rises from the Fens, its hide covered with slate tiles and red clay. Twin tusks of polished bone pierce the skies from either side of a large doorway, curving skyward like the teeth of some felled leviathan.

If rumour held true, the structure had indeed been built around the carcass of an Elder Gargantuan which had attacked the city some thirty years earlier. Defeated by the Red Queen and her allies, the beast had been stripped of flesh and organs over a period of years, while oil and resin and numerous other substances were mined and processed on the site of the deceased Gargantuan. Several bonesmiths had set up workshops inside the carcass, working for years on end to carve and shape the creature's skeletal frame into objects of the most utilitarian function.

The rivalry between bonesmiths quickly moved from mercantile competition to something more brutal. Gangs of smith boys were sent to bludgeon and beat, cut, and murder one another. Skirmishes quickly escalated as three smiths vied for exclusive control over the supply of bone from the Gargantuan to the city. Within weeks, the balance of power lilted toward one of the three smiths, a nameless remade brute who was rumoured to have escaped the Queen's justice, bearing a mechanized arm and bio-augmented organs. Touting the unimaginative appellation *Bonesmith*, the figure quickly rose to victory, crushing his competitors in a gruesome tableau of blood and bone, death and mayhem.

Long years after the bulk of usable bone had been extracted and sold, the Bonesmith and his gang of thugs took up residence in the hollowed-out shell of the Elder Gargantuan. Red clay and pieces of dark slate were fixed to the outer shell of the beast, while its insides were fashioned into several levels of liveable space.

Litmus looks on in sudden dread at the gaping maw of the Gargantuan that was. He walks gingerly across newly swept stones toward a pair of hulking brutes sitting casually to either side of the towering entryway. Both are shaven-headed, well-muscled, and bare chested, and each sports a series of bone affectations—piercings through ear and nose, arm and chest. One of the two also boasts a pair of curved bone ornaments which had been driven through the shoulder to the left and right of the neck. The sight of these thugs makes the little man weak at the knees.

"You lost your way, sweet'art?" one of the guards mews, showing rows of jagged teeth that appear to have been fashioned from bone. "You wanna get out of 'ere, little man, afor somethin' bad happens."

Litmus feels a cold chill run up his spine, freezing him in place. There's a lustful edge to the brute's gaze, as though his limited imagination is making intricate plans that involve the calligrapher's diminutive frame.

"I'm here on invitation," Litmus croaks, "the Bonesmith called for me."

The big man nods, turning to his companion. "Hear that grub, old son? Little man says 'e's got 'imself an appoint to see Smiffy. Says e's 'ere on invitation."

Litmus can't help the hand that rises to meet the bulge in his jacket where his meagre weapon sits tucked neatly away in its makeshift sheath. A foolish move, he thinks on reflection. Even with the blade in his hands, these skilled thugs would have him skinned and filleted before he could strike a blow of his own. More importantly, his paranoia at being discovered with concealed weaponry by the Red Guard, or accidentally cutting some vital organ as he removed the blade, had prompted the calligrapher to wrap the knife in several layers of cloth and pack it neatly in the inner pocket of his jacket. Without any threat of impending violence, it would take him several precious moments just to unsheathe the weapon, let alone put it to any good use.

"What's 'e want then?" the thug continues, addressing Litmus once more. "What's ol' Smiffy want with a little maggot like you then, eh?"

Without waiting for an answer, the hulking brute advances on Litmus, placing two meaty hands to either side of his frame and inspecting him like a piece of meat.

"I...I can't discuss the nature of our meeting," Litmus squeaks, "but I assure you—"

The big man spins Litmus around with an iron grip, almost lifting the little man off his feet in the process. Without warning, meaty fingers begin roughly pawing at the calligrapher's clothes, grabbing at his torso with enough force to take the wind out of him. Litmus tries to protest, but his words are barely audible, punctuated by sharp intakes of breath and the odd cry of pain. The calligrapher feels the ground move beneath his feet and hits the ground heavily, sudden pain bursting from the side of his head.

He rolls over, clutching at his head, fingers now slick with blood. The brute stands heavily above him, unwrapping the meagre knife. The big man lifts the blade with a wicked grin.

"Word of warning for ya, little man," he says, turning the blade to and fro, as though he's about to pick his teeth with it, "ain't a good idea to be walking around the Fens wiff a little pig sticker like this."

He pulls a mammoth machete from a sheath at his belt, holding the frightful blade beside the kitchen knife to comical effect. "Stick a man o' the Fens wiff this little prick and 'e might answer in kind."

With a speed that shocks Litmus to the core, the big man tosses the kitchen knife into the air and brings his machete down against it. The big blade cuts through Litmus's knife, sending shards of metal in all directions. The two brutes roar with laughter, their muscled chests heaving.

The calligrapher's head is running with blood from where it has hit the cobblestones, and his right arm throbs as though he may have broken something. But, as he sits crouched before the hulking bonemen, Ellie's face blossoms in his mind's eye, her long hair cascading in ringlets down the side of her face, eyes dark, and curious features more beautiful than they have any right to be.

The little man slowly stands to his feet, making a show of brushing the dust from his jacket. "You've had your fun and proven whatever point you wished to prove," he says, gritting his teeth in an effort to keep his voice level. "Now, what reason would you like me to give the Bonesmith for being so tardy to our meeting? Should I make reference to your names, or simply explain that the two dullards stationed at the door felt it necessary to beat their chests before permitting my entrance?"

The larger of the two thugs narrows his eyes. The hulk leans in, spinning his machete so that the blunt back of the blade faces Litmus. Fighting panic with every fibre of his being, Litmus clicks his tongue in annoyance.

"By all means, delay further. I'm interested to see what kind of punishment your master deems fit for such stupidity."

The brute pauses and, for a moment, Litmus can picture the man's blade slicing through the flesh of his neck and ending all hopes of his return to Ellie. The boneman's eyes dart toward his comrade who shrugs unhelpfully. The former rolls his shoulders, slowly sliding the machete back to its sheath. Litmus can see the man's mind ticking over, like a partly seized clockwork machine, considering actions, consequences. Finally, he nods to the second brute.

"Take 'im in, I'll check wiff the boss man."

The less talkative of the two brutes leads Litmus through the gaping maw of the deceased Gargantuan, past twin pillars of bone upon which, the calligrapher notes, innumerable figures and symbols have been carved. The work is intricate but haphazard; a seemingly random collection of words and pictures, expertly carved, but showing no broader narrative.

The pair head through a series of thick hanging curtains, dark black and silky to the touch, and enter an expansive lower den, filled with brightly coloured cushions, short wooden tables and a series of etheric lamps that give the space a warm, auburn glow. The bittersweet scent of felweed hangs thickly in the air, a pungent aroma that catches in Litmus's throat and fills his head with an unnerving warmth.

There are people sitting around the tables, Litmus notes, gambling with dice and cards while sucking on the sukkahs which adorn each tabletop. Raucous laughter fills the den, mingling with the sounds of jovial banter and the clinking of clay tankards. Young women, stripped to the waist and bearing a frightful array of bone adornments sashay through the den, serving drinks and courting the attentions of an inebriated clientele. Here and there the girls, hair shaved down one side, and flowing long down the other, sit upon a patron's lap, stroking a beard or mewing supple thoughts into engorged ears.

None of the den's inhabitants noted the pair passing. They continued their reverie with utter abandon. Litmus is led up an ornately crafted bone staircase, carved into what might once have served as the Gargantuan's hip, or thigh, or perhaps some other internal structure unique to the beast itself. No other creatures of its like had been witnessed either before or since its attack against the city. There were rumoured to be creatures of equal size and strangeness out among the Red Wastes and Shadowlands to the north, but none had strayed near the red city—a fact which the priests of the Administratum were quick to attribute to the Red Queen's protective influence.

Litmus and the brute walk through a gantry level, down into the bowels of the building, past still more revellers enjoying strong drink, rowdy conversation, and other, more illicit activities. Here and there, behind dark curtains in innumerable nooks and crannies, Litmus can hear the sounds of intense rutting. He feels utterly out of place, a stranger in a strange land, unwelcome and ill at ease. For a moment, the urgent desire to be rid of this place is overwhelming. He longs to be back in his inkery, surrounded by bound volumes and the memories of Ellie's touch. But the little man braces himself against the desire to flee. If he is to have any hope of freeing Ellie from the Red Queen's justice, he will need to enlist the help of the Bonesmith, and others like him. As distasteful and troubling as this may be, he has to follow this course to its conclusion. For Ellie.

Litmus blinks in shock as a meaty hand strikes him across the chest. He recoils but sees that it is only his escort signalling a halt. The big man is looking ahead into a large circular room high up atop a set of bone stairs which has the look of a curved backbone. The room is surrounded by a series of dark, cloth sheets. The faint glow of amber light sneaks through the gaps between fabric, as does the sound of raucous laughter and general merriment.

Litmus gathers that the silent brute wants him to wait, so he nods and crosses his arms with, what he hopes, is a look of impatience. The brute climbs the bone stairs, pausing at the entrance to talk to a pair of bare-chested guardsmen, then he disappears into the circular chamber beyond. For several minutes Litmus waits, trying to keep his mind from imagining the myriad terrors that await him. The message to meet with the Bonesmith had been delivered only two days earlier, but it was most insistent. Litmus hopes that his delay in arriving has not prompted the slumlord to a violent course of action.

Rumours said a great deal about the Bonesmith: that he stood head and shoulders above any other man, that he had grafted Gargantuan bone into his own flesh such that he was entirely remade from the substance, that he delighted in devouring young children. Whatever the veracity of the more troubling of these rumours, it was widely held that the Bonesmith was given to flights of uncontrollable rage and violent fury. More than this, however, he was a keen strategist and a remarkably successful slum boss. He had managed to hold onto the largest and fiercest criminal organization in all of Rust for decades, holding off both rival gangs and the Red Guard's repeated attempts to dismantle the bonemen and reclaim the Gargantuan site.

Litmus does not know what awaits him in the chamber above, but he is sure of two things. Firstly, that the Bonesmith has a clear motive for requesting the meeting. There is something the Smith wants from him, and

Litmus has not a clue what that something might be. Secondly, if Litmus is to misstep and insult the Bonesmith, particularly in the presence of his men, it's likely that sudden, irrevocable violence will follow.

Time seems to drag on as Litmus waits for his summons. The sounds of laughter have died down in the chamber above, and that thought brings a chill to the calligrapher's bones. Frightful scenarios begin to play out in his mind, each more vivid than the last.

The terrifying imaginings are interrupted by the return of his escort. The big man walks down the stairs, stops in front of Litmus, and then motions for him to head to the chamber. Then, without a word, the brute walks off, returning to his post at the entrance of the establishment.

With more than a little apprehension, Litmus wills his legs to move, climbing the stairs in what he hopes is a measured pace. "For Ellie," he whispers, using the mantra to drive himself forward. The guardsmen stationed to either side of the entrance say nothing as Litmus ducks beneath the dark curtain and into the chamber beyond.

The room is only dimly lit, and it takes a few moments for Litmus's eyes to adjust. There are twenty or thirty people gathered in a circle, reclining on large cushions with polished bone goblets and trays of food at their feet. Directly ahead of Litmus sits a hulking figure on a skilfully crafted throne, a man of intimidating size, augmented with several biomechanical limbs and organs. To the left of the Bonesmith stands a tall, dark-haired man in a long black coat and wide-brimmed hat. He has the look of a gunslinger and brings to mind strange memories of Litmus's old life in the waking world. The man stares impassively at Litmus with eyes of dull flint.

"So good of you to grace us with your presence, calligrapher," the Bonesmith says, his voice surprisingly smooth and welcoming.

Litmus nods, realizing at precisely that moment how unprepared he is for such a meeting. He knows not the proper forms or ceremonies to be observed on meeting the most notorious criminal in the red city. One false move and this encounter will likely come to a swift end.

"Sit, please," Smith says, motioning to a cushion near his own.

Not knowing what else to do, Litmus takes a seat, struggling to look dignified as he slides down onto the cumbersome cushion, almost toppling to the floor in the process. Titters of laughter rise from the room, but the look of sharpened steel that the Bonesmith delivers has them quieted with speed.

"A beverage perhaps?" he asks, clicking meaty fingers at a nearby serving girl. "You must be thirsty having navigated your way through the Fens this night."

"Nothing for me, thank you," Litmus says, straining for a mixture of politeness and strength.

The Bonesmith waves the serving girl away, lifting his own cup gently to his lips and sipping slowly, his one good eye locked on Litmus. He places the goblet on a bone table by his side, licking his lips.

"The nature of my summons," the big man begins, his tone suddenly more serious, "relates to a spate of recent, shall we say, inflammatory activities undertaken by your men."

While he speaks, the room empties of its inhabitants. Driven by some unseen signal, the scantily clad women, muscled brutes, and various hangers-on silently depart. Only the tall figure in the dark coat remains in place, leaning casually against a rib-like bone which curves upwards toward the ceiling of the circular chamber.

"You have me at a loss sir," Litmus replies. "I have no *men*."

Smith rasps with laughter. "Oh, come now, calligrapher. There really is no need to be coy. I speak of the network of recruits you have garnered this past year. The *Scripts*, is it? Truly an eclectic group. Bakers, masons, thieves, and laborers. You have managed to spread word to every nook and cranny in this fine welt of a city yet somehow avoid the attentions of the Red Guard."

"I assure you, sir, they are not *my* men. We merely serve a common goal."

"Ah, a common goal, is it? Well, at least you do me the courtesy of not denying their existence. Call them what you will, calligrapher, you have managed to spread your tendrils wide. They reach even into the Fens and, it is for this reason that you sit before me now."

Remember Ellie. It is all for Ellie.

"We mean no threat to your organization, sir," Litmus says, hands outstretched in a conciliatory manner. "We simply seek information about the Red Queen. Each of us has lost much at her hand, and we—"

The Bonesmith holds up a meaty hand, chuckling. "You misunderstand, calligrapher. Believe me when I say that you pose no threat whatsoever to my own interests. Were it so, we would not be talking as we currently are. No indeed, your body would be floating its way down the blood river. I am aware of your dealings, calligrapher, your collecting of information as you say. You have, I hear, acquired quite the library of artifacts concerning our illustrious ruler and her cadre."

He leans back, scratching at the scar below his blinded eye.

"I summoned you, Mr. Litmus, because it seems to me that we have a certain opportunity here. You have, unknowingly I suspect, laid the groundwork for a far more expansive and important venture than the mere publication of a few dissenting scraps of text. I put it to you, Mr. Litmus, that you have, within your grasp, the perfect opportunity to strike at the very heart of the Red Queen's empire, to rid this city of her wretched *justice* and avenge the abduction of your beloved wife."

Litmus felt his heart stop momentarily. His eyes widened, a cold sweat rising over his body.

"Oh yes, Mr. Litmus, we are well aware of your own personal tragedy. It is by precisely this tragedy that I know you are a principled man, a wronged man seeking justice, yes? Well, let me tell you that justice will never come while you content yourself with acts of petty antagonism and the gathering of information. Such an enterprise is vital, it is true, but without force and weighty execution, your pilfering of myths and rumours will not bring back your wife."

The calligrapher cleared his throat, pushing back the panic that welled up from within.

"What…what do you propose?"

"An alliance of sorts. You have, as I mentioned, laid the groundwork and assembled a sizable, if rather motley, collection of agents throughout the city. With the proper organization and an injection of force, weaponry, and personnel, we could bring down the bloody red queen."

"You want to lead a rebellion against the Red Queen?

The Bonesmith smiles, shakes his head. "Alas, Mr. Litmus, I lack the requisite character for such a noble enterprise. True, I possess considerable resources within and beyond the city. But even if I were to engage the Red Queen with all that is at my disposal, my efforts would fail."

He picks up his mug, moving it in gentle circles as he watches the mulled brew within.

"To lead an effective rebellion, dear calligrapher, I would need far more men. But, more importantly, I would need the populace of this great city to rise up and fight. For this to happen, the downtrodden masses must throw off a thousand years of servitude. No easy task, I assure you. How does one move the masses so?"

The Bonesmith leans forward, prodding a finger toward Litmus.

"You, Mr. Litmus, yours is a story which may ignite the passions of the dull-eyed masses and stir them to action. Already you have assembled a network of like-minded individuals throughout the red city; it's an assembly of the discontented, if you will. These people pay you allegiance, calligrapher, even if you do not yet realize it. Call upon them to rise up at the right time, and they will do so. Strike a blow against the Red Queen, and they will march with you. No, Mr. Litmus, *I* cannot lead this rebellion. It would take an effort of considerable force to have the masses follow me, but *you* they will follow out of love, out of solidarity, taking some small part of vengeance for their own losses."

Litmus sits in stunned silence. This was not the meeting he had envisaged. His mind whirls, considering the distant possibility of rebellion.

"It is an…interesting suggestion," he says cautiously. "But I know little of rebellion. In truth my only interest is freeing Ellie from her servitude."

"And what better way to achieve that goal," the Bonesmith booms excitedly, "than to tear down this rotten edifice and lay waste to the Red Queen's rule? Think on it, calligrapher, if you were to recover your love and whisk her away to the far reaches, would not the Red Guard hunt you down? Would not the Warmaster's brutes sniff you out and slit your throats while you slept? Would it not be just a matter of time before agents of the red come knocking down your door to once more steal your heart's love and render you twice sorrowed? And what manner of life would you lead, the pair of you? Running from hovel to hovel, wandering the red wastes with only the clothes on your back? No, far better that we strike the Red Queen at her heart and, in the bargain, free your Ellie from her enslavement. Thereafter, you may live in peace, working your inkery as before, without threat of violence from the Queen's brutes. I myself would guarantee such safety."

"Even so," Litmus objects, "I know nothing of rebellion, nor do I relish the shedding of blood."

Smith puts down his mug roughly, sloshing dark liquid onto the table. He leans forward. "That, Mr. Litmus, is where I can be of service. My men will fight where fighting is required. I will arm those of your followers who wish to do violence, and," he motions to the tall man standing behind, "my man will oversee all matters of military strategy and the like. You, Mr. Litmus, need only be the face and voice of the rebellion. Your story will solidify the resolve of the disgruntled, the displaced, the oppressed."

The Bonesmith speaks with amicable enthusiasm, but Litmus senses the steel beneath his voice. The man is casting the discussion as a suggestion, an inclination, but Litmus can see that his plans are already well advanced. Feeling more than a little like the proverbial rat nibbling at the cheese in a trap, Litmus begins unpacking the implications of the Bonesmith's words. His eyes dart suddenly to the tall figure behind the slumlord—a man whom, Litmus now notes, carries twin revolvers at his side, their dark handles neatly hidden beneath the folds of his long jacket.

"Do I truly have a choice in the matter?" Litmus blurts, before his mind can stop the words leaving his lips.

The Bonesmith looks down at Litmus with an amused expression which is made sinister by the dim auburn light glinting off his scarred face.

"You are perceptive beyond your reputation, calligrapher," Smith says, all traces of humour leaving his voice. "You see right to the heart of it. In truth, no, you have no choice. You are, quite simply, a tool in all of this, a simple cog in a much larger machine."

The big man rises from his seat, grunting with the effort as he stands to full height. Desperate to maintain some sense of dignity, Litmus likewise stands, managing to stop from falling headlong onto the floor as he struggles to attain vertical posture.

"I am a man of ambition, Mr. Litmus," the Bonesmith says, walking to the centre of the room. "Yet I am hemmed in at every side by the Queen and her cronies. If I am to break the shackles that repeatedly quench my enterprise, I must have that red bitch's head on a platter. Make no mistake calligrapher, we are headed to war, a war that I intend to win. Yet, with you as the figurehead of this rebellion, I can capitalize upon the heat of the moment. The discontent of the rabble is a powerful tool when wielded correctly, and I intend to use that very weapon to my advantage."

He turns slowly, rubbing his chin with his mechanized left hand. "You may rest assured, calligrapher; I am true to my word. Play your part in this enterprise, and I will see that your Ellie is freed. More than this, once power is wrested from the Queen and her lieutenants, I will see that you are at peace for the remainder of your lives together. You need not fear retribution nor strife. I will, as it were, take you under my protective wing. Simply do your part, stir the hearts of the people, and I will do the rest."

The Bonesmith – David Sparvero

***

Litmus is shadowed as he leaves Gargantua. The tall, wordless gunslinger who had witnessed his meeting with the Bonesmith follows a few paces behind, walking at an unnervingly even pace. As he walks through the slums and byways of the Fens, Litmus considers his new companion. The man bears none of the bone affectations of the Bonesmith's men, nor does he show any other signs of affiliation with any of the red city's guilds. He carries himself with the air of a practiced soldier, someone accustomed to the application of violence, yet there is little of Rust to the man.

He is newly woken in the red city, Litmus decides. A criminal from the waking world perhaps, displaced and alone in the world of dreams, he finds solace in familiar criminal company. Recognizing a like-minded individual, the Bonesmith welcomes the man to his organization. Yet, Litmus reasons, the tale makes no sense. Why would Smith bring in an outsider? Why would he promote such a one to a distinguished position within the organization?

"Kane is my eyes and ears," the Bonesmith had said. "Do as he instructs, for it will be as if I myself have given the commands."

On returning to the inkery, Litmus lays out the spare room for Kane's convenience. Without a word of thanks, the tall gunslinger closes the door to the small room, leaving the calligrapher to go about his business. The little man tosses and turns throughout the night, his recent encounter with the Bonesmith providing a chilling outline to the nightmarish forms in his dreams. Unable to sleep, disturbed by the gunslinger sleeping only a few rooms away, Litmus retreats to the larder and fixes himself something to eat.

While he lays red pickles on dark millet bread, Litmus reflects at the peculiarity of his nightmares. It had struck him as a wonder, in his first nights in the Traumwelt, that he was still able to dream even when living in a world of dreams. The little man sits on a round stool, eating, wondering if there is another world, a world of dreams within this dreamworld, to which he might one day find himself drawn.

As dawn emerges, slothful and without clarity, Litmus leaves his stool and begins setting to work, arranging the various mechanical devices and kinetic implements upon which the Litmus Inkery is so dependent. The little man fills ink pots, stokes boilers, greases mechanized arms, and prepares parchments for use, whistling while he goes about his work and, for a time, forgetting his current predicament. The various laborers and scribes under his employ enter the inkery in their usual fashion and set about fulfilling the day's orders with reluctant diligence. Litmus greets each of their number in turn, issuing polite orders and instructions.

It is not until the first luncheon that the gunslinger emerges from his room, sharp-eyed and bearing a stack of scripts in his hands. The tall figure walks out into the inkery and hands the pile of papers to Litmus.

"Find me three of your most dependable men," he says flatly. "They need have no gift with letters but must be widely travelled within the city and available for service for the next three days. In addition, disseminate those scripts throughout your network by day's end."

That said, the gunslinger turns and heads back to his room without another word. Litmus stares at the tall man with a mixture of puzzlement and fear. He looks down at the scripts and begins to read. The words are sharp and brittle, instructing the reader to prepare for coming action and citing the need to take up arms against the Red Queen and her servants. Each script is penned in an excellent hand, doubtlessly written in the dead of night, while Litmus sat sleepless in his larder. The little man lifts the paper to his nose and sniffs at the ink. To his surprise, he notes that each script has been penned with that peculiar indigo ink, of his own devising, which vanishes from vision within a single passing of day and night.

Several troubling questions arise. Firstly, how is it that the gunslinger has managed to locate paper, stylus, and ink in the dead of night, without the aid of candlelight or Litmus's instruction? All items are packed neatly away in their given nooks, and a newcomer to the inkery should be hard pressed to locate said items without difficulty. Further, how is it that the gunslinger has managed to find the indigo ink, secreted, as it was, in a hidden compartment below the storage cabinetry of the inkery basement? Either this Kane is a man of unparalleled luck, or the Boneman's informants are far more detailed in their knowledge of Litmus and his activities than the calligrapher first imagined.

Three dependable men. Litmus reflects, still clutching the scripts.

***

In the weeks that follow, Litmus spends his days dispensing pamphlets, posters, and scripts to an ever-increasing band of followers. The number of discontented souls within his cadre expands as word of the so-called Script Dogma spreads and the Red Guard do all in their power to repress it. Local militias in each city district are given the authority to brutalize any and all who feign knowledge of the Scripts or are heard openly discussing the movement.

Pamphlets are confiscated, houses raided. The steady tide of beggars and loiterers who idle among the cobbled streets of Hallow Square and Rookery

Market are dislodged from their pitiful stools and curb sides, sent to wander among the Fens or dragged into swollen cells in makeshift prisons.

Each day the bruised and battered come to Litmus, swelling the ranks of the rebellion. They come from all quarters and castes, but Litmus himself is surrounded by only a select group of trustworthy souls. Behind the scenes, the gunslinger pulls a thousand threads and masterminds the rebellion proper.

Day and night the gunslinger works to promote discontent and anger among the masses. Yet his efforts are equally spent in maintaining the peerless reputation of the Litmus Inkery. The calligrapher is surprised to see such attention devoted to his establishment, but the gunslinger insists that this mercantile flourishing is essential in keeping Litmus beyond the watchful eye of the city guard and their brutal militia hounds.

With time's passing, the diminutive calligrapher comes to know the gunslinger and, through the fastidious and relentless application of goodwill and obedience, Litmus learns a little of the man's history. Idrus Kane, he discovers, was once a soldier in the king's army—though of which king, Litmus cannot say—called to service amid a brutal war. At some point during the bloodshed, Kane was felled and woke a short distance from the red city. He did not return to the waking world and harboured no particular bitterness at this fact. Saved from death at the hands of his enemies, the gunslinger has been given a second life, and he is most pragmatic in his approach to such an eventuality.

Through some series of events the gunslinger will not divulge, he managed to secure the trust and patronage of the Bonesmith and took up arms on his behalf. The gunslinger has since laboured to secure the Bonesmith's kingdom, helping the organization rise to pride of place among the disreputable guilds of the Fens.

Litmus is puzzled by the gunslinger's remarkable intelligence, his gift for letters and strategy. Yet there is always a hard edge to the man's words and little patience for delay or mishap. While Litmus plies his trade by day and distributes inflammatory words to a trusted few by night, Kane works with folk of an entirely different order. There is violence afoot, although Litmus is kept from seeing it. On occasion he may catch sight of a spot of blood upon the threshold to Kane's room or overhear raised voices in the early hours of the morning, but the gunslinger runs his violent program in the utmost secrecy.

No one can say with any degree of accuracy which act it is that precipitates the Rookery Riots. Rumours speak of a child dashed to the stones by an overzealous militia man, the rising up of women against the brute. Others whisper of bloody murder: a knife to the kidneys of a militia guard, followed by swift and blind retribution which quickly escalates. The most amusing tale recounts the simple purchase of bread from a respected baker, a comment made in uncouth jest by a militia man who scores a baguette across the cheek for his insult, and who returns the bready blow with a wild swing of his cudgel.

Whatever its origin, the riots swiftly swell and are brutally halted by an influx of the Red Guard. When the Rookery Riots are finally suppressed, some thirty souls lie dead and a great many loyal Scripts are swayed from peaceful protest to violent action. Kane is quick to seize upon the opportunity, writing a score of sheets and having them distributed to every corner of the city. For the first time he chooses to write without dissolving ink, and the rebellion moves from the shadows into the light.

***

In the dead of night, Litmus is roused from his bed. A burly man with dark eyes and a bushy beard leads him to the basement where Kane and a circle of collaborators stand huddled over a large map, their forms dimly outlined in amber light. Litmus walks hesitantly, supposing that the gunslinger will order some form of refreshment for his comrades or announce some urgent script to be copied and disseminated.

Kane waves the calligrapher forward.

"Come in, Litmus," he says, drawing the other man close. "Matters are moving swiftly, and it is time you were availed of our plans."

Litmus enters the circle, surrounded by hard stares and hard folk. Several bonemen are in attendance as well as representatives from the air docks, the outer Fens and several crafting guilds. At the centre of the group is a woman of rare height and beauty, dressed in a perfectly cut emerald dress and flowing green cloak which sets her apart from the others in the room. Her eyes are of a startling emerald, and Litmus cannot help but put a name to the face—Absinthe Annie, Madame of Sparrow Boulevard. She glowers at him with something approximating disdain, and the calligrapher finds himself somewhat cowed by her gaze.

Kane points to the table between them and a large map outlining the streets and buildings of Rust. Litmus is taken aback by the sight. It is the first time he has seen the city in such a fashion, laid bare before the naked eye as if recorded by some creature of flight. All but the Administratum priests are forbidden such a holistic perspective of the red city, and any contravention of this prohibition against cartography is punished with brutal finality. No one is sure as to the reason why such map making is prohibited, but there have been sufficient instances of punishment in past years to reinforce an aversion to cartography.

Litmus hesitates, wondering who could have penned such a blasphemous artifact. He feels a strong hand on his shoulder as Kane draws him near. The calligrapher reluctantly joins the rebellious cadre.

"We cannot hope to overcome the Red Guard and city militias in pitched battle," Kane says, addressing the group. "We are simply too few and too poorly armed. However, if we can corral the guard here and here, we may conduct our affairs unmolested. We need only block the Red Guard from advancing for three or four hours. That will leave us the militia to deal with and those guards stationed at key points throughout the citadel. At present the Warmaster and his guard are detained to the northwest, so we will not have those brutes to contend with. Our primary goal is to secure the Clockwork Bridge and seal off the military and Administratum districts at these three points."

He goes on to explain in length. The intricate details of the plan are lost to Litmus. He recalls the poisoning of the wells at Greymaul Keep, night-time assassinations at the makeshift militia barracks of Hallow and Moorn. He hears something of the incitement of violence among the masses at trade squares and temple buildings. The plans are detailed and well thought through. The women and men gathered about the table all nod with grim expressions, aware of the parts they must each play. Only Litmus is lost at sea, sickened by the violence and terror laid out upon the table before them. His head swims, vision blurring as Kane continues his methodical description.

An hour or so passes swiftly, and Litmus is carried away in thought. Horrified by the bloodshed which will inevitably befall the city, his thoughts return to more pleasant times, drifting inevitably toward Ellie. His mind settles upon the days spent working the inkery, the blossoming of their nascent love amid ink stains and newly pressed parchment. He is pulled swiftly from the vision by Kane's voice.

"Litmus? Clear your head, calligrapher, there is work to be about."

The little man finds himself alone in the room with Kane, the other members of their cadre having departed. Litmus stammers apologetically, fearing he has missed some vital detail.

"Worry not about what you have heard, calligrapher," Kane says in a voice that exudes a certain hard compassion. "Our people are in place, and all is in readiness. You need only concern yourself with the sending of one more message."

He holds up a small script, the size of a single hand, penned in crimson ink.

"This missive," Kane says, "will spark the tinder in the hearts of your brethren, calligrapher. It is a call to action, a call to war and blood and freedom. You have played your part well these past months, and there is but a little more for you to do. Simply dispatch this message on the morrow and await word of our success. You have no need to take up arms yourself. We will have further need of you in the days ahead, so you must be kept from harm and disrepute."

Litmus takes the script and reads, but the words pass through his mind like water through sand. He looks up at Kane, confusion and desperation waring within his troubled soul. For the first time since the gunslinger's arrival at the inkery, Kane smiles, and there is nothing false in it. He places a hand upon Litmus's shoulder and squeezes gently.

"I have not forgotten your bargain with the Bonesmith," he says, reassuringly. "As you suspected, she is an indentured clerk within the Administratum. We have her location, and our scouts have confirmed that she is alive and well enough. I have a small squad prepared to apprehend her on the morrow. They will bring her safely to you here, within these walls, in but a few short hours."

Litmus cannot speak. His eyes brim with tears. His throat swells in an attempt to reply.

"Sleep now. We still have a little time. I will wake you at morning and we shall be about our business. And rejoice Litmus, for we are on the very cusp of rebellion."

***

Blood, fire, the rending of flesh and bone and iron.

The masses clot every street and byway surrounding the military district, holding fast the soldiers within by sheer weight of numbers. They cry and chant and lift high their scripts, while those at the forefront, armed with picks and bludgeons, jab and thrust at armoured men in the Red Queen's livery.

There is a time of uncertainty, where bloodshed is held at bay by curiosity, by a momentary disbelief which holds the Red Guard in check. But that moment passes swiftly, and red slaughter soon follows. Those of the rabble who have suffered the remaking of the Queen's justice—men with mechanical arms and piston-driven appendages—resist the soldiers with some small degree of success. The heavy miners, with their coal-fuelled boilers and steam-powered jackhammers, form a solid wall of brute metal which the Queen's Guard cannot easily overcome. The desperate and downtrodden likewise offer some little resistance, buoyed by the presence of armed bonemen scattered throughout the broiling crowds.

For the most part, the Guard cut down resistance with frightful ease. Men and women try to flee but are crushed beneath the weight of their own rebellious masses. The Red Guard tire at the carnage they must inflict, arms growing sore with the slaughtering of the hapless and helpless. Here and there a knot of resistance holds fast, bolstered by some biomechanical abomination or a makeshift barricade, bristling with spears and coarse wire.

Blood floods the streets, mingling with red dust to form a grotesque slurry which serves to further slow the advance of Red Guard soldiers and the retreat of ill-armoured rebels. It is the common folk who pay the greatest price: men and women caught up in the frenzy of mass hysteria. They are poorly equipped and ill-informed, and they die by the hundreds while bonemen and undercity thugs scattered among the crowds shout hard slogans and urge bloody violence.

Among the militia barracks and makeshift prisons, militia men are slain while they slumber. Wells are poisoned, ambushes set, and vengeance sought against the petty brutes who have savaged the city for years. Several bodies are strung up outside the barracks, a ghastly warning which lasts only a few moments as the buildings are consumed with fire.

The militia are unprepared for such mass insurrection. They are quickly overpowered, and those who survive the first wave of violence flee to safe houses or strip off their militia garb and turn coat, joining the rabble they would gladly have suppressed only hours earlier.

To the north, dark waters rise from rebellious reservoirs, flooding the city streets and bringing many of the more decrepit buildings to their knees. The streets sag with moisture and rot, the air is filled with heaving sighs and groans as wood and iron, clay and rock, grind against one another. The swelling aids the rebels, locking the Red Guard in place so expertly that many wonder whether the flooding was achieved by design rather than contingent circumstance. The Scripts have buried and drowned hundreds of their kin, and many more die at the hands of armed soldiers, yet the cause advances among rumours that the rebels have entered the citadel.

Clockmancers and thaumaturgic specialists are employed to hold the Clockwork Bridge open, pressing all their power against the will of the Red Queen who is said to command the ingenious mechanisms that power the bridge. Bonemen and nondescript rebels flood into the citadel, armed with purloined weapons and makeshift armour. Those of noble blood barricade themselves inside high towers and heavily walled houses, watching with horror from above as the rabble pours out into the grand courtyard below. Priests of the Administratum are cloistered away within their hulking buildings while those lounging in the towering spires of the citadel watch the chaos with only mild interest.

The Bonesmith himself is said to appear, crossing the clockwork bridge in triumph, surrounded by a hundred shirtless brutes with bone spears and wicked intentions. At the slumlord's side stands the black-clad gunslinger, tall and imposing, guns at the ready. They advance upon the citadel, meeting early resistance from those soldiers stationed at the entranceways to the five towers. Fighting is brutal and bloody, but the rebels advance.

The crackle of gunfire and etheric discharge ripples through the city streets. Doors and shutters are braced against the sudden violence as women and children hide themselves away. From above the sound of Red Guard, airships can be heard as the vast vessels manoeuvre through the treacherous skies above Rust, relaying intelligence to their comrades below via etheric transfer. The hulking sky ships are unable to lose the full fury of their weapons lest they risk catastrophic damage to the city below. Occasional pops of gunfire can be heard from the ships as soldiers fire into the crowds below, but after several near misses and an eventual collision which brings down two of the vessels, the air ships depart.

Litmus sits within his inkery, chilled by the cacophony of violence that reaches his ears. The fighting is far off to the north, yet its effects can be heard in every corner of the city. Thoughts swarm the calligrapher's head, jostling for position in a mind overwhelmed with emotion and angst. He holds, in his hand, a crumpled sketch of Ellie. He presses the paper against his chest and closes his eyes as though in an effort to shut out the violence outside.

He waits for several hours, but no rebels return with Ellie in tow. The sounds of fighting die down somewhat, but there is a boom somewhere to the north, and the earth shudders at the sound, rattling the windows of the inkery so furiously that several crack. Something inexplicable passes through Litmus, a strange etheric force which carries with it a form of rage so potent that he is momentarily incensed. The emotion dies swiftly, leaving Litmus perplexed as to its origin.

Darkness falls, and Litmus debates the need to leave his inkery and seek word of Ellie himself. He cannot wait another minute. Surely Kane's men should have done their deed now. Surely.

There is a slam as something crashes through the side door of the inkery. Figures move through the darkness, and Litmus quickly moves to light lamps and meets the interlopers. For a brief moment he considers the likelihood that it is Red Guardsmen that he will meet, or street thugs intent on looting while the city is at war. His heart thumps wildly as he skips down the stairs, clutching up a fire stoker on the way through, so as to offer some measly defence if thuggery ensues. He reaches the bottom floor and finds…Ellie…

***

The long-lost lovers embrace for what feels like an age, kissing one another and muttering their devotion. They cling to each other like sailors to a raft at sea, defying separation. After their tears have somewhat lifted, Litmus conducts his inspection.

"Did they hurt you?" he mutters, worriedly inspecting her hands, her arms, her face. "Are you well fed?"

Ellie coos to the little man, insisting that she is in good health and all the better for being reunited with him. She offers her own inspection, insisting that Litmus has grown far too slim in the days since her abduction. The two are lost in their bliss, but that bliss is interrupted by a shadowed figure seated by the doorway; Idrus Kane, looking like he has fought his way through the very bowels of hell. His clothes are torn and bloodied, while one arm lays limp in his lap. There is a large gash at one shoulder and a bloody wound emptying itself darkly from his stomach. Kane clutches his gut, grimacing.

"We have little time," he manages. "They will come for us, calligrapher. We are…betrayed."

Litmus rushes to the man as he passes out. The calligrapher and his lover lift Kane onto a nearby bench and set to work, putting a stop to the man's bleeding. The wound to his abdomen is shallow and should heal with due rest, but there are at least a dozen similar wounds across his torso, and it takes several hours of hard work for the pair to staunch the flow of blood. The wound to the man's shoulder is particularly deep, and Litmus is no apothecary, but he knows enough of basic medicine to see that Kane may yet live. They shift the man upstairs and lay him in Litmus's bed, then pass the night in each other's arms, sharing all that has passed since their separation.

In the morning, Kane awakens. He can barely walk but seems much improved on the previous night. After a light meal, he sits before Litmus and Ellie, eye hard as flint, bandages covering his chest and arms.

"We had…underestimated the power of the godlings," he begins, his tone sombre. "The plan to hold the Red Guard and deal with the militia worked well enough. So too, the securing of the Clockwork Bridge and citadel courtyard."

He smiles, and the gesture seems to cause him pain. "There was no grand mystery to the bridge. The Queen does not control it with her mind nor any other etheric device. It is a machine, worked from a series of substations within the inner courtyard. Truly a remarkable feat of engineering, to be sure, but nothing more."

Litmus listens, one arm around Ellie. His mind drifts, thrilling to the touch of his beloved.

"We were set to attack the citadel when the Red Queen and her godling brethren made their appearance. We had expected one, or maybe two godling princes, but there were a dozen waiting for us. The Warmaster, Avernath, was not occupied in the north as we had been led to believe. He and his Butchers lay in wait at the citadel. Tinsen and the Cloudweaver were also present along with Calaban and his abominable golems. We could not stand against such enemies, and I was forced to flee."

His eyes close a little, as though weighed down by the tale. "Even with reinforcements from the building yards, we were woefully outmanoeuvred. The Bonesmith is dead, as are most of his men. We were trapped like fish in a net. I fled east, to the Administratum and the men I had assigned to find Ellie. Of those men, I found no trace. I and a few bonemen managed to work our way through the Administratum, finding and freeing Ellie with all haste. It took the better part of the night to navigate our way back here."

He bows his head, desperation in his voice. "I fear we are marked, calligrapher. I acted foolishly, firing upon the Red Queen herself in a doltish act of defiance. I fear she has remembered the slight and sent her hounds after me. Already we have encountered one of the Warmaster's brutes. More will be on their way."

Litmus leans forward. "Last night. You spoke of betrayal. You said that we were not safe."

Kane nods. "I saw the heads of several bonemen, traitors to the cause and they may be the least of it. The godlings were waiting for us. Far from being scattered to the north and east as is their usual custom, the Red Queen brought them here to fight, to crush the rebellion and make a show of it. We must leave this place if we are to survive."

His words are prophetic. No sooner have they left his lips than the world erupts in flame and violence. In the moments that follow, Litmus understands only a little. He is deaf and half blind, wandering about the inkery, clutching desperately to Ellie's hand. There is movement among the acrid smoke, figures in midnight-black robes, their faces covered with black iron masks. Litmus feels a sudden burst of pain bloom upon his right temple, feels the floor shift beneath his feet, and hits the ground hard.

What follows is a montage of snatched images and impressions which leave the calligrapher cold and unhinged. He sees Kane, fresh wounds breaking their bandages as he fires at the oncoming enemy with both revolvers, heedless of the smoke and fire that surrounds him. When his bullets are spent, the gunslinger hurls himself into the fray, grappling with masked figures and beating at their heads and chests, his knuckles bloodied, eyes frenzied. A hulking figure enters the scene, bristling from back and shoulder with a litany of barbed and bladed mechanical alterations. The figure strikes Kane, sending the man to the floor in a crumpled heap, all resistance quashed.

The brute turns to Litmus, one metallic eye motionless. He bends down and grasps at something nearby, with the speed of a viper. There is a shriek, the feel of warm hands clutching at Litmus's back. His vision blurs, turning first grey, and then black. For a moment the inkery comes back into view. He sees Ellie, caught in the mechanical grip of the Red Guard brute. Litmus cries out, his throat filling with bitter smoke, choking the cry before it can take flight. He staggers to his feet, reaching for Ellie with all the strength he can bring to bear. A foot, or fist, hits the calligrapher across the back of his head, and all is turned to darkness.

***

Now, years later, the fire in Litmus's heart has waned and gutted out. He is a cog in the machine, not merely in metaphor. The price for his part in the Script Rebellion went beyond watching the life ebb from the body of his lover. For three months he was held at the fleshworks, under the personal care of Calaban, the Red Queen's prize Apothecary and the cruellest of her kin.

Calaban had performed unnatural blasphemies against Litmus's flesh, transforming bone and sinew into biomechanical chimera. Flesh and metal, steam and blood were joined and twisted with etheric mancery—housed within his raw, blistered, excruciated body.

"In truth, the work could have taken little over a week," the Fleshmancer had mused as Litmus's remade body was being taken from Calaban's tent. "But alas, I confess to much enjoyment at the sounds of your bleating."

The final part of his transformation had been reserved for his return to the Inkery. What was once a home and safe haven was now a tomb from which he could never venture. Biomechanical limbs were grafted to printing apparatus and structural beams, such that Litmus himself became one with the inkery. Blood and ink now flowed through his veins and arteries. His bi-folded heart pumped life and liquid to every nook and crevice of his disproportionate body, while steam-driven pistons powered various biomechanical appendages.

It was of little consolation that they had not gone so far as to dictate the manner of his business, those nameless bureaucrats who delighted in the dispensing of the Queen's justice. Litmus was free to take whatever commissions he chose and free to court the custom of whichever benefactors he wished. Surprisingly, demand for calligraphy of his sort had not diminished during his failed rebellion and imprisonment with Calaban. To the contrary, business resumed without missing so much as a step, much to Litmus's consternation.

His clientele did not care a jot for his treasonous activities. Nor did they seem unduly disturbed by his recent transmogrification. If anything, Litmus's imprisonment within the inkery—his becoming indistinguishable from the apparatus of the calligrapher's art—had only served to bolster his reputation among the Administratum priests, whose constant intrigues and internal bickering required a near endless supply of scribal work. Only the stall owners and artisans who lived and worked in Rookery Market looked with misery and sorrow upon the newly remade Calligrapher.

***

From the distant window, Litmus watches shadows lengthen upon the red-brick walls of the buildings opposite his inkery. Fingers and feet do their work, seemingly of their own volition, as he gazes longingly through the grimy glass, tapping at keys, pulling levers and performing the multitude of sundry tasks upon which the inkery's work is founded. The multitude of metallic runners, pulleys and mechanized pistons that enable his movement throughout the building provide for a surprising range of movement in all but one case.

In the cruellest of punishments, Litmus cannot move within five feet from any window or externally facing door. His only view of natural light is that which reflects off the dull red surface of the buildings hunched heavily beside his own.

He watches through the circular portal as darkness falls, then reluctantly leaves his place atop the second story gantry, sliding on brass runners down through the heart of the building and into a large basement, where perpetually stoked boilers fill the air with stifling steam.

A figure waits for him, sitting on a chair and holding a tattered book whose cover is black with soot. The figure looks up at Litmus and grins.

"Good to see that not all the Script's volumes were lost," he says, holding up the charred volume.

Litmus twists his neck to one side, kneading the bulbous flesh of his shoulder with a spare hand, while the rest of his appendages disentangle themselves from the apparatus of the inkery, to the sounds of hissing steam and clanking metal. The Calligrapher's bones ache with constant strain, the muscles and tendons of his remade limbs adding to the cacophony with periodic stabs of pain and unruly spasms.

"Two or three volumes, no more," he says to the visitor in a wet, murky voice, spittle and ink bubbling at the corners of his mouth.

The figure places the book to one side and stands. He is a man remade, much like Litmus, but the transformation for Idrus Kane has been one of internal excruciation. He has no added limbs or mechanical augments. His only affectations are the broken shackles at his wrists, the symbol of his long imprisonment. Those shackles apart, he is a man unchanged from all those years ago, and Litmus cannot help but weep from ink sacks and tear ducts alike at the memories that Kane's face conjures.

Yet, for all his similarity, the man who stands before Litmus now is no mere gunslinger. He may look as he did, but he has undergone a transformation far more profound than the Calligrapher.

"I have it," Kane says, producing a small amber bottle from his jacket and handing it to the spider-monstrosity that is Litmus Shule. The Calligrapher feels his blood heart flutter in anticipation as he accepts the gift with an outstretched hand. In one fluid movement, he unstops the cork and raises the bottle to those olfactory abominations which serve as both nose and mouth. The ink is pungent, brimming with etheric energy.

From a hidden nook elsewhere in the inkery, one of Litmus's limbs produces a long syringe. He fills the syringe with the ink and injects it directly into an abdominal ink sack which sits along his spine. There is a momentary shudder in reality as the ink takes effect, and Litmus closes his eyes. He sits in silence for a time, feeling the warmth of the etherically charged ink as it flows into his second heart.

In the darkness, light blossoms around a feminine face, its outlines etched in threads of golden light. She smiles. "Litmus, my love," Ellie says, her voice ringing out melodiously through the caverns of the Calligrapher's mind. His heart swells to hear her.

"My beloved," he intones, grinning despite himself. "Kane is here. He has brought the ink."

She nods, knowingly. "I feel it, my love. I sense its power. Will it do as you wish?"

"We shall see, precious one. I will return shortly with news."

Gold-etched hands take form as Ellie blows him a kiss. The gesture is simple enough, but it causes spasms of joy to ripple through the Calligrapher's many-limbed body. He opens his eyes, feeling as though the weight of his afflictions have been lifted somewhat. As he prepares his implements for the task at hand, Litmus reflects on the quirk of fate which has given him his heart's desire.

It was Calaban the Cruel who thought to punish Litmus for his love, grafting Ellie into the Calligrapher's monstrous new flesh and killing her in the process. It was a torture so profoundly horrific as to turn the stomach of even the most hardened of the fleshmancer's assistants. Litmus could only watch in horror as Ellie was taken apart, piece by piece, and grafted into his own flesh. She lived far too long as Calaban did his gruesome work. Her screams, first audible and then heard through some inner organ buried within Litmus's new body, were silenced too late in the torturous process of transformation.

Yet, that act of brutality gifted the Calligrapher with his greatest prize. He is monstrous, there is no doubt of that. Yet Ellie lives on, within the ruined castle of his flesh. They commune nightly, entwined within each other's thought-limbs, nestled together where no harm can reach. More than this, it is not some mere facsimile, some etheric echo, which resides in the Calligrapher's body, but Ellie herself. The Fleshmancer has given Litmus this great gift and, unknowingly, granted the Calligrapher the tools which may one day prove the undoing of the Red Queen and her brutal council.

Kane departs momentarily, returning after a time with a young man with tanned skin and a steady gait. The young man bears his right arm, sitting on a seat and laying the arm on a nearby table. There is a look of fiery determination to the lad, and Litmus approves of the choice. Litmus lumbers toward the young man, limbs shuffling, a tattoo needle poised in one hand.

"This will hurt somewhat," the Calligrapher says.

The young man nods solemnly. Litmus turns an eye to Kane, the gunslinger nods. "Haste, I think, Litmus, if you can manage it. Daramus is a runner, so haste would make sense."

"Haste and endurance, with a touch of strength," Litmus agrees. "He will need all three, otherwise he may run himself into an early grave."

Kane nods and Litmus begins his work. The tattoo needle hums beneath his expert hand. As the needle draws near to flesh, Litmus closes one eye, welcoming Ellie forward. In his mind he sees her perfect, gentle hand, cover his own monstrous appendage. As one, they press needle against flesh and begin to etch etherically charged symbols into the young man's arm.

It takes many hours to complete the work, and the young man is forced to eat and sleep before the task can be completed. When it is done, he looks haggard, but grateful.

Several days pass until Kane returns to the inkery. He meets Litmus at their usual time, bearing a second bottle of etheric ink.

"You are to be commended," he says, holding the bottle out to Litmus. "You and Ellie. You have done a remarkable thing."

Litmus nods, a fumbled gesture with his bulbous, distorted head. "The work is Ellie's," he says, voice brimming with pride. "I am merely the vessel for that work."

Kane nods. "Daramus has healed, and we have tested his abilities. He can run without tiring for days on end, and at speeds which outrun the storm wraiths."

"Then the ink works?" Litmus asks.

"It does. And with it, we have our chance at vengeance, old friend. It is time, once again, to stoke the fires of rebellion. But this time, we will not be so ill-prepared."

The shackles on Kane's wrist begin to glow violent red, hinting at thick black shadows at the edges which seem to drift into the air like smoke. The inkery shakes with a sudden burst of etheric power and Litmus feels a momentary cessation of pain among his tethered limbs and tortured organs.

This time he is no mere observer, no hapless soul trapped in the machinations of greater powers. He is *the Calligrapher*, architect of the new rebellion.

The Calligrapher – Charidimos Bitsakakis

Litmus Inkery – Piort Antoniak

11. Temple of Justice: Case 245/115a – Script Rebellion Dogma

Historical Fragment.

Item: Pamphlet Fragment, Third Cycle, Original, 245
Providence: Discovered amongst remains left by a thaumaturgical fire in the northeast Fens. It is assumed that some property of the fire ossified the temporal ink on said pamphlet, providing a permanent record of several legible pages.
Content:
…against the Red Queen and her witchery! And fight we must, for the passing of each cycle sees more of our loved ones imprisoned without just cause.

Say not, "I live at peace in the Red City," and think not that your path is free of turmoil, for none of us know when the crimson cloaks may lay hands upon friend, colleague, brother. Hear, now, the plea of one such soul, and let these words stir you to action!

I, Magnus Baun, speak true and in mine own words. I am a simple worker of metal and glass. Each day I and my brother worked the bellows and bells, fashioning bulbs and tubes for the grand folk of the citadel. Tis hard work which breaks the back and turns fingers to raw meat, but I and my brother and our fellows did not complain, nor cause disruption.

Through error, and no fault of my brother's, the crimson cloaks did come to the foundry and steal him away without cause. I and my brother pleaded for mercy, but the Red Guard are ever deaf to the pleas of the innocent. For my part I earned a bloodied nose and crippled leg, and several others in our crew were likewise treated to the guardsman's rough touch.

I travelled to the Administratum with all good haste, to seek the magistrate and plead justice. But there was no justice to be found, nor was my brother accused of wrongdoing. "Wanted on Queen's business," was all the priests would tell on it. I…

[Burnt fragment – illegible]

…floating in the canal, discarded like a child's plaything. Horrors they had racked upon his body, before his death. I found him not as I remembered him but twisted into a monstrous form. They had taken him for their wicked experimentations, without just cause...

[Burnt fragment – illegible]

...another! So, brothers and sisters I urge you. Do not tarry, for when next the red guard walks your streets it is your kin they may drag to the Red Queen's dark bosom.

Death to the Red Queen. RUST for liberty!

Notes: Antagonist Magnus Baun, apprehended and found guilty of treason, first class. Sentenced to biothaumaturgical reconstruction in service to the Landemere foundry 245.12. Several suspected sympathisers apprehended for public distribution of seditious pamphlets. Various sentences carried out, ranging from reconstruction to brief imprisonment and confiscation of goods and property.

Magnus Baun broke from Landemere foundry restraints some five years into the service of his punishment and was killed attempting to flee the city. Explosive combustion of an etheric storage facility caused extensive damage. Consequently, Baun's remains were not found among the debris.

Additional Notes: Convicted/deceased sympathiser Magnus Braun has taken on some symbolic importance in the recent Script resurgence. Though all evidence points to his death, rumours of his appearance in parts of the lower city in the past year have led the Ministry to reopen this case to ascertain the veracity of these rumours.

12. Shackled Lament

In the darkness, I am remade.

Dark walls rise up around me, yawning open like the great maw of some dire beast. I am a man subsumed; buried beneath a mountain of rotting iron and sun-baked clay.

With the passing of each day, I am lessened. The flesh drips from my bones, falling away beneath the weight of darkness.

My eyes have grown stupid and desperate, searching with manic despair through the absolute black of the pit to which I am chained. They are now organs of invention rather than mere perception. In a sea of nothing, they discern the faint boundaries of my cell; here the glimmer of fetid moisture against a steady sloping wall, there a glint of metal, a hint of form and structure in the interminable darkness. Above, the locked hatchway from which food and water are daily dispensed; a portal of hope which cuts more deeply than any torture.

My sleep and wakefulness are no longer distinct. My mind drifts, wanders through dark and hopeless paths. Yet, of late, such wanderings are infused with novelty. The canvas of my mind has become far more than the dull surface of a pond, into which I cast my memories and imaginings; a fleeting picture which holds its form for no more than a few brief moments. I have borrowed clarity and precision from some dark intelligence, some grand dweller of the pit who seeks communion.

The images of my imagination are made vivid, made strange by those beings who call this darkness home. They speak in swaths of light and colour and leave behind a host of affective impressions. I am unsure now which hand guides and which forces. I know only that my thoughts are not fully my own.

I sense their conflict, the interminably slow clashing of malevolent minds within eternal darkness. Their debates cause ripples that cast me to and fro like a ship amid some vast etheric tumult. I try, with all the force I can muster, to throw my own will into the fray, but such insolence is the baying of an insect at the heels of the gods.

In the darkness, I am remade.

13. Spawn of Shadows

It is commonly thought that the beings who inhabit the Shadowlands—north and west of the red city—come into the Traumwelt ready-made, born out of the nightmares of dreamers and given substance by the peculiar workings of Rust and its cruel patron. And yet, one does not find, among the shadowspawn of that region, much reference to popular film culture in the waking world. One finds no Freddy Krueger or gremlin, no axe-wielding murderer or sewer-dwelling clown. True, there are some reflections of these popular horror personalities, but far too few to suggest that the monstrous aberrations of the shadowlands are derived simply from the dreamed nightmares of sleepers.

I would suggest, by way of contrast, that there is a profound underlying logic to the vast array of horrors which inhabit the storms of the Shadowlands and, on occasion, find their way to the outskirts of Rust. Those who have witnessed the beasts first hand often speak of abhorrent augmentations—gruesome limbs sewn in place with haphazard stitches, organs bound to flesh with crude chains and crooked nails, a blending of flesh and machinery.

Does this not remind us of the aberrations we find in our own city? Does it not bring to mind those poor souls who have fallen victim to the so-called *Queen's Justice*, and been sent to the Fleshworks to be remade into something monstrous? The fleshmancers, under the tutelage of that most heinous of individuals, Calaban, twist and burn, augment and crush, fixate and disperse with the ill purpose of demented gods. We all have seen the results of such hideous experimentation with our own eyes. We have witnessed the man with two heads, the woman with pincers for hands and clockwork mechanisms for organs. We have watched with weeping eyes as our loved ones are transmuted into the realm of the monstrous; miners with piston-powered limbs and boiler-plate bodies, farmers with germinating pouches grafted to their hips and ploughs fastened to their mechanized legs.

What then of the waste? What of the failed fleshworks, the apothecary's chemical miscreants, the biomancer's miserable rejects? They are flushed, it is said, through the sewers of the red city: dispensed through underground caverns into the wastes and forgotten. But what if this self-same bioetheric effluent is bonded with happenstance among the tumultuous storms of the Shadowlands? What if the leavings of the Red Queen's cruellest magicians are given license to take flight, to evolve, to become more than mere waste?

I am aware that my words are more than treasonous. I am aware that, if I am found, these words will be my last, and I will likely fall prey to precisely the horrors I have spoken of. Perhaps Calaban himself will work his miseries upon my flesh? Yet, for all that, I must speak. I must propose a simple idea, at whose heart lies the seed of rebellion. And so, I say it.

The shadowspawn are not born merely of nightmare, but are given shape and form by the etheric abortions and cast offs of the Red Queen's Fleshworks. It is the Red Queen, and her horror hounds, who have brought the shadowspawn to life and, in so doing, have fostered a great and terrible enemy that may yet destroy us all.

- Blind Augur, 7AR

Shadowspawn – Gabriella Nagy

14. Everdawn

The slip of paper protruded tongue-like from beneath the lip of Sara's front door. She plucked it from the ground, noting its roughly hewn texture—strands of interwoven thread pressed together to form a heavy, fibrous pulp. It had an earthy, sweet scent to it, as though it had sprouted from the ground and been harvested by calloused hands. Intrigued by the odd epistle, Sara sat on the doorstep and began to read. Thickly marked words were etched across the aged parchment, harshly penned, dark letters that bled at the edges as though weeping for their own heavy meaning.

To my deepest, darkest love,

The world warps and wanes around you,
twists itself to your every whim and inclination.
Its fibres and sinews are forever touched by your passing.

My mouth aches for the swan's curve of your neck.
My fingers flex with longing, groan and crackle in anticipation.
My heart rages within its shallow prison.

I am come, my love, prepared to tear this world asunder,
To pluck the heart from its chest and ruin all that is, and all that will be,
for the promise of your touch.

Let the worlds burn and our love take flight among their ashes.
Let the cosmos reel around us, let our foes gnash their teeth in despair.

I will possess you my love,
devour you, ingest all that you are,
until we are one flesh.

Dance on, my heart's antinomy.
Spin, and kick, and tarry a while longer,
while I sharpen my teeth and hone my heart's desire.

Yours eternal…

Sara read the words slowly, re-reading the letter several times, savouring its refreshing oddness. She felt a voyeur's wicked delight, viewing the love of another through a one-way lens, laid out so stark and unsettling on the page. She turned the paper over and inspected the parchment for signs of origin but was unable to find the least trace of its author's identity.

The mere fact of its presence beneath her door raised certain questions. Who was this man who wrote with such terrifying passion, who spoke of devouring, ingesting his lover and damning the world around them? Who was the object of the man's crazed affections? What kind of woman could drive someone to such poetic extremes? It was a letter from another age, thoroughly out of place in a world of email and texts and all manner of electronic communications.

The message was delivered by hand, so the postal service could not be blamed for its misdirection. Neighbours on either side were elderly and happily married, so the chance of an impassioned love letter to either party seemed unlikely. Sara ran through the list of her most mischievous friends to find a possible candidate for a practical joke but came up empty. They were all too old, too far away and disinterested to pull such an eccentric prank. It was simply a delicious mystery for which she would search in vain for answers. She tucked the letter in her pocket and set about unpacking her groceries, all the while distracted by the odd words and their mysterious author.

Sometime later, possessed by a peculiar flight of fancy, Sara walked to her bedroom and secreted the letter beneath her pillow. She felt more than a little embarrassed by the gesture, by the wave of protectiveness that had washed over her. There was no logical explanation for her desire to hide the letter away like that. She was not the kind of person to hoard letters or birthday cards, nor was she the type to dote over Hollywood heartthrobs or demand passionate declarations from those men who had served as lovers over the years. This made her actions all the more absurd, yet it was only when the letter was safely stashed beneath her pillow that Sara felt free to get on with the day's affairs.

The day passed with agonizing slowness. Sara returned to the letter more than once as she went about her business, though she could not have said what drove her to do so. She read and re-read the text, puzzling over the identity of its author, as though the letter truly had been meant for her.

Night fell slowly, and Sara longed for the blissful vacuity of sleep. This, perhaps more than anything else, was her furthest departure from normality. Sara Tremaine did not, under any circumstances, in any time or season, go to sleep early. Her aversion to sleep had earned her the nickname "Sandman" during her college years, and many a roommate had been driven to distraction with her various midnight tinkerings and procrastinations. So, as she lay her head on the pillow at seven p.m., a warning bell tolled somewhere in the back of her mind, drowned out by the overpowering need to sleep. Her eyes closed, seemingly of their own volition, and sleep claimed her.

Sara fell into the void where words floated, danced, taunted her with their bleeding letters, words laid bare in her mind like an open wound. The words took form as dark figures gathered in her mind's eye, mighty demigods warring for honour and passion, the clash of brutal weapons, the cry of the dead and dying. She hovered over the battlefield, forced to drink in the horrific violence that burst from every rent shield and shattered sword. The stench of death rose thick in her nostrils, nauseating, causing Sara to recoil within herself. Like the Valkyrie of Norse legend, she drifted above the throng of battle, untouched by the carnage below yet feeling intensely out of place in this violent dreamscape. Flat and unyielding, the landscape seemed to yawn outwards in all directions, red dirt and immutable rock as far as the eye could see. Clouds of red-orange dust swirled around the warring soldiers beneath the heavy brow of a clouded sky. In the waning daylight, Sara felt her dream self gently goaded toward the ground, toward a circle of calm amid the raging tumult.

A man clothed in darkness stood at the centre of the clearing, eyes aflame, a single hand outstretched toward her. The figure called to her from beyond the waking world, striding steadily closer and becoming more vividly real with each passing step. There was no pleading in his eyes, only a voice of absolute command.

"Come to me," he whispered, without speaking. "Come, my love."

Sara felt herself drawn to the man, pulled by invisible threads. She saw the outline of his face, a visage which was at once beautiful beyond measure and terrible beyond description. Something unearthly burned within those eyes, something savage and all-consuming. It was the face of a god made flesh, or perhaps a demon, Sara could not decide which. Each curve and angle radiated strength, filled her with a longing that bordered on physical pain.

Still moving toward her, past warring combatants and the clashing of divine wills, the figure reached out, and Sara felt herself pulled bodily toward him. Her hand found its way to his, descending upon silken skin, electrified by an inexplicable energy transferred by his touch. She felt herself drawn inwards, moved beyond herself, falling into his waiting embrace. The strings of her mind were undone and Sara-that-was became something wholly other, dissolving amid the indomitable fire of those inhuman eyes. She whirled, warbled, felt herself utterly destroyed and then recreated, born anew in a body not yet her own.

Sara woke with a start. She was on her feet, surrounded on all sides by the chaotic sounds of warfare. The sky hung too low, rumbled too loudly, as though she were standing on a mountain top. The clash of metal echoed from a thousand encounters where gods and men fought to the death. Others, she saw, were joined in battle—creatures brought forth from the depths of an unholy imagination, things of tooth and claw, muscle and sinew. All was blood and sweat and the immanence of death, a nightmare incarnate. Unlike the dreamy malaise that had brought her to this place, Sara now felt painfully awake, fully present in the dream.

She realized that something had hold of her arms, locking her in place with a vice-like grip. She tried to twist away, but there was no give in the fingers that held her. She felt her body being turned around, forcibly spun like a plastic ballerina in a child's music box. Slowly, like the rising of a dying sun, the god of her dreams took form in front of her. But this was not the terrifying beauty she had witnessed only moments ago, but a horror. He stood well over seven feet in height, clad in black armour which bore the gruesome stains of combat. His face was covered by a wolf's head helmet, dark and forbidding. Only his eyes remained the same, burning with ferocious intensity, a crimson glow within the dark recesses of the wolf mask.

The god-man scrutinized her with a hunger that bordered on insanity. Her chin, her hair, the curve of her back—the demon inspected her naked form as a farmer might examine livestock. She bore the indignity helplessly, unable to break free of his iron grip. War raged about them, but he felt no need to rush his examination, even when a stray lance or projectile struck calf or flank. He brushed errant attackers aside with the flick of a wrist, his attention focused squarely on the young woman who had answered his call.

After what seemed like an age, the demon faced Sara and drew her up so that her eyes met his. He wore a look of cold disdain that barely masked the churning rage within.

"This is not my beloved," he boomed, his voice cutting through the tumult.

With one hand he flung her aside, sending Sara to the earth with such force that she felt the bones of her left arm shatter on impact. Pain sprang from the fresh wound with gazelle's hooves, stabbing at her wrist, elbow, and shoulder. She cried out in agony; her voice lost in the cacophony of battle. Legs twisted unnaturally, body broken and bleeding, she watched helplessly as the demon bellowed into the night. With dark intent, he hefted the mammoth sword which stood to his left, blade jammed into solid rock. He wielded the weapon with practiced ease, advancing on Sara with death in his eyes. She scrambled to get to her feet, then recoiled in agony at the pain that bit at her from all sides. The demon was on her in three steps. He raised the sword and brought it thundering down toward her throat.

There was a loud *crack* that seemed to split the air around them. The demon's sword was knocked aside, jolting the gruesome figure backwards. His eyes narrowed, hunting the surrounding battlefield for the cause of his aborted strike. A second crack fired, and sparks flew from the demon's hulking chest plate, driving him backwards a few steps. He bellowed in rage, still scouring the battlefield with hateful eyes.

Sara tried to crawl away from him, crab-walking through the dust in desperation. A third shot rang out above the din of battle, knocking the demon's dented helmet from his head and causing him to roar in a mixture of pain and frustration. He turned, stormed off into the fight, swinging his mammoth sword and screaming in rage.

Sara sat in the red dust, tears streaming from her eyes, her body assaulted with pain. From somewhere behind she felt gentle hands upon her uninjured shoulder. She spun, eyes fearful, mind cracking beneath the strain of this new reality.

A figure, lithe and draped in strands of black fabric, loomed above her holding a rifle that stood half a dozen feet in height. Hard eyes looked down at her, but the voice that spoke was soft and kind.

"Need to get you out of here, princess, before someone tries to stick you with something pointy."

***

An hour or so passed in a haze of confused imagery. The pain in Sara's body pulled her from consciousness several times, only to thrust her back into the fray once more.

She was walking, stumbling beside the woman in wrapped cloth, who seemed to half carry her through the desert terrain. Gradually the sounds of battle faded into the background, and Sara felt herself lowered to the ground. The pain in her arm flared as her rescuer lowered her gently to the ground. She felt the world spin and threatened once more to black out, but a warm hand on her cheek kept her from falling.

"Need you to stay with me, princess. It's gonna hurt like a bitch, but if you force yourself to stay awake, you'll get through it."

The woman pulled strips of fabric from her wrist and laid them out on the rock beside them. Sara tried to talk, but the words came out garbled.

"Don't bother talkin', sister. Just stay with me and we'll get this sorted for you."

In her pain-induced madness, Sara witnessed a profound oddity. A small beetle alighted on the woman's shoulder and walked toward her face.

Unconcerned, she kept pulling strips of fabric from her person and laying them out on the ground next to Sara's arm. Then, without warning, her head turned so that her lips were only an inch away from the small, brown beetle. She spoke whispered words while the beetle waited patiently. Sara could not hear the words, but their importance was obvious. Even though she could only make out the woman's eyes from beneath the cloth-wound mask on her head, she read great urgency in her rescuer's expression. All at once, the beetle flitted from her shoulder and flew off into the air, moving with more speed than a beetle had any right to.

The pain bit at Sara's arm once more and she cried out. Lightning fast, the other woman's hand shot out to cover her mouth, stifling the scream before it had a chance to take flight.

"Here, take this."

She shoved a small bundle of cloth into Sara's mouth. It tasted of sweat and dust, but Sara had no time to object. Moving with unnatural speed, the woman caught Sara's shoulder and yanked it forwards. Sara bit down against the pain, screaming into the cloth while a torrent of agony cascaded down her arm. Her body spasmed, limbs flailing wildly. She tried to pull away from the black-clad stranger, but the woman held her fast.

Something cold and flat pressed against her forearm and she watched in horror as the woman began winding strips of cloth tightly around her broken limb. The pain redoubled and Sara let out another muffled screech. The work was done in a matter of seconds, but those seconds seemed to elongate beneath the pain that bit at Sara from all sides.

Slowly, mercifully, the pain began to abate a little. Sharp stabs were replaced by a dull ache that promised violent agony if she moved too swiftly or in the wrong way. Sara let the bundled cloth fall from her lips. Her head lolled to one side, and the other woman held it from falling.

"We're done for now," the woman said, sweat dripping from her brow and trailing down the cloth of her mask. "Your shoulder's back in, and I've set a splint for your forearm. Once we get you back to camp, I'll get the doc to take a look at you, but this should do for now."

Tears fell from Sara's eyes, and she felt the weight of a world press down upon her.

"You did good, sister. You can sleep now. I'll wake you when it's time to move."

Sara let the darkness take her, and once more felt the warmth of the other woman's touch against her cheek as she drifted into a deep sleep.

***

When Sara woke, it was to the gentle swaying of a pack beast's rhythmic steps. She was slung over the beast on her stomach and felt herself pitch left and right in time with its footsteps. Groggily, she lifted her head and tried to sit, managing only to shift her head a little. The pain in her arm was still terrible, but the tight bandage her rescuer had wound around it had helped somewhat.

A face came into view, large and square-jawed, the face of a bald-headed brute with darkly tanned skin. Stone-hard eyes scowled down at her, and Sara realized with alarm that she was not riding a pack animal, but was being carried by the towering brute. She was about to let loose a scream, when gentle hands touched the side of her head, accompanied by a familiar voice.

"Hold on, sister. Everything's gonna be okay."

Sara felt the world around her move as the giant figure laid her gently onto the ground, showing remarkable care not to touch her bandaged arm. The cloth-swaddled woman bent down and carefully examined Sara's arm, gently moving it to and fro as she leaned in to take a better look.

"So, you just popped up out of nowhere back there, princess. I'm guessing that means you've gone and dreamt yourself here, and I'm guessing that Avernath had something to do with it."

Sara felt the dry rasping of her throat as she spoke. "Avernath?"

"Yeah, the big bastard I tried to put a hole in back there. The guy's got a friggin' screw loose somewhere in that mangled head of his. Keeps fishing the waking world trying to find some lost love. Must be half a dozen chick's he's brought back here and killed 'cause they ain't what he's looking for. You're just lucky I was in the area. Bastard would have pulped you if he'd had half a chance."

"I…I don't know what to say…"

"Thank you usually does the trick, princess, but you're probably still in shock, so I'll let it slide this time."

Sara looked from the other woman to the giant standing disinterestedly nearby. He was rippled with slabs of dark muscle, naked from the waist up. "I don't understand. Where am I? What is this place?"

The other woman laughed. "Ah now that's the question isn't it. But it'll take a little winding up to get you to an answer, and most people freak out when they first hear, so how about we start with something simpler."

She stood to full height and placed a hand on her chest. "My name is Daisy, and this big bastard is Rook. He doesn't speak much, so don't get offended."

Sara nodded. "I'm Sara."

Daisy smiled. "Great, well now that the introductions are out of the way, let's get back on the road. Safe house is still a little while away, and I want to make sure we get you there before nightfall."

She pointed to Sara, and the big man bent down and picked her up, just as carefully as when he had laid her down. Sara could feel hard chords of muscle in the man's arms as he held her and marvelled at the man's strength. Near as she could tell, the brute had carried her like a baby for several hours. She wasn't exactly heavy, but it spoke volumes of the man's strength and endurance.

"Okay, so I'm gonna try to explain this nice and simple, princess," Daisy said, walking alongside the brute. "Basically, you're not in Kansas anymore. Like Dorothy, you've fallen down a well or been picked up by a twister or whatever, and your ass has landed way, way out of town. What's the last thing you remember before you came here?"

The question momentarily threw Sara. She thought back through memories that were already murky with pain and confusion.

"I…I think I was asleep in my bed."

"Right, so you go to sleep and you have a crazy ass dream. Only you don't wake up from this dream right. It keeps getting more and more real, and suddenly the bit where you're lying at home in bed seems like the dream, and now this crazy ass shithole is the real thing, yeah? What did he use to pull you here? Some kind of device or something?"

"I'm sorry?"

"Avernath. He must have used something to lure you in here."

Memories came back to Sara in small pieces. She fought hard to make sense of the impressions. The note under her door, those impassioned words.

"It was a letter. A love letter. I didn't know who it was from and…look I'm not normally the sort of person who would hold onto something like that, but the words did something to me. I…I ended up sticking the letter under my pillow…then I went to sleep and woke up here."

Daisy nodded. "A letter."

She tapped Rook on the arm, and the big man looked down at her. "Mean's he's got someone working for him on the other side."

The big man nodded, though the stony expression on his face did not change.

"Well, sister," Daisy went on, "that letter was kind of like bait, and you were the fish. I'm guessing Avernath has a few cronies over there in the waking world who can communicate with the bastard. Must have used inkmancery on the letter. Either he's got thousands of those things and only a few of them work, or he's targeted you specifically."

"But I'm no one special. Why would he be trying to get at me?"

Daisy frowned. "Come on now. No need to talk like that. We're all God's children, so we're all, like, super special and shit."

The young woman's words were thick with sarcasm.

"Look, don't beat yourself up about it, all right? Avernath is a crazy fuck, and there's no telling what reasons he had for picking you. Might have been completely random. Might be that you've got something in you that makes you more able to cross over into the Traumwelt than most other people."

"I'm sorry, the what?"

"Traumwelt. Dream world, in German or Dutch, I think. Some academic coined the term and now we pretty much all use it. Anyway, what I'm saying is that some people can cross over from the waking world to the dream world super easy. Other people can never cross over, and some just flicker in and out from time to time. Odds are you were one of the lucky ones…or unlucky depending on how you take it. Same with me and big Rook here. We weren't born here in this place. We crossed over just the same as you…well, maybe not the same. I kind of took a fast path here, and Rook didn't exactly have a psycho godling write him a love letter, but you get what I mean."

Sara's mind swam. "So, you came to this place the same as I did?"

Daisy shrugged. "Things were a bit different for me. But, like I said, I wasn't born here. Hell, no one is born here. Well, almost. Anyway, most people dream themselves into Rust or somewhere nearby but, like you, I ended up miles away, right in the middle of the Red Wastes if you can believe it. Man called Kane found me and…well that's a story for some other time. Thing is, I came here when I was sixteen, right?"

"What is Rust?"

"Big-ass city. We passed by it a while back, but you were out of it."

Daisy began unwrapping the strips of dark cloth around her face. With each sliver of fabric, a youthful face was revealed. Once the final piece of cloth had been unravelled, she turned to Sara. Daisy was young, barely out of her teens. Clear skin and finely crafted features were offset by several large scars on her face. The right side of her head was shaved, and a bullseye was tattooed into the flesh, while long, dark hair hung down the other side.

"I look like I'm fresh out of school, right?"

Sara nodded.

"That's the thing. See, shit works differently down here in the Traumwelt. Time moves differently and you age a lot slower than in the waking world. I can't give you an exact timeframe, but I'm guessin' I've been here for twelve years or so. Should be closin' in on thirty, but I still look like a fucking teenager. So, the upside of this place is that you get to keep your good looks for a while."

"And what's the downside?" Sara asked.

Daisy laughed. "Give me a couple of weeks and I'll write you a list."

She pointed to a large outcropping of rocks nearby. "Okay, we're almost here. I'll take you in to see the doc and get you some food. Get yourself some sleep tonight, and I'll catch up with you in the morning, okay?"

With her good hand, Sara caught the young woman by the shoulder.

"Thank you, Daisy."

***

The Warmaster stood alone looking out over the red city, clothed only in a simple black robe, blood flowing from a shallow cut to his chest. An image of the woman's face hung in his mind. He had been moments from killing the girl when the rebel whore had fired her wretched weapon. Yet now, as he stood upon the high balcony of his tower estate, the subtle sounds of his frolicking harem drifting lazily from the bedchamber, Avernath the Warmaster was filled with doubt.

There was something in the woman's eyes that haunted him. Something that tugged at the strings of memory, that pulled against the barbed strands of his heart. Perhaps the rebel girl had done him a service? Perhaps he had been too hasty in seeking to dispatch the woman.

Could it be that his long search was over? Could this weak vessel carry the seed of his great love? He flexed the muscles of his arms, twisting his neck to one side with a satisfying crack. On the morrow he would begin his search for the girl, and this time no gun-toting rebel whore would stand in his way.

"Sienna my love," he whispered. "I come for you."

15. Rust – An Etymological Note

Four letters, etched into the ochre clay and badly cracked with age.

R U S T

The word is penned in a hasty scrawl upon the capstone of an ill-shaped archway that marks the entrance to the city's southernmost gateway; the so-called Lion's Maw. None can say whether the word was penned in reference to the sun-baked clay from which so much of the great city is fashioned, or in tribute to the pitted iron shards that mark the city's boundary like some jagged-toothed beast.

Some attribute greater theological significance to the title, found not only upon the capstone of the southern gate, but at innumerable locations throughout the city proper—etched on paving stones, into walls, and cut into the earth itself like echoes rippling outward from the source. It is the sole word upon which every faction of the city can agree. Northmen from the shadow hills, brutes and enforcers of the merchant guilds, the Orst, the Silent Priests, even the Red Queen herself does not forbid the marking of her city with this singular, inoffensive title.

It was not always so, of course. The city was christened *New Dawn* by the Red Queen half a century ago. Newly built at the hand of the Clockmaker and brimming with promise, the city stood as a bastion against the ever-swirling sands of the red wastes. Time and tribulation have worn that city down. Likewise, they have worn down the Red Queen's resistance to the city's new appellation.

The city wilts and withers, its iron towers pitted with corrosion, its red-brick walls crumbling with age and sorrow. The city is eaten away from the inside out, every surface covered with the dull orange hue from which the city derives its common name.

Even the Shackled Man and his followers take no offence at the appellation. To the contrary, they speak the word with pride and anguish—a symbol of their struggle against the Red Queen's tyranny, their desire to see the city freed from oppression.

She has not beauty, nor does she court the visitor with fine phrases, this wounded city, standing resolute among the shifting sands and ethereal vistas of the Traumwelt. Rust is an open wound amid the broken rock and endless winds of the red wastes. What it lacks in beauty, it recovers in blunt resilience. While the many cities and hamlets of the Traumwelt are caught forever in an ethereal flux—becoming more and less substantial in turns—Rust sits like a stubborn welt, unmoved by the rise and fall of dreamed empires, of spectres and phantasms, ghosts and ghasts and all manner of waking nightmares.

16. Seditious Mummery

A wooden stall, painted red, black, white.

A curtain, black, with white stars shining.

A sign, cut with crimson ink, announcing to all who pass, the date and time at which the mummer's act will commence.

Night falls, darkness reigns, and the streets are filled with revellers. Harvest's End is a cause for light debauchery and unbridled celebration. The market squares are filled with masked celebrants, each buoyed with drink and song. The night is one of several throughout the year where the common folk reign supreme throughout the red city: where the Red Priests briefly surrender their hold and the Queen's Guard rarely are seen. Only a few district militia stand guard, the most corruptible of militants who are more likely to give in to the ebb and flow of the festivities than police unruly behaviour.

The mummery begins at midnight, announced by the trumpeting of miniature horns. Curtains open and give rise to a cast of caricatured puppets, moved by ingenious strings and hidden levers. The players are led by a grotesque narrator; a crippled spider of a figure, corpulent and many-limbed, who sits above the stage and to the left—bound to the mummer's apparatus as if by the fleshmancer's art.

Drunken crowds begin to gather as the play is joined. The dark narrator sets the tone—a kingdom in strife, ruled by a cruel king, love obstructed, hope in peril. As the crowd settles, hero and heroine enter the miniature stage. A thin, studious figure who wields the pen rather than the sword, swears his undying love to a figure of unparalleled beauty.

The lovers are joined in blissful union. A smaller, semi-opaque curtain is raised over their bed chamber. An amber light shines from the rear as lover silhouettes perform their intimate dance, much to the raucous delight of the intoxicated crowd.

At this point, by shrewd design, young boys and girls—street urchins clothed in the vibrant red sash which signifies the mummer's company—circulate through the crowd with upturned hats, begging indulgences. Once sufficient coin has been loosed from the purses of onlookers, the mummer's show commences once more.

The lover's contentment is short-lived, brutally cut short at the bequest of a jealous king who seeks to possess the hero for his calligrapher's art. But the hero is cunning and not easily outfoxed, evading all attempts at capture and making fools of the king's guardsmen. Furious beyond reason, the king sends dark knights to apprehend the hero's companion, settling for her art and company in lieu of the calligrapher himself.

The enthralled crowd boos and jeers as the jealous king torments the hero's lover, locking her in chains and forcing her to work against her will. A message is sent to the hero calligrapher, stating that his love will be put to the sword unless he himself attends the king and surrenders his gift.

In the crowd, there are rumblings: the first inclination of discontentment, a hint of discomfort at the parody played out in miniature before them. As the play moves into its final scenes, several militia men—previously disinterested—now watch the play with narrowed eyes and ready cudgels. There is a texture of defiance, of mockery, to the mummer's act which leans too heavily upon real experience. Even the most insensible of onlookers can see the clear points of connection between this fanciful tale and the old rebellion whose scars still mark the red city.

The final act is one of complete abandon. The cunning calligrapher does not merely present himself before the king in the hopes of saving his love. Knowing full well the treachery of the king and his minions, the calligrapher—now proudly displaying a red quill upon his chest; an emblem of defiance which harks back to the scripts of old—rouses the people to fight against the unjust king.

Swiftly, the small stage is filled with riotous figures, led by the calligrapher and storming the king's castle. Horrified by what they see, those few militia men who have not drunk too deeply of the wine barrel, raise their cudgels and begin advancing upon the mummer's stage, shouting above the rabble. They urge the crowd to disperse, but already the puppetry melee has roused something within the intoxicated onlookers. They cheer and shout, raising fists into the air as if in solidarity with the puppets who now assail the king and his cronies.

Militia men continue their advance, shouting now with punctuated swings of their weapons. They struggle in vain to move through the press of revellers, kicking and swigging cudgels with something approaching frenzied panic. It takes a few minutes for the violence on stage to spill over to the street. Once the crowd perceive the brutish behaviour of those few militia men, fists and half-empty goblets become weapons, and an awkward violence ensues.

The moments that follow are confused and charged with fear and brutality. More militia men enter the fray, resorting to projectile weaponry in an effort to disperse the crowd. Blood is spilt and old grievances raised. Forgotten now amid gunfire and panic, the mummer's final act concludes. Lovers stand united, one foot upon the broken body of the dead king, while a dozen figures hoot and cheer around them. No one sees this final exaltation, for the violence in the streets had acted as a sobering agent and now, even the most quarrelsome of citizens is resolved to flight and safety.

When the final tally is counted, three militia men lay dead. A dozen common folk are dead by gunshot or battery. Joined by the Red Guard, the militia men advance upon the mummer's stall, intent upon delivering cruel justice to the puppeteers who have incited such brutal violence. They find no puppeteers, but only a clockwork mechanism of ingenious devising. Incensed, the militia men set about the absolute destruction of the clockwork mummery, beating at cogs and clockwork with hard cudgels. Amid the clang and crash of this battery, some curious mechanism is triggered within the apparatus. The machine splits open, birthing a rapid flurry of projectiles that fly into the air and out of militia reach.

The whirling, insect-like machines divide and disperse throughout the city. Their coiled spring catalysers are short-lived, but of sufficient power to disseminate the clockwork creatures to every corner of the trade district. They fall swiftly, embedding themselves into walls and roofs and the hard stone cobbles of the street itself. Each machine dies on impact, splitting to give birth to its true purpose. Each holds a small pamphlet, a script penned by a single hand. Each script speaks briefly but in powerful syllables.

Remember the Script Rebellion.

Remember those who died.

Free Rust.

Down with the red queen.

17. Salinger

Shadows lengthen as a tall, sinewy figure slinks through the broken remains of the outer courtyard, heading toward the ruined house with deceptive speed. Stray vines and weeds seem to cling to the figure as he moves, welcoming him as one of their own.

Without a word, Salinger ducks through the open doorway and into the house beyond, surrounded by a small cloud of whirring fruit flies that seem to dance about his head as though it were a rotting melon. Shadowfang is the first to speak.

"Some spymaster," she offers, her petite nose scrunched. "I could smell you from halfway across the courtyard."

Salinger grins, showing rows of mismatched teeth that seem stricken with rot and decay, like the moss-covered stones of some abandoned castle. He bows in front of the assassin, pulling something from his waistcoat and handing it out to her wordlessly. A small elephant beetle sits nestled in the palm of his hand.

"No thanks, Sal," she says with a forced smile, "I'd rather eat my own foot than touch anything that's come from your fucking pockets."

She motions toward a nearby doorway. "He's downstairs. Knock before you go in."

Salinger bows once more, grinning gruesomely as he slips the elephant beetle back into his vest. The mist of bugs and fruit flies that hover about his body drifts behind like smoke as the lanky figure heads to the basement. Shadowfang lets out a breath, turning to a squat figure sitting nearby, nestling a rifle between his legs.

"I'm not kidding," she says, sucking in breath, "but that boy smells like a dead cow wrapped in the devil's asshole!"

It draws the usual round of laughter from those seated nearby. Shadowfang grimaces. She can still taste the fetid scent of rotting meat and putrefied flora that follows Salinger like some ghastly aura.

The spymaster enters the ruined house, heads downstairs to a long, dimly lit corridor. At the far end is an old wooden door. He is about to knock, but before his grimy fingers connect with wood a voice comes from inside the room.

"Come in, Sal."

He opens the door and enters a world of sudden, shocking darkness. The light from the doorway streams in, fanning out in all directions, seemingly swallowed by the darkness within.

"Close the door," says the figure sitting in the far corner of the room. Salinger does as he's asked with something approaching reverence. This might be a dishevelled hovel on the outskirts of Rust, but he is in the presence of a living legend, and it pays to be respectful in such company.

"What have you got?" the dark figure asks, his voice hard and weathered, as though left out in the desert too long.

Salinger clears his throat, releasing a sudden swarm of fruit flies as he prepares to speak. His voice is reedy and insect-like.

"We are losing our man at the Greymaul. His mind is going soft, like the others, like recruits. Is what you are saying boss, is no turning back once they leave the Greymaul. Red Guard is all bad…turned bad no matter how they are coming in. She is doing…something to them, something makes them soft in the head."

The spymaster taps the side of his head, sending a flurry of insect life momentarily skyward.

"What of the Shadowlands?"

Salinger nods, zealously. "Yes, yes boss, Shadowlands, yes. We is getting message from the man in Greymaul…before he go soft in the head. He is telling us about project in Shadowlands, something about the red bitch doing experimentations in Shadowlands. She is finding a way to make the nasties stay solid, stay real for longer time. You know boss, the ones coming in from wakers, nasty things from nightmare, she is make them solid and real. She is keeping them in this place for long time, some kind of collar or shackle or thing like that…"

Too late Salinger realizes his mistake. The mention of a shackle was careless, stupid. He shakes his head, inwardly chastising himself for the misstep.

"She's building an army?" the other man asks, seemingly unconcerned.

Visibly relieved, Salinger nods. "Yes, yes, army. This is why we is not finding her much in the city. She is work on project, making army of Shadowland creature. I don't be hearing much more, but I hear some of shadowspawn get loose and kill bunch of Red Guard in the Greymaul. Experiment is gone wrong, and a bunch of soldier is getting killed. I don't hear any else about this though."

"Daisy will take care of it. Tell me about the Fleshworks."

Salinger nods, but there's a hesitation in his speech as he continues. "Is nasty business. All kinds of nasty business."

"And the Cauldron?"

"Nastiest of all, that place," Salinger says, "there is being a lot of augmentation, punishment, all that kind of thing, but is new kinds of thing there too. Calaban is getting people from waking world, not here in the Rust. The bugs have seen it. They taste me…tell me that they is to be bringing in many new people from waking world, new dreamers who getting trapped here. They take them from city and into Calaban's tent and doing all the nasty experiments on them."

The figure in the corner of the room stirs, standing to full height. He takes a step closer, his imposing figure a dark shadow that seems to absorb what little light enters the room through the cracks in the door.

"What does she want with the dreamers?" he asks. "What is she getting out of them?"

Salinger swallows, his heart beginning to gallop. "Is blood ether…so the bugs are to be saying. Bugs say Calaban is draining the juice from dreamers and using it to make trappings for the darklings in Shadowlands. Using this blood ether for other things too, but the bugs don't be seeing that."

The conversation is interrupted by the loud buzzing of a many-winged insect hovering just outside the door. The creature buzzes and taps against the wood, searching for a path to its master.

"Pardon," Salinger says, with a slight bow. He turns, opens the door a crack, and lets the insect in. The bug darts through the door, landing expertly onto Salinger's outstretched hand. The spymaster gently strokes the creature's back with his index finger, and the bug quivers in response.

"Moment," Salinger says apologetically. With frightful speed, he thrusts the insect into his mouth and begins chewing ravenously. In moments the bug is gone, and Salinger has his head twisted thoughtfully to one side. He picks at his teeth with a grubby fingernail, nodding to himself.

"Word from port," he says, his eyes closed. "Trouble at Fens. Red Guard is going house to house…look for something, locking up anyone they telling is part of rebellion."

"Our people?" the shadowed figure asks.

"I think we safe, boss," Salinger says, "but is better I be going to make sure."

There's a slight pause as the other man considers. Deathly silence is interrupted only by the buzzing and chittering of the varied bugs and insects which perpetually crawl about the spymaster's body.

"Very well. Go. Make sure our people are safe. I'll call for you when I need you."

Salinger bows, quickly opening the door and setting off without a backward glance. Kane waits in the darkness for a few moments, breathing deeply as if in preparation for his entry into the light. He slips a pair of dark lensed goggles over his eyes, pulls up the half-mask that covers his mouth and chin, then strolls out into the light.

He walks with a steady gait through the ruined interior of the decaying residence and catches Shadowfang's eye on his way through the twin pillars that mark the remnants of the front doorway. Without a single word, the assassin leaves her perch, snatches up the dark metal rifle at her side, and falls in beside Kane.

They walk wordlessly for a time. Shadowfang can't avoid staring down at the broken shackle dangling from Kane's nearest wrist. The blackened, time-worn metal seems to hum and vibrate with power, sending out faint wisps of etheric energy like amber tendrils of smoke.

"It seems Eva is making her move," Kane says.

The assassin nods. "What kind of move exactly? She gonna purge the city again?"

He shakes his head. "No. She's looking elsewhere. Has her eyes set on the waking world, on her sister. Salinger says she's found a way to trap dreamers here and drain etheric power from them. She's using it to recruit shadowspawn; building a permanent army in preparation for a crossing."

"How the fuck?" Shadowfang says, her jaw wide.

"I don't know."

"Shadowspawn? For fuck's sakes, Kane, permanent shadowspawn? I thought the bastards we had to deal with at Baronsville were bad enough, and they only lasted a few hours. Can you imagine fighting off an army of permanent shadowspawn? I mean, can they even be killed? They're not strictly real after all. Well, I suppose they are *real*, but not really real. Fuck, I'm not making any sense."

"You're missing my point," Kane says, still walking at a brisk pace toward the outskirts of the property.

"Oh really? And what point is that exactly?"

"Her attention is focused on the shadowspawn, on building her army. That means it's not focused on us. That presents us with a unique opportunity. Even a godling Queen can't be everywhere at once."

The words hit the assassin like a brick to the chest. She spins, grabs Kane by the arm and immediately regrets it. An etheric charge bites at her skin like electric current, and she pulls back her hand with a curse.

"She's building a fucking army, Kane. And you know what she's planning on doing with that army? She's going to take it to the waking world. To my fucking world, God damn it! That's not a small thing in my book."

Kane turns, starts walking again, forcing Shadowfang to follow after.

"She has no viable means of traveling between worlds," he says flatly. "Not without drawing the attention of the Old Ones. She won't risk a crossing until she has a stable portal, and all our intelligence says that she's a while away from that. So, for the meantime your world is safe, little one. We should turn our attention to present business, and that is how to take advantage of the Red Queen's preoccupation."

He pauses for a moment, slowing his pace a little.

"I might add, little sister, that the waking world was once my home as well."

Shadowfang snorts. "Dude, you're so far removed from that place it doesn't even count. I mean, can you even remember what a hotdog tastes like? You missed all of *Friends* and *The Simpsons* and you've probably never seen a laptop in your life."

Kane shrugs.

"Plus, I'm still not sure we're from the same world at all. I get that you came from some olden day place, but there could be a hundred worlds which all sound pretty much the same back in the old days. You're all churning butter and hunting pigs and all that shit."

Kane smiles, and the expression is more than a little alarming. "My dear Daisy, I'd forgotten how perceptive you are."

Shadowfang snorts. "That's 'cause you got a bad memory, grandpa."

Kane turns and begins walking once more with Shadowfang keeping pace beside him.

"Where are we heading anyway?" she asks.

"There is something I must show you, something important."

He leads her to a small building hidden to the rear of the compound, past several guards, the local smithy and Rook—bare chested and lovingly caressing a broadsword with a large whetstone. The big man looks up at the pair as they pass by, the slight edges of a smile etched into his oversized features.

"Okay, I'm all for surprises, Kane, but this is starting to piss me off."

"Patience, little one," Kane says, leading her through makeshift walls to the innermost room of the building, which is cut into the mountainous stone that surrounds the compound.

A young man stands by the doorway. Shadowgang recognizes him, but cannot place his name. Besides the young man, a woman lies on a cot, sleeping. Shadowfang turns to Kane, tilting her head questioningly.

"This is Romero," Kane says, motioning to the young man, "an ethermancer of rare skill. His young bride, Brita, sleeps on the cot."

The young man stands in reverent silence as Kane speaks, his head bowed.

"Pleased to meet you," Shadowfang says with a bemused expression. "Wow, this was really special, Kane, are you dropping a hint that I need to find myself a boyfriend?"

"Brita herself is a capable mancer," Kane goes on. "The pair have survived great tribulation and found their way to us by only the most difficult of paths."

Shadowfang moves to speak but is held back by Kane's upheld hand.

"The girl is with child, Shadowfang. Brita and Romero have conceived."

Shadowfang laughs. Turning from Kane to the young man, then back again.

"You're shitting me, right? For some reason you've decided to crack an incredibly unfunny joke?"

"I do not jest, Daisy. She is with child and, from what we can tell, the child is imbued with significant etheric power."

Shadowfang takes a step closer to Brita, who stirs a little, a hand moving protectively to her abdomen. She wakes slowly from her slumber, bleary-eyed, but unconcerned at the newcomers standing over her.

"I don't get it," the assassin says.

Kane nods. "Five hundred years or more have passed in this land, and not one child has been conceived by our kind in all those years. I cannot say what significance this heralds, but believe me, this is significant."

Shadowfang sits beside the young woman, reaching out a hand to place on Brita's belly. The young woman smiles broadly.

"A baby," she says, shaking her head. "No shitting way."

18. Shacklebane

Shacklebane is a man-chimera, a blending of flesh and machine. He is a creature made, not born, just as all things within the Traumwelt are not born. Nameless, until receiving his first and only commission, Shacklebane began life in the bowels of the Red Queen's citadel, amid the obscene machinery and etheric mancery that dwells in that place.

While none who walk beneath the citadel are free to tell what they have witnessed, it is said that a dark sentience dwells there, feeding off the terrible etheric power which leaches down from the Red Queen herself into the depths. Channels of raw power likewise flow from the Apothecarian. Etheric effluent bleeds from the fleshmancer tents into this dark reservoir, spewing forth the abhorrent remnants of failed experiments and excruciations. The dead are given monstrous life, it is said, among the ether-rich stones and broiling waters that churn beneath the red city.

Such tales are mere rumour, yet their veracity is written large upon the tortured flesh of the man-chimera, the bounty hunter born of darkness and demonic intent.

Shacklebane.

19. Red Guard initiate

I am no soldier, no brute who delights in the shedding of blood. I have no skill with weaponry nor hand-to-hand combat, nor any other skill which might prepare me for the role of a soldier, save the will to complete my mission.

I have lost much in the years since my arrival in the red city. A sister came with me to these crimson shores—bright eyed and full of life, my Liza. Born of the same mother, on the same day, we lived shared lives and, on occasion, could even sense what the other was thinking. It is little surprise then that we shared the dream which took us from our native land and brought us to Rust.

We woke to this strange place, alone and afraid, wandering aimlessly until a kindly soul brought us in and gave us food and water. Mama Kel had a heart too big for her body. She was a simple metal smith—a repairer of pots and pans and all manner of tools and trinkets. Traveling from street to street with her tinker's wagon, Mama Kel was well known and well loved, particularly among the merchants and purveyors of the market districts.

In winter she would sell hot soup and stale bread to the port laborers and fenboys. In summer, she would bring ice to the soldiers of Greymaul and the denizens of the Fens. She did not withhold her goods from any man, woman, or child, be they the lowest sewer rat or the loftiest of the Red Queen's nobility. The Red Guard and militia alike, who would delight in finding excuse to brutalize even the most mild-mannered of merchants, left Mama Kel unmolested. On occasion, they even went so far as to serve as unofficial bodyguard to the tinkerer.

A thousand pages I could write of the kindness and cunning of Mama Kel, but alas I have only a little time and only a little space. Suffice it to say that she was a saint in this red city of sinners. She took Liza and I in, gave us food and shelter, taught us the tinkerer's art. We joined her in her rounds of the city and spent our days helping her bend and twist metal. Likewise, we helped Mama Kel dispense soup and bread, ice and sweet tea. In a city of brutes and cutthroats, we found the loving embrace of an old woman of rare courage and strength.

She died not more than three years after we arrived in Rust. An infection, grown for long years up her legs, began to turn black. Too swiftly for medicine to aid, the infection took Mama Kel's heart, and she passed from this strange world into whatever lies beyond.

The city mourned for Mama Kel in its own peculiar way. Here and there, throughout the streets, women hung long yellow sashes from their windows, in honour of the scarf she wore each day. As we continued her tinker's rounds, many folk came to state their sorrow at her passing, some even offering what little money they could spare in her memory.

In just three years we had become Mama Kel's children. In a heartbeat, we had become orphans.

The peace lasted a year or so. We continued Mama Kel's work and, though we lacked her skill and her diplomacy, we were able to secure sufficient money to keep us fed, clothed, and sheltered. Yet the world had grown darker in her absence and the city streets began to take on a vicious edge. Red Guard patrols we encountered looked upon us with disdain, what little goodwill Mama Kel had managed to foster with the soldiers now gone. We were barred from the military district and forced to follow less lucrative paths through the city streets. The local militias, too, forgot their love of Mama Kel and began treating us with contempt.

I worried for my sister. She was strong willed and sharp of tongue, but far too beautiful for a city such as this. I saw, in the eyes of every soldier, every militiaman and brute, a violent lust that spoke of eminent danger. I urged her to dress plainly, to cover her face and conceal her beauty, but my sister was a proud woman and not given to shying away from conflict.

It took the unwanted advances of a drunk militiaman to bring her to sense. The brute had stumbled into our path as we returned home from the port district. Though thoroughly inebriated, he was swift as a serpent and strong enough to overpower me without difficulty. A blow to the head sent me to the ground as he caught Liza by the wrist and began to explicate the horrors he wished to visit upon her flesh. Through bleary eyes, I watched her struggle, watched the brute overpower her with ease and press her against a nearby wall, intent on taking her before my very eyes.

I struggled to rise, but could not intervene, for several of the brute's companions held me to the ground, delighting in the violence of their drunken comrade. It was the good people of Rookery Market who saved my sister from the militiaman's cruel attentions. A local baker, O'Toole I believe his name to be, and several other shopkeepers advanced on us, wielding what weapons they had to hand. First three, then four, then a dozen men—all lean of muscle and used to hard labour—stood against the militiamen and ordered them to release my sister.

For a moment, the world was caught betwixt peace and violence. From my vantage, head down in the dust, I could make out the cold rage which had crossed the militiaman's face—he who still held my sister by the neck. There was blood and horror in those dull eyes, and, for a time, I thought that the night would end only in death and misery. But the baker and his fellow merchants were persuasive, and the militiamen soon tired of their sport, leaving us to our misery with a series of spits and curses.

I thanked the shopkeepers for their kindness and moved quickly homeward with my sister walking in silence. From that day forth, she wore a cloak and hood to hide her face. She spoke little and no longer wore a smile.

In the end, it was not the militia brutes who took my sister, but the Red Guard—those of shield and spear, rifle and polished armour.

I took ill and could not leave my bed. Liza led the tinker wagon without me, insisting that we could not afford to let even one day slip without risking starvation. She worked the Administratum district from dawn till dusk for three days while I fought to purge the malady from my flesh. I was so weak that I could not stand; so helpless that I was reduced to a simple-minded wretch. She cared for me, my sister. Working by day and tending my needs by night, she kept me from death's door.

On the fourth night, as strength began to return to me somewhat, Liza did not come home. I enlisted the aid of a neighbour and pulled myself from bed. Still fevered and shaking for lack of strength, I searched the city streets for some sign of my sister. We found the wagon, toppled and ransacked. We found blood.

Even now, I cannot speak of such things easily. I will spare the details for fear my heart will wrench itself in twain. It is enough to simply say that a cadre of Red Guard took her for their sport and left my sister dead in a nameless gutter.

It is for my sister and others like her that I joined the Shackled Man and took up arms against the Red Queen. I spent two years proving my loyalty, two years fighting against oppression in my sister's memory. I have done all that you have asked and more, yet I find myself hollow. You have said, more than once, that this rebellion must be driven by more than revenge and hatred. While I concede your point, I myself cannot see beyond the rage that still burns within me day by day. I must act and cannot prove patient a day longer.

For this and other reasons, I write to you now to inform you of my own plan for retribution. I act alone, without endorsement from the Shackled Man or his kin. I act alone, so as to bear the punishment for my discovery alone. Should my plans be uncovered, I will die without causing your rebellion ill. However, it is my fond hope that my actions will bring the rebellion closer to fruition. It is my hope that I, in my own meagre way, can aid you in your righteous cause.

I intend to submit myself for induction into the Red Guard. If I am accepted, I will report back to you at every possible juncture to reveal what secrets I can uncover of Greymaul Keep and the brutes who dwell within it. I know not how this venture will end but only that blood will be shed, and I shall have my vengeance.

For Liza. For the rebellion. For myself.

1

Three days and nights have passed since I walked through the gates of Greymaul Keep and voiced my intention to join the Red Guard. Those three days have passed in a haze of pain and darkness. I have learned no weaponry, nor skill with fist or cudgel. I have been fed nothing but the meanest gruel and kept in darkness for all but a few moments each day.

A figure passes outside my door, a monk or acolyte—I know not which—whose duty it is to read out the tenets of service to the blood throne and the demon which I must soon call Mistress. The words he speaks are unduly lengthy and of little consequence in and of themselves—*we serve the Almighty Mother, we give our blood to serve the red throne, she is our life and breath*—and so on he speaks day and night. There is an etheric charge to the words, I am sure of it. While their meaning does nothing but fuel my hatred for the Red Queen, I feel the etheric energy within them press against my soul.

Only after three days and nights have I been allowed to move into the barracks properly. I have been given a small cot, and permitted charcoal and paper, to which I am somewhat surprised. If one of those who watch over me should discover this missive, or those I intend to write in the future, it will spell my death. Nonetheless, I intend to write and use what little talent I have to spirit these messages to you, in the hope that they might one day help to set the red city to rights.

2

Proper training has begun in earnest. Day and night we learn the skills of warfare, though our lessons are painfully restrictive. We are not taught to fight in all manner of ways, but instead are instructed on specific methods which align with our future designations. Those of the rifle and pistol are taught to fight with projectile arms and given only a little instruction in hand-to-hand combat. Those who are set to walk the streets of Rust are taught to hold shield and spear. There is a mind mage of some sort who divines the talents and abilities of each recruit and assigns each to their given rank. Thus, before I have landed a single blow, I am assigned to the Black Fist—a small division of the guard who specialize in the use of explosive force and destructive thaumaturgy.

While others learn to fire weapons from great distances or grapple hand to hand with enemy combatants, I and the few others chosen for the Black Fist are schooled in munitions and the basic principles of thaumaturgical warfare. We are told that brutes will accompany us at all times, clearing the way so that we may work unmolested.

3

The burns on my hands make it hard to write, so this missive will be brief. The art of explosive manipulation is painfully taught. Twice now I have rendered myself blind for a day or more. Three times I have caught fire and once, set a fellow recruit to flame. I have little gift for this work, but the hunch-backed cretin who rules over our division pushes me ever onward, despite my stumbling.

There is no enjoyment in the work, only mindless drudgery. I lack sleep and nourishment, working day and night until my hands shake and I cannot see. Amid the constant pain and humiliation, I remind myself of my dear sister and begin to formulate a stratagem. Each day my mind clings to Liza and my resolve returns.

4

Three more days and nights locked in a cell. Another priest chants mindless platitudes while he paces the walls outside my cell. Darkness surrounds me, but it is a welcome respite from the endless drudgery, the pain and monotony of learning the demolitionist's vocation.

There is a little light for a few minutes while the priest takes his rest, and it is then that I write this message to you. Again, the mind mage's words seem to stir something within me. There is mancery at work, I am certain of it. Though, fortunately, I feel no ill effects.

5

We are to be taken to the red wastes on the morrow. I know not where, nor if I will be able to write again. They intend us to fight some foe, though I know not whom. We have been fed on grain and meat for the past few weeks. My strength returns, and my skill with explosive devices begins to improve.

I have a stratagem but have yet to set it in motion.

6

I have lived in Rust a great many years, but never have I witnessed such horror. Blood and fire and death unquenched. Even now, as I remember those hours spent crawling through rivers of blood and carrion, my hand takes to shaking. It is our baptism of fire—a rending of mind and flesh alike.

I feel myself coming undone and thus cannot describe more fully the horrors they have subjected us to these past weeks. I am a hollowed-out shell, devoid of whatever it was that gave me some spark of joy or satiety.

7

Three months I have spent within these blood-soaked walls, plying my newfound trade, bruised and battered, bloodied and warped beyond sanity. I am less than I was, and somewhat more. I cannot give words to the changes this place has wrought within me, nor the multifarious methods in which the red host has brought their will to bear against my soul. To my shame I have befriended several fellow recruits. To an even greater shame, at times I have learned to relish the fight, to revel in the shedding of blood through caustic thaumaturgy.

The nights I dream of my sister's face grow less. The moments in which I draw courage from her smile arise only fleetingly and without their former vigour. I am less and more and wholly other than I have been. So it is that I set my plan in motion before I am changed irrevocably. Yet, I dare not detail such plans, even in this hidden epistle, lest all be unravelled before fruition.

Now is a time when I remember, so I write these words as testament.

I remember you, Liza. I remember your face, your smile. I remember the vengeance I feel at your passing, the blood oath I have sworn before the walls of this red city. I remember you, dear sister.

8

I am reborn. The All Mother has revealed her love to me, and I am moved to tears. My heart is fit to burst its moorings, for the joy of her gaze upon me. She is the warmth and life at the heart of the etherverse. She is all in all, the one true being of light and purpose and majesty.

My hands serve at her pleasure. My heart rejoices at the thought of her radiance. My eyes forever gaze toward her matchless form. She is mother. She is Mistress. She is the Red Queen.

Note to Kane - SB

This is the last record from our friend at Greymaul. No clear view yet of what changed in those last two notes. Some kind of ceremony or some such—probably with powerful etheric manipulation going on; some kind of mind fuckery to be sure. Whatever it was, our man's mind turned to mush. We figured something like this was going on. That's why we get nothing from the Red Guard when we capture them. Just mindless shit about the red bitch. Butchers are a different breed, but they're hard to catch and not easy to get anything out of. Besides, they stick together, so if you corner one, you soon end up with half a dozen.

A few days after this last missive, there was a sizable explosion within Greymaul Keep. More than one. Took out half the main meeting hall and killed a couple of hundred initiates. Good to see our friend got his vengeance before they broke his mind. Can't say for sure, but I figure he was among the dead.

It won't win us the war, but two hundred dead red guard is not bad for a tinkerer with a grudge. Still don't know how he managed to get the messages out to us. I figure some kind of latent mancery going on, but no idea what it was.

One more brother and sister dead at the red bitch's hands. One more reason to take up arms and end this thing one way or the other.

20. Calaban

He stares at the blade, considering its cruel, twisted steel with a vacant expression which is made grotesque by the warped flesh of his face. Calaban Eru, erstwhile Apothecary to the crimson throne, is a tangle of flesh and sinew, wrapped too-tightly about a hunched, bony frame. A bulbous, swollen nose sits unevenly beneath twisted, weeping orbs. Milky white and half covered with the loose flesh of his eyelids, the eyes are devoid of features, yet their pallid expanse seems to take in everything with hawk-like precision.

He turns from the table and shuffles toward a young woman strapped to a vertical brace against the near wall. Her eyes are red with weeping, her expression forlorn. Eight days and nights she has stood thus—strapped in place with pitted steel, forced to eat, sleep, and agonize, standing with her back pinned to the aged wall of the chamber.

He has kept her well fed, her monstrous host. Each day she is forced to eat a rich gruel, to drink fetid water laced with some noxious concoction that encourages mental compliance and will not allow her stomach to empty itself, however it may buck against the indignities it suffers.

Calaban lifts the curved blade, twisting it this way and that, a short distance from the girl's face.

"Here," he rasps, waving the blade at the girl, "here is the object of which I spoke. A curious blade to be sure. See the turning of the blade here and once more."

He lowers the blade, smiling grimly. "It was not fashioned so, little dove, but fell from the heavens thusly. A twisted shard of sky iron which broke from its kin."

He nods, admiring the blade once more. "The smith who worked this steel did not fight against the grain, little one. You must understand, he sought to harness the blade's natural shape—to enhance rather than rework. Two years, he laboured in his attempts to refine the weapon. In the end, it was only with a second piece of sky iron that the smith was able to sharpen the blade."

Calaban chuckles to himself in a grotesque parody of self-amusement. "Two years it took to sharpen this edge and dull the hilt, just so. And here, in my very grasp, sits a blade which is said to be able to cut the very cosmos in twain."

With surprising speed, he swipes the blade through the air, close enough to the woman's ripped tunic for her to feel the wind of its passing.

"So, it is that I save this particular artifact until the very last," Calaban continues. "First with plier and pin, with needle and a touch of venom. Then to the more—"

A groan rises from the opposite end of the chamber, expelled from between cracked lips. Calaban's eyes narrow. He clicks his tongue, turns to face the darkened corner of the chamber.

"All in good time, young buck," he hisses. "Lie still a while longer while I banter with your lover. Do not stoke my ire with your bleating, lest I be tempted to make a quick end to our play."

The groaning ceases as the young man passes into delirium and Calaban smiles, as though the young man's passing out had been an act of simple obedience.

"This fair blade," Calaban goes on, "is the last and finest of my devices. It is my fond hope that, where knife and hammer have failed—where the cracking of bone and the wrenching of flesh has yielded nothing but childish bleating and the shedding of tears—this blade will divine deeper truths. One cut into the flesh and this, the purest of edges, will sever truth from lie and all that is hidden will be made plain."

The aged apothecary lets out an involuntary cackle, shuddering a little as he considers the import of his own words. Still giddy with excitement, he turns once more to the young woman.

"I tell you all of this, little dove, that you may appreciate the fortune of your station. You will have cause to see with your own eyes the workings of the sky blade. You will behold the rendering of truth from bone and blood, grit and grime. And, in the days to come, you may anticipate with awe the workings of this wondrous device against your own flesh. For such will surely happen in good time."

He waves a finger at her. "Be warned, little lamb, try though you might, you will not persuade me to hasten my application of the blade against your own skin. For that ecstasy you will have to wait."

He sighs, turns to the darkened corner of the chamber. "So now, to work."

***

The torn lovers endure their excruciation in an agonized delirium. The drugs and torments of Calaban's design keep them far from lucidity but, on rare occasions, they catch sight of one another, and recognition begins to dawn, bringing with it unfathomable sorrow. It is for the alleged practice of mancery that the two lovers have been given over to the mercies of the Red Queen's chief Fleshsmith. For his part, young Romero cannot determine whether the charge is simply a pretence or if the Red Queen's agents do actually suspect he and his lover of practicing the forbidden art.

"I am a farmer," he had pleaded in his first moments of captivity. "I sow the Queen's crops and bring in the harvest. Our farmstead is small but productive. We have always paid the tithe."

On and on his words had spilled, while Calaban set about preparing his torments, utterly headless of the young farmer's pleas. Romero had begged the fleshmancer to release his young bride—Brita the raven-haired beauty whom he had wed not more than three months before their capture.

Romero's words fell on deaf ears. The monstrous Calaban was not merely disinterested in their plight, he was, as far as Romero could see, thoroughly mad. In the days and weeks since those first outbursts, Romero's body had been broken, his resolve whittled away with a perverse range of torments. Worse, Brita had been forced to observe his torture, and he hers. Calaban was yet to break the young woman—he seemed to be more interested in soliloquy than brutality in her case—but Romero had no doubt that the fleshmancer would set to work on her the moment that Romero himself passed beyond the veil.

It was that singular fact which kept the young man alive, despite the rending of flesh, the breaking of bone and syphoning of lifeblood that drained him of all vitality. He would cling to life with every fibre of his being, for no other reason than to forestall his lover's own suffering. Yet, the cruel irony was that his act of endurance prolonged Brita's suffering in far more profound ways. For it was she who had to watch her lover brutalized day after day, without hope of respite. So, locked in this grimace of agonies, the torn lovers endure.

***

It is known well that the fates work strangely within the Traumwelt—somewhat more cruelly than in the waking world, but no less capricious for that. It is perhaps for this reason that freedom comes for Romero and his bride, born on the wings of happenstance and accident.

***

A hulking figure enters the Apothecarian Gate, clothed in midnight armour and wearing a wolfs-head mask of pure obsidian. Avernath, the Warmaster, eats up ground with the rhythmic lumbering of his footfalls. A cadre of black guards flank the demigod to either side; masked brutes that shadow the godling general like storm clouds on the horizon.

Those unfortunate souls along the path to Calaban's pavilion, bow and grovel, or are thrown aside as Avernath makes his way through the fetid streets of the Red Queen's Fleshworks. He cannot help the snarl that rises from his throat as he ascends the steps to the fleshmancer's pavilion.

"Calaban! Attend me you worm!" the demigod's voice booms.

Cloaked figures scurry to and fro, like cockroaches rushing to find cover. Torturous pumps and clockwork excruciators cease their machinations as their operators cower away from the enraged demigod.

"Calaban! Attend me, lest I grind this place to ruin and tear you limb from limb!"

The fleshmancer's stooped figure emerges slowly from the dark recesses of the pavilion, moving with maddening slowness toward Avernath and his retinue. Calaban stands before the giant figure, wiping his gnarled hands on a piece of cloth, blood and grease leaving smears across the fabric. He looks up at Avernath, wearing a grotesque smile.

"Brother. It is good to see you. Tell me, what brings you to these hallowed halls?"

Avernath snarls. "I descend into this fetid pit only because my Mistress demands it. She seeks news of the child."

A grotesque aberration of a smile crawls across Calaban's lips. "She is impatient, our Lady, is she not, brother? Still, one can hardly begrudge her. For it is truly a marvel we are witness to."

"So, the girl is with child?"

Calaban nods slowly. "Indeed, dear brother. The babe stirs in her womb even as we speak. I confess, it has taken considerable restraint on my part not to cut the child out of her body and set to work immediately. To see how the little one ticks, as it were."

Avernath looms above the Fleshmancer. "You were instructed to bring the babe to fruition, worm, not tear it to ribbons on one of your grotesqueries. My men did not pluck the babe's parents from the heart of the rebellion simply to have you put the child to death on a whim of curiosity."

Calaban laughs wetly. "True, dear brother. Still, you cannot begrudge me my indulgences. Surely you, of any of us, know a little about obsession, eh? Tell me, have you found your lady love yet, or has the mound of female corpses at your feet merely increased a little more these past years?"

With terrifying speed, Avernath unsheathes a large blade, pressing it against Calaban's throat before the other man has time to react.

"Oh really, brother, I speak in jest," Calaban offers. "Truly you must learn to curb that temper of yours."

The Warmaster leans in close. "And you must learn to bite your tongue, brother."

Backing away from the naked blade, Calaban dabs at the slight cut on his neck and waves a hand toward the rear of the chamber. "You may inform our Mistress, dear brother, that my work here is almost complete. The young woman is indeed with child and, to all accounts, the babe is in good health. The woman will give birth here, under my care, and we will send word to the crimson throne the moment this occurs. In the meantime, please allow me to continue my work. I have yet to determine the *how* of all of this, let alone the *why*. The babe is special, purely by dint of her existence if nothing else, still, there is powerful mancery at work here, and I have yet to divine its purpose."

"Take me to her," Avernath demands, sliding the blade back into its sheath.

"Oh really, brother, you do quite vex me. Must you see the woman at this late hour?"

"Now, Calaban!"

The hunched Fleshmancer shrugs, shuffles toward a narrow corridor to one end of the chamber. "Very well then, brother, follow me if you must. I have focused the bulk of my work on the young father, you shall see, but the woman truly is quite fascinating in her own way. There is an etheric…"

Avernath follows, closing his ears to Calaban's relentless chatter. They walk through a series of corridors, heading down into Calaban's private underground bunker. On reaching the centre of the room, Avernath sees two torture cots, one standing and one lying horizontally. There are blood stains upon the cots and the ground beneath, and the chamber reeks of blood and sweat.

"Oh dear," Calaban says.

Avernath snarls. "What?"

"It appears, dear brother, that our prize has been purloined. The girl and her husband are no longer in my care."

Dead silence fills the chamber, broken only by the slow grinding of the Warmaster's teeth.

***

Alone and contemplative in his private chamber, the Red Queen's personal fleshmancer stares in disbelief at the blood-stained space upon his excruciation table. In the hours that followed Avernath's visit, it is discovered that the captives were freed by a bare-chested brawler and the young assassin Shadowfang. Two rebels entered his inner sanctum and stole his prize without raising the slightest alarm.

Calaban was not a warmonger like his distinguished brother, yet the fleshmancer had laid a dozen etheric wards about his pavilion, and there were personal guards stationed at each entry and exit. Two dozen heavily armed soldiers would have a difficult time performing the rescue, and the slightest sign of treachery should have alerted Calaban immediately.

More than this, someone should have seen something. One did not simply stroll into the Apothacarian without the prying eyes of Calaban's Acolytes giving intense scrutiny. In addition, the Warmaster himself must have been present at the time of the theft. It must surely gall Avernath to have such thievery take place beneath his very nose, and yet, that very theft is an impossibility.

The Apothecary considers the possibility that his brother has instigated the robbery, perhaps to damage Calaban's standing with the red mistress? The Warmaster is surely not above such petty manoeuvres, whatever his purported sense of honour. Yet Calaban had watched him closely as they came upon the scene. Avernath was no dull brute, but he lacked the patience for cultured deception, and Calaban could see nothing of trickery in his brother's reaction to the theft.

Most troubling would be Eva's reaction to the theft. After long years of fruitless obsession, she had finally obtained her prize: a child conceived and in good health. For nearly a century the Red Queen had turned Rust's nobility into little more than a brood den, forcing Calaban to perform countless experiments and alterations in the vain hope of defying the Traumwelt's prohibition against childbirth.

The noble families lived lives of luxury and excess, their only duty to mate regularly and submit to Calaban's various experimentations. A hundred years of trial and error had yielded not the slightest sign of progress. Yet, this humble farmer and his bride manage an impossible feat seemingly by their own means. Calaban was yet to discover whether the conception had been bolstered by the etheric potential within the young pair. In service to the Queen's overwhelming desire for progeny, he had attempted countless etheric manipulations among the captive nobility at the citadel, but all to no effect.

Perhaps some deeper, underlying change had occurred throughout the Traumwelt, and Calaban's various scrying devices and instruments of perception had simply failed to mark the change? Or perhaps there was a dark intelligence at work. Had the Clockmaker God returned to stab at Eva with a false pregnancy? Had one of Calaban's old rivals sought to discredit him by first raising the possibility of a new child and then dashing that possibility to the rocks?

Calaban shakes his head. It matters not what has caused the miracle. Eva's punishment will be severe and protracted. The fleshmancer is determined to put the matter out of mind for the time being. He would let matters take their course. Eva would rail and spit venom. Avernath would grind his teeth and strut hatefully. The godlings would perform their various mummer's tasks, and Calaban would eventually be permitted to return to his work.

The Fleshmancer takes in a deep breath, his attention moving to the promising thought of an evening of excruciation with a pair of female twins he has newly obtained—taken from the fishmonger's district on charges of sedition and unpaid tithes. Yet even as the thought lifts his spirits somewhat, Calaban's moist eyes return to the space on his table where the priceless sky blade had sat. He could forgive the rescue of his prized prisoners, but he would rend the Traumwelt in twain and drown the Red Queen herself in blood to get back that knife.

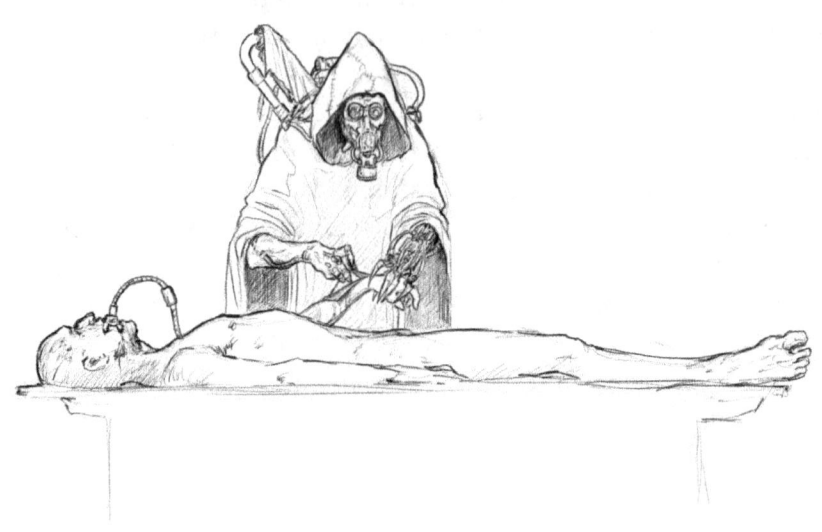

CALABAN
Charidimos Bitsakakis

21. The Butcher

Can a man be more than the sum of his actions? Can a lifetime of slaughter be undone by a few acts of kindness? Is evil used in the service of good any less evil for that fact?

These are the questions which house my misery, which keep me from sleep and prick my conscience with unrelenting frequency. They are, at once, my damnation and salvation, my hell and heaven. Such questions keep me from peace and serenity, yet they also free me from the mindless savagery of my brethren.

I am, and ever will be, a Butcher.

***

Those of us who are not made for the purpose are sent to the Butcher pens in our youth, mere boys and girls with no knowledge of the horrors that await us. We kill quickly and often, without respite. Older boys and girls press the blades to our hands, hold them in place as we are forced to cut the throat of a lamb, a pig, or whatever animal is prepared for slaughter. That first gush of acrid blood stays with us for some time—warm and sticky, filled with the bile from our own throats. Many of us cry, many empty our stomachs, some wail and soil themselves.

Three throats are cut before that first day's end, before we young, innocent children are led to our bunks to weep and cry out through the sleepless night. The next day we slay three more beasts but are forced to cut what we have killed; to carve and slice at the dead with shaking hands held firm by our unfeeling overlords. We kill three beasts on our second day and carve the meat off the bones of one of these victims.

Food is offered, but very few can take it in. Some of us manage to sleep—driven to darkness by exhaustion. Others still shed their tears, still mourn for the dead. Some scrub at their hands until they bleed, wishing to wash away their guilt.

The third, fourth, and fifth days follow in like fashion: three beasts dead, one butchered to the bone. Eat, sleep, kill, bathe, eat, sleep, kill…

With the passing of the seventh day, those too fragile of mind have been removed from the fold, though to what fate we are not privy. We that remain become dulled to the slaughter by dint of sheer repetition. In time the stench of hot blood and torn flesh no longer turn our stomachs. Now accustomed to the slaughter, we begin to live again. Friendships are formed, laughter returns, and we recover a little of what was lost.

We are taught to fight; first with fists, then with weapons. Slaughter in the morning, fighting in the afternoon. We learn to strike swiftly and without mercy. Our bones are cracked and muscles torn. We are allowed to heal and given instruction on the application of healing herbs and thaumaturgical remedies.

After three years, we teach the newly inducted how to kill. We come full circle as we press the blade handle against the palm of the child and force them to cut flesh despite their cries of protestation. It is an odd thing to experience, and we are surprised to feel no great remorse at our duties. We remember our own pain at the beginning but have come to see this as necessary.

One more year we spend in the slaughter yards, learning our lessons, slaughtering cattle. Then, when our bodies start to reach maturity and aging begins to slow, we are moved to the Warmaster's barracks.

***

Our second lesson in slaughter is not like the first. We who think ourselves hardened to the rending of flesh and the spilling of blood, are forced by grown men and women—cruel figures in dark armour—to clutch blades as we take the life of a new kind of beast. The men are traitors to Rust, we are told. For crimes against the red city and her Queen, they have been sentenced to death. And so, we spill their blood. Three men per day.

Though we have slaughtered a thousand beasts each, many of us weep on the night of that first human slaughter. Some empty their stomachs, others cry into the night. The killing of men is something far darker than the culling of cattle for food and survival. Soon it is not merely men that we kill, but women too. We are forced to wrestle with terrible possibilities. Could these souls really deserve such an end? How could this young woman have so offended the city, to find her death in such a place?

For all our unanswered questions, we still do our duty. Once more, we are shadowed by our elders until we demonstrate the willingness to kill alone. Three per day, then back to the study of weaponry, of battle and the dealing of death. Before long the lessons in fighting and our slaughtering duties become one and the same. Our victims are no longer tied and gagged. We are sent to a pit to deal death using the skills we have newly acquired. Here we learn to fight and master ourselves and the other. We are injured, we are cut with sorrowful words as our victims plead for mercy. We kill and are killed, some of us.

We learn to deal death swiftly and without remorse. As the lessons advance, we learn to fight two, then three, then five enemies at a time. We become more weapon than living being. We become the *will* to death, the reaper's blade incarnate.

Again, once we have mastered our craft, we are called upon to teach the younger ones how to kill men. Our duty done, we once more begin to laugh and bond and live.

When our training is complete, once we have slaughtered a thousand souls, our true purpose is made known.

***

We few who live on meet Avernath the Warmaster—slayer of souls, god of steel and fire and retribution. It is Avernath, they say, who expelled the Clockwork God and his traitorous cadre from the red city, executing the Queen's bloody justice against his fellow godlings. It is Avernath who quelled the Script Rebellion, who led the campaign to cleanse the Fens of the Bonesmiths, to suppress the Hammerjack Uprising and lay waste to the Shadowmere.

That first meeting sees three of our number dead. Three of us, he calls out. Three he arms with blade and buckler, stripping the obsidian armour from his hulking frame to reveal scarred muscle and mechanical augmentation. He is a devil made flesh, ravaged by time and innumerable battles: the semblance of man and god transmuted into a deadly horror.

He urges the three chosen to attack and deals swift death to each. He roars in triumph, yet there is nothing of joy in the gesture.

"You are my chosen," he says, addressing those of us who have been spared and donning his armour once more. "You are my right hand and my fist. You are the execution of my will. Yet, you are weak and must be forged in the crucible."

And so, we are forged. We are sent to the Shadowlands to battle dark beasts. We journey through the red wastes, battling shadowspawn and etheric horrors. Our numbers dwindle, yet those that remain are formed of hard-pressed steel. We return to the red city and begin our true work. We are sent to the Fens to dispatch an irksome stonemason. We are sent to the citadel to slaughter a wealthy family whose words have offended the Red Queen in some manner.

We kill infrequently, but with utter finality. We are the right arm and will of Avernath the Warmaster. We are his right arm and deadly fist.

***

What joy we butchers have previously found in comradery, in the sharing of meals or the bearing of torments, is lost to us. We are kept in isolation. We sleep in dark cells and move from place to place, doing our lethal work with masked faces. We have no names, no identities. We are the Warmaster's blade.

And yet…something must remain. Some sliver of humanity or empathy, or weakness. We are told, "The blade does not question the hand that wields it," yet I am caused to question, brought to indecision by a miracle.

Three of us are sent to dispatch a family of rebels. Hidden by the Shackled Man and his comrades, the family are difficult to track, moved often and with great secrecy. It takes three months for us to track the young man and his wife. We find them in the sewers below the citadel, huddled together around a meagre fire, fearful and malnourished. We do not hear their cries of anguish, nor pleas for mercy. We slaughter man and woman without effort and prepare to make our way back to the red city when an impossible cry pierces the darkness.

Bundled beneath the slaughtered body of her mother lies a new born babe, a miracle child squawking and bleating, headless of the death around her. Despite ourselves, we three are mesmerized by the sight. In all our years, we have never laid eyes upon such a thing.

Those who come to Rust by dream or nightmare may be children or fully grown, but never has an infant made such a passing. Nor, in my memory, has a child yet been born in Rust, or anywhere within the Traumwelt. The young may grow to maturity, the mature will age slowly, but no coupling of man and woman has ever brought forth new life in this crimson land.

And yet…

The first of our number recovers quickly, unsheathing his blade and moving toward the babe. Just one more animal to slaughter; one more loose thread to clip. I cannot say what it is that makes me act, but something stirs within me, taking hold of head and heart, moving me to deadly action.

"The blade does not question the hand that wields it," yet I have become more than a mere blade.

With speed, I set my cleaver against the first's throat and end his life. The second does not tarry in response. In moments, we are locked in battle, blades sparring in the dim light of the undercity. The fight is brutal and swift. I suffer cuts to the arm and chest but manage to bring the second down without enduring a crippling blow.

The babe cries and I sheath my knife. I am compelled to take the child in my arms, compelled to brush aside the blood-stained blanket across the babe's face, compelled to cry. I stand for an age, tears falling, babe crying. I am mesmerized, unravelled, remade.

***

I move swiftly, driven by some inner dynamism I cannot understand. As I move through the sewer city my mind periodically reverts to habit; I must return to the Warmaster, must report the success of our mission.

The babe cries, tearing me back to the present, unsettling my thoughts. For the first time in many years I am lost, unsure how to proceed. The child must be fed, clothed. Such thoughts are foreign, they taste acrid and uncertain on my mind's tongue. Like the twisted unfortunates who leave the fleshworks, remade into grotesque parodies of their former selves, I feel myself twisted within. The babe, whose warmth I feel through the thick fabric of my butcher's cloak, has worked some peculiar mancery upon me.

I leave the undercity and head through market streets and plazas, mind racing. The Warmaster will know of my treachery within hours. He will send a score of my kin to hunt me down, and they will not rest until the task is complete. I must find shelter for the babe. I must be free to fight when the time comes.

Driven by forces I cannot yet comprehend, I accost a grocer's wife—a young woman of an age with the child's mother. The woman cries in terror, her screams mingling with the babe's own outcry. I pull her bodily from her home, past wide-eyed purveyors and tinkerers. A pair of guardsmen watch disinterestedly as I drag the woman through the street. Not a soul lifts a finger, for they know well the butcher's garb and dare not risk a blade to the throat.

I instruct the woman to purloin a skin of milk, a basket of juneberries, and some flatbread. We leave through the Administratum Gate and head south at a pace. The young woman's cries have ceased, as though she has resigned herself to her fate, or perhaps hopes that this journey will not end in death. We head out into the night, out of the city and into the red wastes.

After an hour or so, I call a halt. I instruct the woman to feed the babe. She fumbles with goat skin and milk, spilling the liquid across the child's face. She weeps, fearful of my blade's bite at any moment. I tell her that she will not die by my hand if she feeds the babe and ceases her weeping. It seems to help a little, and the brief sounds of contented sucking give me a little time to think.

We head further into the crimson wastes, a trio of disconnected travellers, set adrift by an unnamed storm. All of a sudden, there is a crack which seems to split the night air. Something stabs at my shoulder, tearing through flesh and knocking me back a step. The babe begins to cry. I turn my back, scrambling toward a nearby boulder as a second shot rings out, drawing a puff of dust up into the air to my left. The grocer's wife screams, covering her head with pale arms while she flees into the night.

A third crack cuts through the darkness, sending up sparks from the top of the boulder I and the babe are hunkered behind. There is a pause, and the night is filled with babe's screeching. Something stirs in the distance. A figure approaches, cloaked in darkness, moving swiftly through the night. The figure stops some twenty yards away, rifle held aloft.

"So, what's your story, sunshine?"

The voice belongs to a young woman, but there is iron in her worlds that speaks of long years of hardship and bitter experience.

"I come to speak words with the Shackled Man," I offer, trying in vain to stem the flow of blood in my shoulder, while keeping the babe close to my chest.

She laughs. "Well, sure you do. Hell, who wouldn't want to speak words to the boss man? I mean, he's just such a chatty guy. Loves to shoot the shit, does old Idrus Kane."

"I mean you no harm. I merely wish to speak with—"

"You got a slug in your arm, buddy, and I could quite happily put another one between your fucking eyes, so don't go talking about harm now, okay? It sounds to me like you've got yourself a baby girl there? Don't know how the fuck you ended up with that little treasure, but I sure as shit know she doesn't belong to a fucking Butcher. So, if you could kindly lay our girl in the dirt there and just head back a couple of hundred paces that would be super great."

Her words have an odd twang, newly minted as though she has only recently passed over from the waking world. And yet, her garb and skill with weaponry bring to mind a well-known enemy of the crimson throne. Shadowfang stands before me, I am now certain. Some part of me that still resides with the Warmaster's clan thinks to take the girl's head. Such a trophy would raise one's standing with the Warmaster and win welcome praise.

Even now that thought seems old and stale. It is a false memory, a fleeting desire from some other mind than my own.

"The babe will not leave my breast," I insist, pulling a stiletto from a hidden sheath in my left boot. It will not go well with the Shackled Man if I kill his assassin, but the girl leaves me little choice. I must protect the child and every moment we tarry in this desert, the Warmaster's hounds grow closer.

"Okay, princess, keep the girl for a bit. Just tell me how the fuck you ended up with her and—"

I press my back against the earth, freeing my right hand sufficiently for a swift throw. The blade buries itself in the girl's chest. She clutches at it and staggers back a step. A moment passes in silence, even the babe ceases her crying. And then…laughter.

I lean out past the boulder. Shadowfang is holding the stiletto in one hand, the white of her teeth showing beneath her shadowed cowl. Her laughter peels out into the darkness, echoing into the night. I find myself at odds with what I am seeing. No blood marks her clothes… She has…

"You throw like a fucking girl, dude!" the scout says, tossing the stiletto to the ground.

She advances, training the rifle at my head as she circles around the boulder. There must be some mancery at work here? The girl should be dead.

"Not the first time someone's tried to fling a knife at me, princess," she says, as if in answer to my unasked question. "Now give me the fucking baby, or shit's about to get real unpleasant."

"I will not."

She stares at me for a time, weighing my words. "Ah fuck it. All right, just start walkin', dude. And you better not hurt a hair on that kid's fucking head, or I'll tear your god-dammed face of off your skull and shove it up your asshole."

***

We walk through a series of ridges, twisting through dimly lit ravines and coming to a small settlement nestled within a hidden outcrop. Some trick of mancery must keep the settlement hidden from view, for even in the dead of night I recognize this place. I and my black brothers have rendered our knives to the Warmaster in lands far beyond the red city. I have passed this way a dozen times and never suspected a viper's nest so close to Rust.

We are greeted by a dozen heavily armed guards as we enter the settlement. The assassin leads us to a ruined building at the centre of the compound, down into a lower level where a dozen people sit sharing a meal around a hearth. I am led to a small chamber to one side of the main room, furnished with a small cot and table.

"Sit your ass down," the young woman says, pointing with her rifle toward the table. I do as she asks.

"You can put the baby down now," she says, dropping her weapon and closing the door behind her. She pulls down her hood and begins unwrapping the tightly bound strips of dark cloth that cover her body. Slowly, delicate, pale skin is uncovered, revealing a young woman of some beauty dressed in a simple tunic which does little to conceal her nakedness.

"Seriously, dude, you can put the little one down on the bed, no one's going to snatch her in here. I've gotta take a look at your shoulder. Damn thing's gonna go septic if you don't let me take care of it."

Somewhat at a loss, I gently lie the babe on the cot. She stirs a little but continues to slumber. Before I am able to protest, the assassin is pulling at my butcher's uniform, tugging it free whilst unsheathing blades with her other hand. She works quickly and with surprising gentleness. It is only now that I have laid the babe down that the pain begins to burn in my shoulder.

"I'm Daisy, by the way," the assassin says, pulling the fabric away from the wound.

I grimace as she prods at the shoulder, gritting my teeth against the pain. She works quickly and in silence, pulling a small slug from the wound and sealing it with hands that seem far too delicate for the task.

DAISY

"A Butcher?"

Kane asks the question, but he already knows the answer.

"Yeah, bona fide Butcher. One of Avernath's bastards. He's got the right blades and, now that I've seen him fight, I believe it."

"Wandering the desert in the middle of the night with our new born?"

"Hey, what can I tell you? I was just as freaked as you are. When we lost contact with Romero and Brita, I figured the baby was dead too. Some kind of fucking miracle. One of Avernath's Butchers sees the kid, then just decides to kill both his pals and bring her right to our door. You couldn't make up that kind of luck."

Kane shakes his head. "I'd say there was more at play than mere luck, wouldn't you?"

"What are you saying, that this is some kind of trap or something? You think Avernath sent this guy out just to find us?"

"You misunderstand. I speak of the babe. She is the first child in living memory born of the Traumwelt. Born of powerful ethermancers. Who can say whether the child herself possesses some innate gift for etheric manipulation?"

I can tell this is gonna be one of those discussions where Kane makes me guess at what he's saying rather than just coming out with it. Fucking frustrating, but that's part of the whole brooding, weight of the world on your shoulders deal that he's got going on.

"So, you're saying that the little cherub made Butcher Pete go all nuts and kill his buddies? Somehow the little tyke brainwashed the big man into carting her halfway across the desert? I thought mancery didn't even start to show until you're much older."

He nods, fiddling with the shackle on his left wrist.

"You're still not getting the hang of this whole conversation thing, are you, boss? You see, it works like this: I say something, then you say something. It's really neat. You should try it."

"He refuses to leave the child?" Shackle asks, ignoring my mini-rant.

"Yeah, won't let the little thing out of his sight. It's kind of touching, but a little creepy too. He says he can't go back to Avernath now. Thinks they'll have half the butchers out looking for him, so there's nothing to go back to. I told him we could always use a good fighter, but he's not interested. Just wants to look after the kid. Dad of the fucking year, if you ask me."

"And the child is in good health?"

"Yeah, she's doin' fine. I've got Nina looking after her, helping with the feeding and washing and all that. She had a new born before she got dragged into shitsville, so she jumped at the chance to help. Hell, half the women in this place are chomping at the bit to get a look at the baby. Butcher man is ok with it as long as he's close by."

Silence. Shackle just sits there fiddling with his fucking wrist. I mean, I owe the guy my life a hundred times over, but fuck, this brooding nonsense is getting old.

"Okay, so what do you want me to do with him, boss?"

"Send him to me. Double the scouts and pull back our presence in the city for the next few weeks."

***

The butcher gets his face time with Shackle while I hold on to the baby just outside. Not sure why Shackle doesn't want me in the room, nor why butcher boy trusts me with his precious cargo, but there you have it. An hour later, we leave Shackle to his brooding and head topside.

"So, big man, you got a name?"

He shakes his head.

"They don't dish out names at Greymaul, eh? Suppose you just get a number or something like that."

"I did not attend Greymaul. Nor was I permitted an individual designation, other than my rank and caste."

I give the big guy a stare to see if there's any humour in there. No, nothing. It's like looking at a brick wall. Like looking at Shackle, but not quite as scary. I figure the baby in his arms softens the brick wall a little.

"So, you gotta tell me, dude. Why'd you do it? I mean, you butcher bastards are known for being the hardest fuckers in the Traumwelt, so what the hell made you turn to our side?"

He looks down at the baby, then back at me. "I side with the child, not your rebellion."

I can't help the smile that crawls up onto my lips. Damn it, I like this guy.

"Yeah well, she's with us, princess, so whether you know it or not, you're part of the rebellion now because she's right at the centre of it. I mean, you ever seen a baby before? In Rust, I mean?"

He shakes his head.

"That's 'cause they don't exist, guy. Must be a million people stranded in this place and not one baby among them. I mean, most of these fuckers are ruttin' like rabbits, don't get me wrong, but it doesn't lead to anything. We're all sterile here in the Traumwelt. Except, a little while back, a certain farmer chick starts throwin' up for no good reason. She starts getting dizzy and her back starts hurting and, before you know it, there's a little bump in her belly and none of us can explain it."

I reach over and brush a finger over the baby's forehead. So soft. Her hair feels like it's been spun by angels.

"They took her mother, you know. Calaban, the fuck, and his fleshmancer bastards. Took her mother and father and tortured them. We spent weeks trying to track them down and eventually managed to get them out of there. We figured the damage was already done, but this little girl's a tough cookie."

I pick up her little hand in mine and feel the fingers grab on.

"Almost killed her mother on the way out, but she made it. A goddamn miracle kid. Then the red bitch sent half her fucking army after her. We lost a hundred fighters and had to ditch one of our safe houses to the west. A hundred men and women dead, and we only just managed to get the baby and her parents out alive. Romero and Brita, in case you're interested. Those were their names. Good people. Good fighters too. They disappeared after the attack. Just vanished. I'm guessing they thought their chances were better on their own than with us, and who can blame them. We all figured they'd headed north across the Salt Sea, but then you come wandering into the desert with little sister in your arms, like some kind of dark angel."

We head to the makeshift room where a cot has been cobbled together, and Butcher lays the girl down carefully. God she's beautiful.

"Anyhow, I'm sorry I plugged you in the arm. Just not used to butchers being the good guys, you know."

He smiles, and it takes me a few seconds to register it. Something magical happens to his face when he smiles. Rough slate is transformed into something almost handsome.

"I…saw her face," he says, sitting down next to the cot. "I cannot explain why, for I do not know. But something happened in that moment. I felt…a purpose unlike anything I have felt before. I needed to keep her safe, to protect her from my kin. I acted quickly and without thought."

I wait for a few seconds, but that's apparently all stone man has to say on the subject.

"Okay, so what were you and Kane talking about? Not that I'm prying or anything, I just really want to know…because I'm prying. Also, I've never seen him ask for someone like that. Normally you've got to be with the rebellion for months before you'd even get a shot at seeing the big man, let alone a private meeting."

I sit down next to the butcher, peering over the edge of the cot to sneak a look at the baby's sleeping face.

"We have an agreement of sorts," he says.

"Oh yeah? What kind of agreement?"

"I will not fight in his rebellion, nor will I raise a hand in anger against another unless the girl is endangered. I will stay by her side until she is of age and keep her from harm. In return, he allows me to stay in this compound and promises to provide food and shelter for the babe and myself."

Dad of the fucking year. "Okay, big man. Sounds fair. Now how about we get another look at that shoulder of yours."

SHADOWFANG
by Charidimos Bitsakakis

22. Three Truths

I, the Remembrancer, lay forth that which is true by virtue of quill and parchment. I do so at my own peril, as the red devils beat and batter at my doors and prepare to lay hands upon me and execute the Red Queen's swift justice. In the precious moments I have left, I am determined to right the wrongs of a lifetime spent propagating falsehoods at the behest of an unjust bureaucracy.

What follows is truth, laid bare and true for all who have eyes to see and ears to hear. I offer up, in these final hours, three truths to balance the deceptions of a lifetime. My hope is not for redemption, but merely to light the flame of truth in a world of darkness.

1. On the Omnipotence of the Red Queen

We are told that Eva's* power is absolute, that her dominion over the city states and realms of the Traumwelt is complete and unchallenged. Yet, even a casual glance at our northernmost ports makes folly of such a claim. Note, for instance, the grand galleons and merchant ships which traverse the Salt Sea and red wastes beyond our borders. From where do such grand vessels derive: vessels which are, in truth, far grander than any fashioned in our hallowed city? Such vessels come, it is true, from city states of the north and east, rivals to our own red city, and each ruled by demigods of fierce power.

The greatest of these, undoubtedly, is the abode of the so-called Clockmaker God: the great builder to whom our red city owes its decaying brilliance. Have you wondered, dear reader, in times of thoughtful reflection, how it is that so many clockwork marvels exist within the city (note the cascading lights of the fifth sister, the great citadel doors, the kinetic watchman, and so on) when no new marvels are fashioned?

The kinetic machinations of the Queen's citadel itself were fashioned not by artificers of the red city, but by the Clockmaker God and his acolytes, in an age long past.

Yet, the memory of the Clockmaker and his legacy have been so thoroughly whitewashed, so expertly unwritten over the centuries, that our collective memory of such an entity is all but forgotten. From whence do the galleons and airships of the north derive? From the barbarian settlements and ramshackle hamlets beyond the Salt Sea—so we are told. Yet the whispered words of port traders speak a different tale entirely.

* Note: In my final hour I boldly name the Red Queen, not by her preferred appellation, but by an almost forgotten name, Eva. To speak the Red Queen's proper name is death, yet I am emboldened.

2. The Schism
Were the old records not consumed with fire at the Red Queen's behest, they would testify to the earliest days of the *Traumwelt*, whereupon Eva and her kin were thrust from grace and forced to make new their homes within these arid crimson wastes. Such records would speak not of a single queen and her minions marching in triumph into this new land. Rather, such records would tell of a small, beleaguered host, a clutch of demigods of which Eva herself was one among equals. We know with some certainty (despite the efforts of the Administratum to bury such knowledge) that among this entourage were the Clockmaker, Avernath the Slayer of souls, Tinsen, Salik the Twinned, Cloudweaver, Calaban, and Eva herself.

What other demigods were cast into the *Traumwelt* in those early days I cannot say, though there is evidence to suggest a further six or seven in their number. The early unity of this group is written into the very stones and kinetic mechanisms of our city. From the city's architecture and the uniformity of her earliest design, we can surmise that the Clockmaker himself was chief architect. It is likewise believed that several others of the demigods struck out on their own into the great wastes, while several (such as the Clockmaker, Salik, Avernath, Calaban) gave their allegiance to Eva and sought to build the great red city (though, for what ultimate purpose we cannot say).

We can likewise say that, at some point after the completion of the city proper, tensions sprouted within the Red Queen's circle. Over what point said tensions arose, we can only guess. But the outcome of this tension was a profound schism between the Red Queen and the Clockmaker.

3. The Second Sister

It is well known that the mumblers worship their goddess of fire (our nameless Red Queen, no less), but equally well known is their reference to the second goddess; she of water. We have oft paid too little attention to the words espoused by this crazed religious sect, nonetheless there is truth buried in dogma, and we need only dig a little below the surface to discern its shape and texture.

Where there is Eva, the goddess of fire and ruler of the red city, there is also Eve, goddess of water and a power beyond any of the godlings who make their abode within the *Traumwelt*. It was Eve, legend says, who first banished her sister from the waking world, Eve who opened the way between worlds and cast out the Red Queen and her godling brethren. While little is known of this second sister, her existence is a certainty, her agency in casting out Eva from the waking world undeniable.

So, far from being unique, the Red Queen and her fellow godlings are no more than a band of rogues, cast out of the larger godling host. At the will of greater and nobler beings Eva and her cadre were set adrift within the crimson sands of this broken land.

***

My final moments approach, and so I write this last point in hopes that it will inspire resolve and fan the flames of rebellion once more.

Gird your hearts and bind your minds against the machinations of the Administratum priesthood and the lies they so readily propagate. I myself rose to the position of Second Prelate within that foul institution, and it was only as I was confronted with the truth of our work that I resolved to free myself from blind service to the so-called Red Queen.

We of the Administratum were lauded as stalwarts of the kingdom. The eyes and mouth of the Red Queen herself, dispensing justice and ensuring the safety and prosperity of the red city and its citizenry. We issued countless edicts, statutes and prohibitions, seeking to guide the people of this great city and cut down all forms of destructive thought.

Only when I came face to face with those whose lives were forever changed by such edicts, did I begin to see the truth. There is no justice in the work of the Administratum: only malice, propaganda, and self-interest. The poor and needy lie destitute while those who bend their backs in hard labour are rewarded for their years of toil with petty statues and ever-increasing taxes.

I am ashamed of my former vocation and set forth these words in defiance of those I have served these long years. Perhaps none will read these words, yet I must pen them nonetheless.

The truth is buried deep but may be found for those with the courage to dig deeply. Look beyond the gilded lies of the Administratum and see the godlings as they truly are: oppressors, demons.

THE SHACKLED MAN
by Charidimos Bitsakakis

23. Battle of the Underwood

There is a world within a world, buried beneath the Salt Sea, thick with forestry and flowing with water, rich in minerals. Clothed in darkness, the netherwoods thrive without the sun's warmth or the moon's careful guidance. Large pods of luminescent amber cling to rock and wood alike, glimmering from above like a false sky in the night.

For the myriad indentured loggers and cutters who work the night forests, it takes little more than a week for the eyes to adjust to the faint amber light. That adjustment made, a new world of intricate life and diversity reveals itself.

***

It began with rip, a tear in the fabric of the Traumwelt, wrought by happenstance and the unwholesome blending of etheric effluent: the by-product of countless fleshwork experimentations and thaumaturgical blasphemies. The vast network of sewers and caverns that lay beneath the red city, branching out toward the underground lakes and rivers of the Underwood, carry unholy horrors, etheric abortions and unruly products of rogue mancery. Such a culmination of ruinous power births unpredictable children. On the night before the great bloodletting, the warp and warble of discontented powers cut a hole in the world of dreams, a yawning vortex which swept some two hundred folk from their homes without warning or apology.

A dozen Red Guard, asleep and not garbed in their customary livery, a family of stone masons, a score of port laborers and sewer rats, three Administratum priests and a high-cheeked baroness all were pulled from their places and deposited at the southernmost edge of the vast Underwood. Added to these were a few sundry merchants, a chimney sweep, and a clutch of rebels with an impossible babe in their midst.

Chaos ruled in those first few moments, followed too quickly by violence. The Red Guard, wishing to assert dominance early, ordered the displaced to form ranks, fashioning makeshift weaponry from what sticks and stones lay to hand. Fearful of some rebel-inspired mancery, the Administratum priests set to barking orders, insisting that the Red Guard fulfil their duty and dispense with the enemy combatants with speed. Amid the shouting and posturing, a merchant fell beneath one of the guardsmen's makeshift cudgels, hitting his head against an exposed root. Several of his kin responded with raised voices and heavy fists.

As their eyes began to acclimatize to the dim light of the wood, tempers settled somewhat, and the true nature of their predicament was made known. The swirling vortex, which had deposited them so uncouthly amid the soaring trees and wild ferns of the Underwood, still thrashed about with convulsive abandon. Within moments the rend had sealed, leaving the gathering stranded.

In the minutes that followed, it was agreed that the party should head toward the closest lumber mill and, once there, seek to return to the red city by conventional means. Only the quiescent few nestled to the rear of the group, clinging to the shadows, seemed uneasy at the prospect. When questioned about their reluctance, a particularly sharp-sighted member of the Administratum caught sight of the small treasure nestled in the arms of a hulking brute at the rear of the group. Realizing the importance of their quarry, the enterprising priest ordered three of the guards to escort the bulk of the refugees to safety and issued orders to his fellow priests. The remaining guards were set upon the rebels and ordered to capture the babe without harm.

Within moments, four Red Guard lay dead, their improvised weaponry lying beside bodies quickly draining of blood. The remaining guardsmen backed away warily, as did the priest who had issued the order to attack. At the centre of the carnage stood a towering figure wearing what looked like a Butcher's uniform. The hooded figure stood with the babe in one arm and a bloodied knife in the other.

"Follow us, and you will surely die," the brute barked as his cadre melted into shadow.

**

"We have no choice," Daisy said, brushing aside a large fern as she laboured through the undergrowth. "Got to keep heading out further into the woods and hope that we can find our way to the surface."

Nina frowned. "We could walk for a year and not find a way out of here. This place is at least as big as the Salt Sea, maybe bigger."

"Well, we sure as fuck can't head back to one of the logging camps. That bastard priest had us pegged as soon as he saw us. Little fucker will have called for help and, by morning, they'll have a hundred fucking Red Guard waiting for us. Probably a few dozen Butchers too."

Nina seemed to shudder at the mention of Butchers. "You saw how easily he killed those guards, right? It was terrifying. I've never seen anything like that before."

Daisy smiled. "Yeah, I know right. Pretty fucking amazing."

"It was horrific."

Daisy turned on the other woman, tilting her head as though confused. "It was what needed to happen, Nina. You've gotta start getting used to this kind of shit, sister. It's just the way things work in the Traumwelt. Speaking for myself, I'm glad to have the big bastard on our side. We're gonna need him if a few more Butchers turn up to the party."

"I'm not saying it wasn't…necessary. I'm just not as comfortable with killing as you are."

After a few more steps, Daisy called the group to a halt, waiting for the tall Butcher and a few stragglers to catch up. Of the rebel group only Daisy and the Butcher were fighters, and the others were struggling to keep pace. Daisy let the group rest a while and pulled the big man aside. It took more than a little convincing, but eventually he relinquished the sleeping babe to Nina, who took the girl gratefully.

"Okay, we've gotta make a plan here big guy. We're exposed as hell down here in the Underwood, and we can't keep running, not with these guys lagging behind."

The man she had taken to calling Titus frowned darkly. "Survival should be our first priority. I have no milk for the child, and there is little in these woods to provide nourishment."

Daisy rolled her eyes. "The kid will be fine as long as we keep Nina fed. Look, she's already got her tits out."

The assassin motioned toward the other woman who was sitting with her back against a tree, feeding the baby contentedly. "You just concentrate on getting us the fuck out of here in once piece, okay?"

Titus nodded. "I have some knowledge of these woods. I can instruct the others to harvest edible roots and fresh water."

"Okay, great," Daisy said. "That takes care of the meals, but how the fuck do we get out of here?"

Even as she spoke the words, something caught the assassin's eye. Moving quicker than she had any right to, Daisy leapt forward and snatched something from above Titus's right shoulder. She opened her hand to reveal a small, motley coloured beetle. She smiled, took a deep breath and then shoved the beetle unceremoniously into her mouth. She chewed for a few moments, her expression uncertain, then spat the masticated bug out onto the ground with a look of disgust.

"Jesus, how the fuck does he eat those things?"

Titus looked at her in confusion.

"Salinger, he...oh yeah, you haven't met him yet. He's kind of our Spymaster. Ugly looking fucker, but he's a good egg. Uses bugs and critters to gather information. He eats them and somehow absorbs their knowledge."

She pointed to the bug's remains. "That's one of his. I recognize it. Thought I'd try to see if I could get anything out of it, but no, just tastes like dried shit."

She spat on the ground, raking gloved fingers over her tongue.

"We are alone then?" Titus asked.

She spat again, hunched over, holding up a hand. After a short wretch and a few deep breaths, she recovered herself and turned to the Butcher. "Bug made it through from camp, and Salinger was there tonight. I'm guessing that that stupid portal or whatever it was that brought us here was open long enough for old Sal to get a lock on us."

Titus looked at her blankly.

"Sal knows where we are, big man. That means Kane knows, and that means we're not going to be on our own for long."

She pointed to the baby, still suckling at Nina's breast. "Boss will move heaven and earth to keep that little girl safe, and I'm not talking figuratively. So, we don't have to get out of here. We just have to stay safe and find the boss when he comes looking."

DAISY

It all happens by instinct. I've done this gig so many times; it's second nature by now. Find a nice spot, hidden but with a good view of the ground below. Settle in and get the gun locked in place. Slow your breathing, use the scope to sight up some key distance markers, go for a piss, then sit down and wait.

I'm perched on top of a group of boulders, beneath an overhanging rock cleft, a full view of the woods below and solid stone at my back. I'm not sure if this is the very edge of the Underwood cavern—I doubt it—but it's a good enough spot to make our stand. Titus and the others are nestled in the cave below, securing the baby out of sight. They've managed to rustle up enough scrub and dirt to block off the cave mouth a little. It should muffle the baby's cries, but it won't do much more than that.

I take a few sweeps across the ground below. There's a large clearing of a few hundred feet surrounding the rocks and, even in the dim light, I can make out everything fairly clearly. Good place for a last stand. Still, I'd rather not die today.

I catch sight of Titus, limbering up out in the open. He's pulled off his cloak and now he's going bare-chested. Damn. He's got a back like a fucking panther: all muscle and sinew, crisscrossed with old scars. He's swinging those bastard cleavers around like a motherfucker, some kind of training exercise to get him ready for what's coming.

Watching the big bastard go through his paces I can't help my mind from running the numbers. *Could I take him in a fight?* It's the question I ask myself about just about everyone I meet. He'd be a tough one to bring down, and I'd need a little luck to pull it off, but I reckon I could take him if it came to that.

There's a crack in the distance, followed by raised voices. I snap my brain into gear and scan the surrounding woods. A dozen or so men walk out into the clearing, easy as you please. They're Red Guard scouts by the look of them, all light-armoured and all ready to run like rabbits and toot their little warning horns if they catch trouble.

I watch them waltz out further into the clearing. I check for more, but they look like a single unit. Tricky one, this. If I'm gonna shoot, I'll need to take out as many as I can, as quickly as I can before any of the pricks can raise an alarm. Those horns of theirs have an etheric pulse that's tuned to the Scoutmaster. Only takes a few seconds to get back to him, and there's no way to stop it once it's been blown.

I look for Titus. He's vanished—hiding somewhere nearby, ready to pounce. I press gently against the trigger, lining up the nearest scout. Fourteen or so men, all with horns, and I've got five bullets before I need to reload. Even at my quickest it will take five seconds to load another clip—five seconds too long. I don't even want to think about the other problem. Fifty bullets. That's all I've got, and I'm lucky I was holding my clip belt when that swirly fucker sucked us into the Underwood. Fifty bullets, then it's down to the knives.

The butcher moves so quickly I almost overshoot my mark trying to lock in on him. He takes out a straggler at the rear of the group without a sound, then lets the guy drop to the ground and manages to kill two others before the body hits the earth. They're all clustered together, so he takes them in pairs, charging at another two and stabbing so violently that he knocks them off their feet.

One of the guards at the front of the group sees the trouble and reaches for his horn. Then it's on.

50

I take him through the chest, before he has a chance to raise the alarm. The guards next to him panic, half running, half grabbing at their belts.

49

I plug a second guard right through the forehead, and he drops like a stone. The other one is running, but I manage to track him.

48

47

Fuck it! Two shots to bring him down, and I'm swinging around praying that the others haven't had a chance to get to their horns. The middle of the clearing is in chaos. They're running into each other, scrambling to get away. My finger hovers over the trigger, but I have to hold back. Titus is right in the middle of the group. Smart bastard isn't even trying for the kill. His blade cuts at wrists and forearms—if they can't pick it up, they can't blow their horn.

In seconds the six remaining guards are writhing on the ground, screaming in pain. Casual as you like, the butcher moves over and cuts their throats one by one, leaving them to bleed out. He leaves the last guard alive, cutting at the tendons in the poor bastard's leg so he can't run. Titus looks up at me, points to the edge of the forest, like he wants me to keep an eye out. A little part of me feels like plugging him through the foot. I know my fucking job, dude.

I swallow it and scan the edge of the clearing. Nothing.

Meanwhile, Titus drags the dead bodies out behind the rocks, two at a time like they don't weigh a thing. *Jesus.* Whatever you think about the Butchers, that's one impressive fuck of a man right there.

Once he's done clearing the bodies away, I hear Titus talking to the wounded guard. The voices are too low to hear, but that doesn't stop me leaning over the edge of the rock to try and hear. After a while I give up and get back to scanning the horizon. I keep my eyes fixed on the trees and swap out the clips from the rifle.

Something moves behind me. I drop the gun and pull a stiletto from my boot sheath. Titus is climbing up the rock. He lumbers over and sits down next to me. He's covered in blood and sweat, his eyes locked on the clearing. I slip the knife back into its sheath.

"What did our guest have to say?" I ask.

He twists his neck to one side, giving it a sharp crick. "Twelve such scouting parties have been sent on ahead. The vanguard is yet a few hours behind. Five hundred Red Guard regulars and fifty Butchers, if he is to be believed."

I have to double take at that. "Did you say fifty?"

He nods.

"Fuck."

The carnage I've just seen Titus dish out is still fresh in my mind. I try to imagine fifty of those fuckers in action and nearly wet myself.

"So, we're screwed then?"

He looks at me, something close to a smile on his lips. "Avernath wants the babe unharmed. That gives us an advantage. They cannot simply take our position by force of arms, less they risk harm to the child."

"Okay, so we just wait then?"

He pulls a rag from his waist and starts wiping the blood off his chest. I leave the gun set where it is and move a little closer, taking the rag from him and moving to his back. He doesn't protest when I wipe the sweat and blood from his shoulders.

"So, we have a few hours before it hits the fan then?" I ask, reaching beneath his arms to grab his waist.

He turns around, grabs me, and pulls me close.

"Time enough," he says, leaning in to kiss me.

ISAACK

"Get to it, son!" Hamen booms at me.

I pick up the kinetic turret and start running, slinging spare reams of ammunition over my shoulder. Even though the weapon is built of ether-charged steel, it weighs enough to bring tears to my eyes every time I am permitted to lay it down. The heavy leather pads on my shoulders only do so much to ease the pain of the turret pressing against my body. Should I survive the battle, there will be fresh welts and bruises on the morrow.

"Move, Isaack. Move!" Hamen bellows, jogging alongside me with a turret of his own, slung effortlessly over one mechanically enhanced arm.

Hard to believe he was a baker before the rebellion began. I look at the man now, and all I see is a mass of scarred flesh and crooked teeth: a bulky biomechanical machine whose sole purpose seems to be grinding me into dust on every possible occasion.

We run for hours on end, only loosely in formation, each grouped together in small, dispersed bands so that a sudden attack would be less devastating to our ranks. We've rehearsed this so many times that my body seems to go through the motions without my needing to think it through.

The woods are thick with heavy-trunked trees that stretch up toward the sparkling cavern sky. So much wood, it baffles me why the substance is in such short supply in the red city. I've seen men pay more than a hundred sovereigns for a simple table, yet here lies a whole world of lumber, stretching as far as the eye can see. Just another example of the Red Queen's stranglehold on the red city and its people. The priests sit on cushioned chairs, dining at polished lumber tables while the rest of the city squabbles over splinters.

"Formation!" Hamen booms, pointing a heavy arm to the south. "Edge of the clearing, just there."

We run ahead, Kip and Uther at the front with rifles and bucklers at the ready, scanning the woods for signs of movement. We reach the edge of the forest, opening out into a vast clearing that looks natural rather than man-made. A small creek runs the length of the clearing, dividing northern and southern banks. I set the turret at the edge of the forest, lining up with half a dozen fellow gunners along the tree line. The others dig in around me, hitching up etheric barricades and unspooling ammunition while I prepare for long-range fire. The kinetic turret begins to whine softly as I crack its motivator, humming to life in anticipation of what is to follow.

"*Brace yourselves,*" the words push themselves into my mind, placed by some psychoetheric gift. It is not Hamen's voice but the voice of Absinthe Annie, former Madame of Sparrow Boulevard, now turned lieutenant for the Shackled Man. Her voice is smooth as butter and hard as iron.

"*They are coming at pace from the southwest. A legion or so of Red Guard and a small unit of Butchers.*"

In my head I quickly calculate the numbers. Kip gives me a worried look. She must be thinking the same thing I am.

"*Focus your fire on the regulars and let the tattooed handle the butchers. They'll approach cautiously, so wait until they are across the creek before opening fire. Etheric wards are in place, so we should escape detection, but maintain silence.*"

It seems such an odd thing to hear military tactics delivered in such a melodic, sing-song tone. Though she is likely half a league away, I can picture her face with ease.

"*Remember the fallen dead. Remember your loved ones. A debt is owed that must be paid. Death to the Red Queen and her kinsmen. Long live the Shackle.*"

And now…we wait.

***

They send clockwork scouts into the clearing—small, dog-like automatons with clockwork limbs and kinetically charged senses. They scutter and sniff and circle around the clearing with an almost animal curiosity. Several of the clockwork beasts pass over the creek and head toward the tree line. One of the scouts passes through the trees, heading somewhere behind us.

Panic rises in me. My heart beats wildly. I turn my head, expecting to see the clockwork beast rearing up behind me, but the scout returns to the clearing without event. Whatever etheric trickery Absinth Annie has employed, it has worked convincingly. After a few moments the scouts return to the other side of the clearing, and enemy soldiers begin marching out into the open.

Three ranks of Red Guard regulars march through the clearing, heading toward the creek, their front ranks bearing charged weapons. They walk at a quick pace, reaching the creek before their back ranks are fully exposed.

I can sense the unease around me. There must be a thousand or more regulars, and we've yet to see their tail. I dare not think how many butchers are in attendance, nor what other horrors they have in their ranks.

As if in answer to my fears, a horrific cry peels through the Underwood, coming from somewhere behind the soldiers. They falter somewhat in their rhythmic marching, some of their number turning heads.

"What was that?" Kip whispers.

I shrug. "Some creature of the Underwood?"

She shakes her head. "No, too close. It's something they brought with them, and they don't look too happy about it."

"*Prepare yourselves. Attack on my mark,*" comes Annie's voice.

The regulars continue their march, passing over the creek and onto our side of the clearing. There is a moment of palpable hesitation when the frontline of the enemy ranks seems to suspect that all is not well. And then the wings of chaos are unfurled.

"*Attack!*" Annie's words roared.

Out of instinct, my hands do their work, releasing the turret's kinetically charged load in a hail of blistering death. Even with dampeners, the sound of two dozen kinetic turrets firing at full capacity is deafening. Bullets cut through the air, tearing through the front ranks of regulars with horrible ease and driving back into the mid ranks. Within moments, hundreds of enemy soldiers lay dead and dying, while their comrades scramble to raise bucklers and find safety.

There is too much confusion to allow the enemy to mount an effective counterattack. Here and there the pop of rifles can be heard, but there is no cover, and the turrets are relentless. Only after we have thinned their ranks by nearly half does the enemy rally. There are a series of loud booms, heard over the constant fire of the turrets, and then a sucking of air, and the clearing seems momentarily devoid of sound. A deafening silence settles over the melee, and only the rattle and bustle of the turret convinces me that we are still firing.

On the other side of the clearing, behind the creek, an invisible barrier of some kind comes into being, blocking the hail of bullets and dropping them harmlessly to the ground. Those unfortunates caught on the wrong side of the barrier are quickly mowed down, coating the invisible shield with their blood as their bodies are torn apart.

Behind the barrier, soldiers clamour to establish some kind of order. The wounded are pulled from their ranks, while militant clerics shout orders.

"*Cease fire!*" Annie orders, her voice cutting through the thick silence.

The guns cease their firing, and I start cranking the turret's waste release valve, expelling the build-up of noxious fumes generated by prolonged usage. Along the tree line, other gunning crews do likewise. A dozen waste canisters are ejected silently, dropping to the earth with their bitter poison locked safely inside.

"*Be ready. Commence firing the moment that barrier lifts.*"

In the forced silence I feel my heart galloping. This is not my first fight, not by any means, but none of us have engaged in pitched battle before, and none have faced such a numerous foe.

Something moves on the opposite side of the clearing, tossing aside enemy soldiers like some gargantuan child disposing of unwanted toys. Through the turret's scope I see a mammoth figure lumbering through the ranks of Red Guard, a figure too monstrous to describe. Within moments it has reached the barrier, passing through it as though it were no more than tissue paper. The barrier falters, and all sound is suddenly restored.

"*Fire!*"

I begin firing just as a pair of winged horrors burst from the enemy ranks and charge toward our tree line with terrible speed. Red Guard soldiers are crushed in their passing, torn by the razor-sharp edges of their unfurled wings. Nightmarish skulls adorn skeletal bodies that move with lethal precision, not flying but moving so swiftly through the air that they seem unbound by the earth.

Shadowspawn.

The word comes to me, as it does each of us. We have all heard, but few of us have seen their kind and lived to tell of it. The twin Shadowspawn plunge into our ranks, tearing apart two turret crews before anyone can react. I move to turn, but the sight of the lumbering hulk at the centre of the clearing drains my resolve.

It towers over the tallest of our number, a mismatch of flesh and bone, sinew and gristle which seems to have been sewn together in haphazard fashion. The beast roars through bristling teeth, its blind head covered in welts and sores that seem to pulse of their own volition. In one hand the hulk carries a curved hatchet large enough to cleave a mountain in two, while a second, hooked blade is crudely bound to his other arm, already slick with the blood of Red Guard regulars too slow to move out of its path.

I aim at the brute's chest, trying to forget the bird-like terrors that are carving a path through our ranks somewhere behind. The turret's rapid fire seems ineffectual against the monstrous form, bouncing off his hardened flesh and causing only mild irritation. Within moments, the other Shadowspawn have circled back into the centre of the clearing, stalking to either side of the hulk, their skulls wet with the blood of our comrades.

Four or five turrets continue their rapid firing, but to little effect. The Shadowspawn seem impervious to such weaponry.

"Halt fire. Turret crews, retreat to your second mark."

We obey the command as quickly as we are able. I busy myself preparing the weapon for transport, bracing myself against the blistering heat of its barrel and propulsive core. We work quickly, aided by endless hours of practice under Hamen's relentless instruction and the tattooed runes on our hands and feet. I lift the turret atop my shoulder and lead the crew back into the woods, shutting out the cries of demented shadowspawn that peel through the air.

The sound of kinetic artillery fire cracks, and the woods erupt with violent force. The eerie whistle of thaumaturgically enhanced projectiles is followed by a round of explosions that rend earth and split wood. I'm lifted into the air, the turret torn from my grasp as the world erupts in flame.

***

I crawl on hands and knees, disoriented and unsure of where I'm heading. Blood pours from a wound somewhere on my head, blurring my vision as I drag myself through the underbrush. I reach a clutch of rocks at the edge of the clearing and drag myself into their cold embrace. My head is cocked at an odd angle, so that I see the violence unfolding through an upside-down prism. The three shadowspawn roar and strut at the centre of the clearing, spitting their challenge as kinetic fire continues overhead.

Several figures step out from our line. The tall, emerald form of Absinth Annie, wreathed in a cloud of etheric dust, is joined by the lithe figure of

Giaus and the hulking, bare-chested Rook. They flex their strength before the enemy, and the clearing seems to pulse and swell in anticipation of etheric discharge. A tall man, clothed in black, walks toward the largest of the shadowspawn. His wrists are wrapped in crimson fire, his midnight coat billowing behind him.

Even bloodied and torn as I am, my heart leaps to see the Shackled Man enter the fray.

ABSINTH

He fights like a demon, just as I remembered. Yet, where once there were blazing firearms, here now he uses raw etheric force. There is no honed technique to his brutal warfare, just the impromptu cracking of bone and rending of flesh. His arms seem to blaze with violent crimson light, an etheric power so profound that I can feel it clawing at my mind even from this distance.

Two more shadowspawn are released from the Warmaster's herd. They are dire creatures, but not invulnerable to etheric weaponry. We work well as a team. I bind, Giaus distracts, Rook and the Shackle deal their death blows. It is over swiftly enough, but I sense something moving behind the line of regulars: some etheric disturbance laced with threat.

When he finally emerges from the shadows, Avernath is surrounded by fifty Butchers, all displaying the horrifying signs of Calaban's hand. They are twisted and made monstrous, more deadly than they have any right to be, a blend of flesh and shadow wrought by the Red Queen's unholy fleshmancers. A Butcher alone is a thing to be feared. Fifty reborn butchers is a terror we may not survive.

There are too many. I send to Shackle. *We should retreat to the woods and pick them off one by one.*

He shakes his head. *NO. WE FIGHT HERE AND GIVE SALINGER TIME TO TRACK THE BABE AND TAKE HER TO SAFETY.*

We may not win this engagement. Many of our kin will die if we try.
THEN THEY WILL DIE.

The enemy leaves no room for further discussion. Avernath, dragging his titanic sword through the ground like a plough, heads straight for Shackle. No words are exchanged before the two are locked in battle. The mammoth godling wields his weapon with frightful ease, blow by blow raining down upon Shackle's relentless defence.

I give the order to attack, knowing full well how many men and women I send to their deaths. And then, all is lost in the pure madness of battle, the frantic rending of will and flesh—the theft of life by the hundreds.

***

The battle rages and both sides take heavy casualties. I find myself torn among a thousand difficult choices, assaulted by the cries of the dead and dying.

All at once, she appears in the midst of battle: an apparition, slight and beautiful. A woman of slim frame and radiant form stands between the Warmaster and Shackle, confusion written upon her face. The battle seems to wane a little as all eyes are drawn to the heart of the clearing and the strange apparition who stands in the fray. Avernath stares down at the woman with a mixture of rage and confusion.

"Emma?"

The words are Shackle's. Spoken with such urgent conviction that it cuts through the din of warfare. The woman turns, recognition in her eyes. She reaches for Shackle and he draws near, but before they are joined, the Warmaster's blade rends her in twain. The demon god roars his challenge as his cruel blade splits the woman's flesh, tearing life from her body with wicked efficiency.

"You are not *her!*" Avernath roars. "You are a pretender, a shadow! You are nothing!"

There is a moment when the Traumwelt seems to shudder. Shackle says nothing. His eyes are locked upon the felled girl. Where crimson power surged around his fists, now dark shadow begins to wreath his body. There is a shudder in the air, a drawing of power so immense that my own etherwork is snuffed out effortlessly.

Shadows billow and dance about the Shackle as he advances on Avernath. No words are spoken as they join once more in battle, but there is a howl of terror that rises from the darkness with such primordial force that friend and foe alike are driven to their knees. Amid the swirling shadow, the sudden pressure that threatens to rend sanity from my mind, I catch sight of the Warmaster, writhing beneath Shackle's grip. Yet, the Shackled Man himself has become something monstrous. He stands head and shoulders above the Warmaster, a creature of shadow and death.

I am driven to my knees, unable to keep my eyes open. All light and sound are driven from the world, swallowed by absolute darkness.

ISAACK

When the darkness fades, I struggle to stand. From somewhere nearby, I hear Hamen's voice shouting orders. I force my legs to move, drag myself from the rocks.

We are scattered and bloodied, half of our number dead. Hamen and the other survivors are tending the wounded and gathering what supplies we can carry. No one tends to the dead, for they are too numerous. As I stumble about the clearing, I see that the enemy has suffered far worse a fate than we. Behind the rent bodies of the dead shadowspawn lay a thousand corpses. Red Guard regulars lay scattered by the hundreds, intermingled with the deformed, ether-charged bodies of dead butchers. There are priests too, clerics and other administrators torn asunder by the Shackled Man's power.

There is a crater at the centre of the clearing. The Warmaster's sword lays broken inside the crushed earth, its blade shattered into a dozen pieces. Of the Warmaster himself, there is no sign but the tracks of dragged limbs wending back into the forest. The Shackled Man is gone. Absinthe Annie is badly wounded, but still lives. Giaus is dead and Rook is bloodied, but the big man takes charge nonetheless.

I find Kip and Uther a little way back in the forest. I have no words to speak over their bodies, nor the strength to weep. I lift the kinetic turret onto my shoulder and join the remnants of our rebellion, following the sound of Hamen's voice into the wood.

DAISY

No one will talk about what happened. Not that they need to say much. I can see how many have died, and Shackle's absence tells me all I need to know. Half of our men and women dead. How the fuck do we recover from something like this?

At least the kid is safe. Hell of a debt she's carrying though. A hundred plus lives she owes, and the little thing can't even walk yet.

With Annie and Shackle out of action, it falls to me to lead the group out of the Underwood. Rook can walk, but he's cut up pretty bad, and I can tell he's hurting because of Giaus—the little guy he loved to hate.

We move slowly and a few die along the way. When we get back to camp Shackle is already there, locked in his basement doing some heavy-duty brooding. It takes weeks before things start to get back to normal. With so many dead, we have to reassign jobs, reallocate provisions, and kickstart our recruitment drive. We won, but it doesn't feel like a victory. Shackle blames himself for killing a bunch of our own men, but it had to be done. Ain't no way any of us were getting out of there in one piece if he didn't let loose the mojo.

Before, our people used to be a little standoffish about the boss. Now they're flat out petrified of him. It's gonna take a shit load of time and some new blood to get over this, and the red bitch won't be doing us any favours. Still, the kid is safe, for now.

24. Ode to Emma

She blinks.

Her vision settles, landing upon the dull surface of a brick wall clothed in darkness. The wall is roughly hewn, its bricks uneven and badly cracked.

She stares for a moment, lifts her hands, and turns them to and fro, noting their ghost-like, ethereal texture. She is something more than insubstantial, something less than concrete.

She smiles, turns her head to take in her surroundings.

She stands in a small room, brick walls on each side with rickety stairs leading up to a doorway above.

The scent of wood-fire smoke and curing meat hangs thickly in the air as dust drifts slowly downward through the slats in the wooden floor above.

Only on the second pass of the room does she note the shadowed figure sitting in the corner. Darkness clings to that corner, obscuring the seated figure to such an extent that she second-guesses her eyes.

She steps closer, peering into the shadows.

Her less-than-substantial heart skips a beat as the figure moves, shifting slightly. A man, dressed in a long black coat, his face hidden by the edge of a wide-brimmed hat, settles himself in place. He has not seen her. He seems fixated on something at his wrist.

She leans a little closer, not daring to take another step.

Something metallic clings to the man's wrist, its dull sheen glinting in the meagre light of the cellar. He mumbles something as he sits, fondling the dull grey shackle with something approaching affection.

She sees a second shackle upon the man's other wrist, but neither shackle is bound with a chain. They sit like odd relics, clinging to the man's flesh.

For a time, she simply stands, watching the dark figure at his silent contemplation. Moments lengthen, and her sense of self begins to wane. She feels herself slipping, feels the pitted walls and the shadowed figure fade from vision, becoming something less than substantial.

In the final moment, before the dark cellar vanishes altogether, the figure looks up at her, staring with cold blue eyes that seem locked upon her.

***

Her second coming is more substantial than the first.

She can feel the cold earth beneath her bare feet, can taste the dust and grit which hangs in the air of the basement.

Her eyes adjust to the light, slowly revealing crumbling brick walls, cold earth, the Shackled Man sitting in darkness, the edges of his face cut with thin blue light.

She draws closer, tentative, heart beating wildly.

The man's broken shackles seem to glow with a pleasing aqua-coloured luminescence. He stares down at them as she approaches, lost in some profound contemplation.

She draws a little closer still, hesitant, cautious. Slowly, as if only gradually aware of her presence, the shadowed figure lifts his head. Cool eyes look out from beneath the broad brim of a battered black hat. He stares for a time, saying nothing.

She opens her mouth to speak, but the words dry up before they take flight. She fades quickly, falling from the vision and snatching a glimpse of the shadowed figure's faint smile as her world fades to black.

***

When next she dreams herself into the dimly lit basement in that other world, she stands alone. The figure she had come to expect is nowhere to be seen, so she makes the most of her solitude. Quickly coming to terms with her surroundings and fearful that she will wake too soon, she searches for some way out and finds a set of aged stairs to one corner of the room. She ascends the steps, attempts to open the wooden door at their apex, steps beyond into…darkness…

***

On three further occasions she appears in the basement, each lasting a little longer than the first. On the last of these occurrences, *he* is waiting in his customary place. She does not waste time.

"Can you see me?"

The figure smiles crookedly, nods.

"And you can hear me… Well, obviously you can. What's your name? Where am I?"

The shadowed figure leans back in his chair, sharp eyes examining her.

"Kane. My name is Kane."

She smiles despite herself. "Nice to meet you, Kane. I'm Emma. Can you tell me where on earth I am? I mean, this is a dream, right? None of this is real?"

"And if all that you see is fiction," he answers, "then how are my words to be trusted? For, in such a fiction, would not my own words be fictitious and thus thoroughly untrustworthy?"

"I…I suppose so. Look I'm just trying to piece this all together. I mean, I've turned up here so many times before, in the red city I mean, but never here, in this place. It's all so real, so vivid."

His eyes narrow. "Ah, so I am no longer a fiction, is that it?"

"Sweetheart, I have no idea who the hell you are. Could be just a figment of my imagination, I supposed, though I hope not. What does it say about my emotional state if I go dreaming up skulking cowboys for kicks?"

Unexpectedly, he leans forward, reaching out to take her by the hand. His fingers pass through hers, though there is a moment of resistance, of hesitation. She feels something as his hands pass through, a curious warmth.

"You are not yet real," he says smiling, "though that may change. When you first appeared, you were little more than a spectre."

She frowns. "What do you…"

Something changes.

When next she appears, there is something profoundly more substantial about her body. She feels the weight of her feet pressing against the gritty floor, senses the stifled air in the small basement.

He sits in his usual place, still as a stone, eyes locked upon her. He smiles.

"Now you are made real, a spectre no more."

She moves toward him, flexing her fingers experimentally. Everything is different, infinitely more tangible. She stands before him, holds out a hand, and feels her heart skip as warm skin meets her touch. Kane takes her hand and presses it gently to his lips. He takes her other hand and leads her to his lap. In a daze, she sits, wrapping her arms around his waist, her breath catching.

"You are dreaming, yes?" Kane asks.

She nods, heart thumping.

"Then you are one of the lucky few, dear Emma. You have dreamed yourself into the Traumwelt, the red desert, the world of dreams and dreamers."

She nods slowly. "I know. I've been here before."

He smiles, the hard exterior of his face warming unexpectedly.

They speak for an hour or more before she is called back to the waking world. Emma learns of the red city, the Queen at its heart, the shadowlands, the ether, the rebellion. Kane speaks freely, with an almost cathartic sense of relief. She asks few questions. She revels in his touch, listening wide-eyed to his tale while she clings to his waist.

All too soon their time is over, yet, before she vanishes from sight, he brings her closer and kisses her tenderly upon the lips. The memory of his warm breath lingers as she fades away.

Emma wakes to an empty room. The chair upon which he usually sits is still in its place, but Kane is nowhere to be seen. She waits for him, wandering aimlessly about the basement, brushing her fingers against the pitted brick walls, sitting for a time in the roughly hewn wooden chair.

She is alone, and feels her heart longing, aching for his touch. Minutes pass slowly. She waits.

***

"I waited, but you didn't come," she says, kneeling to look into his eyes, taking his hand.

"I was…detained. The fighting grows fierce, and our strength is divided among too many lines. The Warmaster seeks to force a pitched battle and…"

He looks into her eyes, smiles, brushes a hand across her cheek. She hears the clinking of old iron on his wrists and cannot resist reaching out for the shackle. It is surprisingly warm to the touch.

"Tell me about these," she asks.

He speaks of failed rebellion, of imprisonment in the pit, of curiously wrought freedom. As he speaks the shackles at his wrist begin to glow with a soft amber light.

"They are imbued with power, though I dare not say from where the power comes. At first I thought it etheric charge, some residue caught from the runoff of Apothecarian experiments. But now I fear a darker power is at work."

She looks up at him, her heart opening like a flower. "I want to know everything. Where did you go when you escaped the prison? How did you come here, to this place? Tell me about the rebellion and—"

Her words are cut short by the tender pressing of his lips against hers. For a time, they stay locked in a passionate embrace. When finally they pull apart, Kane speaks of his time in the red wastes, wandering a forsaken land in search of meaning. He recounts his meeting a young orphan girl, stranded in the Traumwelt far from the red city and any semblance of civility. He takes the girl under his wing, teaches her how to survive, how to hunt, how to kill. For a time, they travel the forsaken lands, coming eventually to Baronsville and returning in time to Rust. He speaks of an old friend, hideously malformed by the fleshmancers, of a second rebellion, of freedom from oppression—of vengeance.

He does not guard his words, nor seek to hide the tears which fall as he recounts his tale. Nor does he pull away when Emma brushes soft fingers across his cheek, kissing him gently as he speaks of death and struggle and bloodshed. He empties himself before her, and she responds in kind.

"On the morrow, I intend to take up arms against the Warmaster. The risk is great, but we have little choice. He intends to take the babe from us. Even now, his Butchers advance on our stranded kin."

Emma pulls herself close. "Can't you just run? Isn't there some way you can get out of this without fighting?"

Kane shakes his head. "We must blunt the Warmaster's attack, or he will not rest until he has the babe. Even if I were to send her to the utmost end of the Traumwelt, the Warmaster would find her."

Something shifts, almost imperceptibly at first. Emma senses it in the tensing of his muscles, sees it in the hardening of his gaze. Gently, but firmly, he pushes her away and stands to his feet.

"My love?" she asks.

The shackles at his wrists begin to smoke, spirals of shadow rising in spirals from the aged metal. He looks down at her with cold incomprehension. Something passes behind his eyes and, momentarily, he is his normal self.

"Forgive me, Emma," he says, teeth clenched. "I must leave this place. I do not wish to…"

He walks from the basement, heading out through the doorway without another word. Emma is left with her confusion for only a few moments before the waking world draws her back to reality. Yet, in those moments, a crazed torment plays havoc with her heart.

***

She sees him, sitting not in his customary chair, but slumped against the wall as though cast aside. She goes to him, kneeling before him and reaching for his hands. Dark shadows surround the pitted metal at his wrists, swirling with serpentine grace. The shackles which are his namesake seem to hum with power while shadow spirals around them. At the touch of her fingers to his hand, the shadow ceases its hypnotic dance. Slowly, like the rising of a moon, he lifts his head.

His eyes fix upon her, showing a look of utter disbelief. He reaches for her face, his hand trembling. She presses his hand against her cheek.

"What is it? What's wrong?" she asks, drawn by the sorrow in his eyes.

"I...I saw you dead, murdered at the hand of the Warmaster."

"I don't understand."

He leans forward, gently pulling her head closer, his eyes locked on hers as though searching for some sign of deception. For long moments they sit locked in each other's grip, staring into one another's eyes.

"It's me, Idrus," she says finally. "Whatever you saw, I'm here, and I'm alive."

Some of the manic despair flees his gaze at her words. He slumps back against the wall, and she moves close, leaning into him.

"Tell me what happened," she whispers, tracing the line of his chin with her finger.

He speaks of war in the Underwood, of battle joined with the Warmaster and his minions, of shadowspawn and ethermancy and Emma's appearance at the heart of the battle.

"I saw him cut you down," he says, eyes glazed with memory. "And I became enraged. I could no longer see friend from foe, light from dark. All was crushed beneath the shadow."

He turns to her.

"There is a darkness in me, Emma. That which gives me power and strength also takes from me. The blessings of the Old Ones are not given freely, and I fret that their price may be too steep."

"I...I don't understand."

He takes her hand, his thumb rubbing gently against the top of her palm. He smiles, but there is no warmth in the expression.

"My memories of the pit are...scattered and incomplete. There is a darkness in my mind which obscures what transpired in that place. I was...half crazed, unable to separate dream from reality. A thousand days had passed without sunlight, without companionship, conversation, the touch of another soul. Such solitude turns the heart sour and warps the mind. It was in the midst of my madness that they spoke to me, reaching out to touch my mind from the depths of whatever netherworld such beings inhabit. I cannot pretend to comprehend their words, nor can I unravel their plans for me. I know only that such plans exist and that my life is a thing of simple convenience to them. From time to time, I still hear the words whispered in my mind; dark and unintelligible, they tug at me, pulling at whatever it is that makes a man whole. When I use the power, the words come also—insistent and relentless."

"What do they say? These words?"

"When I try to call them to memory, I cannot bring them to clarity. I feel the sour taste in my mind, sense the pulling of cruel strings upon my heart. But I cannot recall the words, nor speak them. They are insubstantial things, wisps and spectres that seem to multiply as the days pass, hollowing out my soul so that they may call forth more of their brethren to make merry in the halls of my heart. When the power takes me—the shadow—I become something other than myself. I feel no pain, I hear not the words of my brothers in arms, nor the pleas of my enemies. I become death in shadow, the claw that rends flesh and sheds blood without mercy or volition. I fear…when the shadow takes me, that I am nothing more than a tool: a blade for cutting flesh and shattering bone. Though I know not who wields me, nor what purpose they serve."

His eyes lock onto hers, desperate, utterly helpless.

"I do know that the one who wields me cares nothing for the rebellion, nor for those with whom I daily toil. When the shadow comes, I may kill a hundred of my kin or a thousand Red Guard, without discrimination. And it is that thought—the thought of being reduced to a tool for rending flesh—which causes my malaise."

Slowly, she pulls the hat from his head, runs her fingers through his dark hair, pulls his head close. She speaks no words, but hums a simple tune, pressing her head against his and rocking gently. Tears fall from his eyes as they sit, locked in sorrow and passion.

"Many of my kin lie dead, at my hand. Annie lies insensibly…I fear she will never wake. I thank the fates that the girl was not there to see it."

"But you won the battle didn't you," she asks, head resting against his chest. "For all the pain you're feeling, isn't it better that you won? You were able to bring back your people, and the baby is safe. War is horror, but many more of your people would have died if you'd not used your power."

He considers her words, and, for a time, they sit in silence. What little comfort he can draw from her embrace is tempered by the knowledge that this cannot last.

"When I was first drawn to this land," he says, "I met an old man in the desert."

Kane smiles darkly. "I was spared the moment of my death, only to wake in this crimson hell. I walked for a time and then came across the old man. He looked much like an aged Mumbler, his limbs and eyes sewn together.

He spoke of the future and of a dark purpose. I could not understand his words, but one thing pressed into my memory. *When the time comes,* he said, *you cannot save her."*

Emma looks up at Kane, confused.

"In the Underwood, I feared that the old man's words had come to pass. I feared that you had been taken from me."

"But I was not taken from you," she says, drawing him close. "I'm still here. Still alive."

Kane nods, sorrow tugging at his dark features. "Several times since, the old man has appeared to me in different guises. Always he has spoken truth: words that have come to fruition without error. My time in the pit, my etheric gift and the dark gods who seek to use me as their tool; he spoke of all of this."

Emma nods. "And you're afraid that this applies to me as well?"

"No. I have long come to terms with the loss I will bear. What I fear is what I will do when you are taken from me—what I will become."

He takes Emma by the hand. "It was not you who appeared in the Underwood, but some apparition. Who, then, caused this spectre to appear?"

"I don't understand…"

"The dark gods taunt me, dearest Emma. They use you to wrench me from sanity and unleash the darkness within. *That* is what I fear, dear Emma. Though it has been only a short time, I have come to love you most dearly—more dearly than any other. I fear now that this love will drive me to great evil."

Tears fall down Emma's cheeks as she listens to his words.

"So, what are we to do then? Are you asking me to leave?"

He smiles wordlessly as tears begin to fall.

25. A Final Word

A final note then, dear reader, to those of you who have persevered, who have read and listened and opened your heart to the truth of our plight. There are other stories to be told, a great many tales of woe and struggle, triumph and strife. While there is breath in my lungs, I will endeavour to recover those stories and retell them to all who have ears to hear and eyes to see.

Let me be direct at this present juncture then. You who have read these words can no longer lay claim to impartiality. You are no longer mere observers but have become participants in the rebellion by virtue of the simple act of reading. It is not I who determines it thus, but the Red Queen and her cadre. Merely by possessing this volume and refraining from setting it to the flames, you are complicit and culpable. Beware, then, of the words you speak from this point on. Beware in whom you place your trust and to whom you share these stories with.

The Red Queen's agents are many, even in this world, and they are ever seeking to disrupt our efforts, so be wary and keep your wits, dear reader. Take care, but I urge you to find others, to share these tales with those you trust deeply. Prepare yourselves, for the Traumwelt heaves with unpredictability, and the Red Queen is not content to restrain her war to the world of dreams.

- The Chronicler

Rust: The Place and Players

Gargantua by Piotrek Antoniak

Avernath by Charidimos Bitsakakis

Clockwork Bridge by Piotrek Antoniak

Red Queen by Piotrek Antoniak

Rebellion Hideout by Piotrek Antoniak

Hallowed Gate by Piotrek Antoniak

The Shackled Man by Pavel Tymoshenko

Shackled_Man by Baracceanu

Shadowfang by Baracceanu

Nick Holden by Willi Roberts

Red Queen by Queenmercedes

Shadowfang by Moises May

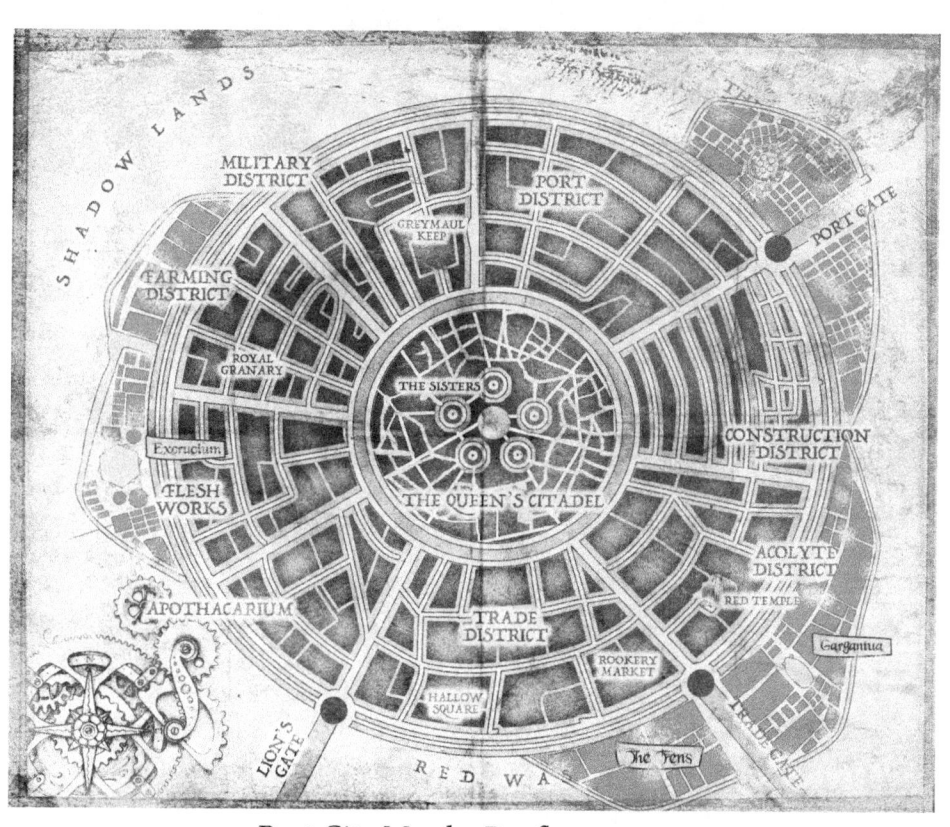

Rust City Map by Renflowergrapx

ALSO AVAILABLE FROM MARKOSIA

WHIPLASH: BOOK 1 – A RUST CHRONICLES NOVEL

Someone or something is killing people in their sleep. The world teeters on the brink of chaos as nightmares begin to spill out into the waking world. Abducted in the dead of night by a mountainous thug and a ginger-haired dwarf, eighteen-year-old Jack Flint soon finds himself at the heart of a war of cosmic proportions, fighting for survival among religious zealots, an underground black ops unit known only as The Bunker, and a renegade assassin with a penchant for over-sized weaponry.

ISBN: 978-1-914926-28-0